On Burning Mirrors

By Jamie Klinger-Krebs

This story is a work of fiction. All characters and events are the product of the author's imagination. Any resemblance to any person, living or dead, is coincidental.

On Burning Mirrors © 2018 by Jamie Klinger-Krebs

Cover design by Jamie Klinger-Krebs
Edited by Signe Jorgenson • signejorgenson.com
Published by J2K-Creative

For more information about the author visit jklingerkrebs.com

ISBN: 978-0-692-11305-9

For Charley Bug

Chapter One

Erin watched as Jules pulled back the curtain and then slipped her gray knit sweater over her head. From the comfort of the bed, Erin felt the vibration of a snowplow as it thundered by on the street below, shaking the ground beneath them. She inhaled slowly and held her breath as Jules glanced toward the clock and then down at the cold hardwood floor beneath her bare feet.

"Are you leaving already?" Erin asked. She pulled the blanket over her chest and propped her head on her hand as Jules moved toward the bed.

"Already? I've been here all afternoon, Erin," Jules said in a low voice. She ran her fingers through her smooth, dark hair to pull it out from her collar. Her eyes scanned the floor and she reached for the black pants that were lying in a crumpled ball near the chair.

"It's snowing like crazy," Jules said. "I need to go before the roads get any worse. It'll take me over an hour to get home in that mess."

"You know, you could stay," Erin said snidely before falling against the pillows.

1

Jules tilted her head and shot a disapproving look in Erin's direction. She sat on the edge of the bed and fumbled for her clothes in the dim light. Erin rolled over and looked toward the window. She didn't want to watch Jules get dressed. When Erin turned back, she could see Jules' face in the faint light from the half-open curtain. She was illuminated in a way that made Erin want to reach for her again. Her mouth went dry, and an acute pain drifted across her forehead. It traveled down her face and then settled, like it always did, directly in her chest. The ache was abrasive. It came from somewhere deep inside and pushed against her with the force of tumbling rocks. A fault line formed inside of her every day. Its jagged edges opened wider and wider every time Jules left the room. Erin knew she was an earthquake waiting to happen as the rumble built beneath her own skin.

Jules reached for her boots. Hoping to stop her, Erin sat up and moved close to her. Erin pushed the hair back from Jules' face, breathing in her warm amber and vanilla smell. Goose bumps rose on Jules' skin, and Erin was gratified in knowing that even her light touch could have such a profound effect.

"You're getting that look again," Erin said as she scanned Jules' face.

Jules laughed and stood up. She zipped her boots and looked toward the clock again. It glared 4:47 p.m. in bold, red numbers.

2

"I'm fine; you're reading into it, but I really need to get going," she said. "Besides, don't you have to work in an hour?"

Erin scoffed and fell back against the blankets. "Yes, I'm working. But it's a bar, Jules; they don't really give a shit what time I get there as long as I show up."

Jules smirked and walked toward her. Erin reached for her, gripping Jules' fingers tightly while trying to pull her back into bed. She wanted to run her fingers through Jules' soft hair and feel Jules' breath on her skin. But instead of lying down, Jules pulled her hand away.

"I wish you'd get the hell out of that place and stop selling yourself short," Jules said, looking down at Erin.

"*Please* don't start that again." Erin turned away and tangled herself deeper in the sheets. "I work at a bar. Get over it. But, if it bothers you that much, I could call in sick."

She sat up and leaned back on her hands. The sheets slipped down, leaving her bare chest suggestively exposed. But Jules ignored Erin's proposition. She ran her hands over her pants and then tried to smooth her wrinkled sweater.

Knowing there was nothing she could do to make her stay, Erin sighed loudly, hoping Jules would notice. When she didn't react, Erin sat up and scanned the floor for her own clothes.

"Looking for these?" Jules asked as she picked up the black bra and gray T-shirt Erin had worn earlier. She smiled facetiously and held them just out of Erin's reach, dangling them before her like some kind of twisted reward.

3

"Very funny. Can I have them, please?" Erin was unable to stop her lips from lifting into a smile.

Jules took a step toward her, but then stopped. "Wait, what will you do for them?"

"Well, Mrs. Kanter, what would you like me to do for them?" She pushed the blankets aside and crawled toward the end of the bed.

"That's very unladylike." Jules laughed. She tossed the shirt in Erin's face and backed away from the bed before reaching for her jacket, which lay on the blue velvet chair that was next to Erin's guitar.

"Don't go yet, Jules," Erin said as she pulled the T-shirt over her head. "I never finished playing you that song."

She felt Jules' eyes on her as she crossed the room in bare feet while weaving her long hair into a tousled braid.

"Next time," Jules said. "I really have to go." She buttoned her coat and dropped her hands to her sides. "Can I see you Friday?"

Erin fell into the chair and pulled the guitar across her lap. "Whatever you say, Jules. You know where to find me."

"C'mon, don't be like that." Jules lowered her chin and looked back at Erin. "I'll see you Friday, and I'll try to call you later, okay?"

"Drive safe, Mrs. Kanter," Erin mumbled while moving her fingers methodically over the strings.

Jules paused. With her hand still on the bedroom doorknob, she turned and gave Erin a somber smile. She stood

4

still for a few seconds, looking at the floor as if pondering whether to stay or whether to go. But then she straightened her shoulders and looked back at Erin. She winked and slipped out the door without another word.

Jules' footsteps moved through the apartment and then down the steep stairs outside. Erin sighed and looked around the room. The cold crept in and a heavy silence filled the air. It always felt that way when Jules left her. The old house, with its small, one-bedroom upstairs apartment, had become a secret sanctuary for her and Jules, but when Jules wasn't there, Erin felt completely alone.

Outside, Jules' car made a distinct "beep" as the doors unlocked. Still dressed in only her long T-shirt, Erin moved through the darkened living room toward the front window. Jules' feet had left a clear path in the snow that covered the quiet street, but with heavy flakes still falling, she knew the footprints would soon disappear. She watched as Jules reached for the car door but then turned and looked toward Erin's window. Almost instinctively, Erin backed away. The familiar ache returned to her chest. Shaking her head at her own stupidity, she stepped back and looked out again. She peered down just as Jules slipped inside the car. Seconds later, her headlights lit the dark street and the wipers pushed a heavy layer of snow from her windshield.

When the car didn't move, Erin contemplated slipping on her boots and running after Jules to try, one more time, to make her stay. But she froze. She thought Jules had turned her head to look up again. But this time, Erin didn't step away. Instead, she placed one hand against the window, hoping Jules could see her. The sting of the cold glass against her palm reminded her of all the reasons that Jules couldn't stay. As she pulled her hand away, she hoped Jules hadn't moved the car because she was reconsidering. But then Erin's hopes fell as the black Acura inched forward and she watched Jules drive away down the snow-covered street.

Chapter Two

Will stared at the liquor bottles behind the bar and took a sip of his soda. Pulling his eyes from the bottles, he looked at the liquid in his glass while the sweet taste still lingered in his mouth. It was unaccompanied by the familiar burn that used to make him clench his jaw.

In a way, he missed that warm flavor and longed for the taste of brandy on his lips, but he knew better than to order one. One would lead to two, then three, and then, before he knew what had happened, it would be ten and he would be passed out in the cab of his truck in the parking lot—or worse, in his own driveway with no recollection of driving home.

The thought churned in his mind as he examined his weathered hands. They were cracked and dry, and they looked almost corpse-like. His wedding band had long lost its shine and was almost like another part of the calloused flesh wrapped over his bones. He shook his head and raised the corner of his mouth in a sarcastic smile, realizing his hands were identical to the way his father's had once looked. Unlike Will, his old man had spent years working in a foundry two towns over. After long hours in that hot, dirty place, Will's father would come home filthy, leaving his black fingerprints on the hallway wall, which annoyed Will's mother so much that she would wipe them away as soon as his father left the room. After showering, he would eat dinner, bark orders at Will and his brother, and then fall asleep in the recliner by the TV, a glass of brandy and water just within his reach. It was the same monotonous routine day in and day out. It was no wonder he wound up killing himself.

Because of his father's size and his loud, domineering voice, Will had feared him when he was a boy. Though Will was just under six feet tall, his father had been a towering man at six foot four. Although Will's hair was wavy and auburn, his father had thick, black hair that was always greased back, except for the Tony Curtis duck tail that fell slightly across the center of his forehead. His father also had a wide, crooked nose, which had been broken in a fight, and he always wore a scowl. Will's face was boyish, though he had a strong, straight jaw, but his father's face looked as if it had been made of weathered concrete that might crack if he attempted even the slightest smile. The only physical trait Will shared with his father was the color of his eyes. They were deep green with a hint of blue, and they were the reason, his mother once told him, that she had fallen for his father when he was just a young man returning home from the Vietnam War.

When he was young, Will would sometimes sit on the floor and watch his father snore while he slept in that old recliner. He looked like a giant, and Will found himself tempted to climb into his lap just to see if his father would wake and devour him. Will wanted to lean his ear against that large, heaving chest and listen for evidence that there was actually a heart beating inside the man. Will's father had the work ethic of mule and was stronger than anyone Will knew, but there didn't seem to be an ounce of warmth inside of him. His virescent eyes always seared through Will with the ease of a sharp knife cutting through flesh. The man's huge, cracked, and grayish-colored hands never offered comfort or a hand-out; they only demanded respect.

As the bar door opened behind him, sending a gust of crisp, frigid air swirling inside, Will shivered and straightened on his stool.

"Snowing again," Ray mumbled. He pushed the door closed and brushed off his hat while shaking his head. "And, it's damn slippery."

Will gave a nod and glanced at his watch. His cell phone vibrated in his pocket before Ray even took his seat.

"Right on cue. Bet that's the wife?" Ray pulled a roll of blueprints from inside his jacket and dropped them on the bar.

Will missed the call as he fished for the phone in his pocket. Squinting at the screen, he was surprised to see it was his mother trying to reach him, not his wife. Before he had a chance to call her back, the phone buzzed again.

"Hello?" He said as Ray unrolled the drawings.

"William, I told you I have plans," his mother began. She was clearly irritated. "Are you coming to get Jillian, or am I supposed to sit here and wait all night?"

"Uh, you mean she—never mind, I'll come get her. I'll be there in a few minutes," he said.

Ray laughed, shook his head, and slid the blueprints back into a tight roll. "Good to see you as always, Will. I guess we'll talk about these plans next week then?"

"Yeah. Sorry, man. I'll call you."

Ray nodded and stared at the liquor bottles.

Will dropped a twenty-dollar bill onto the bar, noticing the tense look on Ray's face. "Buy yourself a few." Will gave Ray a friendly slap on the back and then pushed out the door.

Shivering in the moist, cold air, Will zipped his jacket up to his chin and glanced down the near-empty street. He knew Ray assumed he wasn't taking this prospective job seriously, and he also knew Will needed the work. Ray was already sticking his neck out to help him secure the bid on a remodel that could keep him busy for months, so leaving the meeting without accomplishing anything made Will's resentment toward his wife simmer. Firing the engine of his truck, Will revved it loudly before yanking the phone from his pocket. He tapped his wife's number and waited for her to answer, but when her voicemail picked up after four rings, he hung up. Growing irritated, he pushed down hard on the gas pedal, causing the truck to fish-tail as it slid down the street.

Moments later, while skidding into his mother's driveway, the phone buzzed. Catching it on the edge of his pocket as he removed it, the phone slipped from his hand and hit the floor hard. "Shit," he said, pawing at his feet and trying to

10

grasp it. Again, he missed the call. He expected to see his wife's name appear on the screen when he picked the phone up, but instead it was a number he didn't recognize. He groaned and dropped it into the cup holder before opening the door and stepping into the deepening snow. The front door opened immediately and a light clicked on as soon as he took the first step onto his mother's porch.

"Hi, Daddy," Will's six-year-old daughter said with a wide smile stretched across her Kool-Aid-stained face.

"Hey there, Bug," he responded, mirroring her grin. He opened the storm door and moved inside, shaking off the cold.

The house smelled like toasted bread, as if his daughter and mother had just finished making grilled cheese sandwiches, and he could hear his mother moving rapidly through the house. His daughter smiled and swayed, then reached for the pink snow pants hanging on the doorknob of the nearby closet. "Can we play in the snow, Daddy? Please?"

"We'll see, kiddo, we'll see," he said, quickly wiping his feet on the rug and taking a step forward.

"Oh, no you don't," his mother snapped, waving a finger in his direction. "You get those wet boots off my carpet."

Will smirked and took a step back. Though his father had been gone for years, his mother still ran a tight ship in this house. "Did she call you and tell you she was running late?"

His mother hurried about the room. She mumbled something inaudible under her breath and grabbed her purse

11

from a nearby table before pulling Jillian's yellow jacket up onto her shoulders.

"No. No, she didn't," she said when Will caught her irritated look. "She's been doing this to me a lot lately. I have a life, too, you know."

"You could've called me sooner," he replied, looking away. He slipped Jillian's hat onto her head and playfully pulled it over her eyes, making her laugh and slap at his hands. "She's been working a lot of hours and I'm sure the snow slowed her down."

"Well, I wouldn't want to disrupt her important work," his mother said sarcastically. "If the snow stopped, would you mind clearing my driveway? I have to get going. I'm late for book club."

"Sure, no problem." He gave his mother a salute and winked playfully.

She laughed for the first time and then gave her granddaughter a peck on the cheek before moving around her son and walking out the door.

An hour later, after lugging the snow blower back inside his mother's garage, Will reached for his phone to check, yet again, if his wife had tried to call. Realizing it wasn't inside his pocket, he looked back toward the truck.

He called out to his daughter. "Alright, kid. Time to go." Jillian seemed perfectly content lying in the freshly fallen snow, waving her arms and legs back and forth while gazing at the stars.

"Make an angel with me first, Daddy," she begged. He couldn't resist dropping beside her in the snow. It stung his skin even through his clothes, but he stretched his arms as far as he could to make large, white wings next to his daughter's small imprint.

"You're a huge angel!" Jillian squealed. She sprung up and reached for his hand to pull him up beside her. They peered down at the two figures in the snow, and Will smiled. She always knew how to keep him grounded.

"We better get home to Mom," he said scooping her up and leaning her far over his shoulder.

Jillian giggled when he playfully tossed her on the truck's backseat. His phone, blinking in the cup holder, caught his eye as he clicked her seatbelt. Sliding into the front seat, he swiped his numb fingers across the screen and noticed four missed calls. But, again, none were from numbers he recognized and none were from his wife.

"Well, what the hell?" He exhaled and then barreled the truck out of the driveway toward home.

Turning up his street, Will could see their house ahead. There were no lights on, and his wife's car wasn't in the driveway. He looked down at his phone again. After their talk last night, he was surprised she would work so late without, at the very least, giving him the common courtesy of a phone call. He tapped his fingers on his knee and waited for the garage door to open while fighting the urge to call her again. He glanced in the rearview mirror just as a bright light flashed across it,

13

making him squint from the glare. His stomach fluttered with the relief of knowing his wife was finally home. But when his eyes adjusted, he realized it wasn't her. He switched off the ignition and watched in the mirror as a police officer exited a patrol car. The officer straightened his back, adjusted the hat on his head, and dropped his hand to his holstered pistol before walking toward the truck.

"Stay here a minute, Bug," Will said, fumbling for the door handle. His legs were rubbery as he stepped out of the truck.

"Mr. Kanter?" The officer cautiously approached him, his hand still on the pistol. "William Kanter?"

"Yeah, that's me. Is there a problem?"

The officer cleared his throat. "Are you married to Julia Kanter?"

Will's legs began to tingle. "Yes."

"Can we go inside for a moment, Mr. Kanter? I—"

"What is this about?" Will interrupted. He looked over his shoulder toward his daughter.

"Well, sir, the authorities have been trying to contact you." He cleared his throat again and took his hand away from the gun. "I'm really sorry to inform you, but your wife was involved in an accident this evening. Is there someone you can call to look after your daughter? I'm going to need you to come with me to the hospital."

Will's mouth went dry and he was suddenly nauseous. "Is—is she alright?"

14

The officer looked down at his feet. "It's really best if you come with me, Mr. Kanter. They can give you more information at the hospital."

Chapter Three

Erin wiped down the glossed mahogany bar for what seemed like the twentieth time in the last thirty minutes. She looked out the window at the snow and tossed the rag back in the sink. It was only January, but she was already fed up with the snow and cold. The bite of it had a way of sinking under her skin and stinging her straight to the core. This time of year was always dreary, and because she worked nights, a majority of her daylight hours were spent asleep—at least, she tried to sleep.

"I hope we close early tonight," Jessie said while passing behind Erin. She eyed the credit card lying near the register and then the group of young men playing pool across the room.

"Yeah, I don't think that'll be an issue," Erin scoffed. She pulled the phone from her back pocket and quickly scanned the screen.

"Is Jason coming in tonight?" Jessie asked. Her long, blonde ponytail whipped across her back as she turned toward Erin.

"How should I know?" Erin shrugged and glanced at the TV above the bar. The six o'clock news began with a traffic helicopter panning in on an accident at the Marquette Interchange.

"He's hot. I don't know why you don't give the dude a chance." Jessie leaned back and crossed her arms over her chest. "I know I would if I were you."

Erin shook her head and straightened the liquor bottles below the rail. Because of all the years she'd spent behind a bar taking orders, it annoyed her greatly when the labels didn't face forward so her eyes and hands could move swiftly and efficiently when the bar was busy. Though she had little control over much else in her life, she was insistent on keeping this bar in perfect order.

"C'mon, you've been with a guy at some point in your life, haven't you?"

Erin laughed and tried to appear busy by thumbing through a stack of receipts. "I'm not having this conversation with you, Jessie."

"You mean to tell me he does *nothing* for you at all?" She followed close behind Erin as they walked to the opposite end of the bar. "I've seen him at the gym, and I swear to God I'd rip his clothes off right there if I could. If you're not gonna take that for a spin, then I will."

Erin playfully pushed her away. "Be my guest, because here's a newsflash, Jessie. I'm gay. Remember?" She held her hand toward Jessie with her index finger lifted and her thumb extended, making the shape of an L. "You and I don't play on the same team. Besides, what makes you think he's into me?"

Jessie tossed her head back. "Pu-*lease*—he's in here all the time gawking at you. He told me himself he'd gladly show

17

you what it's like on the other side. And, since we're talking about sports, we even have a little wager on whether or not you've actually been on both teams at one time or another."

"You guys seriously need to find something more interesting to talk about." Erin shook her head. "But, if you really need to know, yes. I'm more than familiar with both sides of the street."

"So you *have* played on both teams. I knew it!" Jessie screeched. "Hell yes! I'm the winner of that bet. I fucking knew it! C'mon, you've thought about riding the Jason train, right? I mean, c'mon."

Erin glanced down at her phone again. "I don't know what you're talking about."

"Uh-huh." Jessie checked her reflection in the mirror behind the bar. She stuck her chest out and pulled her shoulders back before shifting her glance back to Erin. "Kinda like you don't know anything about Jules Kanter either? Is that her you've been waiting to hear from since you got in tonight?"

Erin looked up, narrowing her eyes.

Jessie pretended not to notice the glare. Instead, she tightened her ponytail and ran her fingers over her lips as if she were applying lip gloss. "Oh, Erin, c'mon, you're not as sly as you think you are," Jessie said, turning to face Erin again. She said, "If only we all had as many beautiful people falling at our feet as you do. It must be tough being you."

Jessie raised one eyebrow, looking Erin up and down. "You're such a gorgeous but oh-so-washed-up musician. You almost had it all, but then you let it go. Such a shame." She clicked her tongue and moved past Erin, sauntering toward the kitchen while talking over her shoulder. "Your little story would be perfect for the arts section in the paper, don't you think?"

Watching her go, Erin rolled her eyes. It wasn't the first time Jessie had jabbed at her past or fished for confirmation of her relationship with Jules. Erin knew Jessie meant no harm, but she wasn't about to let those words trap her into a confession. As far as she was concerned, her personal life was off limits to everyone and anyone who asked. She had made that mistake once, and when the truth did come out, her honesty had trapped her more than all of her previous lies combined.

Checking her reflection in the mirror, Erin pulled her braid forward over her right shoulder and then ran her finger over the diamond piercing in her nose. She blinked while looking into her own blue eyes, and she wished she had worn heavier concealer to hide the light freckles on her cheeks. She had always hated those freckles, but they were a trait she shared with her mother, along with her dark hair. The rest of her, including her slight build and no-bullshit attitude, was all from her father.

Glancing at the TV again, Erin noticed that the news was still covering the accident on the interchange. Eyes locked on the screen, she stepped closer and thought she could make out the taillights of what looked like a small black SUV. The front of the vehicle was obliterated and a blue tarp covered the windshield. Moving closer still, she reached for the volume

19

controls, but the reporter reappeared and moved on to the next story before she could turn it up. Stunned, she stepped back and rested her hand on her temple. Jules drove a black Acura, but it couldn't be her. She had left the apartment more than an hour ago. She should be home by now. Eyeing her phone, she thumbed a text to Jules.

Are you okay? Did you make it home?

She looked back at the TV after hitting the send button, but the weatherman had come on now to discuss the sudden January storm that had blanketed the city with six more inches of snow. The next hour ticked by slowly. She checked her phone every few minutes, knowing Jules should have already responded. Finally, unable to take the silence any longer, she picked it up and dialed her number. She knew she shouldn't call at this time of night, but she needed to know if Jules was okay. The phone rang four times before her voicemail picked up, and Erin waited anxiously for the beep.

"Hey, it's me," she blurted. "I—uh, I just wanna make sure you made it home okay. I saw an accident on the news, and I—well, just call or text me when you get this and let me know you're okay. I'm a shithead and I feel bad for not saying goodbye earlier. I know why you can't stay, so I guess, uh, I'm sorry. Call me, Jules, okay?"

Erin hung up, stepped back, and looked at the TV again. There was nothing she could do now but wait. As the night wore on, she tried to stay busy by making small talk with the regulars who strolled in and out. She poured whisky sours,

Leinenkugel's on tap, and shots of tequila, and still Jules hadn't called or texted. She slipped tips in the jar by the register, wiped down the bar again, and checked the tab of the guys still playing pool. They were ringing up quite a bill and getting more drunk as the evening continued. Every once in a while, they looked in her direction and made inaudible comments.

She was sick of guys like these, ones whose attentions were only skin-deep and never reflective of her as a person. They didn't know her, and, for the most part, they didn't really care to know anything about her, but their eyes routinely wandered over her body as if she was there for no other reason than to please them. She enjoyed telling guys like this that she was a lesbian. She found it oddly amusing to watch their brows furl in surprise as they wrapped their shallow minds around the idea that it was possible for a girl like her *not* to be into men like them. "But you're hot; you can't be gay," men like this often told her, almost always followed by, "if your girlfriend is as hot as you, can I watch?" Just the sound of those words rolling off their tongues made her want to lash out and remind them of how incredibly ignorant and egotistical they were. But she would never allow herself to be pegged as a man hater even though she had every right to be one. Instead, she remained calm, smiled confidently, and continued to ask, "Can I get you a drink?"

When Jessie slowly strolled back from the kitchen, Erin watched as the men's eyes followed her, feasting on her curves like a hungry pack of dogs. Jessie was certainly pleasing to the eyes, but she wasn't the type of woman Erin was attracted to. Jessie enjoyed being seen, and though she seemed oblivious to it right now, she ordinarily reveled in the attention. Erin preferred the rare combination of unpretentious charm, intelligence, and beauty, all of which came easily to Jules.

They had met in this very bar on a busy Thursday night when Erin was playing her solo set. Jules and her coworkers had shuffled in and begun slamming shots, downing martinis, and toasting with champagne in quantities that surprised even Erin's manager, who stood behind the bar smiling like the Cheshire Cat. When Erin played her first song, a slow, rough cover of Bob Seger's "Against the Wind," Jules stopped to listen. Their eyes met briefly before they both looked away.

Erin had recognized the smile from Jules' photo in the newspaper; she was the arts and entertainment editor for the *Journal Sentinel* and she wrote a regular column, The Deadline Artist, covering everything related to the arts in the city. Having an arts columnist listening to her sing made Erin uncomfortable, but she tried not to let it show. She read Jules' column often and admired her insight as well as her witty humor—that is, when she wasn't being overly critical of the latest production at The Rep downtown or a new gallery opening in Riverwest. When the set ended, Erin resumed her place behind the bar, but she could feel Jules watching her. When Jules finally emptied her drink, Erin moved toward her.

"Can I get you another?" Erin asked as Jules looked up. Her deep brown eyes were glassy from too much alcohol and her white blouse was unbuttoned just one button too far, so the top of her black camisole peeked out. Only half of the blouse was still tucked into her tight black pencil skirt, and her smooth dark hair was playfully messy.

"No, I'm good. Thanks," Jules said with a sly smile. She ran her hand over her skirt and then pointed toward the small stage at the front of the bar. "Weren't you just up there singing?"

Erin smiled and filled a plastic cup with water, which she used to replace Jules' empty martini glass. "Uh, yeah. I double as a regular bartender and part-time entertainment. You should drink some of that," she said, motioning toward the cup.

Jules smirked and lifted the cup. "You're really good. I mean, *really* good. Have we met? You seem really familiar— and being that good, I should really know who you are."

"Thanks. And, no, I don't think we've met." She smiled widely and leaned flirtatiously forward on the bar, extending a hand toward Jules. "I'm Erin."

She watched the expression on Jules' face shift as their hands touched. Her small fingers were cold, but she had the firm grip of a woman who knew how to handle herself.

"What's the celebration about?" Erin pulled her hand away and scanned the bar for waiting customers.

"Oh, didn't you hear? We, I mean, *they*, won a Pulitzer," Jules said, motioning toward her colleagues, who sat a few tables away.

"Ah. Is that a big deal or something?" Erin winked, pushed herself back, and straightened her shoulders.

23

Jules scoffed and extended her right hand as if she were shooting a pistol. "You're cute. But, don't tell anyone." She motioned for Erin to move closer. Erin did, and Jules' alcohol-laced breath was hot on her face. "Those assholes wouldn't be here if it wasn't for sharp editing and clever rewrites. Excellence in explanatory reporting, my ass. How about excellence in explanatory editing-the-crap-written-by-people-who-use-too-many-goddamn-adjectives-and-have-no-idea-how-to-properly-use-a-fricking-semicolon? There should be a prize for that."

"Is that so?" Erin inhaled a hint of Jules' perfume, making her want to move closer still. "And I suppose you would win that one?"

"Perhaps." Jules once again glanced over her shoulder at the table where her colleagues sat. "The newspaper business isn't quite as glamorous as people might think—well, unless you're them. With the market these days, some of us have to wear multiple hats and do most of the dirty work. But, you know, it's a shared victory and all." She rolled her eyes and made air quotes.

Surprised by Jules' frankness, Erin laughed and tapped her fingers on the bar before noticing a customer waving her over. "If it makes you feel any better, I think your column is pretty good, too," she said backing away. Jules' eyebrows rose in surprise. "Yes, Jules Kanter, a.k.a. Deadline Artist," Erin said with a snide smile, "I know who *you* are."

24

Erin's thoughts drifted away from that night as the ten o'clock news began with a bold "Breaking News" banner stretched across the screen. She instinctively reached for the remote and turned up the volume. Jessie stood beside her, yawning and lazily leaning against the bar.

"We have sad news to report tonight from the Marquette Interchange," the anchorwoman began, her face sober and serious. "The unexpected severity of the winter storm has claimed the life of Milwaukee native and long-time editor and *Journal Sentinel* columnist Jules Kanter."

The blood rushed from Erin's head.

"Oh my God, Erin," Jessie exclaimed. She reached for Erin's arm. From the opposite side of the room, the men carried on laughing and joking as if there was still air left in the room.

"No, that can't be right," Erin mumbled. "Did they just say Jules?" She was faint and hot. Bitter acid bubbled in her throat and she coughed from the harsh taste.

She looked back to the TV screen. The news was showing an image of Jules, the one that ran with her byline in the paper. It was followed by the earlier scene of the black SUV and the tarp draped across its windshield. The anchor continued. "Kanter was traveling westbound and was merging onto I-94 at 5:30 p.m. this evening when a vehicle in the eastbound lane lost control. It slid at considerable speed into the median, causing it to roll into oncoming traffic and directly into the path of Kanter's vehicle. The Milwaukee Police Department has confirmed that Kanter, who was 40 years old, was killed on impact. The other driver was transported to Froedtert Hospital and is listed in serious but stable condition. Employed at the *Milwaukee Journal Sentinel* for the past sixteen years, Kanter served as the arts and entertainment editor for eight years and was best known for her colorful commentary in covering the city's cultural affairs as well as her theater, gallery and music reviews." The anchorwoman paused, looking toward her co-anchor and then back into the camera. "Having the pleasure of personally knowing Jules, who also served as a correspondent and entertainment liaison for this station, I know she will be missed not only by the staff at the *Journal Sentinel* and her friends here at WISN, but, tragically, she also leaves behind a husband and six-year-old daughter."

Unable to keep down the vomit, Erin rushed toward the bathroom as it spilled from between her fingers. When she reached the bathroom, she fell to her knees and gagged uncontrollably. Jessie pulled back Erin's hair and rested a hand on her shoulder.

"I'm so sorry, Erin," she whispered. "I know she was a good friend. I'm so sorry."

Erin sat up and wiped her face with shaky hands. Gasping for breath, she stood and steadied herself against the wall with one hand. She and Jessie locked eyes and stood for a few seconds in a state of shell-shocked numbness.

"I need to go," she said, shaking out of the trance. She shot from the bathroom, rushing toward the bar to retrieve her phone, but her legs felt heavy and awkward. One of the drunk men was waiting as she rounded the corner.

"Yo, Freckles, you gonna get us some drinks or what?" He held a pool cue in one hand while swaying drunkenly on his feet. "I was beginning to think you all went home."

Erin scanned the area for her phone, ignoring him.

"Hey, we need some drinks over here," he said, leaning toward her, growing more impatient.

Looking up, Erin glared back him. "You've had enough. Consider yourself cut off."

"Fuck you, bitch. Get us some drinks, *now*." The man spit angrily through his white teeth and pounded his fist on the bar.

She froze as the anger spewed from her core, making her insides burn. Her skin grew hot like it did whenever a man spoke to her that way, causing a fire-rage that, if left unextinguished, would consume everything in its path.

"You and your fucking frat boys can get the fuck out," she said in a low, guttural voice that didn't seem like her own.

"Whoa, whoa. Erin, calm down," Les, the manager, said as he appeared from the back office where he had been doing paperwork for most of the night. "I'll take care of these guys. Why don't you let Jessie drive you home? It's okay. Just take a breath and get yourself together."

"You need to put a leash on your bitches." The man laughed.

27

Les clenched his fist and kept it close to his side. He picked up the credit card by the register and waved it in front of the man. "I'm swiping this and then you're done, just like she said."

Erin ignored the brewing tension and turned away. She headed to the back room with Jessie following closely behind. "Let me drive you, okay? Please."

"I'm fine. I just need to get out of here," Erin said, snatching her coat from the hook. She moved toward the door that led into the alley.

"I don't think you should drive right now, Erin," Jessie interjected, trying to block her path.

Erin stopped moving. The pace of her breathing increased, as if she might hyperventilate at any moment. "I'm okay, Jessie. Please move," she said. Her voice was calm, but the air escaped from her lungs faster than she could replace it.

"Erin, I know about you and Jules—we all do. It's okay. You don't have to hide it. Just let me drive you. You're upset—I can see it."

Erin inhaled, and then pushed Jessie aside. "You don't know anything," she said as she jogged toward her car.

Jessie called her name, but Erin slammed the door, started the engine, and spun away before Jessie could stop her.

Speeding down the unplowed street, Erin could think of nothing but Jules' face. When Jules had smiled earlier that night, Erin had clearly seen a glint of something in those dark, coffee-colored eyes, but she had ignored it. Just a few hours earlier, they talked like they had done a million times before. Jules had come over that day to listen to new songs that Erin was working through; Jules always had way of improving everything Erin tried to write. But, as usual, they became distracted by each other. Erin had lived in Nashville for five years before coming back to Milwaukee; she'd met countless talented and creative people there, but never had she met someone as naturally gifted with words as Jules was.

Dazed, she stopped the car outside of her apartment and sat quietly, falling snow covering the windshield and blocking the light. She watched the flakes gather in droves and form a thin white layer over her car. It seemed to trap her inside, and it became harder and harder for Erin to breathe. She hated snow—she had always hated it, but now it was suffocating her. Knowing that she hadn't kept Jules from heading home in the storm made her feel as if her lungs were being crushed. If she had just stopped Jules, made her speak her mind, and convinced her to stay, she wouldn't have been on the road at that exact moment when a random car slid out of control. She would still be in bed tangled in Erin's arms. Or, if Erin hadn't insisted that Jules come to her apartment at all, she would have left the office as usual and gone home to her husband and daughter before the storm even began.

Trudging up the stairs to her second-story apartment, Erin wanted to collapse. Her phone rang in her purse, but she ignored it. She wanted nothing more than to stop the guilt from pushing up inside of her, illuminating all the mistakes she had ever made, making them feel vivid and present. The heat of it all left her stunned and confused. She could almost hear a hissing inside of her ears, as if she might explode at any given moment. Shuffling through the door, she dropped her bag and made a beeline toward the kitchen cabinet, where she had stashed the lorazepam. She flung open the door and fumbled past the aspirin and NyQuil to the bottle she hoped was still hidden in the back, but it was gone.

"Dammit," she groaned, then ran toward the bathroom to see if she had moved it. Her makeup case crashed to the floor as she tore through the cabinet, but she didn't care. She sprang into the bedroom, dropped to her knees, and ripped through the bottom dresser drawer, tossing T-shirts and running shorts aside. And then, there it was: the single bottle of lorazepam. It still contained eight pills. Eight small, round, white pills. In the past few months, she'd held them in her hand more than once and counted them out one by one before slipping them back inside the safety of the plastic container. She often moved the bottle around her apartment, sometimes in hope that she would forget where it was, but also so that Jules would never see it.

Lorazepam was the only drug she still kept—it was the only one she allowed herself to keep. She vowed only to use it if the world became too loud for her to handle and she needed something to make it quiet again. As the hissing grew louder inside her head, she snatched the lid off the bottle and the pills spilled into her shaking hand. She pushed three into her mouth and crawled on her hands and knees toward the bed. A black scarf tangled itself around her leg as she moved. Annoyed, she tugged and pulled it off, but then she recognized it.

It was Jules' scarf. She'd worn it almost every day, and she must have forgotten it when she left earlier. Erin held it in her hands, staring at it, running her fingers over the soft fabric. Then she brought it to her face to breathe in the sweet, intoxicating smell of the floral jasmine perfume Jules always wore. Erin curled into a ball, her face shrouded in the scarf, and sobbed. There was so much left unsaid and undone. As the drugs slowly kicked in, Erin's body began to numb and her mind became hazy and unfocused. She blinked and again brought the scarf close to her face. She stared up at the white, cracked ceiling and the fan that now hung perfectly still above her. With tears dripping from the corners of her eyes, she surrendered and drifted into the black that had claimed her countless times before.

Chapter Four

Will sat at the funeral home's large oak table, feeling numb and dejected. He felt as if he'd been forced to play a tragic role in a depressing production but had forgotten all the lines for the next scene. The funeral director was talking, but it seemed foreign to him. The man could have been speaking Chinese for as much as Will was able to comprehend. Beside him, his sister-in-law, Sarah, listened and nodded with tears streaming down her face, but Will couldn't engage in anything that was happening. Pamphlets were spread out before them explaining options in tiers of cost from burial to cremation, from outrageously expensive Cadillac-type caskets to more economical but tasteful pine boxes. There was talk of what she should wear, what jewelry needed to be removed afterward, and how much potato salad would be needed if they decided on a luncheon following a memorial service.

For Will, none of it sank in and nothing made sense. They weren't talking about his wife; they couldn't be. Just a little over twenty-four hours earlier, he had cuddled next to her in their bed as the alarm clock went off. His nose had been buried deep in her dark hair and he had breathed in the smell of her honey-scented shampoo. But now he sat before a stranger trying to decide if she should be buried or cremated, if her casket should be open or closed.

"Do you know where you'd like to have the service, Will?" Sarah's voice trembled.

He looked up and tried to collect his thoughts, but he couldn't make these decisions. He wanted to get up, drive to the house, and lay down until Jules came home. She always came home. Even when the days got long and she worked late into the night, she *always* came home.

"I don't know," he mumbled. "What do you think?"

"I think we should have it at the church. It's bigger, and I think there will be a big turnout, don't you?" She wiped her red face and reached for a Kleenex.

"She wasn't religious, Sarah. You know that better than anyone. Are you sure that's what she would want?" Will looked down at his gray hands. "Maybe we should just keep it at the funeral home, downtown."

Father Tom had been sitting quietly, his hands folded on the table, but now he took a deep breath and looked up. "These decisions aren't easy, not by a long-shot," he said, his voice calm. "She was your wife, Will. Listen to your heart; that's the only thing that's gonna help you get through this right now."

Will laughed and ran his fingers through his hair. He felt the stubble on his face and couldn't recall the last time he had shaved. "My heart tells me I want my wife back, Tom."

Sarah began to sob and Will immediately regretted the comment. "I'm sorry, Sarah. I'm sorry, Tom," he whispered as tears dripped down his cheeks.

Without looking up, Sarah touched Will's hand as he wiped the tears. Though they didn't usually agree, Will had always respected his sister-in-law. She was two years younger than Jules and a successful lawyer, which made arguing with her a moot point at times. Like Jules, she never backed down from a fight.

The overweight funeral director pulled a calendar from a leather binder and placed it on the table. "Have you thought about a date for the funeral, and would you like it all in one day or would you prefer a visitation in the evening and a shorter visitation and service the following day, along with the luncheon?"

Will shook his head in disbelief. Dying seemed like just another day of business for this man. A few hours earlier, Will had identified his wife's bloody and battered body, but this man was all about the process of putting her in the ground so he could collect a paycheck and go home. Not only did Will have to imagine a future without the woman he loved, but he would never be able to erase from his mind the image of her lying on that gurney. Her dark hair, smelling so good that morning, had been matted and caked with blood. Her face was devoid of color and seemed misshapen somehow, as if something had been pressed against it. There was also dark blood, almost rust-colored, smeared on her cheek and across her lips. Stunned and speechless, he hadn't recognized a thing about her at first other than the diamond ring on her finger. He'd uttered her name as if he expected her to open her eyes, but when he touched her hand and realized its stiffness, the earth shifted and he dropped to his knees.

"Will?" Sarah touched his hand again. "Did you hear me?"

"What? No, I'm sorry. What did you say?"

She dabbed her nose with a Kleenex and looked at him with swollen, red eyes. "My mom and Bill are flying in tonight. Do you want to wait and talk about some of this tomorrow when they can help?"

"No, let's do it now. Let's have the funeral on Friday, here at the funeral home, and I think she should be cremated. Can we be done now?"

Sarah blinked quickly. "Are you sure? I think you should think this through. Did she want to be cremated?"

Will covered his face. "I don't know what she wanted, Sarah." He murmured through his fingers before pulling them away. "She didn't tell me what she wanted. She was always busy. We never talked about shit like that. But I saw her at the hospital. I don't know how they can possibly make her look like the woman she was, and I *know* she would not want to look like that."

The funeral director cleared his throat almost obnoxiously. Instantly annoyed, Will glared at him across the table.

35

"Actually, Mr. Kanter," the man said in a deep voice, "once we clean her up, she will look much better, and more like the woman you knew, I assure you. But still, the decision is yours."

Will detested this man and his business.

"I'm sorry, Will, but I think he's right." Sarah looked down at her hands. "So many people knew Jules. I think if it's possible, we should keep the casket open."

"Fine, but I want to see her first. I don't want her looking like some kind of wax doll. She'd hate that. If she doesn't look like herself, then I want the casket closed, or we'll cremate her first and have some kind of service later," he pushed his chair away from the table, slapping his palms against his thighs in frustration.

"I know this is difficult, Mr. Kanter, but we still need to decide on a casket and burial, readings for the service, things of that nature." The director avoided making eye contact.

Will let his head fall back as he laughed and stared at the ceiling. "I *want* her cremated. That's the only logical thing I can come up with right now."

Sarah started to cry again.

"Very well, then. We have some respectable caskets that can be rented for the service," the man said as his sausage-shaped fingers ruffled through the pamphlets on the table.

"Rented?" Will's head snapped back and he glared at the man again. "You actually rent out caskets, like a car or something?"

36

The director shifted nervously in his chair. "Well, yes, actually. For cremation, many families find it less of a financial burden to rent a casket for the showing rather than purchasing one that will be burned during the cremation process. We place a combustible insert inside the rental unit, so when it comes time for the actual cremation, the insert is able to be slipped out and into—"

"Into what? The oven?" Will clenched his jaw. "Tell me, sir, how many dead people have been in the *unit* you're considering renting for my wife's funeral?"

"Will, please stop," Sarah whimpered. "He's just trying to do his job."

Will coughed, shook his head, and stood up. "I'm sorry. You're right, Sarah. I need some fucking air before I puke."

He stomped out of the room as Sarah apologized to both of the men at the table. Once outside, the freezing January air hit Will's face like a splash of ice water on a hot day. The cold was the only thing that felt real to him. He squinted in the sunlight and was nearly blinded by the brightness of the deep snow that blanketed the ground. He wanted to walk away from this place. He didn't know where to go or what to do, but anywhere would be better than here. Going back in there would force him to face the fact that Jules was never coming home.

He paced and kicked at the ground. A slow burning sensation grew from the pit of his stomach, and he recognized the warning sign. It was the hot sensation of the deep urge that haunted him in times when he was most vulnerable. He hadn't had a drink in three years, but for the first time in a long time, he really, truly craved one. Nauseous, Will leaned against the brick building. He knew Jillian was at home with his mom. She was completely devastated at losing her mother, and he had no idea how to console her. He was also unsure of how to console Sarah, Jules' parents, or the countless other people who knew and loved his wife. He crouched down, leaning his back against the cold, rough bricks, and fought the urge to vomit. He and Jules had argued just a few nights earlier. As the scene replayed in his head, he scoffed and almost gagged at how ridiculous it seemed now.

"I just don't understand why you can't make it home to pick up your daughter at least one night a week," he'd said, watching Jules undress before she stepped into the shower.

"I can't help what stories come in and when, Will," she'd said, putting her face into the water. "There's a lot of new, young editors just begging to get promoted, and they're willing to work for a lot less than what I get paid."

She turned and let the water rain down on her hair as she continued. "Contrary to popular belief, my job isn't all about sitting at the theater. I actually have to edit the crap that goes into the paper. You know how shaky this business is, Will. I can't say no when Nancy calls me. It's my job and she trusts me."

He could see the outline of her naked body though the frosted glass. He'd thought about going in to join her, but he

38

didn't. Jillian was just downstairs, and he was more than annoyed with his wife for never being home at a regular time. Since he only worked construction nine months out of the year, winter was his slow time. He was also nervous about lining up more work for the season ahead because he had recently begun to feel like a single parent.

"I'll pick her up on Monday, I promise," Jules said, opening the glass door slightly so he could see her face. Her dark hair was slicked back and she was gorgeous as the water dripped from her long eyelashes. But still, he didn't go in or give her the satisfaction of getting over his anger.

"Don't bother, Jules. You just go on trying to save the paper and you know where we'll be when you're done—maybe." He seethed.

The sweet look on her face instantly melted. "*Maybe?* What the fuck is that supposed to mean, Will?"

"Nothing, Jules. You do what you gotta do." He walked away, wanting the discussion to be over. But it was too late. She was fuming. Slamming off the water, she pushed open the door, snatched a towel off the rack, and followed him into the bedroom, her skin dripping.

"Who in the hell do you think keeps this family afloat in the winter, Will? You? No, I don't think so."

His jaw tightened as he continued to walk, making the muscles in his cheeks ache, but he knew she was right.

Jules continued to rant, following him out of the bathroom. "And whose idea was it to move out of the city and back to *your* hometown? Pretty sure it wasn't mine. I'm pretty sure we discussed what a bitch of a commute it would be for me to drive back and forth and how much time I'd be away from home. You pushed that, Will. You made that decision for both of us."

He ignored her as she stood at the top of the stairs wearing a towel. He wanted to be done with the discussion—it had gone much further than he'd anticipated. They didn't speak to each other for the following twenty-four hours.

Now, crouching like a child in the cold outside the funeral home, there was nothing he wanted more than to have that moment back. He wanted to be standing outside the shower all over again, but this time he would keep his mouth shut rather than waste the precious time neither of them knew was ticking by.

Staring at the frozen ground, Will heard the door creak as Tom stepped outside. Tom exhaled slowly, his warm breath forming a thick, white cloud that quickly dissipated into the frigid air. He reached inside the pocket of his wool blazer, pulled out a pack of Marlboro Red cigarettes, and coughed in the same gruff way he often did at the AA meetings they attended together. He offered a cigarette to Will, and though Will didn't routinely smoke, he slowly stood and then took one anyway. They said nothing as Tom lit Will's cigarette first, and then his own. Will choked as the white smoke circled around them, mingling with their visible breath.

"You know, Will," Tom said, breaking the silence, "when you finally talked at that meeting a few years back and you told us about the problems you and Jules were going through, I don't know why, but I could tell there was something special about the two of you." He paused as he gazed down the street. "You were both different people back then, but you managed to work through a lot together, including you getting sober, and that took a lot of guts on both sides."

Will gave a nod and took another drag from the cigarette.

"This is a hard time, Will, really hard. We all know that."

Tears slipped down Will's cheeks, but he couldn't find the words to respond.

"Jules would want you to be strong now," Tom said. "She chose you as her partner because she knew you were strong, even when you didn't." Tom dropped his cigarette to the ground and crushed it beneath his black Oxford shoe. "That's what brought her back to you when you proved you could be the man she knew you were all along."

"I don't know about that, Tom." Will wiped the tears from his face and dropped the half-smoked cigarette onto the sidewalk. The nicotine was making his stomach turn. "She always knew I was a fuck-up. Maybe this is my penance, or payback, or whatever."

Tom shook his head in disapproval. "That's not true, Will, and you know it. She may have known you were a fuck-

41

up, but she didn't give up, and neither can you. Not now. Not after everything you made it through." He crushed Will's cigarette with his foot and dug his hands deep into his pockets. "If we understood death, then it wouldn't hurt so much, but dying is a part of living. Feeling sorry for yourself isn't going to help you, or anyone around you, Will. You know damn well better than that. When things like this happen, we have to be strong enough to make the decisions for those who can't make them. Sarah needs you to make the decisions in there. That's your job right now, and then you need to go home and hold that daughter of yours, because she's going to need all the strength you've got left."

"And what if I'm not strong enough, Tom? What if I'm still the same fuck-up she left three years ago?"

Tom reached out and placed a hand on his shoulder. "You *are* strong enough, Will. You just need to believe in yourself, just like she did, and just like you did when you gave up drinking for her and for yourself. Are you forgetting that she came back to you?" He shook Will with his large hand. "It's gonna be a tough road, and I know how much you loved her, but I'm here to help you through it. I may wear a collar and talk to God, but you know that underneath, I'm the same kind of fuck-up that you are. I'm no stranger to pain. God is a lot like women, and maybe even alcohol in some ways. He doesn't always make a whole lot of sense, but he never does things without reason, I assure you. He's got your back—and I've got

42

your back, and so will everyone else at the meetings. Don't you forget that, okay?"

Will wiped his face again and straightened his shoulders. "I won't," he muttered. "And you're right. I need to think about Jillian. I don't know what she's gonna do without Jules."

Will drew in a deep, rasping breath and hesitated in the doorway. For a second it felt as if his lungs would never be full. It was as if Jules had squeezed all the air from his body and he would never breathe easy again.

Tom shook him a second time. "I'm right behind you. All you have to do is go in there and tell them what they need to hear right now. The rest will figure itself out."

Chapter Five

Erin's eyes snapped open to the sound of heavy pounding, but she couldn't pinpoint the direction it was coming from. Still groggy, she peered at the clock, which read 6:25 a.m. The sun was just beginning to show through the curtain that Jules had opened the day before. The reality of the previous night started to take shape as Erin felt the scarf between her fingers, and she wanted to escape before it all came rushing back. But just as she was about to pull the blankets over her head, another loud and persistent rap on the door made her shake and sit up.

"Alright, I'm coming," she called, rolling off the bed. She moved through the apartment slowly, her head feeling like lead. She was still dressed in yesterday's clothes, and she hadn't bothered to remove her boots before falling asleep. Even her shirt still smelled like Jules.

"It's Mom and Rose, sweetie. Please open up." Her mother's muffled voice, sounding frantic and breathless, came through the door.

Erin quickened her pace. She had been so wrapped up in her own emotions that it never occurred to her to call anyone, not even her own mother. Tears stung her eyes and she moved

44

toward the door, feeling like she might collapse. Her mother pushed in as soon as Erin unlocked the deadbolt. She immediately found herself in a tight embrace, held against her mother's chest. Erin instantly felt as if she were drowning.

"Oh, sweetie," her mom said, burying her face in Erin's hair. "I've been trying to call you all night. We were so worried."

Erin clutched her mother's shoulder and pressed her face into the soft fabric of her red fleece jacket. She couldn't utter a single word, so Erin clung to her mother as if her life depended on it. Her mother wasn't used to seeing her like this. Erin had learned at an early age how to bury her emotions and trudge through whatever hardships came her way. As her father always said, "That's what good soldiers do, Erin. They keep going, even when it kills them."

She had been through pain before. Pain that, as a teenager, completely gutted her insides, leaving her hollow and undeniably broken. But this pain was different. It was deep and consuming and reminded her, again, how little control she had over her own life. Death seemed like a good alternative.

"We're here now," Rose said, stroking Erin's hair. "You shouldn't have been alone all night."

"Breathe, baby, breathe," Erin's mother said, still holding her tightly. Slowly, Erin's lungs began to fill and the sensation of drowning began to subside. Pulling back from the embrace, she looked at her mother's tired, bloodshot eyes and realized she was standing taller than she had in months. She held her daughter's arm, more to steady Erin than herself. Diagnosed with multiple sclerosis last year, Erin's mother often had difficulty walking or standing for long periods of time. She could no longer safely drive a car, and climbing the flight of steps to Erin's second-story apartment was a challenge she ordinarily wouldn't attempt.

"Wait, how did you get up the stairs?"

"I practically carried her." Rose shook her head and motioned toward her sister. "But trust me, she would've been here sooner had Joe and I not been up in Fond du Lac babysitting for Claire. Your mother almost took a taxi over here last night until I convinced her to sit tight and wait till I got back. Lord knows she would've killed herself on those stairs."

"I heard about the accident and I've been trying to call you ever since." Erin's mother shook her head. "When you didn't answer—I was really worried about you. Why the hell didn't you answer your phone, at least for me?"

"I'm sorry," Erin said. She noticed her purse still lying by the front door. She couldn't remember the last time she checked her phone.

Rose rubbed Erin's shoulders, trying to meet her eyes. "Did you take anything you shouldn't, hon? I'm not accusing you, and I don't blame you if you did, but did you?"

Erin knew there was no point in lying now, so she simply nodded her head and looked at the floor.

"Shit, I was afraid of that," her mother said, sucking in her breath. "Especially when you didn't answer. What was it? How much did you take?"

"Calm down, Violet," Rose interjected. "She just lost her best friend for God's sake."

Erin's mother shot a seething glare at her sister before facing her daughter again. She took her hands and forced her to look up. "I don't blame you, I swear, but we need to make sure you're safe and you're not going to spiral down. That's the last thing Jules would've wanted. Will you please tell me what you took?"

"It was just lorazepam, and only a few, I swear. I just—I needed to get over the shock." Erin glanced toward the bedroom. "The bottle is on the dresser. I swear, that's all I have."

Erin's aunt and mother exchanged glances before Rose headed toward the bedroom and returned with the bottle in hand.

"I'll make you some coffee," her mother said. She handed the drugs to Rose, who slipped them into her pocket.

"No, it's okay, Mom. Let me do it," Erin insisted. "Please, go sit. You can't be feeling good after climbing up here."

Her mother embraced her again. "I'm fine now that I know you're okay. God, I was so worried."

The tears burned Erin's cheeks again.

"Come here. Let's sit—you look awful." Erin's mother led her toward the couch as Rose made coffee.

47

Feeling numb, Erin unlaced her boots and slipped them off before lying down and resting her head on her mother's lap like she did when she was ten years old, before everything turned upside down when her father died. She stared across the room as the coffee brewed and the air filled with the rich scent of morning blend.

"I still remember every detail of the day your father died," Erin's mother said, her voice quiet as her fingers slipped through Erin's hair. "I'll never forget that last conversation we had, the way his eyes looked and how he held my hand. He was never worried about himself, just about us. When was the last time you talked to Jules?"

"Yesterday," Erin said quietly as she covered her face. "She was here. God, this is my fault."

"Oh, baby, don't say that." Erin's mother clutched her daughter's fingers and pulled them away from her eyes. "Jules wanted to be here, otherwise she wouldn't have come. You know that. She was a grown woman. Things like this happen; you can't control that any more than we could control your father's cancer. As shitty as it is, it's just the cards we're all dealt."

"I never said goodbye to her, Mom," Erin said, sitting up and pulling away. "I was pissed off and acting like a spoiled bitch because she wouldn't stay, even though I knew she couldn't. But I let her leave and never said goodbye, and now that's it. It's over."

48

Her mother's face softened. "She knew how you felt about her, Erin, but you know it wasn't easy for her."

Rose sat down beside them and rested her hand on Erin's knee. Feeling these women's warmth made Erin feel protected. Returning her head to her mother's lap, Erin felt her body go almost numb. Closing her eyes, she saw Jules again. In slow motion, she saw her smile, wink, and turn away. That scene would forever be cemented in her memory; trying to block it was no use.

The evidence of Jules was all over her skin, and the memories of being together began to loop through her head on constant replay. She breathed the coffee scent and her mother's fingers softly caressed her face as she recalled the night that Jules first came back to the bar. It was just a few days after they first met, and Jules had walked in with a coworker. Erin had been surprised at the awkward flutter she felt. She hadn't allowed herself to be enamored by anyone since leaving Nashville—and back there she'd left a mess of not only her own broken pieces, but also a few other hearts as well. When Jules crossed the room, she didn't look toward Erin. The two women, engrossed in conversation, simply sat at Jessie's end of the bar without noticing her at all. Erin glanced toward her own customers and then noticed Jessie pouring drinks for a younger couple who kept her distracted with questions about the difference between cheap and high-end vodka.

"I'll get these two," she said as she moved behind Jessie, who glanced over her shoulder toward Jules.

Jessie laughed and shot Erin a facetious look. "Yeah, I bet you will."

Erin shook her head, but she couldn't stop the smile that had begun to spread across her face like fire in a dry hay field.

Jules thumbed through her phone as Erin approached. Erin's stomach twisted, making her unusually anxious and self-conscious.

"Well, if it isn't the Pulitzer Prize-winning *Journal Sentinel* journalists. Back for another celebration, ladies?" She tossed a coaster before each of them. "What is it this time? Did you interview the president or something?"

Jules looked up, her dark eyes fixed on Erin. She wore a curious expression as she studied Erin's face. Looking back at Jules, Erin rested one hand on the bar and flashed the most confident smile she could muster. Jules smirked and glanced at her phone before turning it toward her coworker, who moved her head slightly to peer at the screen. She shot a quick look at Jules and nodded before shifting her glance back to Erin.

"Actually," Jules said, turning the phone in Erin's direction, "I'm here for you. This *is* you, isn't it?"

Erin blinked while looking at Jules' phone. She instantly focused on an unflattering image of herself. She knew the photo all too well. She had tried hard to put that DUI arrest, and everything that came after it, behind her. Dazed, she looked away. She knew Jules had read the story from the *Tennessean*, the local Nashville newspaper. The article had been run the previous spring, accompanied by Erin's mug shot, courtesy of the Nashville Police Department.

"You know, that does look an awful lot like me, doesn't it?" She backed away slowly. The muscles in her throat tightened, but she tried to play it cool. "But I don't know that girl. Not anymore."

"Hmm, that is interesting." Jules brushed the hair away from her face before placing her phone on the bar. "It is incredibly ironic the two of you have the same name *and* look shockingly alike, though I have to say, you do look much better in person than you do in this photo."

"I'm surprised you even remember my name," Erin defensively responded. She placed her hands on her hips and looked Jules directly in the eyes. "Can I get you a drink, or not?"

Jules persisted. "Unfortunately, this story doesn't paint you in a very positive light, does it?"

Erin crossed her arms over her chest and looked over her shoulder at Jessie. Talking to the other customers, she seemed oblivious to the conversation between Erin and Jules.

"You can't believe everything you read," Erin said. "You should know that better than anyone, Deadline Artist."

Jules lifted a knee and rested it against the bar, clasping her hands around it. Her coworker looked down at her own phone, as if she had completely lost interest in the exchange.

"You're absolutely right." Jules nodded, unfazed. Erin eyed the wedding ring on her left hand, but then looked away. "I did notice that you aren't quoted once in that story, but your agent is, and so is the record company that dropped you. Seems like one-sided, irresponsible journalism to me. I'm guessing you didn't even have an attorney?"

"I spent everything I had left on an attorney, but nobody was really interested in what I had to say at the time."

Jules shook her head. "That's a shame."

"Yeah, whatever. It is what it is, and I'm over it. Like I said, I don't even know that girl anymore."

Jules tapped her fingers on her phone. "You know, I wouldn't mind hearing your side of the story. I've got a feeling it was more than just a DUI that led to them dropping you."

Erin gave her a blank stare.

"I mean it. I'd really like to write a piece on you. I looked you up and I'm really curious about what led a talented girl like you, who just happened to have a hit song, to getting arrested and then working at a bar in Milwaukee."

Jules leaned forward, shifted on the stool and dropped her leg to the floor. "There's something that doesn't quite fit with this whole thing. I knew you looked familiar when I was in here the other night, but I couldn't place it. It hit me the next day—I remembered the *Shepherd Express* ran a piece a few months back on a musician who works at this very bar and looks an awful lot like you. I kept the article—I still had it in my work bag actually—and I even made a note to myself to check this girl out since the article raved about her 'raw and untamed talent,' as they called it. I don't like getting scooped by that little rag on artists in my own backyard, and it doesn't make me look good, for that matter."

Jules' eyes shifted upward again and looked directly into Erin's. She was intimidated.

"When I heard you sing the other night, well...let's just say I happened to be in the right place at the right time. So yeah, I looked you up and found out you've got a little more to you than meets the eye, so here I am. I wanna hear your side of the story and what led up to that picture—or, if you prefer, maybe just your story in general, without all the other bullshit. I'll take it either way."

Erin blinked. Her defenses instantly rose against Jules' penetrating brown eyes.

"Everything you need to know about my story is right there. My side doesn't really matter anymore," she snapped.

"I don't believe that," Jules retorted, holding her ground.

"No? Well, the woman who wrote that article did, and people believed it."

Jules leaned back on her stool. "I'm not interested in what that woman wrote. I'm interested in the real story."

"Why? So you can win a Pulitzer?" She shifted on her feet, nervously scanning Jules' face. "No one even remembers me, or that song. It never even broke the top ten, so I'm not the story you want."

Jules nodded and pursed her lips. "I listened to your song, a bunch of times, actually. It's good, and I think it

53

probably could have gone a lot further with the right backing. Did you write it?"

Erin scoffed. "Yeah, I wrote it. So what?"

"Wow, you are a defensive one, aren't you?" Jules laughed and blinked her long eyelashes. "Well, here's the thing, Ms. Quinn. I'm not trying to sell you out or exploit your arrest. I think you're really talented, and it's my job to write about talented, artistic people in this city, preferably before my competition does. If nothing else, a story like that could bring in a few more people to hear you sing and get you a few extra bucks in tips at the end of the night. It's a win-win for both of us—not such a bad thing if you ask me."

Erin looked anywhere but into Jules' eyes. "There is no story. You were here one night and heard a few songs. I'm no more special than any other musician in this town. As for Nashville, well…not everyone makes it in Nashville, either. It's as simple as that. There's probably a million stories down there just like mine."

Jules pursed her lips again. "Yeah, maybe, but I think there's more here, and I'm not usually wrong where that's concerned."

Erin tried to fake a smile. "I'm just a bartender, and they let me sing here. I made peace with all of that other crap a long time ago. I like to leave the past exactly where it is, and I'm not interested in talking about it anymore. So now, Jules Kanter, can I get you a drink or not?"

54

"I'll go with you to the funeral," Erin's mother said, continuing to run her fingers through her daughter's hair. Erin's eyes felt as if they were full of sand. She opened them and gazed across the room.

"I don't know if I should go," she said, slowly sitting up, feeling nauseous and drained.

"Of course you should go," her mother snapped. "You'll regret it if you don't, honey."

"She had a family, mom—a daughter, a husband. I have no place at that funeral. They didn't know who she was."

Rose chimed in. "How can you say that? You need to go, for you and for Jules, Erin." She set a steaming cup of coffee on the table. "If they didn't know who she was, then they won't know who you are either."

Erin placed her hands over her face and then slowly pulled them down. "I don't wanna talk about this right now," she whispered. "You guys should go home, and you should rest, Mom."

"Oh, hell no," Rose laughed as she headed back toward the kitchen. "You're not getting rid of us that easy. You need some actual food in this place, and I'm planning to make some. If you get any thinner, you're going to disappear."

"We're staying, baby," her mother insisted. "We'll watch bad TV and talk about Jules, or not. Whatever you want, whatever you need, but I am *not* leaving you here alone."

Erin exhaled and stared at her feet, knowing there was no sense in arguing. "Okay, Mom, okay," she whispered and lay back down again.

Chapter Six

Sarah dropped a heavy box of pictures on the table as her sons trailed behind her, begrudgingly shaking snow from their boots. Will stood with a steaming cup of coffee in hand, staring at the frozen river behind the house.

"Where's Jilly?" Sarah removed her knit cap and hastily unbuttoned her coat.

"Downstairs with your mom," Will answered. The boys stomp off down the hall.

"Jesus, Will, you look terrible. Have you slept at all?" She came up beside him and placed a hand on his shoulder. Just her simple touch made him want to crumble, so he quickly moved away. He rubbed his swollen eyes and caught his faint reflection in the window. He still hadn't managed to shave and he wore a worn-out flannel shirt with the Carhartt carpenter jeans Jules always hated.

"You know that old Joni Mitchell song, Sarah? How's it go? I wish I had a river to skate away on? Well, there it is." He lifted his cup toward the river. "Did you bring your skates?"

"Maybe slow down on the coffee, Will. You need to sleep." She turned back toward the box.

"I brought pictures for the memory boards, but we have to go through them." She dug her hands in the box and pulled out a handful of photos. "But we don't have to do this right now if you don't want to."

"It's okay," Will said softly, setting down his coffee. "I know she has a bunch of pictures upstairs in the office. We can add some of those, too."

"How's Jillian today?"

"She's up and down," he said, gazing out the window. "One minute she's talking about mommy being in heaven with Sparky, then five minutes later she wants to know when Jules is coming home."

Sarah shook her head and walked toward the coffee pot. "It's gonna take a little while before it really sinks in."

"Yeah," he uttered. "I'll go get the albums."

He was physically and mentally drained as he climbed up the stairs to the second story of their home. He dreaded walking in to Jules' office. When they first built the house, he'd designed the office specifically with the hope that Jules would spend more time working at home, but she never did. Instead, she went to work more and came home later. But, on the rare nights when she was home, she often had trouble sleeping and would quietly slip out of bed when she didn't think he noticed. He often found her in her office either typing away on the computer or scribbling her thoughts in a notebook. He was never sure what she was writing, or why, but he would watch and wonder what she was thinking in the seconds before she noticed him. Her forehead was usually locked in a tight furl and her eyes darted back and forth on the page as they feverishly tried to keep up with her pen. At times, when he mustered the courage to ask what she was doing, she would simply look up, smile sheepishly, and say, "I'm just writing letters to myself, that's all." He never understood what she meant, but that was Jules—always deep and introspective.

The door creaked as he pushed it open. Sunlight beamed through the huge window that faced the river, and the light accentuated the dusty desk where piles of papers were neatly stacked in an order only she understood. He glanced at the towering bookshelves that lined the walls. He had built them with his own hands, and they housed her prized collection of classic novels. Jules loved the smell of old books.

She owned five copies of *To Kill a Mockingbird* alone, but it was Virginia Woolf and the poetry of Robert Frost, Emily Dickinson, and Walt Whitman she loved the most. Though he had never shared her interest in reading and couldn't hold his own in a conversation about anything literature-related, Will knew how important these books had been to her. That's why he had taken special steps to build her these shelves. He may not have been able to interpret the words inside the books quite like Jules was able to, but he could construct a place for her to display them—and for her, that seemed good enough.

Sitting in her leather chair, Will spun around and gazed down at the river again. This view had also been carefully thought out when he drew up the plans for the house. In order to convince Jules to move outside of the city and away from their problems, he knew he had to impress her somehow. It had been a do-or-die relocation that would either bring them together or tear them apart. His drinking had created havoc in their marriage before the move, and it was giving up drinking and building this house that allowed him to narrowly escape losing his family.

He reached forward to grab a photo album off the bottom shelf and felt the familiar ache in is back that made him wince. Jules often caught that same look on his face when the pain seared through him while he worked around the house. She had incessantly urged him to see a chiropractor before doing permanent damage that would make it impossible for him to work. But he never listened and brushed it off. Now she would never ask him again.

Opening the album, he saw the sonogram image on the first page, taken on the day they found out they were having a baby girl. The doctor had been quiet as she moved the wand across Jules' stomach. All three of them seemed to hold their breath before the doctor finally exhaled and smiled.

"Looks like a girl," she'd said, glancing at them over her rimless glasses.

Jules had quickly turned and looked up at him, her eyes glassed over, waiting to gauge his reaction. They had both hoped for a boy, but since Jules had miscarried before, their disappointment didn't last for more than a few seconds. At least the baby was healthy.

"Well, shit." She exhaled, brushing away a tear. He smiled widely and leaned in to kiss her forehead.

"Are you sure it's not a boy with a really small penis?" Will asked, watching the doctor wipe the jelly from Jules' skin. She looked at him with raised eyebrows as Jules nudged his arm.

"Well, Will," the doctor said, "if he's that small, then you should probably get ready for a lot of teasing in the locker room." She laughed, made a note in the chart, and turned to leave the room. "Congrats, you two! See you next week."

Jules was quiet during the car ride home, but her face was peaceful and radiantly calm.

"You okay?" Will reached over and clutched her hand.

"Yeah, I'm good," she said, looking at him as she leaned her head back on the seat. Her dark eyes were still glassy and her cheeks were slightly flushed. "I was just thinking about what it'll be like to have a daughter. I had boy things in my head for some reason. I guess I didn't think about what we would do with a little girl. Did you?"

"Hell no." He shook his head. "I'm really kinda scared of the daughter we're gonna have."

"God, I know, right?" A smile quickly crept across her face. "That kid is either going to be brilliant or a bitch on wheels."

They laughed. He had never seen her skin glow the way it did that day. Trying to have Jillian hadn't been an easy road for them. Between Jules' career at the paper and being slow to conceive, things had certainly taken their toll, but everything was finally moving in the right direction.

61

The album's next page contained images of Jules as she progressed through her pregnancy. Her gorgeous smile beamed brighter, and her stomach grew with each image. He couldn't help but remember how her surging hormones had made her moody and tired, yet she was just as sexy as ever. Though he imagined the sex would end once she became pregnant, her appetite for it surged after those first few months, once she relaxed and was sure the baby was okay. Those were some of the best days of their relationship.

On the album's last page was a photo of the three of them just moments after Jillian was born. Jules looked exhausted. Her black hair was stuck to her moist forehead and her eyes were red from lack of sleep and hours of pushing, yet her smile was so wide and bright. She held on to Jillian like she had just won the most amazing prize. Will was beside her, his arms wrapped around them both as if nothing could tear them apart. He had been incredibly moved by Jules' strength in bringing their daughter into the world. Watching her go through all of the intense pain, knowing there was nothing he could do to stop it, had been among the most difficult hours of his life. But she had endured it all, though he had no idea how. He had always known Jules was strong, but she had proven it ten times over that day.

His mother-in-law slowly opened the office door. "Are you okay, Will?"

"Yeah, yeah. I'm sorry, Deb. I was just getting these albums for Sarah." He slammed the book shut and wiped his eyes.

"Can I get you anything, Will?"

"No, no. Please, sit down."

She crossed the room and eased into the window seat behind the desk. She looked nervous and exhausted. Jules hadn't necessarily been close to her mother, but they had always appeared to be on good terms, or so it seemed to him.

"I've been thinking," she began. Will's head started to ache. "I know you made the decision to have Julia cremated, and I respect that, but I was wondering what you plan to do with her ashes. Do you plan to keep them?"

Will leaned back in the chair. "I really hadn't thought about it yet, I guess."

"Well, I know the church changed its views on cremation and now it's more acceptable and all that, but I'm just not sure I could walk into my home and see her there every day—I mean, if I were you. Do you know what I mean?"

Will nodded slowly, but he was unsure of the point she was trying to make.

"I'm just trying to think how hard it might be for you and Jilly if you kept her here, that's all." She stopped momentarily, as if to catch her breath before continuing. "So, Bill and I were wondering if you might want to consider entombing her ashes. I know Jules had trouble and balked at some of my beliefs—she always did—but out of respect for her grandparents and me, I was wondering if you might want to place her near them?" Her voice cracked and she patted his knee with her small, wrinkled hands. "It's just something to think about. Maybe you'll want to buy a spot there, too, someplace where Jilly can visit you both someday."

"I'll think about it, Deb. Thanks." He reached for another album.

"Will, there's something else," she said. "I know you and my daughter had some rough times, and I, for one, certainly don't believe in second chances. But I know you loved her, even when it seemed like you didn't. She was hard-headed and married to her work and probably not always the easiest woman to live with. God knows she wasn't an easy child to raise." Deb chuckled. "But she certainly didn't deserve the bullshit you fed her before moving out here."

Will looked at the floor, feeling like a scolded child. "I know, Deb. I'm sorry."

"You didn't let me finish." She picked up his leathered hand and held it in her own. "I don't believe people change, Will, I never have. You almost lost her, but you fought hard to become the man she deserved. You're a good father and I'm so proud to call you my son-in-law. I was terrified of what would happen to her if you two got divorced."

"I still don't know how I ever got her to go out with me, let alone manage to keep her." He shook his head.

Deb gazed around the room and then up at the bookshelves. "She always surprised me, and she never did like to give up on things, even when she should have. That was just her way. I don't know how she managed to maintain a relationship with her father, either—not after the bullcrap he pulled. But she did, even when Sarah and I wrote him off."

Will folded his hands. He wondered what his own father would have thought of Jules, had he lived long enough to meet her. For once he might have been impressed by Will's ability to accomplish something, especially since he'd assumed his son would never amount to much. If his father could have seen how incredible Jules was, maybe it would have finally forced him to see his son as a man and not as the lackluster child he'd always believed Will to be.

"I don't even know what to do now," Will said. He lifted his head and looked up at his mother-in-law. "I still can't grasp that she's not coming back. None of this feels right—none of it."

She turned and sat down across from him again.

"You'll breathe and you'll take it one day at a time, just like I will," she said, trying to force a smile.

Will couldn't believe the strength that his mother-in-law exuded. She was handling the situation so much better than he could have imagined. "I don't know how you're doing it, Deb, but now I know what made her so strong."

She laughed and brushed a tear from her cheek. "Oh, honey, that girl was born strong. That had nothing to do with me."

65

Chapter Seven

Erin's mother slept peacefully at the end of the couch, wrapped in a ball-like position that didn't look remotely comfortable. Her breath rose and fell in a constant, steady rhythm and Erin knew she was in a deep sleep. Rose had gone home late last night, but Erin's mother had insisted on staying. Though Erin appreciated the concern, she felt as if she were being observed under a microscope. Her mother was watching her closely, almost too closely. She was reminded of the same suffocating way her mother had watched over her when Erin was a teenager.

But that wasn't until after the time when her mother had passed out cold at the end of another long night of drinking. While she slept it off, her mother's piece-of-shit boyfriend held Erin down in her bed and stole her virginity during an excruciating act that Erin had desperately tried to forget. Her mother had managed to clean herself up after that mess, and she tried hard to repair her relationship with Erin, but her guilt made her suffocating and somewhat overbearing. Though she had been shattered by Jules' death, Erin didn't want it to become a moment where her mother held on too tightly and suffocated her again. Her mother had tried to stay awake as long as possible the previous night, as if to be sure that Erin wouldn't drug herself again, but Erin remained awake when her mother did finally drift off to sleep. It was then that the memories of Jules began to fire from every corner of her mind.

Though Erin resisted doing an interview, Jules continued to stop at the bar, usually on Thursdays when Erin did her solo set. Sometimes she would be with friends or coworkers, other times she would come alone. But Jules would sit on the same stool at Erin's end of the bar each time she came, her dark hair tucked behind one ear and her smile infecting everyone around her. She was always perfectly put together, from the earrings she wore to the shoes on her feet, and Erin often wondered what it was like to be that confident and charismatic. As Erin approached her, and before any words were spoken, Jules would always nod, smirk like the journalist she was, and then ask the same question: "Feel like talking tonight?" It became quiet, almost flirtatious banter, and Erin soon found herself becoming more curious about this attractive and relentless writer.

Then, on a night when Jules was drinking with friends, Erin turned at just the right time to catch Jules watching her. Her eyes grazed over Erin's body, subtly but distinctly. Though she quickly looked away, Erin was surprised and tried to meet her glance again, but Jules didn't turn. She let it go and continued pouring drinks, but she quietly observed as Jules downed three more martinis while laughing and joking with the women around her. Erin could tell Jules was slightly drunk when she began talking enthusiastically with her hands and her hair began to fall carelessly over her eyes. Then, finally, as the crowd began to thin, she looked over at Erin and lifted the corner of her lips into a slight, almost suggestive smile. But, instead of mirroring her attempt, Erin pretended not to notice; she looked away and reached for a bottle of Jim Beam from the lower shelf. She knew how to play this flirtatious game, even if Jules wasn't actually aware of her own participation.

When Jules became caught up in conversation again, Erin smirked and grabbed a napkin from the stack beside her. She scribbled her cell number in thick red digits and wrote "call me," underlined twice. She casually placed it beneath Jules' drink before moving to the opposite end of the bar. Erin pretended to be busy and waited for Jules to notice. When she finally stopped talking long enough to take a sip, Jules focused on the ink. She smiled, picked up the napkin, and shoved it into her purse before anyone noticed. She kept the same facetious grin on her face and looked straight into the mirror behind the bar while lifting the martini up to her thin lips. Then, as if she knew she was being watched, her eyes drifted toward Erin again—but this time Jules slowly blinked as their eyes met and stayed fixed on each other.

Erin leaned back and watched Jules empty the glass. She set it near the inner edge of the rail as if inviting Erin to fill it. But, before Erin could make a move, Jules spun on the stool and walked out the door with nothing more than a quick wave to her friends. Unsure what to make of the sudden exit, Erin wondered if she had completely misinterpreted Jules' actions, or maybe even offended her. She spent the rest of the evening, and most of the next, feeling befuddled and self-conscious.

Two days later, as she tried to push the embarrassing failed attempt at flirting with Jules out of her mind, an unfamiliar number lit up her phone. Running late for work, she was rushing around her apartment.

"Hello?" She pulled on her shoes and scanned the room for her purse.

"Uh, Erin? Did I catch you at a bad time?"

She recognized Jules' voice immediately and stopped moving.

"Well, if it isn't the infamous Jules Kanter," she said coolly. "I have to say, I'm a bit surprised to hear from you after the way you walked out the other night."

Jules breathed into the phone and Erin imagined her smiling in her usual coy way.

"Yeah, uh, sorry about that. I had somewhere I needed to be just then," she said almost flippantly.

"I bet you did." There were muffled voices in the background, and Erin assumed she was calling from work.

Jules let out a playful laugh. "Listen, you gave me your number, so I'm calling you. Are you—?"

"No, I'm still not interested in doing an interview with The Deadline Artist."

Jules laughed again, but this time it came with a more cynical tone. "What I was going to say is, are you free for lunch tomorrow? But, if you'd rather be a smartass, I can always stop in at the bar and wait for the snarky bartender humor you get paid to dish out. Or is this just how you are all the time?"

"Well, I have been told I can be funny, both in front of and behind a bar," Erin replied. "But why would a fancy journalist like yourself want to meet a snarky bartender like me for lunch?"

"You know, I haven't quite figured that out yet, but is that a yes or a no?"

Butterflies rose in Erin's stomach, but she knew this sudden crush could very easily go awry. "As long as you promise not to use your weird journalistic powers to trick me into doing an interview," she said, "then I suppose I'm free."

"Well, I'm glad you think so highly of me," Jules laughed. "But you should probably know straight up that weird journalistic powers are exactly what I use to get everything in life. It's sorta my trademark."

"Alright, alright, Jules Kanter. Where would you like to meet?"

"Do you know Buck Bradley's on Old World Third?"

"Of course—who doesn't? Pretty cliché of you, Kanter."

"I happen to like that place," she fired back. "I like their burgers, and it's close to my office. Meet me there at noon, and do me a favor. Just call me Jules, okay?"

Erin walked toward the front door of her apartment with a wide grin stretched across her face. "Funny, we have

70

good burgers too, yet I've never seen you eat one. But you've got it, Kanter. See you tomorrow at noon." She hung up before Jules could say another word.

The following day, Erin was completely consumed with thoughts of Jules. She couldn't stop thinking of the way Jules' eyes had drifted over her body, and she wondered if maybe she had read more into it than she should have. But, judging by Jules' reaction and her sudden phone call, she also knew Jules had to be at least somewhat curious. Though she tried to stay distant and unavailable, Erin had always been good at luring women in. She would be patient and standoffish, but then she would draw them closer and tease them just enough with her humor and charm before hooking them on the line and keeping them there until she was ready to let go. But Jules had evaded her usual tactics. Sure, she had been wrong before, and Jules definitely wasn't the first straight woman she had found herself attracted to. At the same time, she couldn't shake the feeling that Jules was feeling something too. Was it the prospect of getting a story that kept her coming back to the bar, or was it something else? Either way, she knew she needed to keep things light during this lunch and not give too much away.

Erin reached Buck Bradley's before Jules did, at exactly 11:45. She was nervous and fidgety as she sat at the long, cherry wood bar to wait for her. It seemed odd to be on this side of the rail now; she had never felt comfortable from this vantage point. She preferred to be the one standing, the one in control, but everything about this lunch placed Jules in the

71

driver's seat. Glancing down at the pristine bar, one of the oldest in the city, she suddenly felt the light touch of someone brushing past her. She turned just as Jules slid onto the stool beside her. Her aviator sunglasses were pushed up on her head and she wore perfectly tailored black pants, a sheer black-and-white windowpane blouse, which was tucked in just right at her trim waist, and black peep toe heels on her tan feet. In jeans and a cardigan, Erin instantly felt underdressed.

"Are you always this early?" She tossed her purse on the bar and turned toward Erin with a bright smile. Her eyes were so dark that for a second, Erin thought she could see her own reflection inside them.

"I usually try to be on time, yeah. Don't you?"

Jules smirked and pulled the glasses off her head, allowing her dark hair to spill back against her face. "I'm usually late for everything. Just ask my husband. He'll gladly tell you all about it."

Erin was deflated at the mention of her marital status.

"How long have you been married?"

"Too long," she replied, motioning for the bartender.

"So what's on your mind, Jules Ka—"

"Jules, just Jules," she said, shaking her head and lightly touching Erin's arm with the tips of her fingers.

"Alright then, *Jules*, what's on your mind?"

"Do you really think I have an agenda here? You're the one who gave me *your* number, remember?"

72

Erin nodded coyly. "Yeah, I did, but I wasn't sure you'd actually use it if you didn't think you'd get a story out of it."

Jules straightened her back and tossed her hair over her shoulder. "Oh, come on now. I'm not a predator or anything. Just because I work for a newspaper doesn't mean that's the only thing I'm interested in. I actually think you and I have a few things in common, and sometimes I just enjoy conversation with interesting people. Is that so bad?"

"What do we possibly have in common?"

Jules shoved a pretzel in her mouth as the bartender approached. "Well, for starters, though I'm not a musician, I do know a thing or two about music," she said with her mouth full. "And you, Ms. Snarky Bartender, are one of the best I've seen in a very long time—and trust me when I tell you that I've seen *a lot* of musicians in this city. I'll have a Riesling," she said as the bartender eyed them.

"I'm good with just water," Erin said and then turned toward Jules. "I appreciate the compliment, but is this one of those weird journalistic powers at play here? Because I do mean it, Jules—I'm not interested in you doing a story about me."

"That's not why I just made that comment," Jules said as she leaned against the bar and pointed a finger in Erin's direction. "You are extremely talented. Don't forget that, no matter what a few assholes in Nashville might say."

Erin shook her head and looked down at her water glass, trying not to smile. Though she was unsure of Jules' intentions, she couldn't stop herself from liking her.

Erin snapped back to reality at the sound of her mother's voice saying, "Did you sleep at all?" She found herself staring at her empty, unmade bed. Jules had been in it less than forty-eight hours ago.

"A little," Erin lied, turning away from the bedroom. She crossed the room to where she had dropped her purse on the floor two nights earlier. Fishing through the front pocket for her phone, she realized she had shut out everyone in her world since the news about Jules broke on Monday night.

She eyed her missed calls. Her mom had called seventeen times in a span of six hours. There were also three missed calls from Jessie, one from her boss, Les, and two from an ex-fling, Tina. Ignoring her blinking voicemail box, she checked her text messages. Again, there were several messages from her mom, Jessie, and Tina, who wanted to know if she was okay.

Though Tina was well aware of Erin's relationship with Jules, she had no regard for boundaries and crossed them at any given opportunity. Her sudden concern about Erin's feelings seemed like nothing more than a ploy to tangle her back inside her toxic web of drugs and all-night parties. For Erin, the interaction with Tina had been nothing more than a matter of convenience. She needed something and Tina provided it. Though she'd known this wasn't fair, she'd also known they were both consenting adults. In the beginning Tina had filled a void, and later—in a twisted way—Tina became her weapon for making Jules jealous.

Thumbing through her phone, Erin couldn't stop herself from looking at the last text she had received from Jules, on Monday afternoon. *Running late, be there at one*, was all it said. She sighed and tried to block the guilt that was once again rising.

As her mom struggled to sit up on the couch, Erin heard the familiar thud of the morning newspaper hitting the bottom step below her apartment. It was a sound she knew well. Jules had signed her up for a subscription so that Erin could read her column. She opened the door and peered down the stairs, eyeing two newspapers lying at the bottom wrapped in red plastic. Though for months she had engaged in the same routine of bringing them in to read as she drank coffee, she wished the papers weren't there now. Normally, if she wasn't sleeping after a long shift at the bar, she would have inspected Jules' section of the paper and read her column, if she had one that day. Then, a few hours later, Jules would call or come by the apartment and prod, in a casual, unassuming way, to learn what Erin thought of the day's stories or the topic or performance she had covered. But, instead of giving her the satisfaction of telling the truth, Erin would usually tease her by pretending she had been too busy to read any of it. In reality, however, she would have already soaked in all of Jules' words like a sponge taking on water.

Now, staring blankly at the papers lying in the snow, she realized just how dry her life would be without the stories Jules could spin. Though Jules brushed off her accomplishments and viewed her own writing as nothing more than one woman's opinion on topics she had no right to judge, Erin knew there was much more to the real Deadline Artist than simply met the eye. Though Jules could be precocious and sometimes timid on one topic, she could also be highly critical and opinionated on the next. Knowing the real woman behind the words, Erin understood that the cynical Jules was also the manufactured one. Her true gift was in seeing artists for who they really are—just ordinary people with extraordinary talents. Of course, what Jules usually failed to see, despite the name of her own column, was that she herself was also an artist.

Erin's mom eyed her as she stepped back into the apartment, shaking off the cold. "What's that?"

Erin looked down at the wet papers in her hands and unwrapped the first one, letting the plastic fall to the floor at her feet.

"It's the papers from the last few days," she said, unrolling Tuesday's headlines.

With her hands trembling, she looked down at the front page. There, in the right-hand corner, was a picture of Jules. Her beaming smile and dark, shimmering eyes stood out from everything else, as if she was the most important thing—the only thing—on the page. The bold headline below the image caused her stomach to convulse.

Saying goodbye to Jules Kanter.

Erin couldn't read on. She dropped the newspaper on the table and sank into a chair. Her mother's hands gripped her shoulders and she stood there for a moment before moving away to sit in the chair across from her daughter. She sighed, looked over at Erin, and then unwrapped the second paper.

"They have a look back at her career," her mom said softly. "And it also says her funeral is on Friday, here in town."

Erin couldn't move, but she couldn't cry either. Instead she sat in the chair, completely numb. After that first lunch with Jules, her world had begun to shift. Everything that had seemed bleak suddenly became brighter, and she looked forward to each and every time she saw Jules. Though Jules continued to frequent the bar, they soon began having lunch several times a week, which quickly turned into dinners out. Though she was secretly hoping for more in those early days, Erin knew that Jules only saw what was happening between them as friendship. Erin was six years younger than Jules, but they had so much in common. Erin felt the natural, almost magnetic attraction building between them, but she knew Jules couldn't see it for what it really was—not yet. Though she was open with Jules about her sexuality, it didn't seem to scare or intimidate her like it had with some other straight female friends.

"So, have you thought more about doing the article?" Jules asked one night as they shared drinks at the Newsroom Pub on Wells Street. It wasn't a place Erin would normally go, but when she was with Jules, it didn't seem to matter where she was. As long as Jules was there, she was happy.

"No, actually, I haven't," Erin said, slowly stirring her drink. "Is that why you brought me out here tonight?"

Jules smirked and quickly checked her phone. "No. I wanted to come here because it's quiet and I might have to go back to the office if my boss calls, but I did want to ask you a question—"

"Oh, geez. Here it comes," Erin said sarcastically, leaning back against the hard wood of the dimly lit booth. "Alright, Jules, spill it."

Jules drew in a quick breath and Erin could sense that she was uncharacteristically nervous. "Was part of the reason your record label dropped you because of your sexuality?"

"Why do you want to know?" Erin retorted. Her body instinctively tensed up.

"Honestly, I'm just curious. I mean, I understand what it feels like, to be, well—"

Erin laughed as Jules stumbled on her words. "You know *what*, Jules? What it's like to be gay? I don't think so."

"Why would you assume that?" She looked away, appearing almost wounded.

"Because you're married, Jules; you like men. You don't know what it's like to be gay, or what discrimination feels like, because you've never gone through it."

"That's an unsubstantiated opinion," Jules mumbled while lifting her drink to her lips. She swallowed slowly before

78

continuing. "What if I told you I do understand but just never had the guts to admit it?"

"Admit what? That people like me get discriminated against every day, or that heterosexual privilege is actually a real thing?"

Jules shifted in her seat and fidgeted with the napkin beneath her drink.

"No, Ms. Sensitive. Can you get off your political high horse for a minute, please? What if I told you I'm attracted to women? Would that surprise you?"

Erin felt her stomach flutter with guarded excitement.

"Girl-on-girl thoughts? Well, Jules Kanter, this *is* a much better topic."

Jules laughed shyly and leaned back. "Never mind. Forget it."

"Okay, okay. I'm sorry. I'll be serious. I just wasn't expecting you to say that. I thought we were about to throw down a debate or something." Erin laughed and straightened in her seat. "Tell me what you're thinking. I promise I won't do that again."

Jules took another deep breath and looked around the room before slowly leaning in. "The first girl I ever crushed on was a friend's sister, only back then I didn't really know it was crush. I just thought she was cool and beautiful, and I knew I really liked being around her."

Erin smiled and shook her head. "Jules, that's normal. It doesn't make you gay."

"Yeah, maybe, but when she started dating a guy, I was furious. I don't even know why. I found myself doing the dumbest things to get her attention, and all it did was piss her off and make her avoid me. Eventually I started having these fantasies about her sleeping over at my house, and they weren't necessarily sexual fantasies, but I think I actually wanted to *sleep* with her. I just didn't allow myself to even think it because I was raised Catholic and I thought my bed might burst into flames if I thought about sex with a guy, let alone a girl."

Erin couldn't help but trivialize her story. "Honestly, this is just normal stuff. It doesn't make you gay. If you masturbated to her picture, maybe, but being gay is more—"

Jules cut her off quickly. "My point is, when did you know? I mean, when did you *really* know you were a straight-up lesbian?"

"That's a contradiction in terms." Erin smiled and brushed her fingers across the table before looking into Jules' eyes.

"I always knew, Jules. That's my honest answer. I know it's not unique, or poetic, but that's the truth. I was afraid of it, sure. I denied it sometimes, but when I was around ten, or eleven maybe, and all the girls were starting to care about boys, I was still watching reruns of Charlie's Angels and thinking about what it would be like to kiss Jaclyn Smith. Guys never excited me like girls did. And yes, I did have boyfriends over the years, but it just wasn't the same. I always knew I was meant to be with women."

80

"And what about your parents? Were they okay with it?"

Erin traced her finger along the edge of her glass. "I never had the chance to tell my dad. He died before I came out. As for my mom, well...she was in denial for a while and thought I was going through something because I was depressed, but she came around eventually. Since then, she's always been supportive."

Jules relaxed momentarily. "So, are you still into brunettes?"

"Brunettes are *the* most dangerous kind of women." Erin laughed, and the facetious glint reappearing in Jules' dark and perspicuous eyes. "But, you know," Erin said, "You wouldn't be the first writer in history to question your sexuality." She waved a finger at Jules. "You're in good company, at least. I'm pretty sure there's been plenty of them— Truman Capote, Oscar Wilde, Tennessee Williams, T.S. Elliot, Walt Whitman. Should I go on?"

"Oh, so now it's just because I'm a writer. I see." Jules nodded. "Those are all men, and I think you're just making fun of me now, but you do have a valid point there." She shifted her head. "Did you know that Emily Dickinson had a hot-and-heavy affair with her sister-in-law?"

Erin's insides began to stir. She was enthralled not only with the topic of conversation but also the infectious and fervent way Jules delivered it. "Emily Dickinson? Really?"

"Yeah. They wrote hundreds of letters to each other, and Susan, her sister-in-law, was also the first person to read a good chunk of all her work. Emily herself was quite a recluse and she never married, but let me tell you, if those letters don't capture love to a T, then I don't know what does." Her inflection suddenly turned somber. "Most of the letters were found after both women died, and Susan's family pretty much denied the whole affair, but it's a pretty sad story, if you think about it."

Erin wanted to reach across the table and touch Jules' hand.

"Some writers just knew what they were doing," Jules said softly. "But damn, people just don't write like that anymore."

Erin nodded, watching her closely.

"Eleanor Roosevelt is another one," Jules said, perking up again, as if they were playing a game.

"That one I did know," Erin said as she looked down at Jules' hand. "I wrote a paper for a feminism class in college about Eleanor and her oh-so-scandalous affair—with a reporter, of all people."

Jules raised one eyebrow. "That reporter's name was Lorena Hickok, and I know you'll find this hard to believe, but I have a book about that, too."

"Geez, Jules, maybe you are a lesbian."

Jules' shoulders shook as they both laughed, but something twisted inside Erin. She wanted Jules, but not as a friend. Her inner radar emitted a dim yet distinctive warning as she glanced around the near-empty bar. She had learned all too well in Nashville that it could prove dangerous being too trusting of someone looking for a story, and she wondered if this was Jules' simple attempt to draw her out of her shell. She wanted to believe this budding relationship was authentic and Jules wasn't leading her on for selfish reasons. But, as much as she wanted to touch Jules, Erin's jaded side told her to hold back.

"What is it?" Jules asked when she realized Erin had gone quiet.

Her eyes slowly drifted back to Jules and studied her face. Erin downed the last of her martini. "I've just never met anyone quite like you, Jules," she said after the last swallow slipped down her throat. "I really like hanging out like this, but I have to say, if I didn't know any better, I'd think you were hitting on me right now, or maybe you're trying to trick me."

The smile melted from Jules' face. She dropped one hand to her lap as the other continued to fidget with the napkin. "Why would I want to trick you? Would it be so bad if I were hitting on you?"

"If you were serious, no, not at all, but you're not gay, Jules. You're just curious. That's all it is. I've fallen for straight girls before. It never ends well for anyone."

Jules pursed her lips and her forehead tensed. She seemed surprised and almost disappointed. "Maybe you're right. Maybe I *am* just curious."

83

An awkward silence crept between them and Erin regretted voicing her opinion. While Jules bit the inside of her lip and checked her phone, Erin desperately tried to think of something funny or interesting to say so Jules wouldn't find an excuse to leave.

"Oh, and geez, I almost forgot," Erin blurted. "Every bookworm lesbian knows that Virginia Woolf indulged in the girl-girl side, too."

The corner of Jules' mouth rose into a crooked smile. "She fell in love with another writer, Vita Sackville-West." Jules shifted in her seat and looked back at Erin again. "But, I'm sorry to disappoint you, only a small portion of their relationship was actually physical."

Erin nodded and smiled facetiously. "But it *was* physical, and neither of them denied it."

"True. Some people called Virginia Woolf an experimentalist in humanity, but I think that's just fancy talk for saying she was a brilliant and somewhat tormented woman who needed to experience certain things so she could accurately project them in her art—or maybe that was just a nice way of calling her a part-time dyke. I don't really know."

Erin laughed and shook her head. "Damn, Jules, and I thought I was a book nerd. Maybe you should be teaching literature rather than working for a newspaper."

Jules shrugged and looked off again, seeming unimpressed with herself. "Well, Virginia Woolf is one of my all-time favorites. Did you know she wrote *Orlando* about Vita?"

Erin shook her head and hung on every word as it drifted from Jules' lips.

"Vita had more than a few liaisons with other women even though she claimed to love Virginia," Jules said. "Which, of course, drove Virginia crazy. But instead of getting even, she did the one thing she knew she could do—she wrote about it. Well, she created her own version of it anyway."

Erin nodded and then rested her chin on her hand. Enthralled, she watched Jules drop fact after fact, as if Virginia and Vita were old friends rather than writers who had lived a lifetime before them.

"Virginia developed a character to mirror exactly the way she saw Vita—as both a woman and a man," Jules continued as she leaned in and held Erin's stare. "Vita's own son called that book the longest love letter ever written."

Erin was astounded by Jules' knowledge, and it only enhanced her already deepening attraction. "That's all really interesting, Jules," she said, attempting to be modest. "But if we're getting back to that whole brunettes-are-trouble theory here, wasn't Virginia Woolf a brunette, and wasn't she married?"

"Well, yeah, she was married, but her hair was more light brown, I think," Jules replied. Her face lit up and she lifted her nearly empty glass. "But then again, Vita was also a married brunette."

85

"Uh-huh. I rest my case." Erin leaned back and crossed her legs, unable to wipe the smirk from her face.

Jules tilted her head and smiled. "Well, sadly, Virginia committed suicide when she was only 59, but I think that had more to do with her being bipolar than her relationship with Vita. But touché. I guess you got me on the brunette thing."

A wide smile spread across Jules' face. As Erin smiled back, she became acutely aware that she wasn't the only one feeling the attraction.

Chapter Eight

Will straightened his tie and focused on his clean-shaven reflection in the mirror. Sarah was talking to Jillian just outside the bathroom door. She used the calm, mothering voice she often used with her own sons—that is, when they weren't fighting, kicking each other, or begging for her attention in some way.

"When we walk up to her, it'll look just like she's taking a nap," Sarah said softly.

Will turned on the cold water and let it run through his fingers, trying to block out the conversation, but it was no use. His daughter's voice penetrated the door like a close-range bullet.

"Can I touch her?"

Though he couldn't see his daughter's face, Will felt the weight of her words and his legs strained to keep him upright. He switched off the water and dried his hands before opening the door.

"Um, sure. Sure, you can touch her," Sarah replied, looking up at him. She held his glance and pulled Jillian into a tight hug. "Maybe it's better to just say a prayer for her instead, though, okay?"

Will blinked and hovered near them, feeling queasy. Though he had only been seventeen when his father passed away, he still had a clear image of him lying in the casket. He knew his daughter might not fully comprehend what was happening, but he wished he could shield her from it anyway. Seeing a deceased person for the first time—let alone her own mother—wasn't something she would easily forget. Even cold and lifeless, Will's father had appeared just as intimidating as he had been on the last morning when he left the house for work. The only difference was his attire. Lying in that box, he was dressed in the only suit he owned: a dark navy blue jacket and slacks he reserved only for funerals or weddings. Though his skin was pale and waxy, Will still feared his father's menacing eyes might snap open if he got too close. He worried his father would reach out to slap him across the head, like he had done a million times before.

Though he knew his wife was nothing like his father, Will had put off seeing Jules for as long as possible. He didn't want to remember her in the same empty way he recalled his father. With heavy feet and his heart vehemently pounding in his chest, he slowly walked toward the polished—and rented—white casket.

Will closed his eyes and tried to prepare himself for what he was about to see. He counted in his head, *one—two—three—four—*. He jolted his eyes open on five and found himself staring at an unexpected sight. Just as the overweight funeral director had assured him, he had meticulously cleaned

Jules' face and almost perfectly masked her injuries. While she didn't look exactly like herself, she didn't appear plastic or wax-like. Instead, she was almost as beautiful as she had been in life. Her face was peaceful and her thin lips rested in an expression that resembled the contented smile that's achieved during a deep and tranquil sleep. Will knew the expression well. He had seen it on many nights when he would lie awake watching her as she slept. He wondered how the mortician had managed to capture her presence so perfectly. Unlike the fear he'd had when he looked at his father, found himself hoping Jules would open those gorgeous dark eyes and laugh at him for watching her like a stalker. But then the realization of the moment crept in and warm tears streamed down his face.

After regaining his composure, he went into the other room to be with his daughter and sister-in-law. He stood at Jillian's side and turned to meet Sarah's eyes. She was on the verge of tears, just as unprepared to see Jules as he had been only minutes earlier. "Go ahead, Sarah," he whispered. "I'll take Jilly."

Sarah straightened her shoulders, wiped her face, and gave Jillian a quick smile before letting go of her hand.

Will knelt to his daughter's level and spoke over the sound of Sarah's muffled sobs. "You look really pretty, Jilly Bug." He looked into her chocolate-colored eyes.

Her small hands reached up and felt her double braids, which just touched her shoulders. "Grandma did my hair."

Will nodded and brushed a piece of lint from her black velvet dress. "She did a good job," he said. He tried to smile but had to look away. She resembled Jules so much with her narrow eyes and high cheek bones. He knew he would have a daily, living reminder of everything he lost as she grew older. "We're gonna go see Mommy now, okay?"

"Mommy's in heaven, Daddy," she whispered. She placed her hands on his shoulders and seemed puzzled by his remark.

"She sure is, baby." His throat tightened and he didn't know if he could speak another word without crumbling. Picking Jillian up, he held her close and moved forward, just as Tom had urged him to do a few days earlier.

When they reached the next room, he slid into autopilot. Jules' family gathered around the casket, a circle of flushed faces and red eyes, but they moved aside when he approached with Jillian in his arms. She ignored the sobs around them, as if Jules was the only thing she could see. Jillian's eyes were fixed on her mother, and Will watched his daughter's face glaze over with a wonder he couldn't begin to comprehend. And then, when she finally looked away, he was relieved to see her eyes explode with a new and precocious understanding rather than tears.

"She looks like she's sleeping, Daddy," Jillian whispered.

Will kissed her cheek and held her tighter, and before he could stop himself, he reached out and touched Jules' hand.

90

Regretting it instantly, he pulled back. Her fingers were cold, stiff, and so unlike the ones he had felt just a few weeks before when she had forced him out to see a movie he wasn't interested in. To his surprise, she'd grabbed his hand as they walked toward the car. She hadn't unexpectedly touched him in what seemed like weeks. When he squeezed her fingers, she looked over at him and smiled slightly. Instead of going straight home, they drove to a local pub for a late dinner.

"I was thinking we should take Jilly to Disney this summer," she'd said, dipping a French-fry in ketchup and twisting it between her fingers.

Will had groaned and sunk deeper in his chair. "Really? Do you *really* wanna do that?"

She laughed, shoving the fry in her mouth while continuing to talk. "Um, no, but neither of us went as kids, and we need to give Jilly that memory." She paused to swallow. "Besides, won't it be cool for all of us to experience it for the first time together?"

"Can you actually pull yourself away from work that long?" He mumbled the veiled accusation under his breath.

"Don't do that," she said, wiping her hands on a napkin. She tossed it on the table before pushing her plate away. "I'm trying, Will. I'm here right now, and I'm trying."

He tensed his shoulders and regretted the remark, but he couldn't stop. "You're never home, and when you are, it's still like you're not *really* there."

Jules shook her head. "What do you want me to do?"

91

He leaned forward and reached for her hand, but she pulled it away before he could touch it. "You just seem more distant than ever lately. It feels like you'd rather be anywhere than with us."

Jules picked at the label on her beer bottle and stayed silent.

"What else can I do, Jules? I'm in AA, I'm not drinking, and my life revolves around you and Jilly, but I feel like I still lost you."

Her eyes darted up and met his. "I just need more time to get over some of the things that got us here, Will. That's all."

He sighed loudly and clasped his hands between his knees. "Okay."

"But, you could ask me about it, you know."

"Ask you about what?"

She pushed her empty beer bottle away and shot him a serious look. "Work. You could ask me about work. It's important to me, Will. It's like you're jealous of that or something."

He scoffed as his hands began to sweat. "I'm not jealous of your work. I just wish you were home more, that's all. We need you, too."

She shook her head again and looked away, disappointed.

"Okay, I'm sorry," he said, reaching out to touch her knee. "Tell me about it. What are you working on?"

She took a quick breath and leaned forward before speaking. "Well, awhile back I met this musician and she's really good, so, naturally, I wanted to write a feature on her."

A hint of excitement stirred in her eyes.

"Right now she's working as a bartender downtown, but it turns out she had a record deal in Nashville. Some things happened and she got involved in some shady stuff, and, well…it turns out her story has a few more twists than I was expecting."

"What do you mean?"

"Well, that's kinda what I'm stuck on right now. She has a—well, a sad history, I guess you could say. But in a weird way, it makes her story even bigger, given what she's had to overcome. She's not really offering it up easily, though."

Will nodded as he made his best attempt to seem interested.

"This girl is really talented," she replied, leaning toward him. "She can take any cover and make it sound like something you've never heard, plus her own songs are even better. But, I feel like if I don't tell her whole story, then what makes her so unique might get lost."

She looked away and lowered her voice. "I showed Nancy an early draft. She seems to like it, but she wants me to dig deeper into this girl's past, and…I don't know. I'm just not there yet. It feels cheap to take it that far. I mean, I wanna focus on what it's like to be a gay musician trying to make it in Nashville, or in Milwaukee, but Nancy wants me to keep digging for more...well... more dirt, I guess. I just don't know if I can do it."

She looked up at him as if she were trying to gauge his opinion. "I'd really like to keep writing high-level features like this rather than my column, so I have to get this right. If this story pans out, I could be back to writing about things that mean something to me again, and maybe even take it further and write a book. I don't know. I hate what they've done to my column. That's just not me anymore, you know?"

"People love your column, Jules," he said with a smile. "No one goes to the theater anymore without reading your reviews first."

She scoffed and leaned back. "Whatever. That's not even remotely true."

"It does sound like an interesting story though, honestly." Will said. "But what do you mean when you say 'dark side?' Did she kill someone?"

She snorted and shook her head. "Uh, no. She's just gay, but in the eyes of some people, that's probably just as bad. Her record deal went south, and I'm pretty sure sexuality had something to do with it. She had some problems there, and back here too, but I can't get her to tell me exactly what went down. There's just a lot more to her than I realized when I started this, that's all."

He placed some bills on top of the check and rose to his feet. "Geez, Jules. It sounds like you're diving into some muddy stuff here," Will said. "Are you sure you wanna write about that?"

She reached for her purse and narrowed her eyes. "About what? Homosexuality? Why shouldn't I?"

"No, that's not what I meant at all," he said. "I'm just wondering what people might say about you taking on heavier topics like that, that's all. It's not really what you do, you know? And, on top of that, maybe this girl doesn't want you to dig. Maybe she just got a shitty record deal, and maybe it had nothing to do with her being a lesbo, or whatever." He slipped his hands inside his pockets and hoped he hadn't offended her. "Just don't make it more than it is, that's all I'm saying. If it's not a story, don't make it into one. Don't be one of those reporters."

"Thanks for the vote of confidence," she snapped. "Everyone has a story, Will, *everyone*. Gay, straight, white, black, I don't give a shit who you are, there's a story in everyone. But some lives are bigger than others, and those are the gems just waiting to be found. A good writer can take anyone, or anything, and spin it into a mediocre story; all you need is a few fancy adjectives. But this is so much bigger than that. If it weren't for stories like this, people wouldn't be inspired to do anything. They'd just stay stuck inside their shitty lives and keep walking around half-asleep and act like the world owes them something. But she's not like that. She gives something back without even trying, and that's something worth writing about."

"Jules, I get it," he said defensively. "I didn't mean to insinuate—"

"Do you get it? I don't try to make people into news, Will, and I don't just make shit up as I go along. But sometimes the best stories do come out of nowhere, and they've been under your nose or serving you drinks this whole time and you didn't even realize it. All I need is just one story to get out of this bullshit pigeon-hole they stuck me in. You know this was never where I wanted to be, and I feel like it's now or never to show the paper that I'm more than a dependable second-rate columnist and editor who can paginate faster than anyone else in the newsroom. This is the kind of story that can get me there, I know it."

Will reached for her hand. "I get it, honey. I know how passionate you are about your work, and I love that about you— I do. But I miss your passion at home. We have a story there, too. Don't forget that."

She sneered and stood up. "Gee, how could I forget?"

They didn't speak on the drive home. The heat of Jules' frustration filled the car and pushed them farther apart. Will wanted to understand her passion, but he couldn't. All he knew was that his wife was gone all the time and he wanted her closer. He missed the woman she used to be.

Neither of them moved when he pulled into the garage and switched off the ignition. Jillian was at his mother's, and without their daughter to distract them, they had little left to say to each other. He didn't want to fight, so instead he let his hand slip off the steering wheel and move toward the hand she had rested on her knee. He clutched her fingers tightly and she looked up slowly, a blank expression on her face. The look in her eyes made him realize he had to keep fighting for her attention or he just might lose her again.

"I love you," he said softly. "You know that, right?"

She didn't speak but simply sighed and looked away. He couldn't read her. About to give up and open the door to let her be, she surprised him by grabbing hold of his arm. When he turned, she leaned in and kissed him softly. Without hesitation, he clutched her face and pulled her in closer. He couldn't remember the last time they'd reacted to each other this way. Once inside the house, he pulled off her jacket and pushed her against the wall before leaning into her body. She sighed and tugged at his shirt. He felt the heat of his own breath on her skin as he kissed her neck and inhaled the scent of the perfume he'd bought her for their anniversary last spring. When she impatiently pulled his shirt over his head, he laughed and clumsily kicked off his shoes. She smiled and touched his face with her fingertips. Unable to make it up the stairs to their bedroom, he pulled her down on the stairs and moved himself over her. Her dark eyes glimmered in the dim light as they made love right there on the stairs. He had no idea it would be one of the last times.

Will was brought back to reality when the funeral director approached and whispered about visitors beginning to arrive. As Will set Jillian back on the floor, he said, "You and

97

your daughter will want to stand next to the casket, and her sister and parents will be first in line."

Will nodded, noticing the line beginning to form. The memory boards lined the entryway and he watched as people dabbed their eyes at some of the photographs, then smiled at others. He had no idea how he would make it through the next four hours. Looking at Deb, he recalled how his own mother had appeared during his father's funeral so many years ago. Though they fought constantly and rarely showed affection toward each other, Will's mother had seemed fragile as she held onto his arm to steady herself. He was never quite sure if she'd adopted that appearance because of the attention she received for it or if his mother had truly been devastated by losing her husband. But now, as he peered at Deb and Sarah, he understood the true meaning of loss.

Like Will, Sarah couldn't hide her emotions. Her eyes were swollen and her hands trembled. She wrapped a Kleenex nervously around her fingers. Deb stood at Sarah's side, her hand holding Sarah's arm. Watching them, Will remembered how angry they had been at him once, when they realized everything he had done to Jules. But somehow, he had managed to win them back. He would never be sure if Jules had truly forgiven him, but her mother and sister did. He didn't really know why.

He remembered clearly the night when Sarah had finally seen him for the piece of shit he was back then. When his father-in-law passed away three-and-a-half years ago, Jules had rushed around taking care of details and being strong for everyone else, like always. But instead of being the supportive husband she needed, Will had indulged in one of his disappearing acts—sitting at the bar with friends and not answering his phone. He had become so accustomed to Jules keeping things together that it never occurred to him she might break at any moment.

Though she and her father were on good terms when he passed away, his death was sudden and their relationship had, at times, been less than stellar. For most of her childhood, Jules' father had been a raging, selfish alcoholic who was happiest when he was doing anything but being a father. Though she rarely talked about those days, Will knew it had affected her. When her father died, he assumed Jules would take it in stride, like he had with his father and like she did with most things. It wasn't until Sarah stormed through the doors of the bar that night that he realized how wrong he had been.

"What the fuck, Will," she said, standing directly in his face. Though she was small and pretty like Jules, Sarah was feisty and always more direct.

He looked back at her with glassy, half-open eyes. The smile faded from his face as his friends slowly moved away. He set his glass of brandy and Coke back on the bar and tried not to slur. "Hey, Sarah, what's up?"

"My dad died, remember?" She glared at him in a way he had never seen her do before.

Will looked down and steadied himself against the bar.

99

"Your wife has been trying to call you. You remember her? My sister?" There was heat behind her words. "It's time to go. Get your shit."

As she drove Will back to his and Jules' house in the city, Sarah tore into him like an angry animal. "I don't know why she doesn't leave your sorry ass. How could you leave her alone on the night before our dad's funeral? What the fuck were you thinking?"

Will stayed quiet. He knew he had screwed up this time, but he wasn't quite sure how to dig his way out.

"Goddamn you, Will. You are a piece of shit," she said as she pulled into the driveway.

"I'm sorry," he slurred. "I thought she was okay."

Sarah laughed sarcastically. "Fuck you, Will. Fuck you." She slammed the door hard, making the entire vehicle shake around him.

The house was eerily quiet when they stepped inside. It was well after midnight and Sarah didn't remove her coat. "I'm going home. Get your shit together," she whispered before walking out the door.

Will slipped off his shoes and clumsily made his way down the hall. When he pushed open the bedroom door, he could see the outline of Jules' body on the bed. She was fully clothed and lying in the fetal position.

"Jules," he mumbled, walking over to lie beside her. He gripped her shoulders and then attempted to fold himself around her body like an awkwardly-fitting glove.

"You left me alone," she mumbled. He could tell she was crying.

"I'm sorry," he said. "I thought you were okay. I'm sorry." He buried his face in her hair and squeezed her tight.

"I'm not okay," she whined. "I'm *not* okay."

"I'm here, honey. I'm here now."

"You're never here. You're *never* here for me—just like he never was." Her body went limp. Minutes later, she pulled herself off the bed and walked away. Though he should have gone after her, the swirling confusion in his head—the result of too much brandy—took over and he was soon fast asleep. The next morning, he found Jules in Jillian's bed, nestled beside their daughter.

Recalling that night with disgust, he watched the first people in line greet Sarah with somber, sorrow-filled eyes. He both admired and feared her strength. Though she could never hide her feelings quite like Jules could, he knew Sarah was just as tough as his wife, and he was going to need that toughness now more than ever.

Chapter Nine

Erin felt listless as she helped her mother from the car. "Careful, Mom. It's slippery," she said.

Her mother nodded, reaching for her cane. Once she was steadied against Erin's arm, she gripped it tightly. Scanning the faces of the people who moved toward the brick funeral home building, Erin suddenly found it hard to breathe, and she wondered if any of them knew Jules the way she had.

"I don't know if I can do this," she said, turning toward her mother and feeling panicked.

Her mother sighed and tightened her grip. "You can, sweetie. You have to."

Erin looked at her intently, wanting to escape, but then lifted her chin slightly and begrudgingly stepped forward. She heard the soft murmur of voices as soon as she opened the doors, but her eyes were immediately pulled to the photographs of Jules that lined the boards in the hallway. She veered away, not wanting to see them, and dug her hands deep into the pockets of her blazer.

Her knuckles brushed against a scrap of paper. Without thinking, she pulled it from her pocket. Peering at the name and phone number scribbled on a torn piece of paper, she

102

remembered what it was. Clenching her eyes, she shoved the paper back into her pocket, trying to forget why Jules had given it to her during a lunch at Buck Bradley's months earlier, in August. It was after their relationship had turned physical and, unable to handle the shift, Jules had retreated rather than facing her fears head-on. To add insult to injury, Jules had tried to passively break things off while simultaneously slipping Erin the contact information for a job she thought Erin should pursue. It was the first of many times that Jules would both crush and astound her with one blow.

As her anxiety crept higher, Erin tried to slow her breathing and focus on the gray mosaic-patterned carpet beneath her boots. It reminded her of the floor in the waiting room at the hospital and she recalled the day last June when her mother had collapsed at work. After being admitted to the hospital and undergoing a multitude of tests after temporarily losing feeling in her legs, it became apparent her MS was progressing. The doctors were uncertain if she would regain normal use of her legs. Though her mother had tried to downplay the incident, even she couldn't deny what was happening. As the doctors explained the seriousness of the situation, and what they could expect going forward, Erin sensed the walls slowly closing in around her.

Though she had moved back from Tennessee late the previous March, when her mother was officially diagnosed with MS, Erin's plan had always been to go back once they established a plan for her care. Erin knew she needed to fix the mess she left behind in Nashville. She would never be satisfied knowing just how close she had come to achieving everything she'd worked so hard for, only to end up the quintessential down-and-out story in the gossip section of the *Tennessean*.

But, as time wore on, and after her mother's collapse, Erin realized she might never get a second chance to clear her name. She spiraled down hard before coming home and now, at age thirty-four, she was losing precious time. She was frustrated, worried about her mom, and tired of working at the bar. When Erin finally left the hospital on the evening of her mother's collapse, exhausted and upset, Jules was the first person she thought to call. But by the time Jules reached her apartment after work, Erin was sitting on the couch, a mirror placed before her and three lines of cocaine neatly cut and ready. Though the drug had been her nemesis in Nashville, Erin had stayed away from it after moving home—until now.

"What's going on?" Jules rushed through the door and immediately stopped in her tracks. She still wore her black-rimmed glasses, which she ordinarily wore only at work, and her expression turned from one of worry to something resembling complete shock.

As Jules stood before her, Erin let her eyes drift acutely over Jules' body. But instead of answering, she leaned down and snorted the first line using a tightly-wrapped dollar bill she'd dug out of her purse just minutes before hearing Jules' footsteps on the stairs. Erin sat up quickly and crinkled her nose, warding off the sneeze-like sensation that always followed the first hit.

"Want some?" She wiped her nose and looked Jules up and down.

"What the fuck is going on?" Jules asked bluntly.

Erin gazed down at the mirror. "Have you ever heard of Archimedes, Jules?"

"What are you talking about?" Jules dropped her purse and snatched the glasses off her face. "You are seriously scaring me right now. What is going on?"

"He was a Greek mathematician who said, 'Give me a place to stand on, and I will move the Earth.'" Erin leaned forward and looked at her reflection in the mirror beside the two remaining lines of cocaine. She pushed it toward Jules, who continued to glare at her. "He worked with levers and pulleys and shit, but then he tried to invent some kind of machine that would start enemy ships on fire by reflecting the sun off a mirror. Did you ever try that as a kid? Starting shit on fire with a mirror?"

Jules shook her head and knelt on the other side of the coffee table. "Where is this going, sweetie?"

"I don't know where I'm standing anymore, Jules," Erin whispered, trying to blink away tears. "I don't know where I'm supposed to be, or what I'm supposed to be doing. My mom needs me, but all I can think about is getting the hell out of here again. This place is like a disease that just sucks me back in every time. But where can I go now? Back to where I started from five years ago? And then climb out of the hole I dug myself down there?"

Jules stared back at her, but just as she was about to speak, Erin cut her off again.

"If you really want something to write about, then here it is—they crucified me down there, Jules, and I didn't have the balls to stop it. That label I signed with literally created a person that wasn't me. She sure looked an awful lot like me, and she sounded like me, but I sold out and then I—I couldn't take it—I couldn't. I couldn't lie the way they wanted me to. They wanted the perfect all-American girl, and they thought they were getting Carrie Underwood or something, so they tried to paint that image. But what they didn't realize was that I was really just an all-American piece of white trash that just happened to like fucking other girls."

Jules looked down at the mirror and shook her head. "Wow, Erin, so this is what you're gonna do about it? You think snorting cocaine is going to help change where you've been and where you are now?"

"No," she said leaning forward, taking the second line. She leaned back and rubbed her nose as Jules scowled. "It's just going to numb everything and keep me going until I figure it out. I'm a pro at fucking things up, but it feels good to be numb sometimes. Take some. You'll see."

"I don't think that's a good idea," Jules scoffed. She stood and walked toward the kitchen, clearly irritated by the situation. Erin lifted the mirror and followed closely on her heels.

Jules opened the refrigerator and looked inside.

"What are you doing?" Erin asked.

"When's the last time you ate something?"

"I'm not hungry," she said as she stepped closer to Jules. "Have you ever tried coke? It's not a big deal, just try it."

Jules slammed the refrigerator door. "I'm not doing it, Erin."

Instead of backing off, Erin moved even closer, pinning Jules against the counter while reaching around her and setting the mirror on the counter. She let her arms rest on either side of Jules, her face just inches from Jules' face. Jules' smelled of perfume and had mint on her breath. Jules looked ahead, her hands gripping the edge of the counter behind her back.

"What are you afraid of, Jules?" She moved back just far enough to look her in the eyes, but Jules shifted her gaze.

"I'm not afraid, but you aren't thinking clearly right now. I know you're upset, but this isn't going to help."

Erin laughed and moved away to free her. "Really, Jules? What are you even doing here?"

"You asked me to come," she said turning toward the mirror.

"You know that's not what I'm talking about. What are *we* doing? What is this? Are we friends or are we something else? You know what I am, but what are *you*, Jules?"

Jules' dark eyes averted Erin's glance. "I don't know," she said, looking at the cocaine. Her fingers moved closer to the dollar bill.

"You don't have to." Erin softened her tone and dropped her hands to her sides.

"I know," Jules mumbled before bending down. She sniffed the line before Erin could say another word, then stood up with her eyes closed and her face wrinkled.

Shocked, Erin took a step back.

"Oh God, that burns a little." Jules pinched her nostrils and leaned against the refrigerator.

"Give it a minute," Erin replied, completely astounded by Jules' sudden action. "Why did you do that? I really wasn't trying to make you do anything you don't wanna do. Honestly."

"I know," Jules whispered, still leaning against the refrigerator. Her eyes lifted and she held Erin's gaze. "I really just want to understand you, so if this is what you want, then fine, I tried it."

The raw and irrefutable emotion on Jules' face made Erin move away. She knew that look. Even through her clouded judgment, she knew she could no longer ignore that Jules' felt this attraction too, although she was still denying it. And Erin knew she couldn't have Jules, at least not in the way she really wanted her, so she moved backwards until she felt the wall behind her. Sliding down, her hands moved over the rough finish until she reached the floor. Jules crossed the room and sat beside her. Neither of them spoke for a few minutes.

When Erin pulled her legs to her chest and rested her head on her knees, she studied Jules' profile. There was a slight redness on her well-defined cheekbones, as if she was nervous, and her thin lips quivered slightly. Jules gazed silently ahead, but then, as if she knew Erin was watching her, she turned and their eyes locked. Erin knew Jules wanted to say something, but either she couldn't find the words or she was afraid to say them.

When Jules' eyes drifted over Erin's face and then lingered on her lips before slowly moving back up to meet her stare, Erin lifted her head and leaned in closer. When their lips touched, Jules tensed and pulled back. Erin opened her eyes. Jules' expression was both fearful and surprised, but Erin lifted her hands and held Jules' face, gently pulling her closer and kissing her again. That time, Jules didn't pull back. Erin could taste the mint on her tongue, and her lips were even softer than she'd imagined they would be. Just as she pulled Jules closer against her, feeling her body naturally react, Jules pushed her away and then scampered to her feet.

"Jules," she said, standing up slowly. "I—I'm—"

Jules wiped her lips, ran her fingers through her hair, and walked away.

"Shit," Erin whispered. She rested her hands on her hips and looked down at the floor. Jules stood in front of the bay window, her back to Erin with her hands covering her mouth.

"I'm sorry, Jules, but I can't keep denying this. Please—"

Jules turned to face Erin. "Just so we're clear," she said as she moved closer, "I love my family."

"I know," Erin said quietly. The air had been sucked from her lungs.

"And you don't have to have a pity party just to get my attention—you already have it," Jules exclaimed. Her face was tense, but she moved closer and reached for Erin's hand. "I don't know what this is any more than you do, but I'm here for you. I just don't think we should do something right now that we might both regret."

Erin's eyes glazed over. She didn't want to cry, but Jules pulled her in and held her there, speaking softly in her ear. "You're gonna be alright," she said. "You just have to trust yourself, and trust me. You can always trust me."

As the line crept toward the open casket, Erin thought of those words, *you can always trust me,* and clutched the black scarf that was wrapped around her neck. Though she had questioned whether to wear it, that scarf was the one thing she had left of Jules, and she needed that physical comfort to get through the funeral. Her mother's hand tightened on her arm when their eyes landed on the white casket at the front of the room. Erin held her breath watching Jules' parents and sister greet mourners. But then, noticing Jules' husband and the little girl beside him, she became paralyzed. When the little girl turned, she thought she might collapse. Just like in the pictures Jules had shown her, Jillian was the spitting image of her

110

mother, from her dark, wavy hair, to her thin lips and deep-brown eyes. Erin stopped as the line moved again. "I can't do it, Mom. I can't. I need to get out of here, now."

"No, Erin," she whispered, firmly grasping her daughter's arm as Erin tried to pull away. "You *can* do this, and you will. You aren't walking away from this right now, not like you do with everything else when it gets hard."

Erin glared at her as the line moved forward. She was shocked that her mother would pull out a comment like that now—and here, of all places. Angry, she spun away from her, momentarily forgetting her grief. She looked at the casket and then stepped forward, first shaking hands with Jules' mother and then her step-father. She felt emotionless in expressing her condolences, and it seemed obviously disingenuous. Erin found the courage to look into Jules' sister's eyes as they shook hands, but they didn't exchange a single word. They simply nodded, as if they were passing each other on the street. Erin briefly thought about running again, not caring what her mother would say, but before she could escape, Will turned toward her. Their eyes met and he politely extended his hand, catching her off guard.

"Hi, thank you for coming," Will said in a robotic tone, glancing briefly at the scarf around her neck.

"Hi," she said quietly, her eyes darting away. "I'm so sorry for your loss."

"Thank you," he said, shifting his weight. He nodded again and then looked down at Jillian. The little girl glanced up

111

with pleading eyes that Erin knew all too well, and she couldn't look away. When she knelt, wanting to see the girl's eyes more clearly, Jules' daughter reached out and touched the scarf around her neck. Erin knew it smelled like Jules, and she wondered if Jillian could smell it, too.

"My mommy has a scarf like that," she said quietly.

Erin's heart jumped. "Oh yeah? If you like this one, you can have it."

The little girl's eyes widened as Erin removed the scarf and wrapped it loosely around Jillian's neck in the same way that Jules had always worn it. "There," she said. "It looks really pretty with your dress."

Jillian touched the scarf with both hands. "Thank you," she said shyly, reaching for Will's hand. He turned as Erin rose. Still unable to look at him, she kept her eyes on Jillian. She had asked Jules countless times to meet her daughter, but Jules had refused. Erin knew that meeting Jillian would have solidified something in their relationship that Jules wasn't ready to face. She leaned down and quickly kissed the girl on the top of her head, taking in the familiar oat-and-honey scent in her hair, and then moved away.

Stepping forward, Erin held her breath and looked at the casket. It felt like every eye in the room was on her even though, in reality, Erin knew nobody was watching. None of the people here knew what had gone on between she and Jules, and none of them knew who Jules really was. Or, was it the opposite? Stepping forward, she glanced down at Jules and released her breath. She instantly needed to inhale again, but the air suddenly seemed thin and all she could do was gasp.

Even through the haze of tears that came easily to Erin now, Jules looked almost as she had when Erin last saw her, but at the same time, she looked so unlike the vibrant woman Erin had known so well. Before walking out the door on Monday, Jules had told her they would see each other on Friday, and it didn't seem possible that she was looking at her like this. But Jules had kept her word—like she always did. On Monday they had laughed, touched, and blocked everything out for the entire afternoon—but, for Erin, it wasn't enough. On most days, they thrived in that private world, which was exactly the way Jules preferred it, and Erin had quickly learned that keeping their relationship completely clandestine was the best she could expect from Jules. Now all of it was gone and there was nothing left to discuss.

As she stared at Jules' body, a tingling sensation crept up her legs, as if they had fallen asleep. Just when Erin thought she might collapse, her mother's cold hands clutched her waist. The firm grip forced her to recompose. As other mourners watched, she reached forward and touched Jules' folded hands.

"It's Friday, Jules," she whispered. "And, I'm here."

Chapter Ten

While peering across the table at the stack of papers, angst built in Will's chest. His leg began to twitch, just like it had the day before when he'd tried to sort through all the bills, and the day before that. Jules had always taken care of them.

In the weeks since her death, his complacency toward their finances had become painfully clear. Jules had known what money came in and what money went out, and there had never been a reason to question her aptness or her judgment in financial matters, so he never did. With the wind kicking up outside, the house seemed to tremble, enhancing the inquietude inside his head. He glanced at the clock to gauge how much time was left before he needed to give up, again, to pick Jillian up from school. Though she asked questions and talked about Jules constantly, Will was amazed at how well his daughter was adapting to her mother's absence—unlike him. He felt half alive and deluged with responsibilities he wasn't equipped to handle.

He picked up the credit card bill and looked at the printed words showing through the envelope's clear plastic window. It was an ordinary thing, their names strung together followed by an address, but he knew she would soon disappear from things like this—and so would the lavender smell still lingering on her pillow. Tearing open the envelope, he added up all the trips to the grocery store, gas station, and hardware store inside his head, making sure the bill seemed accurate. He noted Jules' visits to the mall and the restaurants where she most likely ate lunch last month, but one unfamiliar establishment—Catch 22 Bar & Grill—showed up consistently, at least once per week, if not more.

He sighed and tossed the bill back on the stack, knowing he didn't have a clue where to even find their checkbook. The chair creaked beneath him as he moved forward and placed his elbows on the table. He wanted a drink. A drink would make all of this so much easier to bear. He eyed his phone and considered calling his sponsor, or Tom, but there was no time for that; he needed to figure out these bills before collectors started calling.

He also knew he should go to a meeting tonight, before Tom came knocking. He had missed the last two, and he was sure his absence hadn't gone unnoticed. He wasn't trying to isolate himself, but lately he felt like he carried a plague each time he walked into a meeting. What used to make him feel like a part of something was beginning to remind him of how separate he was. He listened to his friends talk about their drinking or the struggles they were trying to overcome, but when it came time for him to speak, he no longer had anything to add. Jules was gone, and talking about it wasn't going to bring her back this time.

Ironically, just two weeks before her death, Will had finally shared the story about when Jules walked away from their marriage—and why. Until then, he had disclosed almost everything else, but talking about the incident that completely broke them meant reliving it. He was ashamed of it and disgusted by it, but he knew it was a vital part of his recovery to accept it and then let it go. It was the darkest moment of their marriage, and explaining it, even with all the time that had passed, still made him feel damaged. Now, sitting in the quiet house and sinking in the quicksand of his own guilt, the memory seeped in again.

He pictured himself outside of the bar, on a night like countless others, with his hand on the door, waiting to pull it open. He had gone there directly from work and ignored Jules' calls, which consistently lit up his phone. He justified his actions by telling himself that Jules was more in love with her job than with him, so it didn't matter that her schedule had changed and she was home early, hoping to see him. Instead, he stood among the crowd of people occupying the bar and ordered the first of many brandy and Cokes. And then Jules' old friend Lisa appeared across the room. He had always been friendly with her and she seemed happy to see him. He reveled in the attention because he received so little from Jules. Lisa, an outgoing blonde who liked to drink, was the complete opposite of Jules in almost every way. And, being the overbearing, fun-loving woman she was, Lisa was quick to express to Will the news of her recent separation from her husband.

"Man, I'm sorry to hear that," he mumbled, noticing her low-cut shirt.

"Nah, it's been a long-time coming," she said, moving closer. Their knees touched and suddenly his hand was on her thigh. They sat together for a long time, discussing the shortcomings of their marriages and pontificating about all their regrets, as if neither were to blame. By the end of the conversation, and after countless drinks, Will was convinced his own marriage was circling the drain. As the bartender gave last call, he realized they were the only two left in the bar.

As he stumbled into the parking lot, Will felt the cool spring rain on his face and realized his level of intoxication for the first time. Lisa, who didn't seem to notice how drunk he was, leaned against his truck with one hand on her hip.

"Um, can I give you a lift?" He asked her pointedly.

She laughed like a vixen, and he liked the way her blonde hair covered her face. Her eyeliner was smudged, but he could see the suggestive look in her hazy blue eyes.

"Uh, yeah. But are you sure Jules won't mind?" She cupped a laugh in her hands like an immature schoolgirl. "Too bad she's not here right now."

"Yeah," he muttered. "Too bad."

Lisa slid into the cab of Will's truck before he could say another word.

Climbing in beside her, Will kept both hands on the steering wheel, but Lisa leaned over, kissed his cheek, and then grazed her lips across his neck, making him almost jump.

117

Though he hesitated for a spilt second, something inside him reacted. He lifted his hand and touched her face, noticing her wet, red lips. And then he kissed her. Though a voice in the back of his mind told him to stop, the alcohol was stronger and pushed him forward. He tore at Lisa's clothes as she bit his neck. His fingertips grazed the lace of her underwear, and beneath them, the warmth of Lisa's skin. But, just as she reached over to unbutton his jeans, a hard fist pounded against the window.

Will's stomach dropped when his drunken eyes focused on the face on staring through the glass, just inches from his own. Jules' black hair was soaked, as if she had been standing there all along, and her eyes were glazed with pure and distinct anger.

"Oh, fuck," Lisa mumbled, quickly pulling down her skirt.

"Oh my God." Will gasped, but Jules turned and stomped away. He could see Jillian's tiny face peeking out from the back window of her car, which was parked nearby. He knew there was nothing he could say to explain the situation, but he scampered after her anyway. "Jules, wait. It's not what you think."

She spun around just as he reached for her arm. Before he knew what was happening, he felt the sting of her hand as it swept across his face and sent him stumbling.

"What the fuck is it, Will, huh? If it's not what I think, then what the fuck is it? I've known that woman for thirty years.

118

We went to fucking high school together and you're screwing her in a parking lot? Fuck you."

Though he knew how wrong it was, the sting of her hand and the force of her words, along with the alcohol surging through his veins, made him lash back. "I wasn't fucking her, Jules, but what the hell do you care? You don't give two shits about me, or Jillian."

Those words sent her into a rage as she lashed out and pushed him with both hands.

"You piece of shit," she seethed. "I'm the one trying to keep us going while you flounder, and don't you *ever* accuse me of not caring for my daughter, you son-of-a-bitch. I'm the one she depends on, not you. You're nothing but a drunk."

"Hey, knock it off," the bartender called from the doorway. "It's time to break it up or I'll call the cops."

"Call them, asshole," Will said, brushing Jules off and reaching for the truck's door handle.

"Oh no you're not," she said, grasping his arm. "You're not driving and taking me down with you when you get caught or kill someone on the road."

He spun around and pushed her before he was able to stop himself, the full force of his anger releasing against her slight frame. She hit the pavement hard, landing flat on her back. She lay there, blinking as the rain hit her face, momentarily stunned. Will had never seen such a wounded look in her eyes, and even in the heat of the moment, he knew he had crossed more than one line. Before he could reach for her,

119

instantly consumed with regret, the bartender tackled him to the ground. Just then, the police pulled up.

Lisa tried to help Jules to her feet, but Jules pushed her off and walked away without saying a word and without looking back. Will spent that night in jail, and then Jules kicked him out of their home. It would be months before she even considered being in the same room with him.

Will brushed off the memory as the old, familiar craving seeped into his bones. He wished he could leave it exactly where it was—in the past.

He took a deep breath and was about to give up on the bills again when he noticed a box sitting on a chair in the hallway. It held Jules' clothes and the other personal items salvaged from her car following the accident. He hadn't been able to look at any of it, or even move the box, since bringing it home. Eyeing the mess on the table, he sighed. He knew her checkbook had to be in her purse—which he knew was inside the box. He stood over it for a few minutes, dreading everything it contained, before finally moving it to the table.

He lifted the cover, one flap at a time, and slowly removed the black Ralph Lauren bag. His legs trembled as he set it down and stared at it. Cold sweat began to pool on his forehead even before he unzipped it. Jules' phone was the first thing that caught his attention. Shockingly, he had forgotten all about it until now. That small device had been like another part of Jules' body most days; it was always with her and she constantly checked messages and sent texts.

The battery was completely dead, so he instinctively plugged it into the wall, just like Jules always did when she came home from work. He powered it up and looked back at her open purse. Inside he found lip gloss, her glasses case, makeup, gum, aspirin, and her wallet, which did contain the checkbook. He opened the billfold to find her driver's license, credit cards, and $27. But, as he thumbed through the plastic-covered photos of Jillian, a folded napkin that had been shoved among the pictures slipped out and landed on the table. The logo—Catch 22 Bar & Grill—immediately caught his attention. There was a phone number neatly written on the napkin in red ink, and the words "call me" were underlined twice. As he wondered why Jules might have something like this hidden in her purse, her phone let out a prominent beep, signaling new messages. Will's stomach turned. Though he had heard that sound countless times before, it was different now. It meant she had unread messages from the night of her death.

Dropping the napkin and wiping the pooling sweat from his forehead, he picked up the phone and moved his thumb across the screen, staring at the numbers. He had no clue what her four-digit passcode might be. He tried her birth month and year first, with no success, then the month of and year of their marriage. Still nothing. When he tried Jillian's birth month and year, the phone unlocked and the home screen appeared. Surprised, Will blinked. With a shaking hand, he realized she had two texts and a voicemail. He tapped the envelope to retrieve her text messages and saw that one message was from her boss, and the other was from someone Jules had labeled with only one initial: E. He opened the message from Jules' boss and their conversation appeared. She asked Jules to make edits to an article and said they would talk about the introduction in the morning, after Jules had slept on it. The next unread message from "E" simply read, "Are you okay? Did you make it home?"

Will scrolled to the beginning of the conversation with "E," trying to determine who Jules had seen before she died. Heat began to rise inside of him as he skimmed their exchanges. With sweat rolling down his face, he read on as the nature of their exchange began to take on a different tone. He felt dizzy and sank into the chair while taking in their playful, almost sexually charged messages. Her responses were like those of the Jules he used to know. They reminded him of when they were first together and newly married. Jules' final message simply said, *Running late, be there at one.*

Will covered his mouth and closed the message app. Nauseous, he tried to wrap his head around what this might possibly mean. He stared at the phone in his hand and felt light-headed, but he needed to know more. With a shaky finger, he tapped the camera icon. He was almost afraid to look as her image gallery appeared. To his relief, most were pictures she had snapped of Jillian; others were from outings with friends and family photos from the holidays. But then, countless photos of an attractive, younger-looking woman with long, dark hair and blue eyes began to appear. He didn't recognize the woman, but he couldn't shake the sense that he had seen her before. There were photos of her on the lakeshore in the city, on the beach smiling, on the sidewalk, and in Jules' car. There were even photos of her lying on a bed, a sheet pulled up to her chest and her shoulders bare. And the next image wasn't a photo at all—it was a video. He closed his eyes and set the phone on the table, face down. Possible explanations for who this girl might be raced through his mind, but nothing fit. Where had he seen her before, and why did Jules never talk about her? He picked up the phone again and pushed play. And then there was Jules, on camera, in a bed, wearing nothing but a sheet, or so it seemed. Her hair fell across her face in an all too familiar way.

"Say hi, Jules," a woman's voice directed. And Jules, appearing completely relaxed, covered her face sheepishly before reaching for the phone. "Knock it off, Erin," she laughed. "Give me my phone." She extended her hand and covered the lens before the video ended abruptly.

"Erin," Will said aloud, nearly dropping the phone. He flipped back to the messages from "E" and immediately connected the dots. He watched the video again and again in a state of shock. He thought, *how is this possible?*

Heart racing, he went back to Jules' purse and dumped its contents on the table. He wasn't sure what he was looking for as random receipts, gum, paper clips, and a flash drive scattered and mixed with the unpaid bills. Then something hard hit the table with a loud *crack*. He stared at the object in utter disbelief. With a shaking hand, he picked up a capped glass tube and

123

inspected it closely to be sure of what he was seeing. But he knew what it was even before removing the cap: cocaine.

The air around him felt thin as he began to hyperventilate. He dropped the tube onto the table, some of its contents spilling out next to Jules' phone. The floor and walls felt as if they were moving, and Will couldn't catch his breath. He grew faint. Collapsing back into the chair, he stared at the mess and covered his face with his hands. "God damn you, Jules," he seethed, trying to catch his breath. "Goddamn you."

Chapter Eleven

Jason's eyes were on Erin as she counted bottles and stocked the refrigerator behind the bar. Though he still came in regularly, she ignored his feeble attempts at flirting. Since returning to work, she'd felt as if she were wearing someone else's skin and nothing seemed to fit. Not her clothes, not her music, not her job—and definitely not men. Without Jules, her life became nothing more than a monotonous routine. If she continued to feel detached like this, it would be easy to slip back into her self-destructive habits. If she chose that road now, she knew there would be no coming back.

Once the beer was stocked, she twisted the cap off a Coors Light and slid it across the bar toward Jason. "Did you get a good enough look, or should I find something else to do so you can stare at my ass a little longer?"

Smiling sheepishly, he picked up the bottle. "What can I say, Erin? I like beautiful women—and here I thought we had that in common."

He raised his eyebrows and took a drink, waiting for her rebuttal. She couldn't help but smile; he could at least make her do that. Across the room, the door opened and a slight chill snuck in, raising the hair on her arms. As Tina moved through the door, Erin's smile melted away.

Dressed in her usual attire—an army-green military jacket, wool scarf, and black slouch hat that was pushed slightly off her forehead to reveal her short blonde hair—Erin's ex-fling Tina loudly stomped the snow off her combat boots, as if to purposely draw attention to herself. She gazed at Erin before striking up a conversation with another group of customers near the door. Erin watched them as they tried to appear inconspicuous, but when they exchanged an awkward handshake, she knew much more than pleasantries were passing between their hands. She looked away, ignoring what she had witnessed. In her current state, she knew that seeing Tina could prove disastrous.

"You have to admit, you do have a nice ass, don't you think?" Jason hadn't noticed her sudden change in demeanor.

Erin scoffed, snatching his money off the bar.

"C'mon, Erin. Come home with me tonight. Give a guy a try. You might just like it." His dimples deepened when he smiled, and she couldn't deny his good looks.

"She's still mourning," Tina said under her breath. She slid onto a stool kitty-corner from Jason and stole another look at Erin.

"I'll go home with you," Jessie remarked, suddenly taking notice of the conversation. She walked over from the opposite end of the bar and rested an arm on Erin's shoulder.

"Hmm, how about you both come home with me?" Jason rubbed his chin between his thumb and forefinger, which gave him the appearance of a deceptive car salesman.

Jessie smiled, slipping her arms around Erin's waist and pulling her closer, as if to kiss her. Erin quickly pushed back. "Don't touch me," she exclaimed.

"Jesus, I was just joking. Relax." Jessie took a step back, glaring at her.

"I'm sorry. I didn't mean—I'm just tired, Jess." Erin reached for her arm, but it was too late.

"Yeah, whatever," Jessie huffed. She spun around and stomped away.

Tina smirked and leaned forward.

Erin glared at her. "Do you want something, Tina? Or, did you just come in here to do your business under my nose and annoy me?"

Tina blinked before looking up with her ice-cold blue eyes. "I just wanted to see how you're doing, Erin. That's all." She condescendingly cocked her head to the side. "But, I can see you're doing great. You look great, anyway."

She moved her fingers up to her mouth, lightly grazing the piercing on her lower lip. "I'll take a gin and tonic, if you have a minute."

Jason eyed Tina suspiciously, but then looked back at Erin. "Are you sure you're okay, Erin? I mean, with what happened to Jules, I wouldn't blame you."

Erin sighed and looked up at the ceiling. "I'm fine. I wish everyone would stop asking me about Jules. Yes, we were friends, but I'm fine, really."

"Uh-huh." Tina cackled, slamming her hand on the bar. "Do you forget I *know* it was more than that between you two?"

Erin turned away. She didn't want to see Jason's reaction or have Tina read her expression. She poured the gin and tonic and placed it on the bar without giving Tina the satisfaction of meeting her stare. Instead, she went back to the register and began straightening receipts, Tina's eyes burning through her. With the receipts neatly in order, she reached for the disheveled stack of lunch menus and unintentionally knocked her keys, which she'd absent-mindedly left on the counter, to the floor. When she picked them up, she remembered the last time she'd almost lost them. Though she was still unclear on exactly how she had misplaced them, her mistake had been a key factor in the closing of a near-perfect day.

It was a warm mid-July afternoon the previous summer and the Thomas Sully exhibit was opening at the art museum. Jules was covering the opening for the paper, and she invited Erin to come along as a guest.

"Don't tell anyone," Jules remarked as they casually walked down the street toward the towering Calatrava, "but paintings aren't really my thing."

"Um, aren't you the *arts* and entertainment editor for the largest paper in the city?" Erin laughed, playfully bumping Jules as they walked.

Jules waved her hand as if the comment were irrelevant. "That was an accident, really," she said, moving ahead to open the door. Erin observed Jules' fitted black capris and wedge heels. She had backed off after the botched kiss in her apartment, but her interest in Jules hadn't wavered.

"I highly doubt you landed that job on accident," Erin replied. She walked past Jules and through the large entryway leading to the exhibit. Jules flashed her press credentials at the attendant behind the counter and they were allowed in with no questions asked.

"Don't get me wrong—I love the theater and music, and, of course, writing, but art is different for me." She reached into her purse and pulled her glasses from their case. "I mean, I can appreciate a beautiful portrait, of course, but sometimes it's paint thrown on canvas with no rhyme or reason that makes me wonder what the hell all the fuss is about."

Erin nodded and smiled. "You know, Jules Kanter, you are full of surprises. I might consider keeping your secret, but let me enlighten you on the world of Thomas Sully."

"And how do you know so much about art?" Jules tilted her head in a way that made Erin want to reach out and kiss her again.

"Well, even though I ended up playing music, my degree is actually in education, and I just happened to take quite a few art history classes—along with those literature classes that you're so fond of," Erin said. A surprised expression spread across Jules' face. "I was a student teacher at Rufus King for a semester, believe it or not. And, here's a little more information about me that just might blow your mind. Before I moved to Nashville, I taught music at an elementary school in Bay View."

129

Jules' smile widened. "Well, who's full of surprises now? I can't believe you've never mentioned this—and why the hell are you working at a bar?"

"Because it pays the bills and they let me play music." Erin smirked and walked ahead to gaze at the paintings. "I've always loved Sully, though. His portraits are amazing."

After finishing the exhibit, they walked the short distance down the lakefront to Coast Restaurant, where they drank wine outside in the cool afternoon breeze. Inspired by Erin offering a bit more about her background, Jules shared how she had worked her way up in the newsroom by writing whatever was thrown her way, but she confessed to truly knowing nothing about art in particular. She had been working in the newspaper's trenches for years when the former arts and entertainment editor retired.

"I'd written a few popular pieces on the rebirth of Summerfest, the growing art scene in the Third Ward, and the urban artist population in Riverwest, and boom, the opportunity landed at my feet. I'd been there so long at that point, and I had a good rapport with our editor-in-chief. I don't think they trusted it to anyone else. That's all there was to it, really."

"Well, I don't know if that's the truth, but I've always thought your column was really good," Erin said. She looked off toward the darkening clouds that were beginning to brew over Lake Michigan. "I think you're just the right touch of funny and serious that this city sorely needs."

"Yeah, well, I'm glad you think so," Jules said as the breeze pushed her hair into her eyes. "Most of my time is spent being told what to write, or editing what other people write. That was never my intention, but in this business, you write less the higher you go in the chain of command. And writing that column definitely isn't as fun as it used to be."

When they ordered their fourth glasses of wine, Erin finally found the courage to bring up the botched kiss.

"So, I think it's time we talk about what happened, don't you?"

Just then, the waiter returned with the wine. Jules immediately picked up her glass and took a long, slow drink.

"I can't keep pretending like this is just a normal friendship, Jules. That's not who I am, and I don't think that's who you are, either. You said it yourself—or was that all just bullshit you were trying to feed me?"

Jules exhaled and avoided Erin's eyes. She looked down at the table, suddenly quiet. Erin reached out and touched Jules' hand, then brushed her fingers over Jules' wedding band.

"I know you're married. I understand that, I really do, but I also know you wouldn't be here with me if you were happy. You don't have to be afraid to tell me the truth, Jules. I need to know what you're thinking."

There was a rumble of distant thunder over the lake as Jules looked down at their hands, which were intertwined on the table.

"Say something, Jules," Erin whispered.

Jules pulled her hand away, cleared her throat, and picked up the glass again. After emptying it, she finally looked back at Erin. "You're right," she said, holding Erin's glance. "But I don't know what I'm doing, and I don't know where this is going. I've never done anything like this, and I really don't wanna be one of those women that just goes off the rails in her forties. But I can't stop thinking about it—or about you. I don't know what I am, but I do know what I want."

Erin's heart jumped. "You don't have to be afraid with me, Jules. I won't make you do anything you don't wanna do, but I can't keep pretending that I don't want to touch you. So if you don't want that, then we need to reconsider this relationship."

Jules bit her lip nervously and looked down at the table.

Erin leaned forward, attempting to make eye contact. "I don't know where we're going, either, but I think we better take a taxi because I'm a little drunk."

Jules laughed loudly. "Me too."

The rain started falling heavily as they slid into a taxi side by side. The electricity built between them as the car turned down one street and onto the next. She moved her hand closer to Jules' thigh, aching to touch her, and Jules studied her face like she wanted nothing more than to kiss her right there in the back of that car. Erin had never been with a woman like Jules, a woman who had spent her life on the opposite side of the fence, afraid to look over. She had experimented in college with straight girls who liked the distraction from immature men, but since then, all of Erin's relationships had been with women who knew exactly who they were and what they wanted from her. Jules was something completely different. Just the thought of getting her back to her apartment made Erin's heart pound faster, like the rain hitting the windshield. Still, Erin knew she couldn't rush this or it just might send Jules running again.

Racing up the stairs to her apartment, Erin fumbled through her purse for the keys as the rain soaked through their clothes. When she didn't find them, she ran back down the steps to her car, which was parked in the driveway below.

"Oh, shit," she yelled, pounding on the window with closed fists. Her keys were sitting in the cup holder behind the locked door. "How the hell did I manage that one?"

Jules sat shivering at the top of the stairs as the heat of the moment began to wane. "What?"

"My keys are locked in the damn car." Erin slammed her open hand on the window.

Jules bent over and burst out laughing. "Well, shit is right. Isn't your landlord home? Doesn't he live downstairs?"

"Yeah," Erin muttered, climbing the stairs with her hands raised in the air. "But he's on fucking vacation in Mexico."

Erin sat next to her and they both laughed as the rain came down harder still.

"What are the chances of that taxi coming back down here?" Jules hugged her legs trying not to shiver.

133

"Wait," Erin said, looking at the window above them.
"I bet if I step in your hands and you lift me up just a little, I can
jimmy that window open and get into the kitchen. I have another
set of keys for my car…somewhere."

Jules wiped the water from her face. "Why can't *you*
do the lifting and *I* do the jimmying?"

"Whatever you say. Just get your ass up." Erin steadied
her back against the wall and then locked her fingers together
before nodding to Jules. "Alright, step up."

Jules shook her head and smiled as she placed one foot
in Erin's interlocked hands while gripping her shoulders. She
jumped quickly, straightening her legs as she reached toward the
window above them. "You know, Jules," Erin said as she
strained to lift her higher, "this isn't how I imagined this
working out when we came back here."

Jules laughed and pulled at the screen. "Shut up
already, before you make me fall. I think I got it."

The screen easily popped off and tumbled down the
stairs. Jules forced the inside window up as far as she could
before looking down at Erin. "I think you're gonna need to lift
me a little higher."

Erin laughed. Her fingers were going numb but she
tried, with little success, to raise Jules higher. Somehow, Jules
found the leverage to pull herself out of Erin's hands and,
almost in military pull-up style, she managed to lift herself up
and struggle through the window. Erin couldn't help but laugh
when Jules' feet finally disappeared through the window and

134

she heard something that sounded like breaking glass on the other side.

"I'm alright," Jules said when her face reappeared, looking down at Erin, who was still on the stairs. "But I can't say the same for the plant you had by this window."

"Just let me in already! I'm freezing," Erin shouted as she scampered up the stairs.

By the time they made it through the door, they were drenched and laughing like teenagers. "I'll get towels and some dry clothes," Erin said, shaking off a shiver. She pulled off her wet shirt and walked toward the bedroom. She opened the top dresser drawer, removed two dry T-shirts, and struggled out of her wet jeans. Just as she was about to close the drawer, a vial of cocaine rolled out from its hiding place. She hesitated momentarily before quickly unscrewing the top and taking a fast sniff from the cap. She looked up as she replaced the cap, catching Jules' reflection in her full-length mirror. Jules had been watching Erin's every move from the bedroom doorway. Although Erin wore nothing but her bra and underwear, the look in Jules' eyes had changed. She rested her head on the doorframe and seemed afraid to come inside.

Erin walked toward Jules, still holding the cocaine. With her free hand, she pulled the straps of her bra off her shoulders and then unclipped it, allowing it to fall to the floor without breaking Jules' stare. Standing before her, she clutched the bottom of Jules' soaked shirt with one hand and pulled it up and over her head. Jules' wet hair fell back against her skin, and

135

Jules shyly looked away as Erin touched her cheek and turned her head so they faced one another. She lifted the cocaine toward Jules' nose, but instead of sniffing it, Jules took it from her and set it on the dresser. Erin moved toward her again, but almost instinctively, Jules moved away.

"It's okay. Just relax," Erin said softly, taking Jules' hands. "It's just you and me here, no one else. If you don't want this, then just say so—it's okay."

Jules moved closer and kissed Erin as if she had been holding it back for days. Erin responded by immediately pulling her close. She grasped Jules' face in her hands, and Jules sighed as Erin kissed her neck and slowly stripped the wet clothes from her body. She gently pushed Jules closer to the bed, and when Jules lay down, Erin positioned herself above, allowing her own wet hair to fall across Jules' face. Erin looked into her eyes and tried to read the expression on her face as her hands moved over her body. Unsure if she should continue, Jules reached up and touched Erin's face with the tips of her fingers, then pulled her into a deep kiss. Erin knew there was no turning back. Jules shivered when she kissed Erin's neck and shoulder, and Erin pressed her body harder against Jules.

"God, you're beautiful, Jules," she whispered. "You have no idea how many times I've thought about this."

Jules smiled, but then turned her head and closed her eyes. Erin inched her hand lower over Jules' skin. When she slipped it between Jules' legs, Jules quickly inhaled and bit down on her lower lip. Wanting to please her, Erin moved her

136

head, following the same path as her hand, and kissed Jules' body until her mouth replaced the area where her hand had just been. Jules' fingers tangled in Erin's hair and her body shook slightly under Erin's touch.

Erin wanted Jules to feel the full effect of her infatuation so she teased and caressed her relentlessly until finally Jules shuddered and breathed heavily, gripping the sheets tightly in her fist. Erin felt the goose bumps on Jules' skin as she moved her hand across Jules' body, lightly grazing her breast. When Jules' breathing finally slowed and she began to relax, Erin moved up to lay beside her. She rested her head on the pillow while slowly running her fingers over Jules' body. When Erin's fingers reached her face, Jules turned toward her and opened her eyes. To Erin's surprise, a tear slipped down her cheek and dripped off the tip of her nose.

"It's okay, Jules," she whispered. She brushed the tear away before moving in to softly kiss her. "There's nothing to be afraid of."

Even with Jason and Tina's muffled voices behind her as she tried to focus on her work, Erin's mind stayed on that afternoon with Jules. She recalled how blank Jules had seemed when she drove her back to her car that day. When Erin pulled up next to Jules' black Acura in the parking ramp, she turned off the ignition and looked at her. Jules hadn't said a word, or even looked at her, during the entire drive.

"Are you okay?" Erin asked.

Jules stared out the window. "I'm fine," she mumbled, then leaned her head back on the seat.

"This doesn't have to change anything—"

"It changes everything, Erin," she said with a slight shake of her head. "It changes everything."

Erin reached out and touched Jules' hair, twirling a piece of it around her fingers. "I don't regret it, and no one has to know."

"I know," Jules said as she turned away. "I have to go."

"You can't leave like this," Erin pleaded. "You're gonna walk away and get weird again, and I thought you wanted this as much as I did."

Jules looked back at her, gently pulling Erin's hand away from her hair. "I did." She leaned in and kissed Erin's lips. "That's why I have to go."

As Erin watched, Jules slipped out of the car and got into her own. She pulled the seatbelt across her chest and started the engine before finally looking over at Erin. She maneuvered her lips into a somber smile, and with that, she was gone.

Erin washed glasses, still attempting to avoid Tina, who sat sipping her drink and occasionally checking her phone. Jason moved to the opposite end of the bar. He struck up a flirtatious conversation with Jessie, leaving Erin and Tina in an uncomfortable silence. Erin knew Tina wanted to say something, but whatever she had to say, Erin didn't want to hear it. After finishing her drink, Tina stood and dug in her pocket.

138

Removing a single silver key, she placed it on the bar and slid it toward Erin with her slender index finger.

"You asked me for this back and I never returned it. I'm sorry."

Picking it up, Erin immediately tossed it in the trash. "Thanks, but I had the locks changed a long time ago."

"Yeah, I know," Tina said quietly. "I tried it once. Well, that was before Jules bitched me out in the bathroom."

"Nice, Tina. You never did know when to quit," Erin scoffed.

"You know, Erin, I didn't like Jules. Well, actually, I kinda hated her," she said, adjusting her hat. "But I know you cared about her."

"Whatever. Don't pretend like you care," Erin said, brushing her off. She placed the glasses in the dryer behind the bar and continued to avoid Tina's stare.

"About her? No, I didn't care about her at all," Tina said, shaking her head. "But even though you completely used me, and then dropped me for a half-straight girl like I was a dirty shirt, I did—actually, *I do*, care about you."

Erin looked up quickly. She hadn't expected Tina to say something like that.

"*You* wanted to get high, and *you* wanted a friend with benefits. I gave you both. But you were sleeping with me and lusting after a woman you could never really have, you were too busy to notice that I actually had feelings for you," she stood up and dropped a twenty-dollar bill on the bar. "But I'm not an

139

idiot. Every time she disappeared and you called me up again, I knew you were never really into me and you just needed something. That's all it ever was. You gave me that key because I gave you drugs. I know that's all you wanted."

Erin blinked and looked away from her.

"And I knew you were head-over-heels in love with her," Tina said while buttoning her coat. "But, just so you know, Jules wasn't perfect. She had her own secrets, and she was never going to leave that husband of hers. And yeah, I was pissed off when I walked in on you that day, so I made it worse by making it seem like we were something more. But I didn't know what you were going through at the time, or what you'd been through. You never gave me a chance to be anything more to you than what I was—an easy lay and a way to score drugs. We could've been more, you know? I could've been there for you if you'd given me half a chance, and I wouldn't have given you the drugs. If I knew the truth…I wouldn't have done that, just so you know."

Erin shook her head. "What the hell are you talking about, Tina, what truth?"

Tina's lips tensed. Erin couldn't tell if she was angry or just disappointed.

"It doesn't matter; all I really came here to say is that I'm sorry you lost her. I'll be around if you ever get lonely again. It doesn't always have to be about drugs or sex, just so you know. I'm more than that."

Erin didn't know what to say. She had never heard Tina talk this way. She looked down at her own scuffed Chuck Taylor sneakers, and Tina loudly sighed.

"Yeah, that's what I thought," Tina said. "I'll see you around, Erin. Take care of yourself—and keep the change."

As Tina walked away, Erin was filled with another wave of regret. She had never allowed herself to feel even remotely guilty about her relationship with Tina. But Tina wasn't lying; Erin had used her, and when Jules became the center of her world, she never looked back. Erin looked around the room as the door closed behind Tina, wondering if anyone had heard their conversation. But no one had. She sighed, picking up Tina's empty glass and the twenty dollar bill she had left behind. She wondered what Tina meant by "the truth." The truth about what?

Tossing the twenty in Jessie's tip jar, Erin tried to push the questions out of her head as she turned toward the refrigerator to arrange bottles once again.

Chapter Twelve

Will slowly stirred his coffee as he waited for Sarah to arrive. The sun was just beginning to set as he peered out the window at the diner's icy parking lot. The hot liquid burned his lips, but it tasted good and reminded him that he could still feel. Since discovering the evidence on Jules' phone, he had barely been able to eat or sleep. He thumbed through her photos, watched the video, and read the texts over and over again, trying to remember details of her behavior or anything she might have said or done that seemed out of place. But nothing came to mind. Yet, based on what he knew now, there was no other conclusion to draw—Jules was having an affair. No matter how many times he turned all of it over in his mind, he still couldn't believe it. Jules had never talked about wanting to be with a woman—at least not to him—and having been married to her for eleven years, he knew exactly how natural she seemed to be with men.

So many unanswered questions flooded his mind. How long was it going on? How did they meet? And, who the hell was this girl, and why did she seem familiar? As his anger rose, everything he missed about Jules was being replaced by pure resentment. Still, even entrenched in that bitterness, Will knew

142

he had helped construct the roughly-built wall that existed between them. But, until now, he hadn't fully realized how thick it was.

Though he hated to remind himself, he knew he was partially responsible for their demise, thanks to his drinking. Jules no longer trusted him after that night with Lisa, and she never let an opportunity pass when she could remind him of how much damage he caused. Other than that push in the rain, he had never laid a hand on her in anger, but there were many times he had cut her off at the knees with just the cunning slip of his tongue. He had done it after late nights at the bar when coming home to face her barrage of questions.

Will had struggled with alcohol even in the beginning of their marriage, but the drinking increased as Jules became more successful in her work and he waned in his own. He had reached the ceiling in his career, no longer finding construction rewarding or fulfilling, and as Jules rose, he sank like a stone and routinely lost out to younger men for promotions and raises. As a result, he became more combative and vocal with his superiors. When they fired him, he blamed Jules.

"I can't stay late or work overtime because you're never home for Jillian, but all those younger guys can," he screamed at her one night, locked in a drunken rage.

"This is my fault?" She grabbed the bottle of brandy from the table and held it by the neck as if she might hurl it across the room. "Don't you dare blame me for your drinking. You did that all on your own."

143

He stepped toward her, snatching the bottle from her hand. "Do you ever wonder why I drink so much?" He paused and narrowed his eyes at her. "It's because of you, Jules. I never wanted to get married. I never wanted any of this. I just wanted to do what I wanted to do, but no, you had to have more."

Jules glared at him, her eyes almost black in the dim light and her lower lip quivering slightly. "*I* had to have more? God, Will, can't you hear yourself? Don't you know who you sound like?" A single tear slipped out, but she quickly wiped it away, as if it had been wasted on him.

"Oh, don't start that daddy-issue psychobabble bullshit on me, Jules. You didn't know him, and I'm nothing like he was—I was happy before you, but you wanted to live in the city, you wanted to get married, you wanted—"

"What Will? I wanted what? Go ahead, say it." She snapped. Her chest began to heave as though she had just run a marathon. "Tell me again how I forced you into marriage and forced you into having a family. Tell me again how *I* ruined your life—just like your mother got knocked up and ruined your dad's life. You were a willing participant in this marriage and this family, William. I forced you into nothing. That fucking bottle in your hand is what created your twisted version of the truth."

Her words only increased his fury and sent him into a rage. He stood inches away and spewed his alcohol-laced breath in her face. "I wish I never met you. I'd have a lot more money and I'd be ten times happier." He stomped away, telling himself

144

she didn't matter and his problems were of her doing. He went to the bar that night, then slept in his truck in the parking lot.

Will continued to stir his coffee and recalled, after countless nights like that one, how hard it had been to convince Jules to give him a second chance. When the alcohol faded, he always realized the impact of his actions and words. He had no idea why he blamed her or why he treated her the way he did. His rage was never her fault, and he knew he was following a familiar and destructive path.

Following the incident with Lisa, and then after losing his job, Will realized what a waste his life had become. He thought of his father's death, and he wondered if this was the same desperation his father had felt when he ran his truck into that tree—the simple yet crushing pressure of domestic life. But still, he wondered why his father couldn't find happiness in everyday things and why couldn't he find them either. There was so much to be grateful for, yet all Will could do was feel the strain of everyday things, and the pressure of them sometimes tightened around his neck like a noose. During those long, lonely nights after Jules kicked him out of their house, Will began to think more about his father and the man he had been. Maybe he had been happy once, but Will had never known him that way.

After Will's grandfather died, his mother had explained, Will's father had been drafted for a year-long tour in Vietnam; when he returned home, he met Will's mother one night at a small bar down by the river. His mother, who was old enough to legally drink but was still in high school at the time, remembered him from school, but because she was a year behind him, he didn't remember her. She said he had the most beautiful eyes, and he had been a star athlete once—he played football and ran track, but after the war, like many of the young men who came home, he was sad and sometimes angry. At times he was distant, like a ghost, she told Will. But most of the time he was just angry. Sometimes, usually when he drank, he would talk about the war and the things that happened there, but it could throw him into fits of terrifying rage. Just a few months after they started dating, she became pregnant with Will. Because of pressure from both of their families, they eventually married. But his father had never been happy, she said. All that came back from Vietnam was the shell of a sad and broken man who resented everything and everyone.

After Jules kicked him out, Will knew he had an important decision to make. He could continue on and become the empty man his father had been, or he could make a drastic change. It was then and there that he finally gave up the bottle for good. Yet he knew that alone would never be enough to bring Jules back to him. He wanted them to be away from the city and from everything that seemed to break them apart. So, in a radical, last-ditch effort, he sold his Harley and borrowed money from his mother to put a down payment on a piece of land along the Rock River, just outside of his home town. Then, without Jules' knowledge, he obsessively began designing her the home of her dreams—the one, when times were good, they

146

said they would have someday. It was a long shot and a gamble, but he knew he had to do something big to win her back. He'd spent years working in construction and drafting blueprints on the side. He was convinced that once he finished this house, the very first home constructed solely with his own two hands, he could launch a new business of designing and building custom homes, or restoring vintage homes, whichever gave him the most work. He only hoped Jules would agree.

It had been a warm fall morning three years earlier when Will finally talked Jules into taking a ride with him to show her just how serious he was with this new plan. Though they had lived apart for months, he was slowly beginning to break down her walls and they were learning to be friends again. As they drove to the country with Jillian fast asleep in the backseat, Will glanced over to see Jules' dark hair blowing freely from the gusts coming through the open window. For the first time in months, he was relieved to see her radiance beginning to return.

"So, where are we going?" She asked as she glanced back at Jillian, who had fallen asleep with her cup still clutched in her tiny hands.

"I told you, it's a surprise," he said. He turned off the interstate and headed south on Highway 26.

"This is the way to your mom's house. If that's the surprise, I think I'd rather go home," she joked, leaning her elbow out the open window.

"We're not going there," he laughed. "But what is your deal with her, anyway? She's always on your side."

"Ha! C'mon, Will. You and I both know you could shoot me in the head and she'd still say it was my fault—no matter what you did." She lifted her sunglasses so he could see her expression.

"I doubt that," he replied as he shook his head. "She's always telling me what I can do to improve myself."

"Does that include improving who you're married to?" She shifted her glance toward the scenery outside.

"That's the one thing she knows I did right." He reached for Jules' hand, but she moved it, conveniently switching the radio station.

When they finally pulled off the highway, Will turned and headed down a dirt road that led toward the river. A makeshift sign propped up by blocks of wood depicted a map of large, plotted-out home sites. The words "Future Home of Blackhawk Circle" were printed in large, black letters.

"What is this, Will?" She glanced at the sign and then back at him.

He smiled and slowly drove over the bumps and large rocks in the dirt road. When they finally reached the end, he pulled into a driveway of crushed rock that crackled and popped under the tires. It was a large, gorgeous lot overlooking the river, and as the largest site in the development, it was lined with trees on either side. Measuring in at just over an acre and a half, it was three times the size of their yard in the city.

148

Jules took off her sunglasses and looked around in bewilderment. "What is this?"

"C'mon, let's get out," he said, ignoring her question. He hopped out of the car and walked nervously toward the trunk.

Jules slowly stepped out of the car and looked toward the water. The soft breeze blew the hair back from her face and she squinted in the sun. She turned as Will approached with rolled-up house plans tucked tightly under his arm.

"I want you to look at these," he said, beginning to sweat. He unrolled the blueprints on the hood of the car as she stepped closer. "It's a modern two-story with an exposed basement. I designed it from scratch—"

"Will," she whispered, lifting her hand to cover her mouth.

"Just hear me out." He talked faster, pointing out the features she always said she'd wanted in a new home, right down to the small wine cellar in the basement. When he finished, he looked over as the tears spilled down her cheeks.

"It's for you, Jules. I did it for you—and Jilly."

She wiped her eyes and gazed toward the river before turning back to him. "How? How can we afford this?"

"I sold my Harley." He stepped forward and clutched her elbows. "And I borrowed the rest from my mom for the down payment."

"And there it is." She scoffed and pulled away.

"Jules," he said as he dropped his hand to his sides. "Can't you see how hard I'm trying, here?"

"So you think building me a house is going to fix everything, Will, is that it?"

"No," he said moving toward her again. "But when we got married, I promised you I'd try to give you the life you deserved. I promised that I'd be better than my dad—and that I'd be better than your dad, and I know I fucked all that up royally. But even if you don't want me to live in this house with you, I want to build it—for you."

She shook her head and looked at the ground. "We were different people when we got married, Will. Now, God, I just don't know what we are—or who I am." She turned and walked toward the water, leaving him with no other option than to let her go.

Feeling defeated, he hastily rolled up the plans and checked on Jillian, who was still peacefully asleep in the backseat. He turned to see Jules standing with her back toward him. She was looking out at the water and he had no idea what she was thinking. He gazed at his feet, disappointed and angry with himself. He had been so sure this plan work. He imagined Jules hugging him. He knew she wouldn't instantly forgive him, but he thought they would plan to make a fresh start at a marriage he knew was worth saving. Now, thinking Jules might already be too far gone, he tossed the blueprints through the open window and leaned against the car, waiting for her to come back. She stood there for nearly twenty minutes before he

150

finally went to retrieve her so they could head back to the city and go their separate ways—possibly for good.

He walked up beside her and looked out at the water. She was quiet and staring at her reflection in the calm, shallow shore.

"We should head back before Jilly wakes up," he said quietly. He lightly kicked at the ground, waiting for her response.

Jules drew in a deep breath before gazing down the riverbank toward a large weeping willow. Its long, green vines touched the water's surface and it swayed lightly in the wind, almost like a dancer who doesn't know anyone is watching. "Can we keep that?"

Will lifted his head, wondering if he'd heard her correctly. "What?"

"The tree. I don't want you to cut it down," she said, turning to face him. She shoved her hands into the pockets of her denim capris and looked him in the eyes.

He stepped toward her. "What are you saying?"

"I've loved you almost half my life, Will," she said as he gently clutched her forearms. "We've already been to hell and back in so many ways. But, God damn it, you really hurt me, and I can't forget that—no matter how many houses you build or AA meetings you go to."

He nodded and looked away.

"But, I am proud of you for everything you've been trying to do. Really, I am. But I also know how fast that can turn

151

around—and so do you. I don't want to be our parents, Will, I really don't. That little girl in there deserves better than that. We worked too fucking hard to bring her into this world only to fuck it up just like they did."

He leaned in and pressed his forehead against hers. "I know," he said. "I'm different now. I promise things will be better. I promise I'm never going to be that guy again. I'm not William Kanter, Sr., I'm not. I'm just me, and I love you, Jules—I love the life we had. We can be that again—I know we can."

"This isn't going to be easy, Will," she whispered. "But, if this means that much to you, I'll try." He held her so tightly that day, and he was sure he would make the most of the second chance she had given him. But, as it always does, life got in the way.

Continuing to stare into the blackness of his coffee, Will now found himself torn between wanting to hate Jules for what she had apparently done with this woman and wanting her back, just to hold her and tell her, yet again, how sorry he was. Though she had agreed to move out of the city to start over, she never truly left it. And though it seemed their marriage had endured, it was apparent their relationship had never fully healed.

"What's so important?" Sarah asked as she slid into the seat across from him.

"Well hi to you, too," he replied, faking a smile.

"You called me at 11:00 last night, Will," she said while unbuttoning her jacket. "I've been freaked out about it ever since, and I don't have a lot of time before I have to pick up the boys, so tell me. What's so important that you need to see me face-to-face?"

Will dug in his pocket and removed Jules' phone, placing it on the table in front of them.

"Did Jules ever mention anyone named Erin to you?"

She thought for a second, but then shook her head. "No, I can't say I know anyone with that name. Why?"

Will nodded and folded his hands in front of him, unsure if he should believe her.

"Was my wife fucking around, Sarah?"

She leaned back, clearly surprised by the remark. "What are you talking about?"

Will tapped the screen on the phone and hit the photo gallery app. An image of the dark-haired woman quickly appeared. "Do you know this girl?"

Leaning forward, Sarah gazed down at the photo. "Mmm…nope. I don't think so. But she's cute. Why, who is she?" She leaned back again and crossed her legs.

Will studied her face, unable to tell if she was lying.

"Can I get you something, honey?" The waitress interrupted as Will continued to glare at his sister-in-law across the table.

Sarah narrowed her eyes at him and then looked back at the stout waitress, who appeared as happy to be there as she was. "Ah, yeah, just coffee please."

"You got it," the woman said before slowly sauntering away.

"What's going on with you?" She said, glancing back at the image on Jules' phone. "Who is that?"

"I thought she told you everything, Sarah," Will said. He took a sip of his coffee before placing the cup back on the saucer.

"Cut the shit," Sarah said. "What's going on?" Will could tell she was growing more irritated by the second.

"Watch this," he said, swiping his finger across the screen. He tapped the play button on the video he had watched repeatedly. He observed as Sarah squinted and then leaned in closer. Her eyes suddenly widened and she looked up at him, covering her mouth with one hand.

"Wait, is that? Is she…? Play that again."

Will hit the play button for a second time.

When it was over, Sarah placed both palms on the table as the waitress reappeared and poured her coffee. "There's gotta be an explanation," she said, stumbling on her words. Her eyes darted wildly before she looked back at him.

"There's more." He swiped to photos the woman appeared to have taken of herself with Jules' phone. Sarah's face turned white. Then he switched over to the text messages. "Now read these and tell me what you think."

154

He continued sipping his coffee. The light from the phone illuminated Sarah's face and her eyes moved back and forth as she read. She brought her hand to her mouth and touched her lips. When she finished, she set the phone down and stared back at him.

"I swear to God, Will, I had no idea. She never mentioned a thing."

He sucked in his breath and held it for a few seconds before letting it out slowly. "So you're thinking what I'm thinking."

Sarah lifted her cup, her hands shaking slightly. "Ah, yeah, the evidence here suggests they were—well, you know."

"Fucking?" Will leaned back hard against the booth.

"Well, I don't know how two women do that," she said with a nervous laugh. "But yeah, it sounds like they were definitely more than just friends."

"Did Jules ever mention anything about women? I don't get this, Sarah. I can't believe this was happening under my nose."

Sarah looked at him blankly. "You know, Will, Jules was always really close with her female friends as a kid, and she didn't date much, but I can't say I ever thought about her being gay or anything. My mother would've flipped out over that."

"Jesus, Sarah," he said. "Did I really fuck up so bad that she switched sides?"

Sarah burst out in an overly-anxious laugh. "God, Will, really? This is my sister we're talking about; did she ever do anything without analyzing the shit out of it? I can't believe she'd just jump in bed with a woman because you acted like an asshole. But you know, now that I think about it, Jules always did love chick singers. I guess in a way it does sorta make sense." She laughed and shook her head. "As a kid she was always sitting in her bedroom listening to Fleetwood Mac or Heart. I just never thought she was *that* into women."

Will glared at her. "Do you think this is funny, Sarah? Really? My wife was fucking around—with a woman. I really don't see the joke here."

He shoved the phone into his pocket.

Sarah's expression suddenly turned serious. "Call her."

"What?"

"Call her—this Erin, whoever she is. Call her from Jules' phone." She motioned toward his pocket. "Call her right now and ask her for an explanation. Maybe it isn't what you think. Jules can't explain it, but maybe she can."

"Yeah right." Will looked away from her. "But, there is something else," he said, lowering his voice. He knew Sarah wouldn't respond well to what he was about to say. "I found coke in her purse."

Sarah blinked and shook her head from side to side. "What? Like cocaine? You can't be serious."

"I can show it to you, Sarah. I found it in her purse." He peered at her dark, bewildered eyes.

"Call her, Will. Call this Erin. If you don't, I will." A hint of anger crept into Sarah's voice. "There's got to be an explanation for that. That's not the Jules I know. She wouldn't do that."

"You do it." Will placed the phone back on the table and pushed it toward her.

Sarah picked it up. She thumbed through the numbers and then put the phone to her ear. "It's ringing."

"What the hell are you gonna say?" He was surprised that she had actually taken him seriously.

She put her index finger to her lips, motioning for him to be quiet.

"Shit. She didn't answer." Sarah lowered the phone but then tapped the number again.

The cold sweat began all over again as Will watched Sarah's face.

Chapter Thirteen

Erin's phone vibrated, but she ignored it. The Marquette versus Wisconsin basketball game had just begun— and so had the evening rush. The bar was filled with college students, and though they didn't always tip great, they were exactly the type of customers she liked to serve. They were young and usually uncomplicated, and they wanted nothing from her other than to help them get wasted. To this crowd she was a star, and she could give them exactly what they wanted as long as she was quick with a pour and even quicker with a comeback. Tonight though, she found herself missing the busy streets of Nashville. Down there, creativity flowed from virtually every open door along Broadway and Fifth Avenue, or from any backstreet bar where undiscovered talent might come together to play music. Here, in the cold of Wisconsin, she felt stifled and uninspired.

The love of her second home had begun six years earlier, during a weekend trip with a friend. She instantly felt Nashville's aesthetic draw. To her surprise, the city was far less country than she had imagined, and she fit in perfectly with its diverse and rapidly forming alternative troubadour population. A few months later, looking to escape both the baggage of her past and her mother's over-bearing attention, she let go of her teaching career and moved to Tennessee. By October of that year, she was living in a crowded house full of impoverished yet happy musicians, and when she stood outside Nashville's iconic Tootsie's Orchid Lounge with her father's beat-up Gibson slung over her back, she finally felt free for the first time in her life.

Truth be told, she had never planned to make a huge mark in Nashville with her music; she hadn't even dreamed of it. But the more she played, the more she seemed to garner attention, and the bug of fame had soon embedded itself under her skin. She found herself becoming thirsty for applause and all the accolades that came along with it. After more than two years of pounding the pavement and playing anywhere from the dirty bars in Printer's Alley to open mic nights at the Bluebird Café, her break finally came in the form of a dark-haired man in black jeans and a neatly-pressed white cotton shirt. With a million-dollar smile and gleaming hazel eyes, the record company scout approached her after a set and handed her a business card. He told her about an open audition for unsigned artists and assured her that if she performed well for his partners during that audition, chances were good they'd sign her right there—and he kept that promise. Though she didn't know it then, that chance meeting was the beginning of the most exciting time in her life, but it also marked the end of her new-found freedom.

As she poured a whisky sour, Erin wished she could retrace her steps and go back to the moment right before she inked her name on that recording contract. As she rang up the drink at the register and placed the change on the bar, a young man slid onto the stool in front of her.

"Hey guys, look who it is! It's Freckles, the foul-mouthed bartender," the man said, pulling Erin from her thoughts. His yellow polo shirt, with an MU logo on the right breast, told her he was just another spoiled rich kid from Marquette University.

Pushing her long hair behind her shoulder, Erin ignored his sarcasm and leaned forward to grab a glass. "Can I help you?"

"You don't remember me, do you?" He rubbed his peach fuzz goatee and gazed at her with a cocky smile.

Erin shook her head. "Nope, sorry. I see a lot of people come and go from this bar."

"Me and my buddies were in here celebrating my twenty-first birthday a few weeks ago. What was it you said? Oh yeah, that's right—me and my fucking frat boys can get the fuck out." He looked her up and down as his friends laughed and nudged each other.

Erin stopped what she was doing, remembering her words. Realizing this was group of young men that had been in the bar on the night Jules died, she took a deep breath and reached for the shot glasses on the shelf below. As they watched, she lined up six glasses and filled them one by one with Fireball Cinnamon Whisky.

"You know, that was a bad night for me. Let's call a truce." She placed a shot before each of the five men and raised the sixth glass for herself. "This one's on me—you fucking little frat boys are welcome to stay."

The young man smiled, lifting the glass. His sparkly-white teeth made her wonder if he was a dentist's son.

"Now that's more like it, Freckles," he said, touching his glass against hers before downing the shot.

"Erin. My name is Erin," she said as the whisky burned all the way down her throat. It was warm in the pit of her stomach as she collected the glasses. "Now, what else can I get you?"

He clutched the fake Rolex on his wrist. "How about your phone number?"

"Sorry, honey," she said, leaning on her elbows before him. "You're too young for me—and, unfortunately, you're just not my type."

"That's too bad," he said, moving closer to her face. "What are you? A dyke or something?"

"That's right. She's my bitch," Jessie interjected, playfully slapping Erin's rear end.

Even though her blood pressure was rising from the ignorant tone in his voice, Erin smiled and straightened her back. "Yup, sorry. I'm already taken." She pushed off the bar and stole a look at Jessie, who winked at her while serving a couple at the end of the bar. Though they were from different worlds, she and Jessie made a good team. They knew instinctively when to save the other from bad conversation with overbearing customers.

161

As the game heated up on TV, Erin remembered her phone and quickly pulled it from her pocket. She swiped her thumb across the screen, noticing two missed calls. She assumed it was her mom again. Though she appreciated the concern, her mother was beginning to hover in that near-suffocating way that had driven her to Nashville in the first place. The bar grew louder as the game intensified, but as Erin stared down at the name appearing under the missed calls notification, everything seemed to slow down and the sounds in the room began to echo. She blinked, hit the home button, and then navigated back to the missed-call log just to be sure she was seeing correctly. There were two missed calls from Jules' phone.

"You okay?" Jessie asked while swiping a credit card near the register.

Erin glanced at the mirror behind the bar. In the dull light, her blue eyes looked tired and her face suddenly appeared sickly white.

Jessie lightly touched her elbow. "Erin?"

"Uh, yeah," she jumped from Jessie's touch. "I just—I need to go to the bathroom. Can you cover for a second?"

Jessie nodded.

Erin was queasy as she darted toward the back room. She slammed the door to the employee restroom and leaned her against the closed door before looking down at the phone again. Bewildered, she shoved the phone in her pocket and placed both hands on the edge of the white porcelain sink. She stared into her own eyes in the mirror and could hear nothing but the

162

persistent sound of blood pumping inside her head. She knew it wasn't Jules who dialed that phone. Someone had discovered their secret, and she could easily guess who it was. Jules was terrified of being caught, which meant dealing with her lies. It was one of the many things Erin didn't understand about her.

After that rainy afternoon in her apartment, Jules had avoided Erin for days. But then, after a few cold texts and several awkward phone conversations, Erin finally convinced her to meet at Buck Bradley's for lunch in hopes of easing the tension building between them.

She was waiting at a table when Jules walked in, neatly dressed as always, but looking tired. Her hair was pulled back in a low ponytail, revealing a new thinness in her face. She seemed uncomfortable and unable to look Erin in the eyes as she approached, but Erin still stood and reached out to embrace her. Jules accepted the hug, but she pulled away quickly and then sat down without looking up at Erin.

"How are you?" Erin asked, her nerves beginning to tighten.

Jules squinted in the sun streaming through the window and glanced at the busy street. She straightened her shoulders and slipped her hands under her thighs. "I'm alright, but I'm really busy, so I don't have a lot of time to talk today."

Erin scoffed. "So, this is how it's gonna be now, Jules?"

She finally met Erin's stare. "Look, I just—I think we need to take a step back from this. I—"

163

"Well, hey there, Jules. Didn't think I'd see you here today." The voice came from behind Erin. Jules' face morphed from utterly serious to a smile that was wide but fake.

"Hey, Nancy," she said. Jules instantly sat up straighter. "Yeah, I'm just grabbing a quick lunch before the budget meeting."

"Me too, me too." The tall blonde woman glanced at Erin, who smiled back and blinked spitefully.

"Uh—this is Erin. Um, she's the musician from Catch 22." Jules looked toward Erin with pleading eyes. "And, Erin, this is my boss, Nancy."

"Of course. It's really nice to meet you in person, Erin," Nancy said as she reached out to shake Erin's hand. "Jules has been filling me in on your music career. You have quite an interesting background, but be careful what you say to this one," Nancy said as she glanced toward Jules. "She's always looking for a good story."

"I don't doubt that," Erin replied sarcastically. She looked up at Nancy and tilted her head to the side. "But I'm not interested in being just another story for The Deadline Artist."

She could feel Jules' eyes burning through her from the opposite side of the table.

Nancy laughed awkwardly, then looked back at Jules. "Hey, can you make sure you bring your story list to the meeting today? I wanna make sure we walk through that."

Jules nodded.

"Oh, and I want you to stop in my office before the meeting. There's a few other things we need to talk about."

"Yeah, yeah, of course," Jules said. "I have the list ready to go."

"Great. I'll see you later, then, and it was so nice to meet you, Erin. Good luck to you." Nancy nodded and turned to join a group of business-looking people a few tables away from them.

Jules shifted nervously in her seat.

"And you were saying?" Erin asked coldly.

Jules rubbed her temple. "I can't believe you just said that to my boss. What the hell was that?"

"She didn't get it, Jules, but really. You're gonna pull this we-need-to-pull-back shit on me now? What the hell is *that*? I wasn't the only one in the room that day, and I don't remember you putting up a fight."

Jules ignored the comment and looked down at her purse. She pulled a small piece of paper from the front pocket and placed it on the table between them. The scrap contained a name and phone number, written in Jules' scribbled handwriting. It looked like she had torn it from a legal pad. Jules said, "Can we talk about this later? I can stop at your apartment after work, if that's okay. I do want to talk to you logically about this, but not here, not now. Okay?"

Erin crossed her legs and glared across the table. "Yeah, sure. Whatever."

Jules pushed the paper toward her.

"What the hell is this?" Erin stared at it, refusing to pick it up.

Jules took a deep breath and exhaled slowly. "It's the name and number of the superintendent over at Riverview Elementary. They have an opening in the music department for a teacher's aide. It's not much, but I made a couple calls. If you contact them, send a resume, and mention my name, they'll give you an interview. I did a story on their alternative learning arts program last year. It gave them some great PR and helped boost their funding—they owe me a favor."

"Are you fucking kidding me right now, Jules?" Erin's blood began to boil.

"Look," Jules said nervously. "You said yourself you weren't sure where you were going. This is a good job, Erin. You have a degree you're not using, and this is in the music department. You have the experience and you have the talent. You'd be perfect for it."

Erin's eyes seared through her. "You don't have to take care of me. I'm not your little project. I'm not something you need to fix just to make yourself feel better about what happened between us."

Jules exhaled as if Erin had knocked the wind out of her. "That's not what this is. I'm just trying to help you. All I did was make a few calls; the rest is up to you. You can still move back to Tennessee, you can still play your music. This is just something to get you out of the bar and make better money—for now."

Though she knew Jules was trying to help, Erin was furious. They exchanged few words as they ordered and then picked at their food in complete silence. She watched as Jules stole quick glances toward the table where her boss sat. But afterward, as they walked out onto the street, Jules stopped and the look in her eyes softened. "I'll stop over later. Is that okay or not?"

"Whatever," Erin said, looking away.

"Please, take this. Just think about it," Jules said, handing over the paper. Erin shoved it in the pocket of her blazer with no intention of ever making the call.

Jules gently kicked at the ground, then glanced over her shoulder as if to determine whether anyone was listening. "Look, I'm sorry. I've just been doing a lot of thinking, and I'm really confused. I—I just don't know how I feel about all this, but I do owe you an explanation. Can we talk later?"

"You always know where to find me, Jules. It's not tough to figure out."

"I'll stop at your place later, I promise, but I have to go." She reached out and lightly touched Erin's arm before turning and heading up the street. Erin stood alone, watching her go. She couldn't believe how quickly things had changed between them or how fast Jules had slid back into denial about their relationship. It made her feel both cheap and responsible for pushing Jules too fast and too far. But, Erin had made her intentions clear and Jules had followed willingly. As she walked back to her car, Erin's hurt and anger rose inside her. Maybe

Jules was right. Maybe sleeping together had been a huge mistake—but even through her anger, Erin didn't regret it.

Jules dropped by the apartment later that evening, knowing it was Erin's usual night off. As soon as she came through the door, Erin could read the guilt-ridden look on her face.

"I don't regret what happened," Jules said, "but I just can't do this to my family." She paced back and forth, hugging her body with her own arms.

Erin sat on the couch, following Jules with her eyes. "I don't want to be friends with you, Jules. I've already made that clear," she said through clenched teeth.

"What do you want from me?" Jules stopped moving and faced the window, her back toward Erin.

"I want you to stop lying to yourself," Erin shot back, her voice rising. "Every time something happens between us, you run away. Why don't you just face what you are?"

Jules didn't turn. "What am I, Erin? Can you answer that for me?"

"You're a woman who fell for another woman—just like me. You don't have to label it, Jules. There's nothing wrong with finally being honest with yourself—or with me." Erin rose to her feet and stood directly behind Jules without touching her. "We didn't do anything wrong."

Jules looked down and closed her eyes. "I'm married, Erin. It's not that simple. I *did* do something wrong."

Erin let her nose graze the back of Jules' hair, and she lightly touched Jules' arms with her fingertips. "I can give you everything you need, Jules, if you would just let me."

"I can't, Erin. I just can't." She turned to look Erin in the eyes. "But I don't want to lose our friendship. I really do care about you, and I mean that."

"Friendship?" Erin stepped back, as if Jules had just stabbed her in the chest. "Fuck you, Jules. Get the fuck out and go back to your family. Keep telling yourself you're fine. You're not fine—I can see it. You wanted that afternoon just as much as I did. You're a liar, Jules. You're living a complete lie and we both know it."

Jules brought her hands to her face and rubbed her temples. "You've never been married, Erin. You don't have a child. You think you know me and have it all figured out, but you don't know me as well as you think you do."

"Yeah, I know you wanted a story, but this wasn't quite the one you bargained for, was it? I sure hope your husband realizes everything he has, but something tells me he doesn't. Get out, Jules."

Tears formed in Erin's eyes, but she quickly brushed them away.

Jules stared at her. But then she simply shook her head, picked up her purse, and walked out the door without another word. When Erin heard Jules' car start and then drive away, she dropped to the couch, feeling drained. There was no way to make Jules understand how deep her feelings ran, and though

169

she wanted nothing more than for Jules to leave her husband, she did know and understand that it wasn't easy. Still, she felt so connected to Jules, as if everything in her life was just a way to pass the time until she could see her again. It wasn't about sex; it was the level of understanding and the electricity that built between them. They were like two sparking high-voltage wires every time they were in the same room. Erin wanted nothing more than to breathe the same air Jules breathed, to sit close to her and laugh. To smell her, and touch her—but Jules was pulling away.

Later that night, as she sat alone in her dark apartment, Erin regretted telling Jules to leave. She didn't want to be friends, but she couldn't bear the thought of not seeing her again. Though she tried to resist and let the situation be, she finally swallowed her pride and sent a short and simple text.

I'm sorry. I don't want to lose you.

She glanced at the clock and realized it was well after midnight. She set her phone down on the coffee table, thinking Jules wouldn't respond that night, or maybe any other night. But when her phone lit up almost instantly, she picked it up. *It's okay, you have a right to be angry. I never meant to hurt you.*

Erin didn't see her again for weeks.

During Jules' absence, Erin tried to deny how out of control her life had become. Her drug use escalated and Tina, who had become a regular customer at the bar, became the perfect indulgence in more ways than one. Erin was aware of Tina's business habits at the bar, even though Tina tried to keep

170

them hidden; she also knew Tina's interest in her went beyond the drinks she poured. Tina routinely followed Erin with her eyes, and she always talked to her too closely, leaning over the bar when the music was loud. Soon Tina started offering Erin small "tastes," as she called them—a hit of speed here, a capsule or two of Adderall there. It wasn't long before eight balls of cocaine found their way from Tina's hand into Erin's pocket. Then, one night just before closing, Tina followed Erin to the bathroom. Cornering her in a stall, Erin allowed her to slide Ecstasy into her mouth, and before she knew what was happening, Tina's hands were on her body and their clothes were on the floor. Soon after that, Erin started inviting Tina home. She was always ready and willing to spend the night, and she kept Erin supplied with Ecstasy, cocaine, or any antidepressant of choice.

Erin eventually gave Tina a key to her apartment, and Tina frequently used it when she needed a place to crash, or if she wanted to warm Erin's bed. But through it all, Erin couldn't erase her feelings for Jules. No matter how many drugs she took, or how many nights she spent with Tina, she still wanted Jules. She missed how important Jules had made her feel. Tina would never see her the way Jules had. One particular Friday night, after Erin had worked the day shift, she sat alone in her apartment, thinking—as usual—about Jules. She couldn't shake the yearning of wanting to see her again. She had reached out to her several times in the past weeks, but Jules hadn't responded.

171

Though she knew it was probably useless, Erin picked up her phone and tried again.

I miss you...can you come over, please? I need to see you.

Erin expected the text to go unanswered, but as she sniffed a line of cocaine and leaned her head back, the phone unexpectedly vibrated.

What time? The message was short, but Erin's heart leapt.

Right now. She wrote back with trembling fingers and stared at the screen, waiting for Jules to respond. When it didn't come instantly, she wondered if Jules had changed her mind. After ten minutes, she set the phone down again, disappointed. And then it vibrated again.

Be there in 30.

Erin couldn't believe it. She'd been almost certain Jules had disappeared for good. Between the kick of the cocaine and her anxiety and excitement over seeing Jules, Erin sprang from the couch and began pacing the room. She needed to relax, but she couldn't slow her heart rate. The minutes slipped by agonizingly slowly. Her body quivered when the knock finally came, but she took a deep breath and slowly opened the door.

She smiled as Jules looked back at her, and though Erin instantly wanted to embrace her, she held back and simply welcomed her in. Jules hesitated at first. Her hands were deep in the pockets of her gray pinstriped trousers, as if she was nervous. She wore a tight black blouse and the same black peep toe heels, but her hair was slightly shorter than it had been. It had the familiar shine and it perfectly framed her tan face, but Erin noticed the change.

"Hey," Jules said when she finally stepped inside.

"Hey yourself," Erin said. She drank in the sight of her, letting her eyes move over Jules' body.

"How are you?" Jules asked, turning toward Erin, catching her eyes.

"I'm better now," she said with a smile. She reached out and gently tugged Jules' hair. "You got your hair cut."

Jules smiled sheepishly. "Yeah, I needed a little change."

"I like it," Erin said, moving closer to Jules. She expected her to pull away, but Jules held her ground as Erin placed her hands on her hips and pulled Jules toward her. Erin leaned in and whispered in her ear. "I missed you."

To Erin's surprise, Jules took her hands from her pockets and wrapped her arms around Erin. "I missed you, too," she said softly.

Erin pulled away and then brought her hands to Jules' face. She kissed her softly at first, but then she pulled her in forcefully, as she had become accustomed to doing with Tina.

"Whoa, slow down," Jules said as she pulled back. She looked at Erin's eyes and then stepped away. "You're high right now, aren't you?"

Erin reached for her again. But Jules grabbed her hand before she could touch her face. "Aren't you?"

173

"Did you come here for me, or for the coke?" Erin shook out of her grasp and turned away. "It's right there if you want it."

"I came here for you," she said, stepping closer. "Erin, why are you still taking drugs?"

Erin dropped on the couch. "You didn't seem to have a problem with me doing it on the day I got you in bed. Oh wait, I'm sorry, you disappeared after that, and you want to pretend like that day never happened."

Jules looked at the floor and then ran her fingers through her hair. "You're right," she said softly. "I shouldn't have disappeared, and I don't want to pretend like it never happened, but I was confused, Erin. You have to understand, it was just too much all at once. I was so wrapped up in you, and home, and work—Jesus, I almost lost my job."

Erin looked up. "What?"

Jules sat beside her, biting her bottom lip.

"Do you remember when we saw my boss that day and she said she wanted to talk to me?"

Erin nodded.

"I missed some pretty big mistakes in a few stories and they went to print that way. Nancy was really pissed off." She briefly looked up. "She was also pressuring me about another story I promised to finish, but I couldn't meet the deadline she set. She said I seemed unfocused and distracted, and she wanted to know what was wrong. I told her nothing, that everything was fine, but she kept looking at me like there was something else she wanted to say."

Erin's mouth went dry as Jules talked.

"Someone saw us, Erin," she said in a near whisper. "At Coast, after the art museum. I don't know who it was, or how, but they mentioned it to Nancy, and then she saw us together that day for lunch—"

"So what?" Erin shook her head. She reached out and touched her hand. "We weren't doing anything."

"You were touching me at Coast, Erin, just like you are right now."

Erin pulled away. "So that's why you've been ignoring me? Because you're afraid someone might think we're sleeping together?"

"No," Jules said, turning toward Erin. "I've been avoiding you because I can't afford to screw this up. Nancy told me that whatever was going on in my personal life, I needed to straighten it out and get it together or she was going to promote someone to help me with my workload, and I know what that really means."

Erin shook her head. "So why are you here now, then, if you're so scared of getting caught?"

Jules closed her eyes. "Because I cannot stop thinking about you."

Erin reached for her again. "Jules, I—"

"I can't be everything you need me to be right now," Jules said, cutting her off. "But you're right—I can't deny this.

I've waited so long to understand this side of myself and to experience what we did that day, and I don't regret it—I never have. But this is complicated, Erin. I don't know what to do."

"You could've just told me all this. You didn't need to disappear," Erin said softly, intertwining her fingers with Jules'.

"I know," Jules replied. She slipped her shoes off and pulled her knees to her chest. "I just needed some time to think."

"Honestly, Jules, you think too much. That's your problem."

Jules looked at her as Erin reached out and twirled a piece of her hair around her finger. "But I do love your haircut."

Jules laughed and looked away. But, when Erin let her fingers fall away from her hair and trail down her neck to the first button on her blouse, Jules leaned her head back and seemed to relax. She blinked when Erin unbuttoned the first button, and then the second. She moved in to kiss Jules' neck as she undid the remaining buttons and then, when Jules leaned forward, she pulled the blouse from her shoulders. She moved toward Jules slowly, but when their lips touched, the electricity took over and Erin pushed Jules down on the couch. Jules grabbed at Erin's T-shirt, quickly yanking it over her head, and then she pulled Erin on top of her, moving her hands over Erin's back and pulling down her bra straps. As they lay there, completely wrapped up in each other, neither of them heard the key slip into the lock. When the door swung open, it was too late to hide what was happening.

176

"What the fuck?" Tina sneered as she slammed the door behind her.

Jules shot up and instantly reached for her shirt. Out of breath, Erin sat on her knees, irritated by the interruption.

"What the hell are you doing here, Tina?"

Jules turned away and began buttoning her blouse. She shot Erin a stunned and questioning glare.

"You gave me a key, Erin, and told me to come over anytime I needed to, remember? Are you seriously screwing around with *her*? Weren't you just crying to me about how she fucked you over?"

"Don't listen to her, Jules." Erin said as she grabbed her shirt off the floor. "This is Tina. We're just friends and she crashes here sometimes, that's all."

"Really?" Tina sneered and then glared at Jules. "Yeah, and sometimes I fuck her brains out, that's all."

Jules looked both angry and terrified at the same time. She smoothed her shirt, ran her fingers through her hair and then straightened her collar while staring back at Tina.

"Yeah, I should go," she said, briefly looking back at Erin. She picked up her shoes and looked around for her bag.

"Jules, wait," Erin said, stepping toward her. "Please, don't go. There's nothing between me and her, and she's not going to say anything to anyone. I just gave her a key, and sometimes—"

"Oh, it's nothing?" Tina scoffed. "Well, that's news to me—"

"You don't have to explain it to me," Jules said as she raised her hand. "I knew I shouldn't have come here. I don't know what I was thinking, and I didn't know you were seeing someone."

"No, don't say that. You're not gonna do this again, and it's not like that, Jules, I swear." Erin grabbed Jules' wrist.

Jules stopped moving and tried to pull away, but Erin refused to release her grasp. "I can make her leave, Jules. You're the one I want, not her."

Jules looked at Tina before pulling out of Erin's grasp. "No, don't. She should stay. I need to go home. I'll see you around."

And with that, Jules slipped away—again.

As Erin's thoughts pulled away from that night and returned to Jules' number appearing in her call log, she checked her reflection in the mirror and wiped her fingers across her cheeks. The ache in the pit of her stomach made her want to crumble right there on the floor of the bar bathroom. She glanced at her phone and cleared the log before unlocking the door. Whoever it was that had called from Jules' phone didn't matter. She knew it wasn't Jules, and it would never be Jules again.

Chapter Fourteen

When he reached the city limits, Will's muscles tightened. He hadn't been there since the funeral, and he'd put off retrieving Jules' personal items from her office for as long as possible. Though they were trying to be respectful, Will knew the paper was eager to replace her. A light snow began to fall as he pulled into the parking ramp just up the street from the *Journal Sentinel* building. He wound his way upward through the concrete structure until he found a place to park and stepped out of his truck only to breathe in the heavy smell of exhaust in the air.

He knew this was the same routine Jules had followed each day, but he was claustrophobic within the confines of these cement walls. After bounding down four flights of stairs, he stepped out onto the street as the cold wind whipped against his face. Busy people shuffled past him, Starbucks coffee in hand, scarves neatly tied around their necks and their visible breath filling the air. They didn't seem to notice him, as if he were a ghost. This was a world he'd never felt comfortable in. Jules loved the city, but to him it was too loud, too busy, and too crowded. Walking toward his wife's office, he realized what a different woman Jules must have been when she moved among these strangers.

Shaking off the cold, he pushed through the newspaper building's main entrance and approached the massive front desk, which seemed to fill the entire room. The pretty young woman behind it smiled, but to him it looked as though the lobby swallowed her whole and she was trapped inside the bowels of this newspaper that he had grown to hate. She wore bright red lipstick and held her iPhone in her hand as if he had interrupted her in the middle of a text or an important Facebook conversation.

"Can I help you?"

"Uh, yeah. I'm here to see Nancy Whitmann." He nervously glanced at the pictures lining the walls.

"Is she expecting you? Can I have your name?" She adjusted her headset and tapped a button on the switchboard.

"I'm Will Kanter," he replied. Her expression changed as her eyes darted to meet his. "Yes, she's expecting me."

The girl turned away and spoke quietly into the headset, as if Will couldn't hear her. "Hi, Nancy. Uh, yeah, Jules' husband is down here. Yeah, um—okay."

The girl hit another button and spun back around. "She's just finishing up a meeting. She'll be down in a few minutes."

Will tapped his fingers on the desk and nodded his head. "Okay, thanks."

The young woman eyed him and nervously straightened papers on the desk. "I, um…I'm really sorry about Jules," she said, struggling to meet his eyes. "Everyone really liked her."

"Thanks," he said, faking a smile. He dug his hands into his coat pockets and turned toward the chairs in the waiting area. He wrapped his fingers around Jules' phone and anxiously began to sweat. Looking around the room, he thought of how he and Jules had met and how different she was before this job had taken over her life. They began dating when she was a senior at the University of Wisconsin Milwaukee, right before she became an intern at the paper. Back then, Will had been working with a construction crew downtown, so he and Jules frequented the same bars. The first time he saw her, he was blown away by how her face lit up when she smiled. Jules always had a spark about her that attracted people. It was this natural charm that made her perfectly suited for a career in journalism. She could draw out the truth and hide deep questions in simple conversation. Though they were often in the same bars at the same time, Jules never seemed to notice him, and it took weeks for Will to build up the courage to even speak to her.

While waiting for his opportunity one night-, he watched as the friend Jules was with went to the restroom. Attempting to seize the moment, Will slid onto the barstool beside Jules and ordered a Miller Lite on tap. She sat quietly, stirring the ice in her drink, lost in her own thoughts. He still hadn't said a word when his drink arrived. His confidence faded, and he turned to walk away at the exact moment the girlfriend returned to reclaim her chair. As they collided, the beer in his hand splashed all over the three of them.

"Oh my God. I'm so sorry." Will apologized profusely. The expression on the friend's face turned to utter disgust and she looked like she might explode.

"Nice, asshole. Thanks a lot," she said, wiping the front of her sweater.

Jules was drying her bare arm with a napkin. She looked up at Will with a quizzical smirk, and he couldn't help but notice that her eyes were the color of a dark, aged whisky.

"I'm really, really sorry," he said, looking from Jules to her friend and then back at Jules again. "Can I buy you both a drink?"

"Yeah, I think you better," her friend replied, then huffed off toward the bathroom.

Jules smiled and handed him a napkin.

"Really, I'm so sorry about that," he said, sitting beside her again.

"Stop apologizing. It's fine, really." She laughed as he motioned for the bartender.

"Well, your friend looks like she wants to rip my face off."

"Yeah, she might. Men aren't really high on her list right now." Jules slid back on her stool and crossed her legs.

182

Her eyes scanned over him and the corner of her mouth rose slightly, as if she were trying not to smile.

"I'm Will," he said, extending a hand toward her. She hesitated slightly but then relaxed her shoulders.

"Julia," she replied. "But most people just call me Jules."

Will couldn't stop the giddy feeling in his stomach when they spoke that first time. He felt awkward and clumsy, but she seemed amused by it, and they stayed there for hours just talking, drinking, and laughing. Jules didn't seem to care when her irritated friend left.

Will had fallen hard that first night, and in a rare moment of bravery, he asked Jules for her number and she easily gave it. He called her the very next day, and soon they were spending nearly every weekend together. Though the early days in their relationship were good, and he soon spent nearly every night in her bed, Jules wrapped herself deeply in her work even back then. By the time she graduated, she was a full-time employee at the *Journal Sentinel* and had dove headfirst into the life of a busy reporter. That was long before she took on the editor and columnist roles and completely immersed herself in her career.

Now, sitting in the newspaper's waiting area with his foot twitching nervously, Will couldn't believe how much he and Jules had both changed from who they were all those years ago. He stared ahead as his resentment for the place slowly built. He often wondered if the newspaper was Jules' actual first love, and he questioned whether she had ever really loved him at all. As he leaned his head back and looked up at the ceiling, the elevator dinged and the doors slid open. He turned just in time to see Jules' boss, Nancy Whitmann, the newspaper's editor-in-chief, walk toward him. She was a powerhouse woman, always in a business suit and heels, her hair perfectly in place and her makeup flawless. As her heels clicked across the floor, Will stood and pulled his sweaty hands from his pockets.

"Will," Nancy said. "It's so good to see you." She opened her arms, offering him an unexpected hug. "How are you? How's Jillian?"

"We're getting by," he said with a shrug, looking down at the shiny floor tiles.

Nancy pursed her lips and touched his shoulder. "Gosh, we miss Jules around here. It's just not the same without her."

Will nodded and shoved his hands back inside his pockets.

"Well, why don't you come upstairs with me," she said, turning back toward the elevator. "We've left her things pretty much as she left them, since we wanted to wait for you to—well, you know."

Will began to sweat even more as they entered the elevator.

"Is it still snowing out there?" Nancy asked, an awkwardness beginning to form between them.

"Uh, yeah. Just lightly, though."

The elevator moved up two floors. When the doors opened again, Will and Nancy stepped out into a busy, open room. He was greeted by the light tap of fingers on keyboards and the murmur from televisions, strategically hung throughout the room, each tuned to a different news channel. The room was distractingly loud as people talked on phones while leaning back in their chairs and staring at computer screens. A few raced around the room with papers in hand, looking like droid ants going about their normal routine. As they walked by another unoccupied desk, Will heard the chatter of a police scanner.

When they reached the back of the room, near what he assumed was Nancy's office, he could feel eyes watching him as Jules' co-workers noticed he was there. When he and Nancy approached Jules' desk, Will's chest began to constrict. Nancy hadn't lied; her things seemed to be untouched. A beige cardigan, which he instantly recognized, was draped across the back of her chair, and her keyboard was still slightly crooked, as if she had pushed it away when she last left the office. Even her nearly empty coffee cup sat untouched with a lip gloss stain still visible on the side. A yellow Post-it note was stuck to the bottom of her computer screen. In her handwritten scribble, it said *Jillian dr appt - Thurs @ 4:00*. Her desk at work was cluttered, just like her desk at home. Near her phone there were two framed photos, one of Will holding Jillian on his lap, both of them laughing, and one of Jillian alone, smiling her big, sweet smile, hair blowing across her face.

Nancy placed a hand on Will's shoulder as he touched the back of Jules' chair. "I'll get a couple boxes," Nancy said quietly, then walked away.

Will sat in the chair and slowly opened drawers filled with files, each labeled at the top in pencil—all in Jules' handwriting.

"Hey, Will." The voice came from behind him and he turned to see Alice, one of Jules' oldest and closest friends from the paper. He stood quickly and she moved in to hug him. Alice was a petite, pretty woman with thick, light brown hair and huge, bright eyes. She and Jules had climbed the ranks of the paper together, and Alice was now one of the managing editors. "It's really good to see you. Are you doing okay?" pulled away but kept a firm grip on his forearm.

"Yeah, hanging in there, you know." He shrugged, nervously looking around the room.

"And how's Jilly doing? She back in school?"

Nancy came up behind them and placed two empty photocopier paper boxes on the desk.

"Yeah," Will said. "Jillian's doing okay. You know kids. They seem to have a way of bouncing back better than us grown-ups." He ran his fingers across the top of the desk.

"I have a quick conference call," Nancy said, almost apologetically. "But please just let me know if you need anything. I'll be back out soon."

Will smiled slightly, and then looked back toward Alice.

"Let me help you," she said, reaching for the coffee cup. "I'll go get this rinsed out."

Will pulled Jules' phone from his pocket and placed it on the desk beside the boxes. He picked up the framed photos and removed the Post-it note from the screen. Instead of throwing it in the garbage, he dropped it in the box as well.

When Alice returned, she placed the cup in the box with the frames. The lip gloss stain was no longer there.

"How're Paul and the boys?" Will attempted to make small talk as Alice opened the bottom desk drawer.

"They're good. The boys are getting big—ten and twelve already, if you can believe that," she said, placing Jules' flash drives and notebooks in a stack. "And Paul is working on his master's now, hoping to finish up his MBA this spring."

"That's great, Al. That's really great," Will took the cardigan from the back of the chair and folded it.

"You should come out and have dinner with us sometime," she said, continuing to clear out the drawers one by one. "Bring Jilly. I'd sure love to see that little thing."

"Yeah, yeah. We'll have to do that soon." It was a lie. Will knew he would never call to make plans.

When she finished placing Jules' things in the box and slowly lowered the lid, Alice turned and leaned against the desk. She was fighting tears. "God, I just can't believe she's gone," Alice whispered, crossing her arms in front of her. "Seeing her desk empty like this makes it seem so final. Before, it just looked like she might be on vacation, or something."

187

Will nodded and picked up the cell phone. "Hey, do you by chance know this girl?" He showed Alice the same photo he'd shown Sarah.

Alice narrowed her glance and her face tensed slightly. She quickly looked away quickly before meeting Will's gaze.

"So you do know her?"

"Well, um…not really. I mean, I know who she is, but I don't really know her." Alice stammered, suddenly uncomfortable.

"Who is she?" Will's heart raced.

"Uh, well…she's a bartender down at Catch 22." Alice slid back on Jules' desk and looked at the floor.

"A bartender?" He instantly thought of the credit card bill and how often Catch 22 had appeared on it.

"Yeah. I mean, I don't really know much about her, but I know Jules was working on a story about her. She's a singer or something, I think." She looked anywhere but into his eyes. It was clear she was hiding something.

"Wait a minute—a singer? Is she the one from Nashville?" He suddenly recalled the conversation he'd had with Jules a few weeks before. He had almost forgotten that discussion entirely, until now.

Alice leaned forward, her feet dangling over the side of the desk. "Yeah, I think so. I know Jules has been working on that story for a while now, and I heard she was at the funeral, but I didn't see her there."

"*She* was there? This girl," he said, holding up the phone again. "She was at the funeral?"

Alice looked around the room quickly before nodding her head. "That's what I heard."

He shifted his weight as scenes from the funeral flipped through his mind. Sure, Jules knew many people he had never met, and it was entirely possible this woman could have slipped by him unnoticed. Then he remembered a pretty young woman who had spoken sweetly to his daughter but barely looked at him. She had given her scarf to Jillian. At the time he had been moved by the gesture, but there were countless kind gestures that day from people who knew and loved Jules. And, considering the young woman never really looked at him, he hadn't noticed the deep blue eyes that now seemed to mock him from the screen of Jules' phone. The realization of kind, scarf-offering woman's identity hit him like a shot and made him dizzy.

"Are you okay?" Alice asked, sliding off the desk. She stared back at him, clearly concerned.

"How far is this bar—what's it called? Catch 22?" He glanced at his watch.

"It's over on Milwaukee Street, between Mason and Wells," she said, eying him carefully. "Why do you ask?"

"Just curious. Did Jules go there a lot?"

Alice shifted nervously and tapped the box lid with her fingertips. "You know, Will, Jules and I were both busy and we

189

didn't get to connect as much as we used to. I can't really say if she went there a lot, but I met her there for drinks a few times."

Will shook his head as Nancy returned. She held a large, black hardcover book in her hands. Jules' name was written across the front cover in gold script lettering. Alice shoved her hands in her pockets and lowered her chin as Nancy held the book toward Will with an astute look in her eyes.

"We put this together for you and Jillian," she said, her voice cracking slightly. "It's a compilation of Jules' work here over the years, and some fun pictures we found of her from around the office. There's even a few notes about her from each of us."

Will took the book and opened it to a black-and-white photo of Jules, fifteen years younger, when she was that cocky, aggressive reporter he had fallen in love with. The youthful spunk in her eyes burst from the page. "I don't know what to say, Nancy. Thank you."

"She was a big part of this paper, and she always will be. I just want you to remember that." Nancy dabbed her eye with her finger.

Behind him, Alice sniffled. The room fell oddly quiet as most of the employees stopped working to listen. As he glanced around, he became acutely aware that this place was the biggest part of Jules that he had never really known or understood. He didn't share her interest in writing, or even reading for that matter, but for the first time realized what a presence she had been here.

"She loved her work, more than you know." He looked down at the book and closed the cover.

"You'll always be a part of this family," Nancy said. "Anytime you need anything, just call." She moved in to hug him again.

He pulled away, placed the book in an uncovered box, and turned to glance around the room one last time. He imagined Jules here, consumed by her work and completely in her element. As much as he wanted to understand, it only made him sad to think he could never fulfill her the way this place seemed to.

He felt almost heavy as Alice walked him toward the elevator. She hit the button and turned toward him, attempting to smile. She held the lighter of the two boxes. He could sense she wanted to say something, but instead she simply looked at the floor.

"Why don't you just put that box on top of this one? I can take it from here," he said, faking a smile.

"Are you sure? I don't mind carrying it out—"

He cut her off. "It's fine, Al. I've got this. Really." He could tell she was on the verge of tears.

"Okay," she said placing the box atop the one Will held as the elevator door slid open. She kissed him on the cheek before he stepped inside. "Will," Alice said, placing her hand over the door to stop it from closing.

"Yeah?" He hoped she was about to step inside and offer him some answers to the questions swirling in his head.

She had to know more. But, as if she'd changed her mind, she brought her free hand to her mouth and shook her head slightly.

"Take care of yourself and call us for that dinner," she said. Her eyes filled with tears as she pulled her hand away from the door.

"I will," he lied as the doors closed. He was left holding Jules' life work in two cardboard boxes and staring ahead at his own reflection in the stainless-steel doors.

Chapter Fifteen

Erin stared at her reflection in the mirror. She unscrewed the top of the mascara bottle and slowly brought the brush to her lashes. It was Thursday, and almost time for her regular shift at the bar. It was also the night she played her usual weekly set. It wasn't much, but it kept her singing, and if the crowd was good, it also brought in extra money. Ordinarily, she loved doing this set. It was easy and it gave her a chance to throw out remixed covers of popular songs people didn't expect to hear from a solo chick with a guitar. It was a trick she'd learned in Nashville—take a popular song everyone knows and completely change the tempo. If it was a slow song, speed it up; if was a pop dance tune, slow it down. The same lyrics could mean something entirely different depending on how they were sung.

It wasn't necessarily a unique talent, but it was enough to build her success on the indie circuit before she was signed to a label. Tonight though, she wasn't in the mood to sing. All week long, she'd practiced a slowed-down acoustic version of Maroon 5's "Love Somebody" and a somber version of Don Henley's "Boys of Summer," both of which she planned to debut tonight. She'd begun working on these songs months ago—changing the measure, slowing the verses, and making sure the chords were perfect. Jules loved them both, and she was always more than willing to tell Erin when her songs weren't quite right or when they were flawless. It didn't seem right to play them without Jules there.

She finished applying eyeliner and ran a brush through her hair before staring at her reflection again. With each passing day, had a few more thin but distinct lines on her face. She knew thirty-four wasn't old, but she was beginning to see and feel the effects of her bad choices. She thought about her first taste of cocaine, over four years ago now, and thought about how her love-hate relationship with that addictive stimulant had begun.

It was her thirtieth birthday, which she'd spent with friends at the No. 308 bar in midtown Nashville. Having played that bar before, she knew the eclectic crowd that hung out there, but when she walked into the ladies' room and witnessed a group of young women passing around a small tin filled with white powder, she found herself plunging into a new and untamed world. Erin felt invincible on cocaine—as if fear or consequences didn't exist. Though her addiction didn't happen overnight, the more she indulged in the drug, the more she believed in her ability as a performer. When she was on cocaine, she believed she could write better, play guitar better, and sing better. Soon after she'd started using the drug regularly, her stage presence began to grow; slowly but surely, so did her success.

There was a time when she believed she couldn't perform without using cocaine—it became a crutch and an ally at the same time. But as her name got bigger, so did her dependence. Before long, her drug habit became another camouflaged version of the truth that she hid alongside her sexuality. Then, just as one of her songs began to receive airplay and quickly climb the charts, the mask of lies that she consistently wore slowly began to disappear.

She revealed too much information one night during a drunken conversation with the friend-of-a-friend who, unbeknownst to her, was a freelance reporter for a small but respected Nashville publication. When the story about her sexuality and recreational drug use came out, she denied the conversation ever happened. But rumors soon began to fester and her record label set in motion cover-ups to protect her reputation. Just as her music career had begun to move full-speed ahead, it stalled. As if things weren't already bad enough, they completely derailed with the flash of red-and-blue lights and the cold, stinging click of handcuffs around her wrists.

After how hard she'd worked to get there, she couldn't believe how quickly she lost her chance in Nashville by doing something as stupid as driving drunk and abusing drugs. After her arrest, she couldn't imagine her life could possibly get more out of control. But she was wrong again. Her biggest fall had occurred right here, in this apartment where she now stood—and it was Jules who finally stopped her from slipping off the edge entirely.

Jules had briefly stayed silent after the incident with Tina, but when she arrived at the bar one night in early September, Erin felt an instant change in their relationship. Jules claimed it wasn't because of Tina, and said she wasn't jealous in any way, but after that, she stopped shying away from the physical side of their relationship. Though Jules still insisted on secrecy, Erin wondered if the thought of losing her to someone else had made Jules see their relationship through new eyes. Things became easier, almost natural, and it sometimes seemed as if they couldn't get close enough to one another.

But still, no matter how much Erin begged her to stay, Jules went home every night. And when she did, Erin would turn back to the drugs that, unbeknownst to Jules, Tina still supplied her with. Though Erin wasn't sleeping with Tina anymore, she couldn't seem to give up the drugs that kept her numb. Even as she took them, Erin knew she was dancing dangerously close to becoming the person she'd left behind in Nashville. But during those low points, she couldn't stop her mind from spinning backward, pulling her into memories she desperately wished to forget.

This was the side of Erin that Jules didn't know. Though she wanted Jules to understand her from every angle, she couldn't find a way to tell her about being raped by her mother's boyfriend as a teenager. The anger of opening that wound could easily drive her deeper into self-destruction, and if Jules knew how damaged she really was, Erin was certain it would change things between them. Erin couldn't bear the thought of Jules looking at her in the same way the nurses, doctors and police officers had so many years ago.

Some nights, when Jules wasn't there, Erin endlessly paced her apartment, unable to block the vivid image of her teenage bedroom and the smell of a man's sweat as it dripped on her skin. That memory, combined with remembering the look of disappointment on her agent's face when he handed her the official, lawyer-approved document ending her relationship with her record label, and the realization that Jules was at home lying next to her husband instead of being there with her, Erin became consumed by self-loathing and jealousy-induced fits of rage. On those nights, depending on how she mixed them, the drugs brought her back down and helped push those harsh realities back to the corners of her mind. Though Jules didn't know it, the drugs helped to erase the slowly passing time until Erin could see her again.

As Erin's feelings for Jules increased, so did her detest for Jules' husband. She couldn't understand why Jules stayed with him or why she insisted on leading such a complicated double life. At times, she found herself wanting Jules to make choice, but she resisted the temptation to push for it because she was terrified of what Jules would choose. And then one night, as she and Jules lay face-to-face under the blankets of Erin's bed, Jules had described her marriage during the years when Will was drinking heavily. A question slipped off Erin's tongue before she could stop it.

"Why don't you just leave him?"

Jules rolled on her back and stared at the ceiling. Her dark hair spilled across the pillow and she rested one hand above her head. "You don't understand how complicated it is," she murmured softly.

"You're right, I don't." Erin said. She touched the side of Jules' face with her fingertips. "But I know I'm in love with you, and I would never do anything to hurt you like that—ever."

Jules sat up and swung her feet over the side of the bed, holding the sheet over her chest. The dim light illuminated the smooth skin of Jules' back as she leaned forward and picked up her clothes.

Surprised, Erin reached for her arm. "What are you doing?"

Jules stopped moving. She covered her face with her shirt and then pulled it away slowly, shaking her head. "You can't say that to me," she said under her breath.

"Say what? That I love you?" Erin leaned back on her arm. "So, we can't be honest now?"

Jules shook her head again and laughed sarcastically. "Honest? Yeah, let's be honest, Erin. I know you're still fucking Tina, and I'm still married, remember?"

"What? Jesus Christ, Jules, I haven't slept with Tina in months—not since *you* decided to be in this with me, so where the fuck did that come from?" She flung the sheets aside and flew out of bed, snatching her own clothes off the floor. "And you constantly remind me of the fact that you're married, Jules.

198

It's getting a little old. Are you reminding *me* of that fact—or yourself?"

Jules stayed silent and looked at the floor.

"I'm not forcing you to come here," Erin said, attempting to swallow her anger. They were quiet for a few minutes before Erin sat down beside her.

When Jules looked up, she had a dismal expression on her face. "So what if I did leave my husband? What then?"

Erin touched Jules' hand and then clutched her fingers before looking into Jules' eyes. "We'd figure it out, and we'd make people understand."

"Understand what? That I left my husband and now I'm a lesbian? That's not what I am, Erin. I don't even know what the hell I am anymore."

Erin slowly exhaled and looked at their intertwined hands. "You know, Jules, you keep telling me what you aren't. Why are you so hung up on the label? It's just a fucking word."

Jules sighed and looked away.

"You told me that *this* was what you wanted. I didn't make you do anything," Erin said. "You said you wanted to be with a woman, but now that you are, you don't know what to do with it. I get how that feels, I really do, but I realized a long time ago that I don't have to answer to anyone but myself when it comes to who I choose to sleep with. Sex isn't always about love, unfortunately, but love comes when it does, and it rarely comes easy—at least it doesn't for me. It took me a long time to be honest with myself and everyone around me about my

199

sexuality, so I understand your hesitation, I do. But I couldn't hide who I was in Nashville, and I won't hide it now—and I *know* how I feel about you."

Jules closed her eyes and held her breath.

"Talk to me, Jules. Tell me how you feel. You lay here and talk, but I don't think you ever really let me into your life, or even in your heart," Erin said. "Maybe you're not a lesbian. I don't know. That's not my determination to make. But considering what you and I do together, you definitely aren't straight either, and you know that. You need to stop trying to put a label on this and trying so hard to understand it. It just is what it is, and it's not wrong. It's just who you are."

Jules opened her eyes and exhaled slowly. "It doesn't matter how I feel, and it *is* wrong, Erin. It's very wrong." She pulled their hands apart and quickly slipped her shirt over her head. "And, you haven't told the whole truth about yourself either—I know you haven't, so let's not play games here, okay? Don't feed me this bullshit about honesty when you can't even come clean about who *you* are. I can't leave Will, not now, not after everything we've been through. It just wouldn't be right, even if he does deserve it."

"I'm not the one hiding and lying, Jules. If there's something about me you wanna know, then you can ask me and I'll tell you the truth. But if you don't plan to ever leave Will, then what are we doing here? Is this just a game for you?"

Jules stood and quickly finished dressing. Defeated, Erin leaned back on her elbows and watched as a nervous twinge fluttered in the pit of her stomach.

Once dressed, Jules held her breath and then sat down again. "I don't know what this is, but it's definitely not a game. I'm sorry I accused you of sleeping with Tina. I didn't mean it, and even if it were true, I have no right to be pissed off about it." She touched Erin's bare thigh with her fingertips before continuing. "The truth is, when I'm here with you, I feel alive and awake, and I haven't felt that way in such a long time. I've never felt this way about anyone in my life, including Will, and it's so…I don't know. Intoxicating, I guess. I know that sounds stupid," she said, looking away. "But there's a lot you and I don't know about each other, and Will and Jillian—they're my family, Erin. They need me, and how could I ever explain this to Jillian if I did leave?"

"Don't you think she'd want you to be happy?"

Jules fell back against the bed. "God, what do you want me to do?"

"I just want *you*, Jules, the real you. That's all I want." Erin whispered, "Come with me to Nashville, just for the weekend. I really need to get out of Milwaukee for a few days and check things out down there, just to see if there's a chance of ever fixing that whole mess I made. We won't have to hide or worry about anyone you know seeing us, and then you can see how good it can be to just be who we are—out in the open. My jig is up down there, there's no denying the gay thing for me now."

Jules continued to stare at nothing, as if she were considering the idea. Then she slowly lifted her head and sat up. "I can't do that, Erin, I just can't."

"Do you love me?" Erin asked, her throat tightening as if she'd swallowed sand. She didn't want to seem desperate or clingy, but she needed to know the truth.

Jules stood up and sneered.

"Do you?"

"*Yes*." Jules's response was sharp, but she quickly softened her tone. "I do love you. But I love Will, too. I don't expect you to understand that, but I do, okay?"

The air seeped from Erin's body as if she were a balloon someone had forgotten to tie. "Are you ever going to tell him about me?"

Jules relaxed her shoulders and dug her hands deep inside her pockets. "What would I say? 'How was your day, honey? Mine was good. I wrote some good stuff today that no one gives a shit about, and oh yeah, I'm fucking a woman on the side. She wants me to go with her to Nashville for the weekend.' Is *that* what you want me to say?"

"Whatever, Jules." Erin walked out of the room, completely deflated by Jules' condescending tone. She stomped into the kitchen and opened the cabinet, reaching for the bottle of lorazepam. Jules watched as she flipped off the cap and downed two small pills with the glass of wine she hadn't finished earlier.

Jules reached for the pill bottle. "What is that now?"

"None of your business," Erin said, pulling it from her grasp. "It's nothing."

"Then tell me what it is," Jules said. She opened a kitchen drawer to see the mirror and a vial of cocaine. She shook her head and slammed it shut.

"Don't get all righteous on me now," Erin scoffed. She walked into the living room, picked up her guitar, and dropped onto the couch. "You loved taking a detour on that white highway with me once."

Jules laughed sarcastically. "Yeah, but I'm done with it now. I realized how stupid it was. And isn't that shit what ruined your career in Nashville? Don't you think it's time to grow up a little, maybe, and stop using that as a Band-Aid for your problems? What was in the bottle?"

"It's for anxiety, that's all."

"For anxiety?" Jules sneered. She put her hands on her hips and glared back at Erin like angry parents glare at their children. "Here's a thought. If you have too much anxiety, then stop doing coke."

"Go home to your family, Jules," Erin said her tone calm as she continued to play her guitar. She wasn't about to be lectured by the married woman she'd slept with less than hour earlier.

"How much coke are you doing, Erin?" Jules asked, stepping closer.

"Does it matter?" Erin stopped playing and stared up at Jules. "You've made it clear what you want from me. I gave it to you. Now get the fuck out."

Jules took a step back as if Erin had just punched her in the stomach. Her dark eyes narrowed and she seemed wounded from the blow. "What I *want* from you? Did you seriously just say that to me?"

Erin stood and walked closer to her. She breathed softly on the skin of Jules' neck and gently tugged her hair with her fingers. Her anger slipped away as the drugs slowly numbed her. "Tell me you don't love how I touch you, Jules. Does Will touch you like that?" She kissed Jules' neck and pulled her closer, moving her lips to Jules' ear. "Tell me you don't love the way my tongue feels between your legs. Go ahead, try and deny it."

Jules pushed her away. Disgusted and angry, she stormed into the kitchen and began opening cabinets and drawers. "This isn't you talking. What the hell else do you have in here?"

Erin cackled like a child and followed behind her. "Oh, c'mon, just admit it. You're only here for the sex. It makes you 'feel alive,'" she said, making air quotes with her fingers as she used Jules' own words against her. "It makes you feel good to stick it to your pathetic husband, just like he stuck it to you, only you decided to take it one step farther and fuck a woman. Bravo,

Jules Kanter. You have everyone around you completely fooled—you even managed to fool yourself."

Jules froze. Her back was to Erin, her shoulders rising and falling as she breathed heavily. "You're wrong about that," she said before turning to face Erin.

"Wrong about what?"

Jules wiped away a tear as it slipped down her cheek. "I'm not trying to fool anyone, and I never came here to hurt you. This was never about sex for me," she said, walking past Erin. She picked up her purse from the table near the door. "You made this about sex. I told you from the start that I still loved my family. But if this is how it's going to be, then we're done here. The drugs are getting out of hand, Erin. I've already been down this road with Will, and I won't do it again—not even for you."

"You just said there's no place for me in your life anyway, Jules, so what difference does it make?" Erin calmly poured herself another glass of wine. She took a long, slow drink without looking at Jules.

Jules shook her head and looked up at the ceiling. "Call me when you're sober."

"Tell your husband I said hi," she said as Jules slammed the door.

Using the mirror to stare into her own eyes, Erin wished she could take back the things she'd said during that argument. Jules had only tried to be honest, and Erin had crucified her with her words.

Though Jules had disappeared from her life before, it was after this fight when Erin wondered if Jules would ever come back. Still, she had tried to be stubborn and talked herself into believing that it was Jules who refused to take their relationship to the next level and decided to end it. With Jules gone again, Erin slid deeper into the dark corners of her mind. The old memories began to haunt her even more and, once again, cocaine became a daily habit. It gave her the short bursts of invincible energy she needed to make it through the long nights at the bar. But when she came home at 3:30 a.m., still wired and unable to sleep, she would stare at her phone and stop herself from calling Jules. Instead, she started calling Tina again. Tina warmed her bed and she never asked questions. But, just like before, it wasn't enough because Tina wasn't Jules. Jules had a way of seeing right through her, and even in bed, they had a connection unlike anything she had ever experienced. Jules touched her so naturally, so tenderly, and there was no way she could erase the sound of Jules' voice or the smell of her skin from her memory. But again, Jules stayed silent, and as the days passed, Erin wondered if Jules had forgotten her altogether.

And then it happened. On a random Saturday night and after a long shift at the bar, Erin came home wired and edgy, as usual. She had become accustomed to a new routine of taking lorazepam to bring her down from the cocaine, but as her cocaine use accelerated, so did her tolerance to the downers. The constant counteraction between stimulants and anti-anxiety meds left her exhausted and lacking clear judgment.

That night, she wanted to call Jules. She picked up the phone and then set it back down, only to pick it up again. She had already taken three pills, but they weren't working. She paced while holding her phone, wanting to dial. She knew it was late, and she knew Jules would be asleep—asleep next to Will. She grabbed the bottle and took four more pills to stop herself from thinking too much about whether she ought to call. Unable to fight with herself any longer, she hit Jules' number and listened to it ring. Jules didn't answer; when her voicemail picked up, Erin ended the call and shut her eyes tightly. Then she snapped them open and hit the number again. Still nothing, so she hung up and dialed again. Finally, after three tries, Jules answered, her voice hoarse and irritated.

"Do you know what time it is?"

"I'm so sorry, Jules," Erin mumbled. Her body began to relax. The drugs were finally taking hold.

"Erin, I can't do this right now. It's four a.m., and you woke Will."

Tears slipped down Erin's cheeks. "I didn't mean what I said. I'll do anything you want, just please come back. I'll tell you every secret you ever wanted to know. I'll tell you all of it."

Jules sighed heavily on the other end. "What are you on right now?"

Erin felt herself beginning to lose consciousness.

"Erin?"

"Come back to Nashville with me Jules," she slurred.

"How much did you take?" Jules said, more forcefully now. "Jesus Christ. What the fuck are you doing to yourself?"

The next thing Erin could remember was lying on her side in the emergency room, choking on a tube that was being pulled from her throat. She vomited violently, black liquid seeping from her mouth into a pan beside her.

"That's right, it's okay. It's just the charcoal coming out, that's all," a nurse said, holding her shoulders and pulling back her hair. "You're okay. Just get it out."

Erin choked again. It felt as though everything inside her body was about to come out of her mouth. She wildly looked around the room and had no idea how she had gotten there.

"You're at the hospital. It's okay," the nurse said. "A friend called the ambulance and you made it here in time. Your mom and your friend are just outside. Everything is gonna be just fine."

Remembering that horrible night as she got ready for work and her solo set, Erin looked away from the mirror and walked out of the bathroom. She sat on the edge of her bed and noticed her guitar across the room. God only knows what would have happened if Jules hadn't called the ambulance.

She remembered the look on her mother's face as she sat beside Erin's hospital bed hours later. It was a wounded, worried, and devastated look.

208

"I'm so sorry, Mom. It was an accident, I swear," she whispered. Erin's mother clutched her hand with silent tears streaming down her face.

"There's a lot I can take in this life, sweetie," she said while rubbing Erin's hand with her cold fingers. "Losing you is not one of them. I know part of this is my fault because of what happened to you, because of what I *let* happen to you, but God dammit, if you need something, then tell me. Talk to me, Erin. Don't lie to me. I can't take that—not from you."

Erin leaned her head back on the pillow and closed her eyes.

"It wasn't your fault, Mom, it wasn't. I just lost control, that's all. I can stop—I'm going to stop."

"I've heard that before," her mother said, ignoring Erin's pleas. "Your friend Jules is outside. She's the one who called and brought me up here, and you're so damn lucky she did. We had a long talk about what's been going on with the two of you. She thinks this is her fault this time."

Erin opened her eyes and looked at her mother's tired face. "It wasn't her fault. It wasn't *anyone's* fault. I just got in too deep. It was just a mistake."

Her mother wiped the tears from her face. "Then you need to tell her that, and don't you ever do this to me again. If you don't kick it this time, then we're putting you in rehab. It's either that or I'd rather you leave and go back to Tennessee and get focused on *your* life again. But you just can't stay here in limbo and slowly die in front of my eyes, honey. I can't deal with that."

"Mom," Erin said. "I—"

"I don't wanna hear it, baby," her mother said. She leaned down and kissed her daughter's hand before struggling to stand up. "I'm gonna go get some coffee and call your aunt. I'll send Jules in."

Erin felt nauseous watching her mom leave the room. Her throat was dry and irritated, and as the minutes passed, she wondered if Jules had decided to leave.

When the door finally opened, Jules walked in and kept her eyes on the floor. She wasn't wearing makeup, and Erin had never seen her so look so tired and disheveled. She nervously bit her lip and sat in the chair next to the bed before looking up.

"Jules," Erin stuttered. "I—"

"Save it." Jules cut her off and leaned forward. "What the hell were you thinking?"

"I wasn't. I'm so sorry," Erin said, her voice cracking. "It wasn't your fault. I swear, I wasn't trying to do anything."

Jules looked away. "You asked me to leave. So I left. Then you called me three weeks later, at 4:00 in the morning, stoned out of your mind, begging me to come back, and then you pass out on the phone. What did you expect me to do, Erin?"

Erin covered her face and tried to stop herself from sobbing. "I don't know."

"If this is too much for you, then we can't keep doing this, but I can't walk away unless I know you're okay." She stood up and moved closer before gently pulling Erin's hands from her face.

"I don't want you to walk away," Erin said through her tears. "I shouldn't have said those things to you."

Jules exhaled and relaxed her shoulders. "Please tell me you didn't do this because of me."

"I swear, it was just an accident. I didn't mean it. I should've just called you and told you the truth—the whole truth, but I didn't know how."

Jules wiped her eyes. "I don't want to walk away either, but we have to be honest with each other—and no more drugs. If you do drugs then we can't be together. I can't do this again."

Erin held her hands tighter. "I promise."

"I need to figure out some things with Will, okay? You need to give me time."

Erin nodded again.

"If you need me, call me before you do something stupid like this, okay?" Jules spoke in a whisper. "I'll be there for you, I promise."

Walking into the bar with her guitar case slung over her back, Erin was greeted by the normal Thursday night crew. Jessie stood behind the bar, her blonde hair flowing over her shoulder and her T-shirt one size too small for her chest, while their manager, Les, loitered and flirted with her. Jessie always reciprocated the playful conversation but kept Les at arm's length. Erin often wondered if they'd hooked up at some point, but she never cared enough to question Jessie about it. The college-age waitresses both smiled in that bright-eyed, naïve way as Erin walked into the back room.

"What's on the set list tonight?" Kat asked, tossing her curly, auburn hair over her shoulder. Erin instantly noticed her nose piercing.

"Oh, you know. A little of this and a little of that," she said, pulling off her jacket. "I see you finally did it," she said tapping the diamond stud in her own nose.

"Yeah. What do you think?" Kat asked as if Erin's acknowledgment gave her some sort of reassurance.

"Yeah, it looks good. Doesn't even look swollen," Erin said unzipping, her guitar's soft case. She pulled out her Gibson Firebird Custom and then closed the case again. The guitar was the only thing she owned that was worth anything. She'd bought it in Nashville as a gift to herself when she penned her record deal.

"Whoa, playing the Firebird tonight," Becky exclaimed while tying her apron tightly around her waist. "Pulling out the big guns, hey?"

Erin slipped the strap over her head, pulled a pick from the front pocket of the case, and tested the strings. "Well, I have it. I might as well play it. It sounds better than my old Gibson anyway."

212

"You sound good no matter what you're playing." Kat smiled nervously and straightened her necklace.

Erin sneered and started strumming the opening of "Smoke on the Water," making both girls laugh and nod their heads along with the rhythm. Kat flashed Erin another look, one Erin knew all too well. It was the same look Jules had given her on the night they met. Though Kat was nice enough, Erin was in no way interested in going down that road.

"Yo, ladies. Are you working or having a coffee klatch back here?" Les stepped into the room and hurried them along.

"Yeah, yeah, we're coming," Becky mumbled while popping a piece of gum into her mouth. "Good luck, Erin. Break a leg."

Erin nodded and smiled. "I don't dance, I just sing."

Kat smiled and quickly looked Erin up and down before pushing her way out the door.

"The mic is set up for you, Erin," Les replied hurriedly. She turned to face the full-length mirror that hung on the back of the bathroom door, checking her reflection one last time.

"There's a decent crowd starting to roll in, but no pressure." He winked and slipped out the door.

Erin closed her eyes and began moving her fingers over the strings. She hummed lightly and remembered what it was like to be on stage in front of bigger crowds in Nashville. Though she was rarely nervous during these Thursday night sets, something seemed off tonight. She glanced at the clock, which read exactly 7:00, then drew in a deep breath and slowly

213

exhaled. She turned and slid her guitar down toward her hip as the door opened again and Jessie sauntered in holding a shot glass. "Your usual Fireball shot, my lady," she said bowing playfully and handing Erin the glass.

"I was wondering when you were gonna show up," Erin smiled. She dipped her head back and let the hot liquid slide down her throat. She clenched her teeth and handed the glass back to Jessie. "Thanks."

"You got it. Now go knock 'em dead, tiger," Jessie said, leaning against the door to hold it open.

Erin winked at her before making her way across the bar. Les hadn't lied. The room filled nicely and her heart pounded as she walked toward the small, makeshift stage at the front of the room. Les saw her coming and stepped up to the microphone.

"Alright people," he said, rocking back and forth on his feet. "It's Thursday night at Catch 22, and that means our lovely and talented singing bartender is about to take the stage. Let's give a warm welcome to the Milwaukee native and former Nashville recording artist who now happens to be our very own talented bartender, Ms. Erin Quinn."

A decent amount of applause erupted in the room as Erin stepped onto the stage and took the Gibson from her hip.

"Thank you, thank you," she said, her voice echoing slightly throughout the room. "Yeah, *former* Nashville recording artist, ain't that the truth." A few laughs came from the crowd. "There must be a lot of regulars in here tonight, and you're just

214

clapping because you like my good pours, but don't tell Les."
She smiled at Les, who assumed his position behind the bar.
"Don't worry, though, I'll be back in bartender mode soon, but
first you'll have to suffer through my singing, so let's get it
going."

Sliding her fingers over the strings, she started right
into Taylor Swift's "I Knew You Were Trouble." She'd learned
it shortly after she met Jules and it had become their inside joke.
She glanced around the room as the customers began nodding
their heads and singing along. It was always energizing to gain
the crowd's acceptance right from the gate. She scanned the
room, and just when she had begun to feel more at home on the
stage, she noticed a man sitting alone in one of the back booths.
His back was to her, but he seemed like the only one in the bar
not watching her. He had wavy auburn hair and wore a tan
carpenter's-type jacket, but he seemed out of place. Her eyes
landed on him occasionally throughout the set, but he never
turned her way.

"Alright," she said upon finishing what would
normally be her last song. "I so appreciate that most of you
stuck around through this." She took a quick sip of water and
pulled up the stool that was behind her.

"If you don't mind, I'm gonna sit for these next two
songs—it's the only time I'll get to sit since I'll be standing
behind the bar for the rest of the night after this." Some of the
customers chuckled again as she adjusted the microphone. "So
most of you know these next couple songs, but I put my own

215

little unique spin on them. They remind me of someone who taught me how to pick myself up when I didn't think I could." The room fell eerily silent, and even Jessie and the waitresses turned to listen. "Sometimes we all need someone to remind us of what we're capable of. She did that for me, so these next two are for her."

Starting into the slow version of "Love Somebody," she quickly surveyed the crowd's reaction. Jessie gave her a wink, but Kat simply averted her eyes and made her way toward the man in the back booth. He turned his head slightly, but she still couldn't see his face. As the words slipped out, she closed her eyes and imagined Jules sitting at the bar with a bright, sweet smile stretched across her face. Erin knew she would never find someone else who intrigued or haunted her the way Jules had. When she finished the song, the room was silent for a few seconds. She opened her eyes to see everyone staring in her direction, and for a moment she was unsure if they'd hated the way she played it or if they had actually enjoyed it. The clapping started slowly, and then it came faster, accompanied by a few loud whistles. Some of the patrons even stood up from their chairs to give her a standing ovation.

She smiled, stood up, and bowed her head slightly. "Thank you," she said, motioning for people to retake their seats. "Now shut up and sit down. I have one more." They laughed again as she led into "The Boys of Summer." Jules had loved this song, but Erin never would have considered playing it until one afternoon when it came on as they were driving along

216

the lakefront on North Lincoln Memorial with the windows rolled down in Jules' car. Erin had reached over to change it, but Jules gently slapped her hand away.

"No, don't you dare. I love this one," she said. Erin had teased her at first, telling her the song showed her true age, but when she watched Jules sing it, with her hair blowing in the wind and her eyes hidden behind her aviator sunglasses, Erin realized the song fit their relationship perfectly.

She watched again as people in the room began to sing along. Though she had been nervous and unsure when she stepped onto the stage, she knew now that she was meant to play these songs. Somehow, and from somewhere, Jules was listening. When she finished the last verse and played the remaining chords, the nervous energy seeped from her body. She let out a long, slow sigh as applause filled the room one last time.

"Thanks so much! Really, thank you," she said, bowing. "In case you forgot, I'm Erin Quinn. I'm just a lowly bartender, and I'll be back on that side in just a few minutes. I appreciate you sticking it out for the last hour."

The clapping continued when she stepped off the stage and made her way toward the back room. With the door closed behind her, she pulled the guitar off her shoulder and sank into a chair. She was suddenly consumed by the deep ache of missing Jules, and she wondered if the sharpness of that feeling would ever go away.

The door opened behind her as Les peeked his head in the room.

"You okay?"

Erin quickly wiped her face and began putting the guitar back in its case. "Yeah. Yeah, I'm good. I'll be right out."

"That was the best set I've seen you do so far. People loved it," he said as their eyes met in the mirror. "Jules would've loved it."

Erin smiled and tried to hide the tears that filled her eyes, but they slipped out anyway. "Yeah, probably."

"Come out when you're ready. I'll give Jessie a hand till then," he said, reaching out to touch her shoulder.

"Yeah, I'm sure you will," she said, pushing him off playfully. Though she would never admit it to them, this tight little group at the bar had become almost like family to her.

When Erin finished packing the guitar, she stood and took a deep breath. She exhaled before changing her shirt and weaving her hair into a braid. After she fixed her smudged eyeliner and quickly applied lip gloss, she made her way toward the bar. Some of the customers clapped when she reassumed her position. She reached for a towel, stuffing it in the back pocket of her skinny jeans before leaning toward them.

"Alright, kids, what can I get you?"

Customers immediately began reciting their drink orders, but when she turned and grabbed some glasses off the shelf, she noticed Jessie smiling at her as she poured a beer.

218

"Check out your tip jar," she said, motioning toward the nearly overflowing jar near the register.

"Well, would you look at that," Erin exclaimed. "It must be my lucky night."

The clock continued to wind as Erin stayed busy making small talk and pouring drinks, but there was still an odd heaviness in the air. She tried to ignore it and simply kept smiling and cracking her usual jokes, but she realized something was about to shift when Kat approached the bar with a perplexed look on her face.

"What's up?" She asked as Kat set down her tray and glanced over her shoulder.

"There's a guy back there. He keeps asking about you," she said. She seemed uncomfortable. "He said he wants two glasses of straight Korbel, and he wants you to bring it to him."

Erin scoffed and looked past her. "What's he asking?"

"He asked if I knew what you like to drink," she said, lowering her voice. "And then he asked me if you're gay."

Erin cocked her head and laughed nervously. "He's probably just some guy who saw the set and he's getting drunk and mouthy. Whatever. Tell him I'm busy."

"He's been drinking Coke all night, until now," she explained. "He's not drunk at all. He said he has something he wants to talk to you about. Maybe he's a talent scout or something? I don't know, but he's kinda creeping me out."

Erin pulled the towel from her back pocket. She looked toward the bouncer, who sat on a stool near the front door.

219

"Where is he?"

"The last booth on the left," Kat said, looking nervous.

Erin nodded and poured two glasses of Korbel. She looked at Jessie, who was talking to regulars at the end of the bar.

"Special delivery, I guess," she said holding up the glasses and nodding toward the back of the room.

"Okay. I got it," Jessie said before turning back toward the customers. The crowd was beginning to thin.

As she walked toward the booth holding a Korbel in each hand, Erin's mouth grew dry. She hated the scent of brandy. It didn't matter if it was cheap brandy or a top-shelf brand; the smell of earthy wood mixed with the bitter scent of red wine always made her stomach turn. It reminded her of the man who raped her, and even though she tried to block it out, she saw his face each time that harsh aroma hit her nose. Approaching the table, she was distracted by that thought, but then she realized why the atmosphere had seemed off all night.

When the man in the booth turned toward her, it seemed as if the air in the bar evaporated. The drinks in her hands nearly slipped to the floor, and her first thought was to run—but it was too late. The eyes that locked on hers were the last she'd expected to see here.

Chapter Sixteen

"So I take it by the look on your face that you know who I am?" Will's voice was cold. Erin looked away quickly; it was evident he'd caught her off guard. Her eyes were filled with sheer panic.

"Have a seat," he said, motioning toward the empty booth across from him.

"I—I'm working," she stuttered. She set the drinks on the table with nervous and unsteady hands, spilling some of the brandy.

Will looked her up and down and then straightened his shoulders. "Look, I'm guessing you know a whole lot more about me than I know about you, but I do know you were fucking around with my wife, so the least you can do is sit down and talk to me for a few minutes."

Erin looked back toward the bar and locked eyes with Kat before apprehensively sliding into the booth across from him. She kept her hands at her sides and took a deep breath before slowly looking up at him. He could read the guilty look in her eyes, and even if she wanted to, there was no way to hide the truth from him now. He had spent hours studying her face on

Jules' phone, but seeing her in person, so close up, increased his anger to a completely new level.

"You were at the funeral, weren't you?" He touched the glass of brandy with the tips of his fingers.

He watched Erin nervously shift, but she gave no reply.

"You gave Jillian a scarf. That *was* you, wasn't it?"

Erin didn't respond, and she dodged looking at him again.

"You don't have anything to say to me?"

Erin finally looked up, but instead of responding, she leaned back against the booth and crossed her arms over her chest. He stared at her in disbelief. He hadn't planned on meeting her this way, but he suddenly found himself struck by the vibrant blue of her eyes. They were the color of tropical ocean water and looked so much brighter in person than they appeared on Jules' phone.

As their silent standoff ensued, Will pulled Jules' phone from his pocket and placed it on the table between them.

"You're the singer from Nashville she was trying to write about, aren't you? Actually, you don't have to answer that one. Your whole gig up there gave that away." He tapped his fingers on the table, hoping to jar her into saying something. "She did mention your story, though she conveniently forgot to explain that her interest in you went a little beyond her work."

Erin blinked quickly, but said nothing.

"What do you think I found on her cell?" Erin's eyes locked on the phone, but she held her ground.

222

"Still nothing?" He reached in his pocket again. This time, he pulled out the vial of cocaine and slammed it on the table. "Okay, then maybe you can explain why she had this in her purse?"

"Jesus Christ. Are you insane?" She quickly snatched the vial from the table and shoved it into her pocket while glancing around the room. "There could be an undercover cop anywhere in here."

"So you do speak," he said, leaning back and crossing his arms, mirroring the same position she had just moments ago.

"It wasn't hers, okay?"

"Why did she have it?" His thirst for the brandy increased.

Erin shifted nervously again. "Because she didn't—"She briefly closed her eyes.

"She didn't what?" He shrugged his shoulders unsympathetically.

"She didn't want me to do it anymore. It was mine, okay? She took it from me."

He laughed aloud as Erin glared at him.

"Oh, you've got to be kidding me. Goddamn Jules had a thing for wanting to solve other people's bullshit problems, didn't she?"

Erin didn't respond. She looked at the brandy and then back at Will.

"Don't you dare judge me," he hissed and leaned forward. "I haven't had a drink in almost three years."

He picked up a glass and then pushed one toward her.

"I don't like brandy," she said, crossing her arms.

Will laughed again. "No wonder Jules liked you."

He drank the brandy quickly and nearly choked as it hit the back of his throat, but the burn of it felt good.

"So tell me, Erin, was my wife a lesbian?"

She scoffed and pushed the brandy back toward him. "Well, she definitely wasn't straight. I think that's obvious."

"But you are—a lesbian, I mean." He picked up the second glass and slammed it almost as quickly as the first.

"Not that it's any of your business, but yes, I am."

"Well, that's good to know. So my wife apparently liked to play both sides of the field then. That's reassuring. So tell me, when the two of you were fucking, which one pretended to be the man?" He looked away from her and motioned for Kat.

Erin leaned forward and looked him straight in the eyes. Her eyes appeared darker so close up, as if his comment had drained their color completely. "Well now, you see, that's the whole idea of two women in bed together," she said through a tightly-clenched jaw. "We don't need a man to satisfy us, or to give us *exactly* what we need."

Will laughed again as Kat approached the table. She cast Erin a worried glance. "Everything okay?"

"Oh, she's totally fine, aren't you, Erin?" He tone was sarcastic. The alcohol was beginning to take hold. "Bring us another round, would you please?"

"It's okay, Kat, I'm fine," Erin said, glancing up quickly. "We're just talking."

Kat nodded and smiled apprehensively before walking away.

"How long was it going on?" He began spinning Jules' phone with his fingers.

"Does it matter?"

"I guess not. But was she planning to leave me?" The tone of his voice softened and he was unsure if he wanted to know the answer.

"If she did, she never told me," Erin sneered. "For some reason, she actually loved you."

Will's head swirled. "Did she love you?"

"You know, I have to get back to work, so why don't you just cut to the chase and tell me what you want?"

Will shook his head. "I just wanna know how the hell my wife ended up having an affair with a woman. Can you explain that to me? I don't understand how this happened. Did she love you or not?" His words began to slur slightly.

"Yes, she did. Does that make you happy? Does that give you some sort of closure? Somehow I doubt it. And, yeah, I loved her, too, but it doesn't matter now, does it? She's gone."

"Yeah, she sure is, isn't she," he said as Kat set two more glasses of Korbel on the table. She held Erin's stare momentarily, then motioned toward the bouncer who stood near the door, but Will didn't care.

"Did she even tell you she was married?"

Kat narrowed her eyes and quickly walked away.

"She didn't need to tell me. I noticed the ring on her finger the first night I met her," Erin said, pushing her braid back over her shoulder.

"And that didn't stop you?"

Erin scoffed. "You act as if she walked in here and we just slept together right off the bat. It didn't quite happen that way, despite whatever twisted fantasy you have in your mind."

"Well then, why don't you explain it to me?" He pounded another brandy and slammed the glass on the table, making the second glass spill slightly.

"Don't you think you should slow down on that?"

"Tell me how you started fucking my wife, Erin Quinn." The brandy blurred his vision, and he couldn't see her clearly as he chugged his fourth drink.

"Why are you doing this?" She shook her head as the bouncer approached the table.

"Because she never let me forget what a fuck-up I was, not ever." He was slurring and his insides had begun to churn. Will hadn't tasted alcohol in a long time, and it had hit him with the force of an unexpected and violent squall. He was unsure if it was the weight of Erin's words or the alcohol surging through his veins that suddenly made him want to faint. "And now I find out that she was lying to me all along. Do you know what that feels like?"

Erin shook her head and looked up at the bouncer.

"Of course you don't. You just said she loved you, and you loved her. Ain't that fucking swell?"

"Look, buddy," the bouncer said, sternly reaching for Will's arm. "I think you've had enough and Erin's heard enough. She needs to get back to work. Let me get you a cab."

"Fuck you and fuck her," he said without looking up. Instead, Will clenched his fists and rested his head on the table.

"Time to go, man," the bouncer said, yanking his arm again.

Before he could stop himself, Will flew out of the booth and lashed out at the bouncer, awkwardly swinging arms that didn't feel like his own. The bouncer easily dodged him, and Will stumbled into a nearby table, sending glasses and bottles crashing to the floor.

"C'mon man, don't make me call the cops." The bouncer calmly reached down to help Will up, but Will pushed him and stumbled toward the door as everyone in the bar stopped talking and turned to watch.

"Screw all of you," he mumbled as he shuffled toward the exit.

"Wait," Erin called from behind him. "You're not driving are you?"

He laughed, pushed the door open, and stumbled onto the street. The cold air felt sharp on his face and he quickly inhaled. The chill of the dry winter air stung his nose and made him cough. He felt the full effect of the alcohol now, and acid began to bubble in his throat, making him choke on his own

227

saliva. The door opened behind him as he hunched over and heaved onto the sidewalk.

"Oh God," Erin exclaimed walking up behind him with one hand covering her mouth. "Seriously, you can't drive. Please, can I just call someone for you?"

Will stood and wiped his face. "Why do you fucking care what I do?"

"I don't," Erin shot back, shivering in the cold. Her blue eyes were fixed intently on him. "But I do care that you have a daughter at home. Hasn't she lost enough?"

Will's rage surged he lunged toward Erin. He wanted to wrap his fingers around her throat and strangle the life out of her, but instead he pushed his face just inches from hers. He was so close he could smell her perfume; it was the same familiar scent that often lofted off of Jules.

"Don't you ever talk about my daughter," he said under his breath. "You have no idea what this has been like for her."

He turned away just as the bouncer came out to the street. "Erin, you want me to call the cops?"

"No. It's okay, Jeff," she said. "I'll give him a ride."

"Are you nuts?" The bouncer said, walking toward her. "You don't know this guy. I can't let you leave with him."

Will leaned against a streetlight and brought his hands to his face. He couldn't see clearly; all he wanted to do was lie down. "God, I hate you, Jules," he mumbled.

"He's not gonna do anything to me," she said, turning toward the door. "Just let me get my car. Watch him and don't let him leave."

"Erin, no way. You can't—"

"Jeff, he's Jules' husband, alright?" Will slid down the pole while they argued.

The bouncer turned back toward Will. "Aw, fuck, man. Stand up," he said, slipping his hands under Will's armpits to lift him. "If you try to hurt that girl in any way, I will hunt you down and kill you myself. You got that? I don't give a flying fuck whose husband you are."

Will could barely comprehend what was happening as Erin pulled her car up to the curb. The bouncer opened the back door and pushed Will into the backseat with little empathy. "This is a bad idea, Erin. A bad idea," he said, closing the door. "You call me when you dump this asshole wherever he needs to go. If you don't, I'll call the police myself."

The car pulled away just as the blackness closed in on him.

229

Chapter Seventeen

Erin lay on her bed listening to the low rumble of Will's snoring in the next room. She couldn't believe the irony of the situation she now found herself in. Since he'd passed out cold in her backseat and she didn't know where he lived, she had no choice but to bring him back to her apartment and garner the help of her landlord, who lived below her, to help drag him up the stairs. She was drained both physically and emotionally. She knew now that it must have been Will who had called from Jules' phone a few nights ago. Jules had left the evidence of their relationship all too visible in the one place she didn't think anyone would look.

"I can't believe you were that stupid, Jules," she whispered aloud.

She wondered how Will would react when he awoke to find himself in the home of the woman who'd tried to steal his wife. She knew he was drowning in anger and grief—and she knew she was partly to blame.

As Will continued to snore, she turned on her side and pulled a pillow over her head. When she shifted positions, a lump in her front pocket dug into her leg. She reached down and remembered the vial of cocaine that she'd taken from Will at the bar. She shut her eyes tightly and pulled it from her pocket. This tiny object seemed harmless, but it was like a demon just waiting to possess her. She knew it would be best to flush it down the toilet before it found a way around her self-control, but she didn't move. Instead she remembered the look on Jules' face when she had taken it from Erin's hand.

"If you do this, I'm gone. That's it," Jules had said, and Erin could still hear her voice as if she were in the room.

"You're gone anyway, Jules," she whispered, reaching through the darkness to place the vial on the nightstand next to a framed photo of her and Jules.

After her brief stay in the hospital, Erin had quit doing drugs cold turkey. It hadn't been easy, and there were many near relapses, but Jules stood by her. She had been supportive when Erin needed it and tough when she needed it more. When Erin was working one particular night, but still feeling vulnerable and coming in and out of periods of withdrawal, Jules stayed close and kept an eye on Tina, who sat at the opposite end of the bar. The more obnoxiously Tina laughed and nonchalantly conducted her business, the more Jules honed in on her like a hawk. Though Tina had heard about Erin's overdose after she missed an entire week of work, Tina made it clear that she would be more than willing to supply Erin with something to take the edge off if she needed it. But on this particular night, Jules was having none of the snide remarks being tossed in Erin's direction by Tina and her drunken friends. When Tina stood and walked toward the restroom, Jules seized the moment and spun off her stool, making a beeline behind her.

"Jules," Erin called, hoping to thwart a confrontation between them. But Jules ignored her. By the time Erin made it around the bar and into the small, dimly-lit restroom, Jules had Tina backed against a wall. Jules' face was just inches from Tina's, but her hands were shoved deep inside her own pockets as if to keep herself from touching her. Jules' dark eyes were locked on Tina's face, but Tina looked at the floor. Her shoulders were hunched down, as if Jules' words had landed a hefty punch.

"Jules, don't. I don't need you to do this for me," Erin said as she stepped toward them. "This wasn't her fault. I did this to myself."

Tina glanced up at Erin but then quickly looked away.

Jules didn't waiver. "Tell me you understand what I just said."

Tina looked up at her and then nodded. "Yeah, I get it," she said quietly.

Jules took one step back to let Tina slide out. She brushed past Erin without saying a word. Surprised, Erin watched her leave before turning back to face Jules in the mirror.

"What the hell did you say to her?"

Jules stared back at her through the glass. "Actually, I just saved her ass. The guy at the end of the bar is an undercover cop—and he was watching."

232

"How the hell do you know that?"

Jules turned to face her. "I just do, and I could have turned her in, but I told her to leave you alone or next time I'd tip him off myself."

On another weak day, when she nearly relapsed again, Jules had come over to find Erin frantically tearing through every drawer in her apartment looking for the cocaine that she knew was still there—somewhere.

"I had a bad day. I just need a little, Jules. I'm tired as hell all the time. I can't take it," she said, feeling anxious and overly agitated.

"It's just the withdrawal. A little will put you right back where you were," Jules said while closing drawers and following behind Erin as she darted for the bedroom and opened her bottom dresser drawer.

"No, I can handle it. I just need a little."

When she saw the half-empty vial stuffed between two T-shirts at the bottom of the drawer, she snatched it up and spun around to find Jules facing her.

"You can't do this, Erin," she said, motioning for her to hand over the drugs.

"I'll never touch it again after this, I promise." Erin pleaded, clutching the vial in a closed fist. "I'm just exhausted and I can't keep up. I need this, Jules. Maybe I just need to cut it back slower."

Jules dropped her hands to her sides. "If you do this, I'm gone. That's it," she said sternly. "A little is exactly how

233

you started before. I told you, I've already been through this with Will and my dad. I won't do it again—not for you, him, or anyone else. Ever."

Erin knew she was serious. The look in her eyes, though calm, was austere. Before she could change her mind, she handed Jules the vial and sank down on the bed.

Jules shoved the cocaine into the pocket of her black pants and sat down beside Erin. "Is there anything else in here you need to tell me about?"

She flopped backwards, closed her eyes, and shook her head. But it was a lie. She still had lorazepam hidden in a drawer. Jules leaned back and rested her head on her hand, looking down at Erin. "You should eat. Want me to run out and grab some Chinese or something?"

Erin felt nauseous, and the thought of food only made it worse. "No. Please do not make me eat."

"Okay, well, it's gorgeous outside. What about a walk on the lakefront? I have something for you that might actually make you feel better."

Erin laughed sarcastically. She knew Jules wouldn't let up until she agreed to do something other than lay there. She pulled herself off the bed and grabbed her sneakers from the closet. "Well, I can't wait to see it," she mumbled. "Are you planning on walking in your fancy editor pants?"

Jules sat on the bed, still leaning on her hands with a sly smile stretched across her face.

234

"I'm sure you have something I can wear," she said, beginning to unbutton her blouse.

Erin eyed her carefully. "You know, Jules, normally I'd be down with you getting naked in front of me, but right now I think we better just go for a walk."

Jules laughed and tossed her blouse on the bed before reaching for one of Erin's T-shirts from the still-open drawer. "Shut up and find me some sweats. My running shoes are in the car."

As they walked the winding path at Atwater Beach, along the shore of Lake Michigan, Jules seemed calm and more at ease than she had been in months. She kept her purse slung over her shoulder, and though Erin's head ached and she still felt nauseous, she couldn't help but wonder what Jules was hiding.

"Why are you so damn cheery all of a sudden?" Erin finally asked when Jules stopped to take photos of the lake with her phone.

Jules smiled, turning toward her. "I didn't realize it was so out of the ordinary for me to be in a decent mood." She snapped more photos, making Erin blush and turn away.

"I didn't mean it that way," Erin said. "It's just that you seem oddly chipper today. What, did you kill the dreams of some young reporter or something before you came over?"

"What the hell?" Jules laughed. "First of all, I'm not that kind of editor. I actually try to help the ones who aren't completely full of themselves. And second, it's a beautiful day.

I'm here with you, and yes, I started writing something that I'm feeling pretty good about for a change."

"Well, it must be good. Please, do tell," Erin said. She sat in the sand and wiped the sweat from her forehead.

"Nope, I can't. Not yet." Jules bounced around as if she were about to sprint off.

Erin couldn't help but be amused by this sudden child-like burst of energy. "Um, Jules, in case you forgot, you don't really run—like, ever. I don't know why you even have those shoes."

"Well, maybe I'll start." She playfully kicked Erin's thigh before dropping her bag and doing jumping jacks in front of her.

"Seriously, Jules, did you snort that coke when I wasn't looking? Because I'll kick your ass if you did and you didn't share it."

Jules laughed and finally sat down beside her. "Now, that's not funny. But you know, for the first time in a long time, I *do* feel a little optimistic. I put some words down today that I think might actually mean something. Well, maybe. It's not finished yet, but I'm shocked at how good it felt to write how I *really* feel."

Erin liked the way Jules looked wearing her old UW-M Panthers T-shirt, and she could get used to the newfound smile that made her eyes soften and her face seem brighter.

"So, are you gonna tell me what it is, or do I have to beat it out of you?"

236

Jules shook her head and slipped her hand into her purse. She pulled out a tattered-looking book and leaned closer to Erin, staying just far enough away so that someone walking by might not realize what they really were.

"I told you, I can't say anything yet, but, this is what I wanted to show you." She looked at the object in her hands. "Remember how we were talking about Virginia Woolf and Vita Sackville-West awhile back?"

Erin nodded as Jules handed her the shabby-looking book. It had a green cover.

"This is a 1964 copy of *Orlando*. I found it at a little bookstore in Lake Geneva. It's a tenth impression, and not really worth much, but it is a Hogarth Press edition, which was Virginia and Leonard Woolf's printing house. Open it—check out the dedication."

Erin lifted the cover and turned the page.

To V. Sackville-West was all it said, but the words gave Erin chills and she shook her head slightly.

"Yeah, it sure is something, isn't it?" Jules looked out toward the water. "That book was originally published in 1928. It's hard to believe they struggled with the same issues back then that, as a society, we're still struggling with today."

Jules combed her fingers through the sand. "Virginia used Orlando's switching gender to imagine what it would be like to let go of our physical identity and just love for the sake of being in loved, regardless of who we're in love with, you know? Vita certainly did love both sexes, and she had plenty of affairs with both, so really, it's a beautiful testimony to how Virginia saw her."

Erin leaned in and kissed her cheek as Jules playfully pushed her away. Erin thought she might sink in the sand right there as Jules reached for her hand. "I want you to keep this copy. I have another one, but it's not in quite as good of shape as this one."

Erin held the book in both hands and looked back at Jules, wanting to cry. No one had ever given her such a meaningful or unexpected gift. "God, you really blow me away, Jules. Do you know that?"

Jules scoffed, stood, and shook the sand from her pants. "Well, it's just an old book—and let's not forget that even though they were brilliant, talented, and extraordinary, those two women were still fucking crazy. Now get your ass up and I'll race you back to the top."

As Will's snoring turned to steady, heavy breathing, Erin wondered how on earth Jules had managed to sleep next to him night after night. There were countless times when Erin had watched Jules sleep, right here in this bed, and she had selfishly wished Jules would stay asleep and forget to go home. She couldn't understand how Jules could love her so passionately and then simply get up, get dressed, and go home to live a completely different life. She understood that being a mother was Jules' first priority, but she didn't understand why Jules couldn't be honest with herself and leave Will. Erin had kept her end of the bargain; she had stayed away from drugs. But Jules hadn't left him, and she wondered now if Jules had ever intended to leave him. Maybe Will and Erin weren't so different after all. They both loved the same woman, but Erin wondered now if either she or Will had really known Jules the way they thought they did.

Lying completely still in the darkness, she remembered how guarded and sheepish Jules had been at the beginning of their relationship, but in the end she had become so audacious and sensual in bed. Erin looked up at the ceiling fan, her thoughts drifting back to an unusually warm Friday evening in October when she and Jules had taken Erin's mother out for dinner. Though her mom had always accepted Erin's sexuality, she had never seemed interested in anyone Erin dated and had certainly never bonded with any of Erin's partners. But, things were different with Jules. They seemed at ease with each other and, for once, Erin could see the approval in her mother's eyes. For some reason, though she had never needed it before, that validation made her want Jules all the more.

When they had come back to her apartment after dinner, Erin sat on the couch, kicked off her shoes, and watched Jules open a bottle of wine in the kitchen. Erin leaned back and let her eyes take in the natural curve of Jules' shoulders and the slender shape of her back. She was small, feminine, and breathtakingly beautiful in a natural way, as if she didn't really need to try. On that night, she wore a pair of dark twill stretch skinny jeans that fit her body just right and a sheer blue button-down blouse with the cuffs rolled up on her tan forearms. Her dark blue camisole was visible underneath her blouse in a subtle but sexy way. As Jules turned, wine glasses in hand, she noticed Erin watching her.

"What are you looking at?" She smirked while lifting an eyebrow and handing Erin a glass.

"Nothing. I just like your jeans," Erin coyly replied as Jules sat down and pulled her feet off the floor. She tucked her legs close to her body as her cell phone vibrated on the coffee table.

"You gonna get that?" Erin asked as Jules' eyes landed on the phone.

She didn't move toward it. "Nope," she said. "Not right now." The corner of her mouth tensed, making slight creases appear on her skin.

Erin leaned back and placed her bare feet on Jules' legs. "I don't know how you did it, but you sure made quite the impression on my mom."

Jules slipped her hand under the leg of Erin's jeans and gently touch her skin. "Well," she said, "you and your mom are a lot alike, so it shouldn't surprise you that she's a good judge of character." Her fingers slowly massaged the back of Erin's calf as the phone buzzed again.

"Seriously, you're not gonna answer that?" Erin said, growing annoyed. She pulled away from Jules before standing up.

Jules sighed and reached for the phone. Lines appeared on her forehead when she tapped the screen and read the messages. Without responding, she set the phone back down and glanced at her watch.

"Is it work?"

"Uh, no, it's not," she said, skimming Erin's body with her eyes.

"It's Will?"

Jules shrugged and looked away.

"Do you have to go?"

Jules looked up at Erin before rising to her feet and moving toward her.

"No, he can wait," she said, her voice soft as she gently backed Erin against the wall.

Erin could feel the texture beneath the palms of her hands and she knew Jules was waiting, like always, for her to make a move. Erin leaned in and teasingly grazed Jules' cheek with her lips before whispering in her ear. "Is there something you're waiting for?"

Jules returned her stare, moving her hands to either side of Erin's face before pulling her into a deep kiss.

"What's gotten into you?" Erin asked after pulling away, surprised by Jules' forcefulness. "You're not usually the instigator."

Jules didn't reply. Instead she let her hands fall to the bottom of Erin's sweater and then she slowly lifted it over her

241

head. Her hair fell back over her shoulders as Jules touched her face again.

"You're like my drug," Jules said softly, letting her hands slide down to Erin's shoulders. "I am so addicted to you."

Erin held her breath as Jules kissed her neck and then moved down slowly until she was kneeling before her. "Be careful. You're getting pretty good at this, Jules." Erin exhaled. Jules smiled and unbuttoned Erin's pants.

Jules continued to undress and tease her until Erin could barely stand it—but then Jules' phone buzzed again from across the room. Ignoring it, Jules continued to touch Erin, and the passion built between them. For the first time, Erin let Jules take the lead and allowed herself to fall completely under her command. Though Erin usually preferred to be the one in control, she felt safe with Jules, and Jules knew exactly how to put her at ease by touching her softly and slowly. When Jules brought her to the edge and then kept going, Erin's muscles naturally reacted, and it wasn't just her body that surrendered.

"Holy shit, Jules," she whispered when her body began to relax. She pulled Jules to her feet and clung to her tightly. "That was incredible."

Jules laughed and leaned into her before slowly backing away. She began to unbutton her own blouse when her phone buzzed again.

Annoyed by the interruption at such a profound moment, Erin rolled her eyes. "Seriously, answer that damn thing or turn it off." She pushed herself away from the wall and

242

walked toward the bedroom. Flopping on the bed, she pulled the sheet to her chin as Jules appeared in the doorway with her phone in hand.

"What the hell does he want?" Erin scoffed as Jules set the phone down on the nightstand. Jules sighed and sat on the edge of the bed, looking toward the window. Feeling guilty, Erin sat up and moved closer to her. She grazed her fingers along Jules' arms and worked her way up until she slowly slid Jules' blouse off her shoulders, letting if fall to the floor beside them.

"Jillian wants to know when I'm going to be home," Jules replied, looking at her crumpled blouse.

Erin stopped. She rested her chin on Jules' shoulder and slipped her hands around her waist. "Maybe you should go," she said quietly, though she didn't really want Jules to leave.

Jules drew in a deep breath and exhaled slowly before turning toward Erin. They were only inches apart as Jules ran her fingers across Erin's cheek. "I don't want to, not yet. I told him to tuck her in and I'd be home in a couple hours."

"Where does he think you are?" Erin moved her hand under the back of Jules' camisole, caressing the small of her back.

She let her hands fall away from Erin's face, then gripped Jules' camisole and pulled it over her head. "He thinks I'm having drinks with friends from work."

Erin stared at her face and tried to read her expression. She knew Jules was torn between staying and going, but when she reached to touch her, Jules dipped her head slightly.

"Jules," she said gently. "I don't wanna make things harder for you. If you need to go and be with Jillian, then go."

Jules grabbed Erin's hand and lay down beside her. "I'm here because I want to be here," she said somberly. "I just don't wanna hurt you, and I don't wanna hurt them, but I know there's no way to avoid it. In the end, someone is going to get hurt."

"I'm here because I choose to be, too," Erin said. "Of course, I want more from you, but I've learned to take what I can get—and, you just gave it to me pretty good in there."

Jules rolled onto her back and groaned slightly. "God, that makes me sound like a piece of shit."

Erin laughed. "Well, you kinda are, but I still love you, and what you just did was pretty incredible. Honestly, Jules, I've never let anyone take me over like that—at least not when I've been sober."

Jules' shoulders shook as she laughed. "You know, if I decided to come out in the open about this, I don't even think anyone would believe it."

Erin leaned on her elbow and stared down at Jules' face. "Are you thinking of coming out with it?"

Jules looked into Erin's eyes and ran her fingers across Erin's forehead, pushing Erin's hair to the side of her face. "God you're beautiful, and I do love you," she whispered. "I'm so tired of all the lies."

Erin sighed. "Then why don't you just do it? Just come out with it. You're not going to feel better until you do. Who cares what people think?"

Jules' eyes drifted away again. Her hand fell away from Erin's face and landed above her head.

"What, is it the gay thing again?"

Jules scoffed. "I'm just not as tough as you, Erin. Where I grew up, you didn't entertain the thought of being gay. You pushed it away and tried to forget it, but now...now I know I can't deny it, but I still don't know what the fuck to do about it."

She took a deep breath and rolled on her side to face Erin. "There was this guy I went to high school with—his name was Danny—and I don't even remember why, but all of sudden everyone started calling him a fag and saying he was gay and all that," Jules said. "I remember thinking to myself, well, so what if he *is* gay? But I never said that out loud because I didn't want to be on the same side he was. I wanted to stay quiet and laugh right along with everyone else. Only I didn't laugh, and I never made fun of him, because I knew I was just like him."

Erin nodded and touched Jules' fingers.

"I couldn't tell anyone how I was feeling, so I just kept on pretending I was someone I wasn't. But as I got older, the feelings got stronger." She leaned back again, looked at the ceiling, and ran her fingers through her hair. "There were a few

245

girls in college I crushed on, but nothing ever happened, so I thought maybe it never would. Then when I met Will, I just kind of pushed it all away. I focused on my work and on starting a family—I just kept thinking those feelings would disappear. But they didn't, and I think it was always a matter of the right woman coming along to bring it out."

Erin smirked. "So did you ever find her?"

The corner of Jules' mouth rose slightly. "If you really wanna know the truth, I knew on the first night I saw you sing that you could be dangerous for me. You're talented, beautiful—and a complete smart ass, which is exactly what kept me coming back for more."

"And all along I thought you just wanted a good story and you screwed your way in to get it." Erin laughed and unbuttoned the top of Jules' jeans.

Jules grabbed Erin's hands and stopped her. "But it doesn't change the fact that if I come out with this, not only will it destroy my marriage, but it could affect my position at the paper. There's a lot of nasty conservatives out there who would just love to slam me if they found out—and the paper for that matter. For my employers it's not just about readers, it's also about advertising, and some of the big companies in this city aren't as forward-minded as you might think. They could pull out if they thought the paper was getting too liberal. It sounds like a stretch, but it's not, Erin. That's how shaky things are right now, and I'm just not sure the paper would be willing to go to bat for me like that when they could risk losing precious advertising dollars."

Erin pulled her hand away and studied Jules' face as Jules took off her pants and tossed them on the floor.

"So it was me who opened Pandora's Box, then? Is that what you're getting at?"

Jules turned toward her again. "I didn't say I regret it. I just don't know if I can admit it to anyone. Not yet."

"I'm sorry, but that sounds like a load of crap to me, Jules. I don't want to keep asking you this, but I kinda need to know where you see this going."

Jules held her breath and closed her eyes.

"I'm not giving you an ultimatum," Erin whispered as Jules let out her breath and blinked. "There's just things I want too, like stability—and kids."

Jules met her eyes and held her stare. "I don't want to hold you back from those things."

Erin laughed and leaned in to kiss her. "For a smart woman, you are so stupid, and you have absolutely no idea how beautiful you are. Everyone can see it but you. I would wait for you forever if that's what it took."

"I don't want you to do that," Jules said, slowly pulling herself up. She brought her knees to her chest and hugged them to her body. "You have too many things you need to do, and I don't want you to wait for me to do them. You need to get back to Nashville and get your career on track."

Erin shrugged and shook her head.

"My music career isn't what's important to me anymore, Jules. You are. And if you wanna talk about nasty conservatives, have you ever met a southern conservative? There's a reason they wanted me to play the straight card down there. The old-school, solid south bigots aren't about to accept people like me into their world, and the pray-it-away mentality is still very much alive and well in a lot of places down there. After all, even though that city's eclectic population is changing, it's still smack-dab in the middle of the fucking Bible Belt. I never really wanted to be pegged as a country artist. They put me in that box before I even knew what was happening, and then they tried to squeeze the gay right out of me in the process. Only too bad for them, because it didn't really work, did it?"

Jules turned toward her. "What happened to you down there, Erin? Why can't you just tell me?"

"Nothing happened to me, Jules. There really is no story there—contrary to what you might think." She lifted her hands in the air. "I'm just one of many who happened to hit at the right time with an attitude, the right look, and a good song, but in the end that's all it was. At first, when they thought I might be the next Taylor Swift, they loved everything about me and they put their money in my corner. But I lied, Jules. I pretended to be something I wasn't, just like you are right now."

Jules exhaled and closed her eyes.

"It all blew up in my face when my manager and a possible tour sponsor walked into the studio and found me kissing a girl who worked for the label. We'd been flirting for weeks and she was in the closet too, but that afternoon it just happened. We were alone and all she wanted was to hear me record, but then they walked in and there was no way to hide it anymore. Everything changed after that. Well, that and I ended up running my mouth to someone I thought I could trust, and a whole shit storm of rumors started after he wrote a story about it."

Jules suddenly looked up, seeming surprised.

"Yeah, you heard me right. That's why I don't want you to write about me. I'm just done with it. They never gave me a specific reason, but after all of that, the tour sponsor decided to go with another artist. All of a sudden my manager and agent started pushing me to go out in a public with a guy they hired for my band." Erin sighed and leaned on one arm, watching Jules' expression. "They made it pretty clear that if I wanted to make it in *that* business and in *that* city, then being with girls wasn't something they were going to tolerate. And yes, there are plenty of country artists out there who *are* gay, but let me ask you a question. Can you name one?"

Jules looked away again, shaking her head.

"No, you can't. Being out is dangerous sometimes, Jules, and it's scary, so I understand your fears even though you don't think I do." Her voice was firm as she tried to prove her point. "I can name a few country artists that are out, like Chely Wright, for one. She spent years living in the closet and giving up on the woman she loved because she had to choose between her career and who she really was. I read her book and it scared

249

the shit out of me. There's a strong force in that industry that still doesn't support open homosexuality, even now."

Erin moved her arm and dropped against the pillow as Jules turned to face her.

"I love that city, Jules," she continued. "Some of the most talented people I've ever met in my life live there. But if you're gay and trying to make it with a major label in Nashville, well, good luck. The radio people can make or break a career down there, and if you can't suck up in the right way—and trust me when I tell you that *a lot* of women actually suck up to the radio guys—you're not gonna make it." Erin rolled onto her side and Jules relaxed slightly, lying down beside her. "I was doomed before I even got off the ground in Nashville, for the most part. I wish that wasn't the reality, but it is. I've accepted it. I couldn't live a lie, and neither should you." Erin gently tugged Jules' hair.

Erin continued. "Pretending to be something I'm not is what destroyed me. And, it will destroy you, too, if you don't face it. Maybe it won't be the same tornado that hit me, but it'll catch up to you at some point. I tried to be what they wanted me to be, but I couldn't pull it off. I tried so hard that I did date that drummer for a while—even had sex with the guy—but I hated ever single second of it because it wasn't me. That's when I started drinking more and hit the drugs even harder. I thought I could be better if I just had that little extra boost. Little by little, it all just started to fall away and I got pegged as the lesbo party girl."

Jules watched her intently, not saying a word.

"But then, the final straw for everyone was when they found an empty coke bag and snorting tube in my car during my DUI arrest. They couldn't exactly pin me with possession, because lucky for me, I'd snorted the entire bag over the course of a few days. They still called it paraphernalia, and I wiggled out of a major felony by the skin of my teeth. But it didn't matter. My career was over. My record label dropped me without even offering the chance of going to rehab, like they would've done for any other up-and-coming artist they really believed in."

Jules pulled her closer. "God, I'm so sorry that happened to you. You didn't deserve it."

"Maybe I did, maybe I didn't, but it doesn't matter anymore—all I need to make me happy now is you."

Jules closed her eyes and sat up again. "Erin, please don't bank on me to give you a future. The only thing I can promise you is today."

"What are you saying?" Erin's stomach turned. All she wanted was a straight answer.

"Just promise you won't wait for me to do the things you need to do," Jules whispered. "You can't wait for me to figure out my life. You have so much potential and talent, and you're stronger now. You can show them that all of the other crap is behind you now, if that's what you really want."

Erin ran her fingers down Jules' back, and she quivered under Erin's touch. "This conversation is getting way too

251

serious." Erin sat up, unclasped Jules's bra, and leaned in to kiss her shoulder. "I really don't wanna fight with you, and right now I don't care about newspapers, record deals, or any of that shit. That was never why I played music anyway."

Jules turned toward Erin and leaned in to kiss her. "Hold on a minute," Jules said as she slipped off the bed and walked toward the bathroom while playfully flinging her bra over her shoulder.

Erin flopped back onto the bed just as Jules' phone buzzed again. Erin groaned, looked over at it, and then glanced back toward the closed bathroom door. Then she laughed, picked up the phone, and quickly swiped her finger across the screen. Unable to unlock the passcode, she hit the camera icon on the lock screen and began snapping pictures of herself, giggling as she did. When the bathroom door opened, Jules walked toward her wearing nothing but her black lace Victoria's Secret boy shorts. She looked incredibly sexy. Erin hit the video record button just as Jules slipped in bed and pulled the sheet up to her chest.

"Say hi, Jules," she said playfully, making Jules laugh and shyly put her hand up to her face.

"Knock it off, Erin. Give me my phone." She chuckled and grabbed the phone from Erin's hand. She tossed it onto the floor as Erin rolled on top of her. With a wide smile, Jules stared back as Erin pinned her hands over her head and kissed the side of her face.

Chapter Eighteen

Will awoke to the smell of coffee. His mouth was dry, as if he had swallowed dust, and his head pounded—slowly at first, like the light taps of a mallet, and then intensely, like the precise hit of a hammer to a nail, over and over again. He opened his eyes slowly, looked around the room, and instantly panicked. He had no idea where he was. He shook off the red fleece blanket that covered him and sat up to find his boots placed neatly beside the couch. He still wore his jacket, along with all of his clothes.

When he was about to stand, Erin stepped out of the bathroom. Her hair was damp, as if she had just showered, and his heart dropped as he tried to remember the previous night's events.

"Oh shit, you're awake," she said, eyeing him cautiously.

Will ran his fingers through his hair and looked around. Acid began to churn in his stomach, making him feel nauseous.

"How the hell did I get here?" His voice was hoarse and he attempted to stand, but he sank back into the couch because of the light-headedness.

"You passed out in my car," she said as she walked toward the kitchen. "I was going to give you a ride somewhere, but I didn't know where to take you."

"So you brought me here—to your place?" He looked toward the window, realizing they were on the second floor.

Erin poured two cups of coffee and eyed him like a nervous cat. "Here, this might help."

She handed him the coffee but avoided his eyes.

Will took the cup, keeping his eyes on her as she took a seat in the chair across from him.

"I would've left you in the car, but you would've froze to death and I don't need that on my conscience," Erin said, glancing up at him before taking a sip from the cup in her hand.

"How did you get me up here?"

"My landlord was nice enough to help," she replied. She leaned back and pulled her legs up off the floor.

"Great. I'm sure that looked fantastic to your neighbors." He leaned forward and held his aching head.

"Do you want some aspirin or anything? You were slamming brandy pretty hard last night."

"Yeah, if you don't mind." He clenched his eyes closed. It was as if everything he'd worked for with his sobriety in the last three years had come crashing down hard and the pounding was just the aftershock.

Erin disappeared into the bathroom. Will opened one eye when she approached him with an outstretched hand. He couldn't help but notice now how attractive she was. Her dark hair brought out the stark brightness of her blue eyes and her cheeks were accented with light freckles. Still, he didn't want to look at her. She reminded him of everything he didn't understand about Jules.

"Where's my truck?" He tossed the pills into his mouth and took a gulp of the hot coffee, which burned all the way down.

"Wherever you left it, I'm guessing with a few parking tickets by now," she said. She sat back down, not meeting his eyes. He could tell she was nervous.

He stared at her and remembered the sound of her voice as she sang. "So those two songs you sang—they were for Jules?"

Erin sighed, rubbed her temple and sipped her coffee before answering. "Yeah, they were."

Will ran his fingers over his stubbly face and looked around the room. "Is this where she spent all her time? Here—with you?"

Erin looked down at the cup in her hand. "She spent some time here, yes."

Will's anger began to bubble inside of him, but right now, all he wanted was answers.

"How did this happen between the two of you? How did I not see it?"

Erin looked back at him as if she were contemplating the question. She let one foot fall back to the floor while the other remained tucked under her leg. "I don't know how to explain it to you, but I can tell you it wasn't because she didn't love you. I know she did."

Will laughed out loud. "Did she? You know, I've spent so much time being pissed off at her lately that I can't even remember the good things about her."

Erin shook her head and looked away.

"How did it start? Can you tell me that?" He picked up the mug and leaned back on the couch.

Erin shrugged and touched the diamond stud on her nose. "We met at the bar when I was working. It started out innocently. She wanted to write a story about my music, and it just grew from there."

"And you knew she was married."

"Yes."

Will clenched his jaw. "And that didn't stop you?"

Erin sighed again and swallowed slowly.

"How long was it going on?" He leaned forward, trying to meet her eyes. She clammed up and avoided his glance, as if she were afraid to answer. "I think you owe me the truth. I'd much rather have this conversation with Jules, but since she's not here—"

"Almost a year." Erin looked up and nervously wiped the palm of her hand on her leg before softening her tone. "It was almost a year."

"A year?" Will exhaled. It felt as if someone had punched him in the stomach. "God, it all makes sense now. I don't know how the hell I missed it. I knew she was acting different, but chalked it up to work as usual. Shit, even in bed she was different."

Erin looked up and her eyes narrowed slightly.

"Oh, wait. Did you not know she was still sleeping with me, too? I *am* her husband—or did you think you were the only one she was fucking?"

Erin leaned her head back and pursed her lips tightly. "Look, Will, you should know my relationship with Jules wasn't just about sex. Sex is only what separated us from being friends, but she talked to me. We had an emotional attachment that was bigger than either of us expected. All she really wanted was acceptance."

"Acceptance?" Will shook his head. "I've known that woman for almost seventeen years. I was married to her for eleven years. Are you trying to tell me I didn't accept her, or that I didn't know her?"

"Did you know she struggled with her sexuality?"

Will clenched his jaw again. "I thought you said she wasn't gay."

"I don't think she really knew what she was, but sometimes that's an even tougher one to understand because you don't know if you're one or the other. It's hard to make sense of it all."

"Oh, I see, so I should feel sorry for her because she decided to have a sexual awakening? And let me guess. You just came in and saved the day. Is that it?" He glared at her as his anger began to spill out and leak all over the room. "Or, maybe you just took advantage of her emotional state."

Erin scoffed and stood up. "Yeah, that's it. I just took advantage of her. You've got it all figured out. Maybe I should just take you to your truck."

Erin crossed the room and slammed her mug on the countertop. Though his head felt as if it might explode at any minute, he wanted answers, so he drew in a deep breath and tried to regain his composure. He clenched his teeth and tried to back-pedal the conversation.

"Look, I'm sorry. I'm just so pissed off at her right now and I—" The tears began to come, but he fought them off and momentarily paused. Erin studied his face. "God," Will said. "I just miss her. I fucking hate her right now, but I miss her so much."

Erin's shoulders loosened. She blinked slowly before sighing and sitting across from him again. She placed her elbows on her knees and clasped her hands together. "I'm sorry," she said quietly, looking up to meet his eyes. "I don't know if I can give you the answers you're looking for, but I do know she loved you and Jillian—she said it all the time, honestly."

Will laughed. "But she was still here with you, wasn't she?"

"And she went home to you every night, didn't she?" Erin said, leaning back. "Don't think for a minute I didn't want her to stay with me, but she never did."

"That still doesn't make it right," he said reaching for his boots.

"You can't play the victim here, Will." She seethed and leaned forward. "You spent years with her, and you pushed her away with your drinking and all your other bullshit. She never came looking for me. She just happened to stumble onto something she didn't know what to do with. You can't blame her for that. She told me she fought her attraction for women since she was a kid—that's predisposition. She couldn't fight that forever."

"Wow. You really think you knew her, don't you?" He stopped lacing his boots and looked at her. "She may have told you about the drinking, but did she tell you how we got there? Did she tell you how obsessed she was with her career? Or how long we tried to have a baby and how that changed her? I never had a choice in either of those things. She disappeared before my eyes. Not all of that shit was on me."

Erin stared at him blankly.

"When we finally did get pregnant, were you the one who found her on the bathroom floor in puddle of blood when she miscarried at seven weeks, and then the second time at four weeks? Did you hold her through all that and then feel like it was your fault she was falling apart?"

Erin looked away.

"No, I didn't think so," he said. "Because you only saw what she wanted you to see. She was an expert at pretending to be okay and then pushing everything away and blaming me."

259

He looked toward the window as a lump grew in his throat.

"Yeah, I was an asshole. Yeah, I drank and almost cheated on her one time—*almost*. But she left me long before that. I thought she came back when we had Jillian. For a short time, she was the woman I used to know, but then she turned into a fucking cold workaholic that I didn't even recognize anymore." His voice cracked and he didn't want Erin to see his pain. "So yeah, I did some bad shit. But I realized what I had to lose and I gave up drinking. I faced my demons and I did that because I loved her. I wanted to be the husband she deserved, the one I promised her I would be, but she never gave me a chance. And then the best part yet—you turn up."

Erin brought her hands to her mouth.

"What, she didn't tell you all of that?" He glared at her now, unable to stop the words as they spilled from his lips. "I can go on. Did she ever tell you about her dad? He was a drunk too, did a real number on her by never being home, and when he was there he was an asshole who embarrassed her in front of her friends." The color drained from Erin's face, but he kept firing.

"He made sure she and her sister knew he never wanted kids, and especially not two snotty little girls who would never amount to anything because the only thing girls are good for is screwing—*his* words, not mine. He never laid a hand on her, but she never got over those words. She had a real hard time getting close to men, thinking they would all turn out just like him. I should know. It took months for me to break down her

260

walls when we first started dating. I guess I shouldn't be surprised she eventually turned to women."

"Stop. *Please stop.*" Erin leaned forward and closed her eyes.

"Why? Because now you know that it wasn't all my fault?" His voice cracked slightly as it rose. "Jules was a brilliant, beautiful woman—but she was damaged. She didn't have the first clue about how to face her problems. She loved being a savior to everyone else. She loved fixing every broken part of every goddamn person she knew, but she never turned and looked at herself or realized how fucking broken she was. I tried to get her to do that. I tried to make her get rid of the weight inside that made her incapable of loving anyone but Jillian, but all she wanted to do was hide. And apparently she hid right here, in this room—with you."

Hot, silent tears streamed down Will's face. He knew Erin had no way of defending herself against his words.

"I'm sorry," she said in a low voice. "I didn't know."

"Of course you didn't, but you did know she was married. Didn't that bother you?"

"Yes, it did, and she tried to end things between us more than once, but—"

"But what?" He wiped his tears with the sleeve of his jacket.

"I wouldn't let her, I guess."

Will laughed out loud. "You know, you don't have to take all the blame just because she's dead. I know damn well that when Jules wanted something, she'd get it."

Erin glared at him like an angry child. "It wasn't like that. My feelings for her were real. I didn't ask for that, and neither did she."

"Uh-huh," he said mockingly. "So the cocaine in her purse, that was yours?"

Erin nodded and looked toward the window.

"How'd she get you to quit?" He eyed her and rubbed his chin. "Let me guess, she gave you an ultimatum, it was either her or the drugs?"

Erin continued to stare at nothing and didn't respond, but it didn't matter. He already knew the answer.

"See? She did it to you, too." Will looked into her suddenly vacant eyes. "She tried to fix you but refused to fix her own problems. She was a mastermind in that way, she really was."

"She helped me. I'll always be grateful for that," Erin said quietly. "If you hated her so much, why didn't you just divorce her?"

Will shook his head and finished lacing his boot. "I don't know. Maybe I should have. But if there's one thing I'm sure of, it's that as much as I hate her right now, I loved her one hundred times more."

They were silent for a moment and it seemed to Will as if the air had slowly dissipated from the room.

"I'll drive you to your truck," Erin said. She stood and despondently walked toward her bedroom.

"There's one more thing I need to know," he said, his voice firm. Erin stopped in the doorway. Her shoulders slowly rose and fell as she drew in a deep breath and turned around. "Was she here that night, the night she died? I saw the message on her phone and I know she was here at some point that day, but were you the last person she saw before she got in her car?"

Erin swallowed hard and steadied herself against the wall. She kept her eyes on the floor while nodding her head.

Will shook his head again. "Did you sleep together that day?"

Erin looked up, her eyes glistening. "I asked her to come over and listen to some songs I was working on—"

He cut her off. "That's not what I asked you," he said. The pain and regret was written on her face, but for some reason he needed to hear her say the words.

"Yes, we did," she said softly.

"Okay. That's all I need to know." He stood and straightened his back.

They didn't speak as she drove him back to his truck. When they pulled up alongside it, there was a bright yellow parking ticket stuck beneath the windshield wiper.

"Shit," he grumbled, tightly gripping the door handle.

"Well, you're kinda lucky it wasn't towed," Erin said, not looking at him. "The cops are pretty strict about the winter parking around here."

263

Will scoffed and opened the door. "Lucky is one word I would never use to describe myself."

"I can't take back what happened," she replied. "But I *am* sorry. I—she never meant to hurt you."

Will stared at her, unsure if he was angry or finally relieved to know the truth. "Thanks for not letting me freeze to death."

She smiled slightly. "I did that for Jillian. But seriously, take care of yourself. Don't go back to the bottle. It's not too late."

"Yeah, and don't you do that blow," he said with a cocky smile before slamming the door.

Erin gave him a quizzical look and then drove away. He watched her taillights and took a deep breath of the freezing air, which burned his lungs, before sliding into the cab of his truck. He felt heavy as he stared at his green eyes in the rearview mirror before firing up the engine to head for home.

Chapter Nineteen

"Mom?" Erin called as she stepped into her mother's kitchen through the side door. Right away she noticed the bread on the table, along with a gallon of milk. She sighed and scanned the cluttered room before twisting the cap onto the jug and placing it inside the refrigerator.

"I'm in here, honey," her mother called from the sewing room near the front of the house.

A walker was shoved against the hallway wall, and the rug beneath it was curled in a twisted mess. Erin quickly unjammed the walker, rolled up the rug, and placed it in a corner.

"Hey," she said as she walked into the room. Her mother nodded but didn't look up. She sat in the rocking chair near the window, a befuddled expression on her face as she peered at the quilt spread on her lap. Her glasses were perched on the end of her nose and she held a needle and thread in her small, shaky hands.

"What are you up to now?" Erin asked as she flopped into the rocking recliner and leaned her head against its soft cushions. Reading the frustration in her mother's eyes, Erin knew she was pushing herself too hard. Making quilts had been

265

her specialty for years, but it had become increasingly challenging, a near-impossible task for her to complete alone.

"I just want to finish this damn thing for your cousin's baby shower next month," her mother mumbled.

She examined the needle while trying to steady her hand enough to thread it.

"Here, let me do it," Erin offered. She took the needle and pushed the thread through the small eye with ease before quickly knotting it and handing it back.

Her mother eyed her over the rim over her glasses. "Hmm. You're getting pretty good at that."

"I've watched you do it a million times," Erin replied. "What's with the walker in the hallway? You have a little traffic jam in there?"

Her mother's shoulders heaved slightly. "I told Dr. Stein I don't need that damn thing—it's nothing but a pain in the ass."

"Uh-huh. Well, it'd probably work better if you rolled up the rugs. You don't need all those rugs, Mom. They're just gonna trip you up more."

Her mother rolled her eyes. "I don't need the walker either. I get around just fine."

Erin slowly rocked back and forth. The chair steadily creaked as she looked at the dingy white ceiling. There were cobwebs in the far corner, and she made a mental note to get them down later. The room hadn't been updated in years and it desperately needed a fresh coat of paint.

"What's on your mind, kid," Erin's mother asked. "I can see something has your undies in a bunch." She lowered the needle and removed her glasses. Erin cleared her throat and stopped rocking. She looked toward the window so she wouldn't have to see her mother's eyes peering through her.

"Will Kanter stopped in at the bar the other night."

Her mother's eyes widened and she gripped the chair's arms. "You're joking! Did he come to see you?"

"Well, he sure didn't end up there on accident or come to hear me sing," she said. She met her mother's glance before shifting her eyes toward the floor. "He found pictures and texts on Jules' phone."

"I see." Her mother exhaled. "So he knows what was going on between the two of you?"

"Uh, yeah...you could say that," Erin scoffed. She looked out the window at the snow-covered street. "I'm still not sure how he found me, but he's drinking again and I ended up taking him back to my place."

Her mother glared at her. "You did *what*?"

"It wasn't like that, Mom. Seriously." Her tone was defensive. "He asked me a bunch of questions about Jules and he was pounding brandy. I was gonna give him a ride somewhere, but he passed out. I didn't know where to take him, so I took him home. What was I supposed to do?"

"Well, I don't know, but, honey, that was dangerous. What if—"

267

"He didn't do anything, Mom. Seriously, it wasn't like that. I'm fine. He just doesn't seem to be doing well at all. He's so pissed off at Jules, and he was drinking. I'm just really worried about Jillian. Jules wouldn't want this for her."

"Sweetheart, you can't get involved in this." Her mother's tone was sharp. She shook her head and leaned forward. "Will has to figure this out on his own. He has family and friends, and of course he's angry—anger is a part of grieving, you know that. But, he's Jillian's father. You're not part of that."

Erin looked into her mother's bloodshot eyes. "He said so many things about her, Mom, so many things I didn't know. It's almost like I didn't know her at all."

"You knew her in a different way than he did. You always knew that."

"Did I?" Erin leaned forward and clasped her hands. "She barely ever talked about her past, beyond her marriage anyway, and the things he said—I just never knew any of it."

"Honey, you can't blame Jules for not wanting to talk about the past. It was *her* past. It had nothing to do with your relationship." Erin's mother shook her head. "We all have a past—*you* of all people should know that, too. You never told her about your past. Am I wrong?"

"Mom, please don't start that. There was no reason to tell her about what happened. She didn't need to know." Erin looked away. "But Jules had two miscarriages. *Two.* All the times we talked about kids, or when I told her I wanted kids, she never mentioned that—not once."

Her mother sighed. "Erin, you need to stop this. You cannot let his grief undo everything you felt for Jules. It's not fair to you, and it's not fair to her. You just said there was no reason for her to know about the things you went through, so maybe she felt the same way about telling you what she went through. Those are painful memories. Maybe you both would have been able to talk through it all in time."

"But she never left him, Mom. Why? Why didn't she leave him? I have no idea what the hell we were even doing anymore."

"She never said she would leave him, honey. She never said that."

Erin studied her mother's face. "What are you talking about? She said she needed to figure things out with Will, and—"

"And what, Erin? Did she ever promise you a future? Did she tell you she was ready to leave her family and start a life with you?"

Erin couldn't believe the words she was hearing. "Whose side are you on?"

"Your side, honey. I am *always* on your side, but you know Jules loved you, and you also know she didn't make promises she couldn't keep. Will knows more about her past, but that doesn't mean you didn't know her. You just knew her in a way he never did."

Erin leaned her head back on the chair. "I just feel like she knew almost everything about me, and I thought I knew her, but now...I just don't know."

Her mother shook her head again. "You never told her the most excruciating part of your past, Erin. Don't you think you should have told her that? Don't you think that would have helped her understand your problems just a little bit better? You hid that from her."

Erin glared at her mother. She wanted to stand up and walk out, but something stopped her. They hadn't discussed her rape in what seemed like years. It was usually a dark cloud that hovered over them both, but it was rarely addressed openly.

Her mother softened her tone and tried to meet her eyes. "Either way, honey, I don't think it's a good idea for you to talk to Will again. You need to remember what you and Jules had together, not what she was with Will. What's done is done. Don't question yourself." She placed her glasses back on the end of her nose. "She managed to get you off of drugs, and for that she will always rate as pretty fricking awesome in my eyes."

Erin scoffed remembering the cocaine sitting on the nightstand in her apartment. "There's something else I want to talk to you about."

"Now what? I know I need to get my hair colored," her mother joked. "I can see the gray roots, so you don't need to harp on me about it."

Erin laughed. "Well, that's not it, but now that you mention it…"

"Very funny. What else is on your mind?"

"Well, I've been home almost a year now, Mom, and my lease is up this spring. I was thinking—"

Her mother cut her off, lowering the quilt as she spoke. "I think you should go back to Tennessee."

"What? That's not what I was gonna say. I was going to ask if I can move back in here for a while. I think you could use the help." She motioned toward the walker in the hallway.

"No, absolutely not." Her mother's voice was stern. "I will not have you move in here to take care of me. That wasn't part of the deal when you moved home, and I didn't want you moving back here just for me. I've told you that. I'm fine, and you need to get your ass back down to Nashville and start living for yourself."

"Mom, seriously, I don't need to—"

"Yes, you do. It was one thing when Jules was here, sweetie, but she's gone, and I will not be the reason you stay here. I won't. I know you're unhappy and you're not doing what you should be doing. You're hiding from your life because you feel responsible for me. I won't have it."

"Who's going to take care of you if I'm not here?"

"I have your aunt and uncle if I need anything. They're close, and Nashville is only eight hours away. It's not like you'd be in Italy or something."

"Mom—"

271

"Dammit, Erin Elizabeth, I said no! You are not moving in here with me, and I mean it," the stern look on her mother's face and the use of her full name made Erin hold her tongue. "You figure out what you need to do, but it's not going to include moving in here."

"Seriously? You're just gonna make this decision without even allowing me to discuss it with you?"

Her mother sighed. "Someday you'll understand what it's like to be a mother, Erin. If you think I would choose for you to be that far away from me, then you're wrong. But I know you. In some ways, I know you better than you know yourself. You have talents that reach beyond anything I could've imagined for you. Those are *yours*. You developed them on your own, and when you sing, you go to a different place. I can see it—everyone who watches you can see it. That's what attracted Jules to you in the first place." She paused and swallowed hard before continuing. "But, it's time for you to go back to Nashville and see where that takes you, or you'll always be here wondering and thinking about what could've been. I don't want to be the reason you don't follow through with what you started. I know how close you came to making it there, and even though it wasn't everything you thought it would be, they never doubted your talent, and you know that. Your talent is what can prove them wrong again."

"Jesus, Mom. For the five hundredth time, everything was a mess down there. I needed to come home just as much as you needed me to be here. I needed to clean up my act. Besides,

I can't go back there and be worried about you. What good would that do? I'm singing here, and I'm doing fine." She got out of the chair and paced momentarily before turning back toward her mother. "After everything we've been through, I *want* to be here for you. I lost dad, and I lost Jules. I can't lose you, too." Erin knelt next to her mother, placing her hands on her mother's knees. "Like it or not, Mom, we're stuck with each other. I don't want to leave you here again."

Her mother lifted her hand and touched Erin's face. "It was so hard to watch you leave the first time, and watching you go a second time won't be any better. But when I saw you in the hospital, I realized how far you fell again. You're not happy here, Erin. I can see it—and Jules could see it."

Erin shook her head and tried to speak, but her mother stopped her.

"I know what happened to you all those years ago was my fault, and I should've been there to protect you, but I wasn't." She squeezed Erin's fingers and lifted her chin slightly. "I can't take that away, but I won't sit here and watch you waste your life because of me. You were happy in Nashville before all the craziness took over. That's what you need to find again. Right now you're working at a bar, singing for people who forget you the next day. Just go—*please*. Go back and find yourself again. Get back with the like-minded people who make you feel complete and sing on every street corner if you have to—just get back to where you were before. That's what I want. I need to see that light in your eyes again. That's what will make me better. In the meantime, I'll be right here, in this damn chair, probably still working on this stupid quilt. If you feel like you need to come home again, we'll talk."

"God, why do you have to make everything so hard?" Erin shook her head and then rested it on her mother's bony knees.

"Because I'm your mother, and it's my job," she said as she ran her fingers through Erin's hair. "You'll always be the most beautiful thing that came out of my ridiculously screwed up life. But, could you do me a favor, please?"

Erin lifted her head.

"Could you get your ass off the floor and go get me some ice cream?"

Erin laughed and playfully slapped her mother's leg. "You know what? Why don't you get your skinny ass up, go fetch that walker in the hallway, and put your own damn milk away?"

Her mom tilted her head and peered around her toward the hallway. "Screw that walker. Nothing is going to slow me down, dammit. Not MS and not those damn rugs."

"Uh-huh," Erin said. "So what flavor do you want? Chocolate Chip Cookie Dough?"

"Nah, I'm in the mood for something fruity." Her blue eyes grew larger. "How 'bout Blueberry Swirl or something fun like that?"

"Okay. Anything else, boss?"

"Nope, I'm good. Just hurry back, please." She winked and looked down at the quilt.

Before leaving, Erin sat in the car for a few minutes and stared back at the house. On the outside it looked virtually the same as it had for the past thirty-four years. For most of her life, this small, ranch-style home with its plain white siding and black shutters had been the only home she'd known. It held priceless memories of her dad teaching her how to play his guitar in the front room, and she remembered perfect Christmases when it was just the three of them decorating a tree and watching *It's a Wonderful Life* on TV. But once her father passed away, and during those dark years that followed, that house had also been hell on earth.

At one point, when her mother completely lost control and things had gone from bad to absolute worst, Erin left that house and lived with her aunt, uncle, and cousins two blocks over. It was a time in her life she didn't like to revisit, and she never talked about it, not with anyone—not even Jules. If there was one lesson she had managed to learn from those vacant, awful years, it was that you never really get over some things in life —you just learn to live with them and move on. She refused to let the incidents of that time define her.

Now, though, she knew there was no learning to live with her mother's disease. With no cure for MS, Erin knew it was just a matter of time before her mom couldn't live on her own, and the thought of leaving her was almost unbearable. But still, she couldn't help entertaining the thought of being back in

275

Nashville. Her mom was right. She'd left good things behind there, too, and she had been happy there once—more so than she ever had anywhere else.

Staring ahead, Erin remembered a conversation she'd had with Jules back in December, only around six weeks before Jules' death. They were eating lunch at Swig in the Third Ward and, in her typical journalistic way, Jules had begun to pepper Erin with questions about Nashville. With steady snow falling on the sidewalks and holiday decorations adorning every streetlight, Erin had divulged for the first time how much she missed her second home.

Jules sipped a steaming cup of coffee and looked at Erin. "So, what would you be doing for New Year's if you were still down there?"

"Well," Erin said, pausing to think as she looked out toward the street. "My roommates would probably be throwing a house party since the tourists would be taking over downtown."

"Oh, so you've never been a tourist in that city?" Jules smiled. She raised one eyebrow and stirred her coffee.

"I'm an interloper. That's completely different." Erin laughed. She reached for her water glass and raised it to her lips.

Jules nodded. "How many of you lived in that house again?"

"Well, before I left there were four," she said, straightening her shoulders. "But I think Kasey might be leaving soon. Sounds like he landed a full-time gig playing in a traveling band."

Jules nodded again, but her forehead tensed. "Do you miss it? The house and your friends, I mean."

Erin shrugged and looked across the table at Jules, who appeared well put-together as usual in her neatly-pressed white blouse and sanguine-colored cardigan. "Yeah, I do. They're a great group of people who really pulled me through a lot of shit. But why are you asking me about this?"

"I'm just wondering," Jules said. "I guess I just wonder if you're happy here, or if you've been thinking of going back, that's all."

"Uh-huh. Well, I haven't really thought about it, at least not with the shape my mom is in."

Jules touched the saucer beneath her coffee cup. "Is your mom the only reason you're staying?"

"Well, I mean my job at the bar is *really* amazing and I'm *really* going places," Erin said. She leaned forward and gripped Jules' hand. "And then there's this hot brunette who keeps distracting me."

"Are you suddenly into guys now? What's his name again, Jason?" Jules mocked while brushing her hair over her shoulder.

"You know I wasn't talking about Jason."

"Yeah, I know, but he sure seems in to you," Jules said, then pulled her hand away and reached for her phone.

Erin scoffed. "Uh, are you trying to pick a fight with me, Jules? Because if you are, do I need to remind you that you're still married?"

"No, I just want you to be careful, that's all." Jules avoided Erin's eyes and slipped her phone back inside her purse.

Erin leaned back and crossed her legs. "Are you about to lecture me? Because if you are, you can save it. Last time I checked, you and I aren't exactly exclusive, or are we?"

Jules put her hand to her face and gently rubbed her eyebrow. "I wasn't going to lecture you, I just—I don't know. I just want to make sure you're being safe."

Erin threw her head back and laughed out loud. "Seriously? Are you insinuating that I'm sleeping with other people? Is that it?"

"That's not an irrelevant question, Erin." Jules lowered her voice. "I'm not trying to piss you off. I just...I don't know what you do when I'm not around."

"Okay, well, here's a newsflash." Erin glared at Jules and lowered her voice. "I'm not an idiot, and don't worry, I'm not sleeping with anyone but you. I won't give you any STDs that you'll take home to your husband, if that's what you're suddenly concerned about."

Jules took a deep breath. "I'm sorry. That's not what I meant."

Erin shook her head and took a deep breath, trying to push away her anger. "Sometimes it really drives me crazy when you try to act like my mother, Jules. You don't need to

278

worry about me. When you're not around, I do actually know how to take care of myself."

"I know, I know. It's a bad habit. But I do worry about you. I can't help it," Jules said. She tried to reach for Erin's hand just as the waitress walked up and placed the check in front of Jules before collecting their plates. Jules turned and reached for her purse.

Erin grabbed the check before Jules could pick it up. "That's another thing. You don't always have to pay for me. Just because I work at a bar doesn't mean I don't have any money."

Jules took her hands off her purse and raised them in the air. "Alright, alright. Be my guest."

Erin softened her tone and tilted her head to the side. "I know this might come as a surprise to you, but I actually have quite a bit of money saved. I managed not to blow all the money I made from gigs and a few record sales—believe it or not."

"Why would that surprise me?" Jules asked. She crossed her arms and bit her bottom lip.

"Because you always try to pay for everything, I just assumed you thought I was broke."

Jules smiled. "Well then, Money Bags, what are you saving for?"

"I was saving for a house. I had my eye on a little bungalow-style place in the Twelve South neighborhood, but I'm sure it's long gone by now."

Jules' face softened. "You do miss it, don't you?"

279

Erin shrugged her shoulders. "It doesn't matter."

"Yes it does. You know, it's okay if you want to go back. I wouldn't blame you."

Erin looked out the window and then back at Jules, who watched her intently.

"It doesn't matter. I can't leave now. I can't leave my mom like this." She looked away from Jules and reached into her purse for her wallet.

Jules wrapped her black scarf around her neck without taking her eyes off Erin. "Your mom wants you to be happy, like me. She worries about you

"You know, you could come with me —you and Jillian, and Mom." Erin avoided Jules' eyes as she dropped cash atop the bill. "That city has so much to offer—we could buy a house, settle down, buy some sperm from a trendy musician-slash-artist-type-guy so I can pop out a few kids. Vanderbilt has some of the best doctors in the country for Mom—"

"It sounds perfect," Jules said, but then she shifted her glance out the window.

"Yeah, it does," Erin said, feeling foolish for indulging in the fantasy out loud. "Too bad it's just a dream."

As the memory faded into reality, Erin wondered if Jules and her mother had discussed the notion of her moving back to Tennessee before all of this came about. Jules had been sly, but Erin began to contemplate that perhaps Jules was trying to find a way to rid her from her life. They had discussed Nashville countless times after that day, and her mother had

280

been right—not once did Jules promise she would go, or even entertain the thought. Now, sitting in her car and staring at her childhood home, Erin wondered how long Jules would have strung her along before cutting her off completely.

Chapter Twenty

Will sat on the bed while Jillian splashed in the large Jacuzzi bathtub in the adjoining bathroom. He loved listening to the way she played with her toys, giving each one a name and having conversations in different versions of her own little voice. Nights like this made him feel anchored, as if he had a purpose. But something inside him still burned with anger. He sucked in his breath and leaned back on the bed. He had gone to an AA meeting earlier in the day but still had the fiery urge to drink. Today, for the first time in ages, he had spoken at the group. He confessed his recent relapse and everything Jules had done. The room was eerily quiet when he finished, and though he kept his eyes on the floor, he knew everyone was staring at him. He was ashamed, not only for falling off the wagon but also because he hadn't seen Jules for who she really was. As usual, it was Tom who finally broke the silence.

"Well, Will, the thing about wagons is they're only built to carry so much of a load. When the load gets too heavy, the damn thing just falls apart." Others in the room nodded. "But, with the right tools and with the right help, you can put that wagon back together, piece by piece, and maybe even get some help carrying that load, too. Once you get it back on the right track, it'll hold itself together. The key is just staying on that track—even after you fall off."

Tom had a metaphor for everything, and it made perfect sense to Will. But right now he felt as if he were still dragging that load. It was heavy, and he hated Jules for leaving him with it. Before meeting Erin and hearing the facts straight from her mouth, he'd thought the truth just might help him move on. Now that honesty burned him deeper than not knowing had.

"Daddy," Jillian called from the bathroom.

"Yeah, honey, I'm here," he said, rolling off the bed. He felt heavy as he stepped into the bathroom. "Ready to get out?"

"We need to wash my hair first," she reminded him, pointing toward the bottle of strawberry-scented shampoo.

"Oh yeah, of course we do, Bug." He picked up the bottle and squeezed the liquid into his hand. Only a small glob leaked out, and then nothing but air. "I guess we need to get some more."

"Mommy always bought me the other kind. I don't like the strawberry one," she said wrinkling her nose.

"Well, next time you can pick one out, how's that sound?"

Her face lit up with innocent excitement.

While lathering her dark hair, he thought of all the nights Jules hadn't been home to do this in the past year. At least two or three nights out of every week she worked late, not getting home until it was time to tuck Jillian into bed, or most times even later. Now he knew she most likely hadn't been working at all but was with Erin instead. Though he never had a problem picking up the slack where Jillian was concerned, he often resented Jules for not being more present, both physically and mentally, in their life together. He couldn't understand why, after all they had been through to have Jillian, she would put work and this affair with Erin above her daughter.

After rinsing Jillian's hair and lifting her out of the tub, he wrapped her in a fluffy towel and stared into her big brown eyes. "So what book is it gonna be tonight, kiddo?"

"*I Love You Forever.*" she giggled.

"Ugh. Again?" Will groaned. He picked her up and lifted her over his shoulder, then let her flop onto the bed.

"It's Mommy's favorite," she said as she slipped into her pajamas. "We have to read it every night so she doesn't forget."

"So Mommy doesn't forget what, Bug?"

Jillian stared up at him with those dark, innocent eyes that always melted him. "So she doesn't forget that we love her."

Will sucked in his breath and sat down beside to her. "Jilly, she won't forget that, not ever."

She begged. "I want you to read it, Daddy. Please?" Will had read it so many times he knew the book by heart, but he nodded anyway.

"Okay, I'll go get it, but you have to brush your teeth first."

She smiled, jumped off the bed, and ran back toward the bathroom as if he had just lit a fire under her little feet.

Walking out of his bedroom to retrieve the book, he remembered all the nights when he had peeked in as Jules sat on Jillian's bed and read that story. *I Love You Forever* and *The Giving Tree* were two of Jules' all-time favorites; when she was home, she read them to Jillian over and over again. Seeing them together like that was one of those Polaroid-type memories he hoped would never fade.

As far away as she felt to him now, he needed to remember Jules for the mother she had been, for Jillian's sake. Looking around Jillian's cluttered room for the book, he noticed the black scarf hanging on her bed post. He gripped it in his fingers, remembering how Erin had taken it off at the funeral and carefully placed it on Jillian's neck. At the time he had no idea how significant the gesture had been, and he almost wished he could go back to that moment—before he knew who she really was.

Though his anger at Jules was hard to tame, he suddenly couldn't erase Erin's face from his mind, and for some reason, he no longer harbored the same resentment toward her that he still kept for Jules. Maybe it was the way she'd looked at him when he spoke or the chance she had taken by bringing him back to her apartment when he passed out, even after the way he had spoken to her, but he realized now that Erin was just as

285

wounded as he was. Though he couldn't wrap his head around why Jules had done what she did, he realized that he wasn't the only victim. It was almost as if Jules had swallowed both him and Erin with her lies.

"Why do you have my scarf, Daddy?" Jillian looked at him and then picked up a stuffed animal from the floor.

"I was just looking at it," he replied with a half-smile. "I'll put it right back here."

"That lady gave it to me." She crawled up on Will's lap and pulled the scarf close to her face. "It looks like Mommy's."

"Yep. It sure does, Bug. It sure does."

"Can you read to me now?"

Will groaned, lifted her up, and then dropped her playfully on the bed. He tucked her in tightly before picking up the book and lying down beside her. He recited the book line by line. Her eyelids fluttered, then closed completely, and her little body went limp beside him. He sighed and listened to the sound of her breathing, knowing she was a million miles away.

When he looked toward Jillian's bedside table, his eyes landed on a photo of Jules. Consumed half by anger and half by agony, he recalled making the decision to start a family. They were young, naïve, and completely in love. It was before his drinking had spiraled out of control and before the real cracks in their relationship began to show. They were sipping piña coladas on a beach in St. Martin while watching a storm cross the sky and head toward them. Jules had turned to him, a bright smile stretched across her gorgeous, sun-kissed face, and she had asked him plain and simple, "Do you wanna go make a baby?"

He laughed, assuming she was drunk, but as she swung her tan legs off the chair and leaned over him, placing both hands on the armrests, she moved in slowly and kissed his face. When she pulled back, her dark eyes glimmered and she looked at him with an unwavering glare. "I mean it. I stopped taking my pills last week and I didn't bring any on this trip."

"Are you serious?" He placed his hands on her waist and pulled her closer. "I thought you wanted to wait until things calmed down at work?"

"Yeah, I know what I said, but I don't wanna wait," she whispered.

"Jules, I just wanna make sure you're ready. I mean, I know I am, but I don't want you to do this unless it's really what you want."

"You're seriously killing the vibe I have going on here," she said, straddling him on the chair as if no one was watching.

He sat up slowly and pulled her hips over his groin. "So sorry about that." He breathed into her ear. "But I'm more than ready, and I can go for it right here in this chair if you want me to."

She smiled suggestively, stood, and looked him up and down. "Then I suggest you take me upstairs."

He laughed nervously and looked around the half-empty beach. "I might need to wrap your towel around my waist to get back up there."

She snickered, reaching for her towel, and then she held it in front of him, just out of his grasp. "Come and get it."

"Jules, dammit." He chuckled. "Just give me the damn towel."

She took her time packing up her magazines and slipping on her flip flops before finally tossing the towel in his direction. They walked to the building hand in hand as Will gripped the towel around his waist. Jules giggled like a teenager when they stepped into the elevator. Mirrors surrounded them on every side and she backed up against the far wall, motioning for him to come closer as the doors slid shut. She pulled his face to hers and slipped her hand into his shorts as the elevator began to move. Just the feel of her hand on his body made him shiver and he couldn't remember how they even made it back to their room. That night they made love like they never had before. They both knew the chances of conceiving early were slim, but the possibility made the moment more sensual than he could have imagined.

What followed that decision was something neither of them anticipated. Months of sex were accompanied by months of disappointment when Jules couldn't seem to get pregnant. Though her doctor had told them not to worry at first, that these things can take time, there was fear in Jules' eyes and the sensual act soon turned methodical. Nearly a year passed before complications became evident and Jules' doctor recommended further testing. They learned that Jules' ovaries were prone to cysts and her ovulation cycle was erratic. More often than not, her body was unable to produce viable eggs. Through it all, Will had told her everything would be fine and it didn't matter if they ever conceived; he would love her just the same. But it was obvious the toll the news was taking on her. She felt incapable and frustrated, and those were emotions she didn't wear well.

And then finally, after fifteen months of trying for a baby, Will came home one evening to find Jules sitting at their kitchen table, dinner made and three place settings neatly set out.

"Are we expecting someone for dinner?"

The corner of her mouth lifted into a slight smile. "Well, I just figured we might as well get used to having three settings at the table."

He quickly walked to her and knelt. "What are you saying? Do you mean—? Are you? Are we?"

"Yeah, we are." She gripped his face in her hands. "And it's about fucking time."

"Holy shit," he whispered. He pulled her closer and hugged her tightly, both elated and consumed with fear. "See? I knew we could do it. No problem."

She pulled away and wiped tears from her face. "Yeah, that was a lot of sex," she said, laughing.

"Please tell me we don't have to stop doing that," he murmured. "I was enjoying every minute of it."

She scoffed as he stared into her eyes and brushed the hair from her face with his calloused hands. He had never loved her more than he did at that very moment.

For the next few weeks, Jules was more radiant than she had been in months. Her smile was brighter, her steps were lighter, and she finally laughed again in the deep, happy way she had before they started this journey. The weight of worry she had been carrying for so long had instantly vanished. But during the sixth week, without warning, things began to change. Her newfound energy was soon replaced with exhaustion. They both assumed the pregnancy was beginning to wear her out, but then the bleeding started.

"She said it's normal, we just need to keep an eye on it," Jules explained after speaking with her doctor on the phone. But there was worry in her eyes as she looked at Will, almost pleading for reassurance.

"It's okay, honey," he said as he pulled her to him, his tone confident. "You just need to take it easy. I think you should stay home from work tomorrow."

"No, I can't. Alice is on vacation and I have to cover two sections tomorrow." She pulled away from him and crawled into their bed looking pale and exhausted.

"You're gonna have to slow down and you're gonna have to tell them you're pregnant," he said, sitting beside her and running his hands along her back.

"I know. I will, I promise. I just want to wait a little longer," she whispered before closing her eyes and falling asleep.

She awoke the next day feeling somewhat better and with more color in her face, but Will still pleaded with her to stay home.

"Honey, I'm fine. I'll be home early, I promise," she said, pecking his cheek with a kiss before picking up her work bag. She was out the door before he could say another word.

When he returned home from work that night, he was relieved to see her car was already in the driveway. He assumed she had taken his advice and left early to rest, but he could sense something was off as soon as he walked through the door. The house was dim and oddly quiet, and it didn't exude its usual warmth.

"Jules, you home?"

There was no reply.

Her purse sat on the table next to her keys and her work bag had been dropped carelessly on the floor. This wasn't like her; she always hung her bag on the hook near the door.

"Jules?" He walked through the dimly-lit living room and into the hallway that led to their bedroom. Light from the bathroom seeped into the dark bedroom through the crack beneath the closed door.

"Honey, you in there?" He knocked softly and then slowly turned the knob. He was struck with by the smell of copper as soon as the door creaked open, and his wife was lying on the floor shivering.

"Oh God, Jules." He gasped, pushing his way inside. Her face was ghostly white and she was trembling.

"Something's not right, Will," she said, straining for breath. Her pants were saturated with blood, and there was blood smudged beneath her on the white tile floor.

"Okay, honey, it's okay. I'm here." He attempted to lift her, but she moaned again and curled back into a ball.

"There's cramps," she winced. She was gripping the phone tightly in her left hand.

"Let me call an ambulance," he said, trying to pry the phone from her fingers.

"No, it's okay," she mumbled. "I called the doctor. She said we should wait and see if the bleeding gets worse."

He realized Jules wasn't fully aware of what was happening. "Jules, honey." His voice was calm as he pulled her closer and tried not to alarm her. "We need to get you to the hospital."

"It's okay, Will. The cramps are getting a little better now." She looked up at him. The color had left her face completely, and he could tell she was close to losing consciousness. He cradled her in his arms and she looked down at the floor. "Is that blood?" She began to shake. "Oh my God, Will, is that blood?"

He pulled the comforter from their bed around her, picked her up, and rushed her to his truck.

Once at the hospital, their worst fears were confirmed. Jules had miscarried. She had developed a high fever along with the severe cramping, which altered her judgment and left her unable to analyze the seriousness of the situation.

"It's a good thing you came home when you did," the doctor told him. "Her fever was over 103 and she was completely dehydrated. There's nothing we could have done to save the pregnancy, but she was slipping into shock. Things could've gotten much worse. We're keeping her overnight to keep an eye on her and get some fluids back in."

Will sat at her bedside. There was a blank stare in her eyes and the glow, which had been so evident before, had been completely extinguished. "I should've listened to you and not gone to work," Jules whispered. Will held her hand and traced her wedding band with his fingers.

"It wouldn't have mattered," he said, leaning in to kiss her hand. "These things happen, Jules. It wasn't your fault."

"God, I'm fucking defective." She exhaled and stared at the ceiling with tears dripping from her eyes. "You married a defective woman that can't give you kids."

"Stop it, Jules, this isn't your fault," he said softly. "We can try again. This stuff happens all the time."

"I'm sorry," she whispered, laying her head back on the pillow and closing her eyes.

Hearing her apologize for something beyond her control had nearly killed him that night, but now, as he lay next

293

to Jillian in the empty darkness, an apology was all he wanted to hear from her now.

She had returned to work quickly after the miscarriage and, as always, she refused to talk about what had happened. They carried on as usual, and to their surprise, they learned they were pregnant again only six months later. Though she was happy, Jules was guarded, and for good reason. When she started bleeding just two weeks in, they both knew what was happening. After almost two full years of trying and two miscarriages, Jules was ready to give up.

"I don't think I can do this again," she had whispered as they lay awake in bed following her second D & C procedure.

He felt helpless because there was nothing he could do or say to take away her pain. A couple days later, Jules went to work again and shut him out of her grief. They didn't discuss the miscarriage, or trying again. But then, the following year, out of the blue, they became pregnant for a third time—without a plan, without discussion, and without consciously trying. Though they were happy, they were also cautious. It wasn't until she reached her twentieth week of pregnancy that Jules was finally able to breathe easier and accept that they just might pull this one off.

Thinking about those times made Will remember how much Jules had smiled back then. Since her birth, Will had thought of Jillian as the glue that held him and Jules together, but now he wondered if their daughter was the only thing that kept them fused.

Sliding slowly out of his daughter's bed, careful not to wake her, Will stood and marveled at what he and Jules had created. This tiny, feisty, and perfect little girl was everything he had hoped for. He knew that he and Jules had managed to destroy just about everything else in their relationship, but Jillian was the one thing they had done right. She was the spitting image of Jules but had her father's fighter instincts.

As he slipped out of Jillian's room and trudged down the stairs into the kitchen, the cold sweat returned as Will thought of nothing but the taste of brandy.

Just one, he thought. *I just want one.*

Still, he knew one was one too many, and one more would never be enough to kill the animal inside of him. He sank heavily into a kitchen chair and stared at his reflection in the glass doors, resisting the urge to scream Jules' name out loud. As he glared into his own eyes, he wanted to throw something, anything, at his reflection in the doors. He looked like his father. He loathed his father—hated him, even—because he made Will feel incapable of being loved. Through his coldness, Will's father had made him feel weak. Will wondered why his father had married his mother when it was clear he never wanted that life at all.

Will remembered when his mother had received the phone call explaining that his father had slid off the road and rammed his pickup truck dead center into an oak tree along old Highway Y. Though his mother had crumbled to her knees, Will sat stoically at the kitchen table. An odd flood of relief came

295

over him as he looked down at his geometry homework. It was Will's brother who moved first and helped their mother to her feet. Will had never told anyone about how relieved he felt that day. It was like he'd become lighter somehow. But now, staring at his father's likeness in the glass, he stood, grabbed a large hardcover cookbook from the counter, and pulled his arm back, ready to launch it into the glass and destroy the angry reflection that looked more like his father than like him.

But then, out of nowhere, he became acutely aware of the object in his hand. Jules had been a horrible cook; she'd hated everything about cooking, yet she had dog-eared half the pages in the book with recipes she never made. The thought made him pause, and as he stared at the heavy book, he realized it felt just like the one Nancy had given him when he picked up Jules' things from her office. Other than when she handed it to him, Will had never looked at the book. He had brought it home, dumped it in Jules' office, and closed the door, wanting to forget the entire experience of that day. But now, his heart racing in the deafening silence of their home, he wanted to understand Jules, or at least try.

Making his way up the stairs in the darkness, he felt nauseous and almost light-headed. He pushed through her office door and flipped on the light. The box was on top of the desk, right next to her briefcase, exactly where he had left it. He touched the leather bag with his fingers; he had given it to her two Christmases ago and had her name engraved on the metal tag. Prior to using this case, she had carried the same messenger bag for years; it was tattered and torn, but it held half of her life inside. When he gave her the new bag, he told her it was time to start looking the part for the job she had risen to achieve. It was one of the few times he ever complimented her for her work.

He'd meant to look through the book Nancy had given him, but he was distracted by Jules' bag. When he opened it, he found several manila folders, a paper-clipped collection of papers, and her leather-bound portfolio notebook. He pulled everything out of the bag and stared down at it. Opening the notebook first, his eyes instantly fell on her scribbled handwriting. The first few pages were filled with names, dates, phone numbers, and random jottings. He flipped through and found interview notes from stories she must have been working on, but just as he was just about to close the book, he turned one more page and noticed that she'd written "Dear Jules." Though he had never read one, he remembered her familiar phrase of "writing letters to myself."

Will sank into her chair and read her words. They were poignant, poetic, and even prophetic, yet he couldn't pinpoint their meaning. She had written about mirrors and reflections and the river, but what did it all mean? It didn't sound like a letter at all, but more like poetry.

When he finished, he slowly closed the notebook and leaned back in the chair. Jules had never been an easy woman to understand, and he couldn't begin to interpret the meaning of her words. Shaking his head, he set the notebook on the desk and stood to retrieve the book that Nancy had given him from

297

the box where he had left it. He ran his fingers over the outline of his wife's name on the front cover and quickly flipped it open.

He thumbed through the highlights of Jules' career and the pages of stories she had written. He had never seen most of these photos or read any of these stories, and he realized just how little he had paid attention to her job. Each of the book's sections was labeled by year, like a neatly organized scrapbook. He knew it would be a priceless gift for Jillian when she grew older. Without it, he would never be able to explain the talented and hard-working woman her mother had been.

Closing the book, Will's eyes were drawn to the paper-clipped papers lying on the desk. They were marred with red-inked corrections, and he wondered if this was the article Nancy had mentioned in her last text to Jules. He picked it up and began to read. It was the story about Erin, the one Jules had told him about just weeks before her death, and the one Alice said Jules had finished. There was a note, written in red, at the top of the page: *Jules – Please see me about this. Thanks, Nancy.*

He remembered the passion in Jules' voice when she'd told him about this story, and now he knew why it had meant so much to her. As he flipped through the pages, a photo of Erin slipped out and landed on the desk. It was an image of her on stage, and as he picked it up, he was struck, yet again, by how stunning she was. Even wearing jeans, Converse sneakers, and a black Johnny Cash T-shirt, Will could see that she was beautiful. She held the guitar in her hands as if she was about to play it, and her long, dark hair was pulled into a braid that hung forward over her right shoulder. Erin was smiling in the photo in a way Will hadn't seen her smile in person, and he couldn't bring himself to look away from her bright blue eyes for some reason. He wondered why, in the midst of everything else they had discussed, Erin hadn't mentioned seeing this article or even knowing about its existence. And, more importantly, knowing just how much the story meant to Jules, he wondered why Nancy hadn't run it—or was she still planning to run it? He glanced at his watch, which read 11:39 p.m. Nancy wouldn't be in the office now, but he clamored out of the chair and yanked Jules' phone, which he now carried with him at all times, from his front pocket. He thumbed through the numbers until he found Nancy's office phone. The blood pumped inside his head as her voicemail picked up.

"Uh, hi Nancy, it's Will Kanter. I know it's late and you're not there right now, but I wanted to talk to you about one of Jules' stories. Please give me a call when you have time. I'd really appreciate it."

He sank back in the chair and stared at Erin's face in the photo. He couldn't believe how far apart he and Jules had grown—there was so much he didn't understand about her now. Picking up the story, he again he began to read. Jules wasn't there to explain to him the person that Erin was, or how their relationship began, but maybe her words would help him to understand.

Chapter Twenty-One

The cold wind whipped up behind her as Erin climbed the snow-covered stairs to her apartment after another long shift. She opened the door to the dark room, dropped her bag on the floor, and then closed and locked the door again. The silence was deafening and she almost regretted leaving work. Quiet and stillness always gave her an uneasy feeling that made the walls seem as if they were closing in. They kept her confined in a prison that was filled with bad memories and voices she wished she could forget.

She was home earlier than usual because it had been a slow night at the bar, but she had still managed to put in a ten-hour day. Though she was surrounded by people who laughed and talked all day long, she had never felt so displaced. Now, surrounded by the loneliness in this room, moving back to that loud and crazy house in Tennessee didn't seem like such a bad idea after all. She had just over two months left on her apartment lease, and other than her mom, there was really nothing else keeping her in Milwaukee. Flipping on the living room lamp, she looked around the small, drab room. For the first time in weeks, she didn't feel like being alone.

She contemplated calling Tina, but it was almost 12:30 a.m., and she knew Tina would stay all night. Erin wasn't in the mood for awkward morning small talk, especially after the strange way that Tina had acted during their last encounter at the bar. Though they had good sex, she knew Tina wanted more from her, and she wasn't interested in taking that relationship any further. Tina would never be enough to replace Jules. Still, she craved the feeling of having another body beside her. She longed for the warmth of another woman's skin, and that need was slowly beginning to drain her.

She picked up her phone, but instead of dialing, she looked back at her saved messages from Jules. She hadn't read them in weeks. The last one, from January 25th, was the nonchalant *Running late, be there at one.* It was typical Jules, always behind schedule. Erin had been annoyed with her that day. Jules had promised to meet her for lunch, help her run a few errands, and then listen to Erin's new songs. Jules had been unusually busy and distracted in the weeks leading up to her death, and Erin had begun to feel pushed aside. When she received that message, she was sitting right here, on this couch, with her guitar on her lap, growing increasingly irritated and staring at the clock.

Jules was already almost a full hour late, and she knew Erin had to work that night. Erin felt slighted and squeezed into Jules' already jam-packed schedule. When she read the message, she groaned aloud and tossed her phone on the couch in disgust. Jules was wasting time they didn't have. As the clock

301

ticked, Erin knew Jules would only give her a few hours before rushing off to another appointment or heading home to her family. By the time she heard the familiar sound of Jules' feet on the stairs, Erin was too annoyed to even look up as Jules pushed through the door like a tornado.

"I know you're mad. I'm *really* sorry," she said with a sheepish grin spreading across her face. Her hair was windblown and she gripped a bag of Chinese food in one hand. She stumbled while wiping her black riding boots on the rug near the door.

Despite her anger, Erin couldn't help but chuckle at Jules' clumsiness, but Jules didn't seem to notice. She dropped the bag on the table and began to unbutton her gray pea coat. "Geez, what a morning I've had," she said, out of breath. "Jillian was in a mood so I got out of the house late, and then we had a new reporter starting this morning, and of course IT didn't have the computer ready, and Kristie was supposed to train this kid, but of course she called in sick because it's Monday, you know, and then Nancy was late for the budget meeting and axed half my section this week, and—" She sensed Erin's heated stare. "You *are* mad. Shit, I'm sorry. I swear, I tried to get out of there on time. I swear I did. I told Nancy I had appointments all afternoon, but she gave me a shitload of corrections to make on a story—"

"Whatever," Erin mumbled. "I'm getting used to it." She tuned the guitar and pretended not to care.

302

Jules groaned and flopped down beside her. "Don't be like that, please. Don't be like Will."

Erin glared at her again. "Please do not compare me to your husband."

"I'm here now. You have my full attention. I turned off my phone, and I don't have anywhere else I need to be."

"Yeah, until you go home."

"Alrighty then. I can see where this is going." She stood and began to button her jacket. "I really don't need this today, Erin. I'm sorry I was late and I'm sorry you're pissed off, but I can't be in ten places at once."

"I only need you in one place," Erin shot back. She looked down and moved her fingers over the guitar strings, starting into a new song she was writing. She hadn't named it, or finished the lyrics, but she watched as Jules stopped buttoning her coat. She turned back as Erin stopped playing.

"That sounds really good. Is that the new one?"

"Yeah, it is. Are you going somewhere?"

"Well, you seem rather pissed off, so I was thinking of just going back to the office."

"I see. Well, then don't let me keep you." Erin stood and walked toward the bedroom. She leaned the guitar against the wall and began folding a pile of laundry she had tossed in the chair the night before. She could feel Jules hovering in the doorway like a shadow.

"Erin," Jules said softly. "Please don't act this way. How many times do we have to go through this?"

"You have a whole life that doesn't include me. I get it," she said, tossing a shirt back on the pile. "But when you tell me you're gonna be here, then just be here. That's all I want. I don't think that's too much to ask."

"You're right," Jules said empathetically. She stepped inside the room and moved toward Erin. "I'm a complete asshole, and I know I'm totally unfair to you."

"Well, at least we finally agree on something," Erin muttered. She turned and tugged at the black scarf wrapped around Jules' neck. She slowly pulled it off before looking into Jules' eyes. "Are you coming, or going?"

"That sounds like a loaded question," Jules smirked, unbuttoning her jacket. She slipped it off and tossed it onto the chair.

"It's just a question, Jules. You can do whatever you want."

"I already told you," she said as she moved closer. "I don't have anywhere else I need to be."

They never did make it out to run errands, and Erin never did play the rest of her songs for Jules that afternoon. They spent the next four hours in Erin's bed, kissing, touching, making love, laughing, talking, and reading passages from *Orlando*. Erin loved listening to the sound of Jules's voice as she read through lines from that book. While her head rested on Jules' lap, and while Jules' fingers slid through her hair, Erin closed her eyes and imagined living inside that beautiful and twisted story.

304

It wasn't until the room grew dark, when Jules got up and looked out the window, that they even realized it was snowing. Erin watched her, silhouetted in the soft light that seeped from behind the curtain. It shimmered off her bare skin, and all Erin wanted was to reach out and pull her back to bed. But when Jules began dressing and slipped her sweater over her head, Erin knew she was going to leave. There was a slow burn in the pit of her stomach, partially from anger and partially from the simple longing of wanting Jules to stay—just once. And she knew Jules felt it, too. She could see the look in her eyes as she sat near the edge of the bed. Still, Erin couldn't convince her to stay, despite her best efforts. The last words Erin had said to her that day were "drive safe." After everything they had weathered, those cold and prophetic words were the last Jules had ever heard her say.

As she thought about that afternoon, sitting alone on the couch in her apartment, Erin rested her phone on her chest and stared at the ceiling. She realized what a stab in the heart it must have been for Will to know that Erin was the last person Jules had seen before the accident. She wondered what Jules had been thinking when she drove away that night. Was she upset? Was she thinking of Erin? Or, was she thinking of all the work she would need to catch up on the following day because she had wasted the entire afternoon in Erin's bed? If fate hadn't intervened, Erin knew she and Jules would have exchanged texts and a few phone calls over the next few days, and then Jules would have been back at Erin's apartment, and in her

305

arms, that Friday. God knows how long they would have continued on that way, never moving forward. Ever since the talk with her mom, Erin had begun to hone in on certain aspects of their conversations and she wondered if—or when—Jules was planning to push her away for good. On that last day, Jules had mentioned Tennessee again, asking if Erin's friends knew about their relationship.

"Why would I tell them?" Erin shot back sarcastically. "Have you told your friends about me?"

"That's completely different." Jules' voice was condescending. "I would have *a lot* more explaining to do than you would."

"I told them I was seeing someone, that's it."

"Don't they wonder why you aren't coming back?" Jules lay on her side with her head resting on the pillow. One hand was tucked under her head and the other was on of Erin's forearm.

"They know why. They knew things weren't good with my Mom when I left, not to mention all the other shit that went down with me."

"Sweetie, your mom is doing okay. You know that, right?" Jules slowly moved her fingers over Erin's skin.

Erin sighed. She was growing annoyed with the repetitive nature of this conversation. "What are you getting at Jules?"

"I just wonder sometimes if you're using her as an excuse not go back. Your mom has a lot of support with your aunt and uncle. Is there another reason why you're staying?"

Erin tossed the book on the nightstand and rolled away from Jules in the same patronizing way Jules normally did when Erin questioned her. "I'm not going back because I can't be in two places at once— just like you. She's sick, Jules, and she's not going to get better. I know she says she's fine, but we all know she isn't. I'm glad you two get along, but don't let her fool you. She's not fine. I can't be that far away and not know what's going on with her."

"Okay, okay." Jules let up and reached for Erin's hand. "She just wants what's best for you, and so do I, so don't be afraid to be honest. That's all I'm saying. You're moving backwards here. No one wants that for you."

"God, why can't you just give it a fucking rest?" Erin asked, growing angry. "What the hell do you know about it anyway? You don't know my mom, Jules. When my dad died, I was the one who took care of things while she was out drinking and getting high. I couldn't wait to get the hell out of there, I admit it. But we put all that behind us, and I owe it to her to be here now."

"Erin, you don't owe anyone—"

"Yes, I do, Jules. I don't expect you to understand why she and I are the way we are, but when she cleaned up and got sober, she worked her ass off to put me through college. But then she hovered over me and tried to get me to talk about

307

things that I didn't wanna talk about, so I completely ditched her and moved to Tennessee on a total whim. I was all she had, and I just left her without even thinking twice about it." She sighed and looked at the ceiling. "Besides, maybe I like where I am now. Maybe it's a dream of mine to be singing at a bar and fucking around with a married woman, so just drop it, okay?"

Jules gripped Erin's hip and pulled her back to face her. "Consider it dropped," she said, looking directly into Erin's eyes. "I don't want you to go, but I do want you to be happy. That's all I'm saying."

Erin knew that both Jules and her mother were trying to protect her, but she also knew the real reason she was staying. She couldn't imagine being in Tennessee without either of them now. But they were right; she wasn't moving forward. If she wanted to reclaim her career, she needed to make a change, but she didn't know how.

Now, lying alone on her couch, the familiar fear of making the wrong decision crept up inside. Her heart raced until she could barely catch her breath. On the verge of hyperventilating, she wanted to stop it all and simply be numb. She ached for the lorazepam her mother had helped her to flush down the toilet the day after Jules died.

Erin sat up and rubbed her face, knowing she wouldn't get any sleep. But, she also knew there was cocaine readily available in her bedroom—the vial Will had found. She hadn't been able to throw it away, even now. Her legs shook, and she fought the urge to race toward the nightstand. She knew if she did just a little now she would be wired all night, but maybe, just maybe, it would help her find a way to channel her anxiety. Maybe she could play her guitar, finish the songs she'd started, and accomplish something that made her feel alive again.

She stood, briefly paced the apartment, and then turned toward the bedroom, convincing herself that doing just a little cocaine was fine and she would be okay. Then, just as she was about to step into the room, her phone lit up. Jules' face flashed across the screen. It was a photo Erin had snapped at the bar months earlier. She was laughing, her dark eyes squinting and her lips curled into a wide smile. Erin loved that picture. She knew it wasn't Jules calling, but she couldn't resist answering it.

"Hello," she said, clenching her eyes shut.

"You're awake," Will said softly. "I—I didn't expect you to answer, I hope I didn't wake you."

"Yeah, I'm awake—I was still up." She sank to the couch, waiting for her heart rate to slow. "Is everything okay?"

"Uh, yeah. I mean, well, you know." He stumbled on his words, clearly nervous.

"Are you okay?"

"No, not really. This house is just so quiet at night. Drives me crazy, you know?"

"Yeah, I do know," she whispered, leaning back on the couch. "Why are you up so late?"

"Uh, well, I was looking through some things Jules was writing." Pages turned in the background as he spoke. "I don't

309

even know why I'm asking you this, but I was wondering why you didn't mention the article."

"I'm not sure what you mean." Erin rubbed her forehead and glanced at the clock, which now read 1:43 a.m.

"The article she wrote about you—you never mentioned it. I mean, Jules told me she was working on it, and I know they didn't run it yet, but why didn't you say anything about it?"

Erin quickly sat up. "She—what? I seriously don't know what you're talking about. What article?"

"She didn't tell you?"

"Uh, no. She asked me a million times if she *could* write an article, but I made it clear that I didn't want that. Are you telling me she did it anyway?"

"Um, yeah. It's all right here, sitting in front of me."

Her head began to pound. "I can't believe she would do that."

Will sighed. "I don't know what to tell you, but it's all right here. It's actually a really good story."

Erin felt nauseous as the acid began to bubble in the back of her throat. *Damn you Jules,* she thought.

Will cleared his throat. "Did she ever mention anything to you about writing letters to herself?"

"Honestly, Will, the only thing she ever mentioned was that she was trying to do something new at work, but she didn't go into a lot of detail."

"Yeah, she was good at being elusive," he mumbled.

"Yeah, I guess so," she said. "Why are you asking about these letters?"

He softly breathed into the phone.

"She sometimes wrote letters to herself," he explained apprehensively. "She would do it when she was stressed out or upset, usually, but she would never let me read them. Probably for good reason."

"She never mentioned that to me."

"I found one," he said quickly. "But I don't know what it means."

"What did it say?"

"Uh, well…" He stopped short.

"What is it?"

He took a deep breath before beginning again. "Um…do you wanna come out here? To the house I mean, and take a look? I know that sounds like a weird question, especially given the circumstances, and I'll understand if you say no."

"Will," Erin mumbled. "I—"

"I know. It's a dumb thought, but I really don't know what to make of all this." He briefly paused. "I'm not a writer, and honestly, I was never into reading like she was. I only see things on the surface, you know? So…I don't know…maybe you can help me make sense of this? I'd come to you, but my mom is out of town and I don't have anyone to watch Jillian other than Jules' sister. But I don't want her to know about this yet, or that I've even talked to you."

Erin held her breath. She began to sweat and feel even more anxious. "You want me to come to your house?"

"Well, if you wanna see this stuff," he replied. "I mean, again, you don't have to, but I don't really wanna show this to anyone else until I understand what it means, and then you can see the article, too."

Erin leaned back and closed her eyes. She couldn't believe Jules had written the article after all the times she'd told her not to. And then she never mentioned it—not once.

"Are you sure you want me there—at your house, I mean? What about Jillian?"

"Jillian doesn't know about any of this, and I'd like to keep it that way." He sighed again. "She does remember the scarf, though—the one you gave her at the funeral. All she needs to know is that you're a friend of her mom's, that's it."

"Okay," she said. "It's my weekend off, but I have some things going on in the morning with my mom. Can we make it later in the day, on Saturday maybe?"

"I'll be here all day."

"Okay. Does 5:00 work?"

"Yeah. Do you, uh…do you know how to get to my house?" He was baiting her.

"No. Can you give me the address?"

He recited it quickly, but she didn't write it down— she didn't need to.

"Alright, then. I'll see you Saturday." He exhaled slowly, as if he were relieved to be through with the conversation.

"Sounds good. Get some sleep."

"Yeah," he scoffed. "You too."

After hanging up the phone, Erin sat stoically. She was shaken, yet again, by Jules' dishonesty. She knew her mother would tell her not to go, but she had to see for herself what Jules had done. Plus, the sound of Will's voice had been oddly comforting. He was the only person who truly understood how alone she was. Though they were on opposite sides, they were the only two people who could really understand the black hole Jules' death had created. They both loved her and hated her, but neither of them knew how to move forward without her.

Erin left the lights off, picked herself up from the couch, and walked slowly into the bedroom. She slipped into bed, fully clothed and exhausted, but once her eyes closed, she could only see Jules' face. Rolling over, she fought the urge to open the nightstand drawer. *Not tonight*, she thought. *I don't need it tonight.*

Chapter Twenty-Two

Will sipped his coffee and stared out at the frozen river. It was early March, and though most of the snow had already melted, a cold chill in the air kept a solid layer of ice over the water. He couldn't wait for the cold to give way to warmer weather so he could get out of the house and take Jillian fishing. Though Jules had never liked to fish, he wanted to share those quiet moments with his daughter and teach her the art of sitting still and waiting for a bite. Though he and his father could barely stand to be in the same room, fishing was the one thing they managed to do together. It didn't require speaking; it only required silence and patience, which they both ordinarily lacked. Drifting off into the thought, his buzzing cell phone snapped him back to reality. He glanced at his watch as Jillian hummed and played with her toys while eating her cereal.

"Jilly, you need to hurry up or you'll be late for school," he said before answering the phone. "Hello?"

"Will? Hi there, it's Nancy," Jules' boss said. "I'm sorry to call so early, but I got your message and I'm heading into a meeting, so I wanted to get back to you before the day got crazy." Her voice was muffled, and Will could tell that he was on speaker phone.

Will cleared his throat. "It's no problem. Thanks for calling me back so soon. I didn't really expect to hear from you right away."

"Well, we really miss Jules around here, so I can only imagine what it's like for you," she said. There was a click on the line, and suddenly her voice was close and clear. "If there's anything I can do for you, I just want you to know I'll try my best."

"I appreciate that," he said, glancing at his watch again. "So, what can I do for you?"

Will looked at Jillian, tapped his wrist, and pointed at her cereal, signaling for her to keep eating.

"I—well, I was looking through the book you gave me—and thanks again for that. It's really amazing."

"You're very welcome," she said in the managerial way she always spoke. "It was really a collaborative effort with the staff; Jules was an important part of this newspaper, but I don't need to tell you that."

He shook his head as if Nancy were standing right there in the room with him. "Well, I also found an article in her bag. She'd told me about this story, and I—I guess I just wondered why you didn't run it. I know that story meant a lot to her."

Nancy fell silent, and he thought they might have been disconnected.

"Nancy?"

"Uh, yeah. I'm still here. Which story do you mean?"

315

"It's about that singer, Erin Quinn."

Nancy slowly exhaled on the other end of the line. "Well, Jules and I had some disagreements about that piece. I liked it, I really did. I think it's a great story, but I just didn't think it was ready yet."

"Really?"

"Well, Will, to be honest, I thought there were a few missing elements to that story. Plus, that piece was taking her section, and her focus, in a new direction. She really wanted to do more of those in-depth features," Nancy said. "On top of that, in the past few months she kept insisting that we fade out her regular column. I just wasn't in agreement with that."

"I don't understand," Will said, looking out the window toward the river. "Did you not agree with that story, the new direction of her work, or that she wanted to back off of writing the column?"

"I didn't agree with any of it," Nancy answered quickly. "I liked what she was thinking with these new feature stories, I really did, but at the time I needed her to stay in the role people were used to seeing her in."

"She was burnt out on that column, Nancy. You know she was."

"Her job was to cover arts events in the city and keep up the witty, charming—and yes, sometimes critical—voice she's always been." She sighed before continuing. Her chair creaked on the other end of the line and Will pictured her shifting uncomfortably. "I know she hated being critical, but

316

honestly, that's what she was best known for, and people trusted her opinion, whether she liked to believe it or not. And, more importantly, that's what the advertisers in her section were paying for. Her byline was the most important thing on that page. Those advertisers were there because she brought them in, but it was also her responsibility to keep them there with the content she wrote and what she chose to run. We couldn't take the risk of losing any more money—if we did, she might not have had a section left to work on. I would've had to demote her, Will, or move her to a different section entirely, and neither of us wanted that."

"I don't know your business, Nancy, and I don't even fully understand what new direction she was going in, but I knew Jules, and she valued her job—maybe even too much, if you ask me."

"We were going to revisit her ideas, Will," Nancy replied somberly. "I just needed her to give me a little more time for the market to turn again. The winter is always hard on this business, and she *knew* that. Well, that and I thought maybe she should try some other subjects for those features before we ran the one on the bartender."

"The article on Erin Quinn, you mean?"

"Yes—I thought she should try interviewing more high-profile members of the arts community first, just to test the waters. But you know Jules, she always loved the underdog, and she wanted it her way or no way."

317

Will held his breath. "I understand all this, Nancy, but I need to know—was there any other reason you didn't want to run that story?"

Nancy was quiet again, but he knew she hadn't hung up.

"Nancy?"

"Because I thought it was a conflict of interest," she said abruptly, as if the words would sting less if she said them quickly. "She was too close to the source, and she knew she was. It was unethical, and I couldn't allow it."

"So you did know about their relationship?" He closed his eyes and leaned his head against the cold window glass.

"I knew they were unusually close, that's all. There was talk about a relationship going on between them, but that was really none of my business and she wouldn't admit it to anyone—not to me, not even to Alice. But she didn't have to." Nancy's tone softened. "They were seen together on more than one occasion, and regularly at events Jules was covering. I questioned her about it but she denied it, and she wasn't herself for the last few months. I could tell she was—I don't know, just off somehow. When she brought me that story, I initially considered it. And I did tell her that she needed to dig into it more. But the more I learned about their relationship, the more I realized that she may not have been approaching it impartially. I told her I thought her personal feelings were getting in the way of her professional judgment. We're not in the business of doing favors for the people around us—no matter who they are. We

318

have to stay unbiased and cover all sides of the story. For the first time in her career, I don't think she did that with the Quinn story."

"I see," he said.

"I'm really sorry to be the one to tell you all this, Will. I really am."

"Do you really believe she was writing that story as a favor for Erin Quinn? I'm not so sure about that."

"Well, considering how close they were, I don't know why else she would have done it," Nancy replied. "I thought the Quinn girl was trying to make a comeback in her music career, or something like that. Wasn't she?"

"I really don't know, but I talked to her and she didn't know anything about this article being written. She said Jules had asked her for permission to write a story, but she told her she wasn't interested."

Nancy coughed in surprise. "Are you sure? How did Jules get that information, then? That story was pretty in-depth. She was well aware of the lines in this business. I can't believe she would present something to me for publication without permission or affirmation from the source—especially with a story like that. That's incredibly risky, and it doesn't sound like the Jules I knew."

"I don't know what she was doing, Nancy—I really don't," he said quietly. "But I believe Erin. I don't think she had any idea what was going on with that article."

"I don't know either, Will, but like I said, Jules didn't seem herself for quite a while."

"What if I want you to run that story, Nancy? Can you do that?"

On the other end of the line, Nancy's breathing almost ceased. "Uh…well…considering what you just told me, we'd have to contact Erin Quinn and corroborate the facts in the story and get her permission to run it. But besides that, are you sure that's what you want? Regardless of what it meant to Jules, I do not want to be disrespectful to you and your—"

He cut her off. "The story doesn't say they were fucking, Nancy, even though you clearly knew they were, but I appreciate your attempt in concealing it." Will was more calm when he began speaking again. "It's just a story about Erin. I don't understand what was really going on between them, but I know Jules would hate leaving something undone in her work. I'm really trying to see things from her side, which is what I should've done a long time ago, I guess. If I can get approval from Erin, I want you to run it. I don't know why, but I just want you to do it—for Jules."

Nancy sighed. "I've known Jules a long time, Will, and I don't understand what she was doing either. But if there's one thing I did know about her, it's that she was plagued by empathy. That empathy gave her an uncommon depth that was different from most writers I know but, at times, it also made her soft. She really was gifted at seeing people's raw talent, but where most of us in this business can write a column or a story and leave it behind, Jules had a hard time with that. The people she wrote about stayed with her, and that was always her downfall in this job. That's precisely why I had a hard time letting her write like that."

"She gave everything to that paper," he mumbled. "I still don't know why. I just wish she would've given half of that effort to her family."

"I understand how you feel," Nancy said, her voice cracking. "She was one of a kind, albeit stubborn and sometimes a pain in the ass to work with, but she was definitely one of a kind. Let me know if you talk to Erin Quinn, and I'll talk to my team and see what we can do. John was looking to roll out a new look for the arts section early next month. If we could start with something written by Jules, we'd all be happy with that, and I think our readers would be, too."

"Thanks, Nancy, I appreciate it. I know Jules would really like that."

"You bet, Will. Take care of yourself and give Jillian a hug for me. We'll talk soon."

He sank into one of the kitchen chairs and hung up the phone. Jillian was still lollygagging with her breakfast, but he was too distracted and mentally exhausted to care. He was so tired of trying to figure out what Jules had been doing, and he just wanted things to be simple again.

As he watched Jillian, he thought about the last Sunday night when Jules had been home. She was in her office combing through stories, preparing for work the next day, and ignoring

321

him as usual. He had stood in the office doorway watching her. She was focused on the computer screen, her glasses low on the bridge of her nose and her dark hair pushed behind her ears. She held a pencil between her teeth and her notes were spread all around her. To him, it looked like unorganized chaos.

"Dinner's ready," he said, but she didn't flinch.

"Jules?"

"What? I'm sorry. Did you say something?" She dropped the pencil and turned toward him. Her fingers were still on the keyboard, as if he had stopped her mid-thought.

"I just said dinner's ready. Are you gonna work all night or actually come down and eat with us?"

"Yeah, I'll be down in a few minutes. I just need to get this finished tonight. I have to get it in to Nancy by ten. I have meetings in the morning and appointments all afternoon tomorrow." She pushed the glasses back up on her nose.

He sighed. He knew a few minutes never actually meant just a few minutes. "Did you forget that you promised to pick up Jillian from my mom's tomorrow?"

She wrinkled her face and rubbed her eyes. "Oh, shit, that's right. Can you do it? I'll grab her on Tuesday, I promise."

"No, I can't, Jules," he said, growing annoyed. "I'm meeting Ray at the bar tomorrow to go over the bid for that Victorian remodel. I told you that. I need to get some work lined up soon for spring, or maybe even later this winter if we're lucky."

She leaned back and lowered her chin. "At the bar? Are you sure that's a good idea?"

"Really? I haven't had drink in three years. Are you really gonna throw that in my face right now because I asked you to pick up your daughter?"

She set her glasses on the keyboard. "I didn't mean it like that—I just don't know if it's a good idea for you to meet him at the bar, that's all."

"I do it all the time, Jules. I can handle sitting in a bar and not drink, contrary to what you might believe."

Her eyes narrowed.

"Yeah, just one of the many things you don't know because you're never here. I go to AA, I don't have a drop of liquor, and I don't even talk to anyone you wouldn't approve of, but yeah, I sometimes sit at the bar and enjoy conversation with someone other than our six-year-old daughter."

She exhaled and looked up at the ceiling. "I don't wanna fight," she said quietly. "Can I just finish this quick so we can have dinner, and yes, I will pick up Jillian tomorrow. I'll figure it out, okay?"

"Fine." He down the stairs.

Thirty minutes later, after Will and Jillian had finished eating, she came down to join them. Will was angry and pushed his chair away from the table. It scraped loudly on the tile floor, but she pretended not to notice. Instead, she smiled, sat down next to Jillian, and began picking at the food on her plate.

"Your dinner is cold, Mommy." Jillian straightened in her chair.

"I know, Bug." She winked. "That's the way Mommy likes it."

Jillian smiled and finished her few remaining peas. Will glanced over his shoulder, watching them while loading the dishwasher. A quizzical expression suddenly crossed their daughter's face.

"Allison's mom had a baby," she said, looking up at Jules, who had just taken a bite of her food.

"Is that so?" Jules replied, chewing slowly. "I didn't know that."

"Mommy, when are *we* gonna have a baby?"

Jules choked and then laughed. She looked at Will, and he couldn't help but smile at the directness of the question, despite how annoyed he was with his wife. Jules met his gaze. She raised her eyebrows and nodded toward Jillian as if she were hoping he would chime in on the conversation. But he didn't give her the satisfaction. He wanted her to take this one all on her own.

"Well, sweetie," she began with a quick clearing of her throat. "God decided you were more than enough for Mommy and Daddy to handle, so we were blessed with only little ol' you."

Will smirked and turned back toward the dishwasher.

Later that night, Will had fallen asleep in his chair while watching TV in the living room. When he woke hours later, he realized the house was oddly quiet and Jules hadn't asked him to come to bed like she normally did. He slowly walked to their bedroom, but then realized she wasn't in their neatly-made bed. He peeked toward her office, assuming she was still working, but the light was off there, too. Realizing there was only one place left where she could be, he slowly opened the door to Jillian's bedroom. There they were, cuddling and fast asleep. Jules' glasses had slid down on her nose, and *I Love You Forever* was still resting on her chest. He didn't have the heart to wake them so he simply walked to the bathroom where he began to splash cold water over his face. Seconds later, Jules slipped her hands around his waist. Startled, he stood and stared at her sleepy reflection in the mirror before she rested her head against his arm.

"What's wrong?" He turned toward her and she leaned her head on his chest.

"What's going on, Jules? What is it?"

"I'm sorry I didn't give you more kids," she whispered. "And I'm sorry I've been such a bitch to you. You really have given us everything you said you would, and I've never even thanked you."

He wrapped his arms around her and kissed the top of her head. "I have everything I need," he whispered. "And you don't need to thank me. I was a fuck up, but I'm so glad you're still here."

"I *am* still here," she replied, pulling back and looking into his eyes. "Whatever happens, just remember that, okay?"

325

"What do you mean?" He shook his head and narrowed his eyes. But she leaned in and softly kissed his lips. He could tell by the way she was acting that she wasn't going to explain what she'd said. Instead, she pulled him closer and sighed, allowing him to kiss her neck and explore her body with his hands. They hadn't touched that way in far too long. She took a step back, peeled off her T-shirt, and dropped it to the floor before pulling him toward their bed.

"I love you so much," he whispered, but she didn't reply. Instead, they continued to explore each other and then made love slowly and intensely. She opened her eyes when it was over, smiled sweetly, and touched his face with her fingertips. She said, "We always did know how to do one thing right."

The next morning, still tangled together, they awoke to the sound of her alarm clock. Will's nose was buried deep in the back of her hair and warmth radiated from her skin. She groaned, slapped off the alarm, and lay still for a few minutes before stirring and breaking from his grasp. She slid out of bed and stepped into the shower without a word. He lay there, deflated, knowing things would return to the normal once she walked out the door—the challenging routine that always left them running in opposite directions. As the morning progressed, he felt her slipping away again. Just when she was about to walk out the door, Jillian tugged on the sleeve of her mother's jacket.

"Mommy, can you take me to school today, *pleeeaasse*?"

"Baby, I can't," Jules said, bending to kiss her daughter. "Mommy has a whole lot of boring meetings today, and then I'm gonna come right back home and pick you up from Grandma's house, okay?"

"Noooo, I want you to take me to school."

"Jilly Bug, Mommy has to go. Daddy will take you to school. Go to the window and wave to me, okay? I love you. I'll see you tonight."

She kissed Jillian again, smiled at Will, and practically jogged out the door. Jillian raced to the front window and watched her car back out of the driveway. Jules smiled again, blew Jillian a kiss, and then drove away.

Until then, Will had completely forgotten what she had said to him the previous night. Like always, she managed to distract him with the perfect weapon: sex. It didn't matter what she had said or did. When he was upset with her and she didn't want to fight anymore, she would turn on the charm and seduce him every time. Still, her comment had been so vague.

I am still here. No matter what happens, just remember that, okay?

Had she been planning to come clean about her affair? He thought of the words she'd written in her letter and shook his head in utter frustration. He realized he might never know what Jules had meant, or why she'd said it.

Chapter Twenty-Three

Erin gripped her mother's hand, helping her from the car. She glanced toward the busy crosswalk and handed her the cane. "Are you sure you wanna do this today? It looks busy," she said.

Her mother slid her hand around her daughter's arm and nudged her slightly. "It's Saturday— of course it's busy. And yes, we're doing this. It's the Public Market, it's your father's birthday, and I want some damn seafood."

Erin nodded and recalled her father's weathered but handsome face—she shared his eyes and his smile. This year, she missed him more than ever.

"You know, from what I remember, he didn't really care about his birthday." Erin laughed as her mother gripped her arm. "I think it was you who always made him do things like this on his birthday."

"Oh, he liked his birthday alright. He just liked to pretend he didn't want us making a big deal out of it." Her mother limped along the sidewalk, a reminiscent smirk on her face. "Remember that time you tried to bake him a cake and burnt it to a crisp? Gosh, you were so young—maybe only eight—but gosh if you weren't determined to bake him that

328

cake, Then you got distracted watching TV, and I forgot all about it."

Erin smiled and looked down at the concrete. "I remember. He ate it anyway."

"Yeah, he did, and I still don't know how he did it without gagging. That thing smelled like burnt dog shit, but he choked it down and told you it was the best cake he'd ever eaten. There was nothing you could do wrong in his eyes."

Erin smiled, remembering the sight of her father sitting at the kitchen table that day. When they placed that God-awful cake before him, his face lit up like he had just won the lottery. Her mother lit the candles as Erin slid onto his lap and sang "Happy Birthday" as loudly and as boldly as she possibly could. His eyes glassed over, though she had no idea why back then.

"I could listen to you sing all day long, little girl," he said, kissing her cheek. Then he blew out every candle on the cake but one. As the flame flickered, he let out a deep, guttural laugh and bounced her on his knee. "I guess that one is up to you."

She blew it out before her mother attempted to cut that crisp, blackened cake with a butter knife. "I don't know, Erin," she muttered. "I think it might just be a little too burnt."

"Aw, no, Vi," her father insisted. "I think it's just right. I always like things a little well done."

He winked and reached into his pocket, retrieving the Swiss Army knife he always carried with him. He opened it to

329

the sharpest blade and easily sliced into the cake. "See, this cuts right through it—just like butter."

He cut a huge piece of the charred lump and ate every single crumb. Erin's mother was right—her father had always known how to make her feel like anything was possible.

Erin wondered what her father would think if he could see her now. She had been able to talk to him about almost anything when she was a child, but when she grew a little older and began to question her feelings toward boys, she couldn't find a way to ask him what that might mean. It was the one thing she was afraid he wouldn't understand. But knowing the good-natured and fair man he was, Erin regretted not having that conversation with him now that she was an adult. Not telling him about her sexuality made her feel incomplete, as if his not knowing made her less whole. Her father had been a quiet, hardworking man who enjoyed the simple things in life, and even though she never once heard him raise his voice or talk poorly of other people, she didn't know his views on homosexuality. She longed for the talks they never had and all the advice he'd never had the chance to give.

What would he have thought about Jules, or the fact that she was married? And, would he have been supportive of Erin pursuing a career in music? Her father had been the first person to introduce her to piano, and then guitar, when she was just seven years old. Though she caught on to piano quickly, it was the guitar she felt most drawn to. When she first held that old Gibson acoustic guitar in her hands, it immediately fit and felt right. Back then, her father's guitar was almost bigger than she was. She had no idea how to play it, but he had smiled at her with his big, toothy grin and positioned her small fingers between the frets to show her a few chords. She begged him to teach her, and she quickly mastered the instrument.

Erin's dad had learned to play from his own father, and though he did it purely as a hobby, Erin always loved listening to him pluck away at those strings. He was an old soul who reveled in the music of Johnny Cash and Elvis. He worked as a mechanic by day and always came home smelling like gasoline and motor oil, but when he picked up that guitar, Erin would stop whatever she was doing and sit at his feet to listen. His hands were always dirty and, his fingernails caked black with grease, but when they played that guitar, the sound was always pure and clean.

As Erin and her mother pushed through the doors of the Milwaukee Public Market, Erin immediately regretted their decision to come. Though they came here often, Erin hated when it was busy. The market had a warm and almost hippie vibe when it was quiet, but, like every other place in the city, it was easy to get swallowed by the crowd when it was busy. The aisles, which lined both of sides of the large, two-story building, easily became congested, making them more narrow and difficult to maneuver, especially when walking against the crowd. Given her mother's walking difficulties, it was even more challenging for them to make it from one side of the market to the other.

"Hold on to me," Erin said, moving ahead of her mother. They held hands and pushed through a sea of shoppers toward the St. Paul Fish Company, which was at the opposite side of the market. She knew this trip wasn't easy on her mom, but she also knew it was pointless to argue with her once her mind was made up. Though Erin loved her mother, their relationship had always been different than the one she had with her father. Both Erin and her mother were stubborn, and being so much alike sometimes made it hard for them to get along.

After buying barbecued shrimp and fresh scallops, Erin clutched her mother's hand again and led her toward the exit doors.

"Where do you think you're going?" Her mother pulled her hand away, eyeing the doors. "Oh, no," she said. "We're going upstairs and eating here."

"Seriously, Mom? We have to fight that crowd again? Can't we just eat at home?"

"Hell no, kiddo," she insisted. "We're going up there."

Erin groaned and glanced up at the second floor mezzanine. Getting up there meant battling the crowd to reach the elevator near the doors at the market's opposite end.

"It's for your dad, so let's get up there. Maybe that cute old guy is playing the clarinet again up there. I just love him." She smiled.

Erin shot her a dirty look. Going upstairs had nothing to do with her father; it was just her mother's unwillingness to let MS control her life. Erin took her hand and started into the sea of faces again.

"This place wasn't even open yet when Dad was alive, so don't go blaming him for this," she said.

Her mom laughed and limped along behind her. Occasionally, Erin's mother intentionally nudged her with her cane. This only annoyed Erin more. When they reached the elevator, she punched the button and turned to see her mother smiling from ear to ear. She couldn't help but shake her head and smirk.

When the doors slid open, Erin found herself face to face with Jules' boss. Erin recognized her immediately but instinctively looked away.

"Uh, hi there. Erin, right?" Nancy seemed equally surprised to see her.

"Yeah, hi." Her voice betrayed her nerves. As Nancy stepped out of the elevator, she looked as if she were about to say something, but then she stopped. She gave Erin a slight smile and then walked away.

Erin helped her mother into the elevator. As the doors slid closed, her mother said, "What was that all about? Who was that?" She wore a puzzled expression.

The stainless steel doors distorted Erin's reflection. "That was Jules' boss," she said.

"Ohhh."

They were silent as the elevator went up. Between fighting the crowd and seeing Nancy, Erin began to grow

333

anxious. She was still agitated when they finally found a table and sat down. After what Will had told her, she realized Nancy probably knew more about her than she was comfortable with.

"You seem a little uptight. Everything okay?" With a shaky hand, her mother pulled the shrimp from the bag and began eating.

"I'm fine. I just hate it when this place is crowded."

Her mother nodded. "Anything else going on? Have you thought more about what we talked about?"

Erin leaned back and crossed her legs. "Alright, is this why you dragged me up here? So we can have another heart-to-heart about me moving back to Nashville and getting on with my life?"

"I'm just simply asking if you thought about it, that's all. I only wanted some seafood. No need to get all pissy about it."

Erin took a drink of her coffee and swallowed hard. "I *have* thought about it, but I haven't made a decision yet, okay?"

"I see. And what are you waiting for?" Her mother looked toward the man playing clarinet in the corner.

"Mom, why are you being so forceful about this? It seems like you've been laying it on pretty thick lately, almost like you have something on your mind. If you do, can you please just spill it already? I'm really not in the mood for bullshit right now."

Her mother's narrowed her eyes. "I told you, sweetheart, I just don't want you staying here—"

334

"Because of you. Yeah, I get it." She exhaled. "Ironically, that was the same line Jules gave me every time she brought it up."

Her mom popped another shrimp into her mouth and tilted her head to the side as if she had no clue what Erin was talking about.

"Did you and Jules have something going behind my back, Mom?"

Her mother laughed and swallowed. "Baby girl, Jules wasn't my type. I'm completely fine with the fact that *you're* a lesbian, but honey, I am totally hetero. Jules was cute and all, but really, I'm not into that."

Erin snorted and nearly spit out her coffee. "You know that's not what I meant."

Her mother smiled and leaned forward to pat her knee. "No, Jules and I did not have something going on behind your back," she reassured. "We just happened to agree on a few things, mainly that we just want you to be happy. In case you forgot, that whole drug thing was pretty scary for both of us."

Erin nodded. She knew her mom was right.

"Speaking of Jules, I got a call from Will the other night."

"Erin, honey, why are you still talking to him?"

"I just told you, *he* called me."

Her mother rolled her eyes. "And? What did he want this time?"

335

Erin eyed her mother carefully. She didn't want to give too much information about what Will had found until she was able to see it for herself.

"He found some things Jules wrote and he wants me to take a look to see if I can help him make sense of it. Something about letters she wrote to herself. I don't know, though. She never really talked to me about that stuff."

"Hmm. So, are you gonna take a look?"

Erin straightened her back and set her coffee back on the table. "Actually, I'm driving out there this afternoon."

Her mother's demeanor instantly changed. "You're doing what?"

"It's fine, Mom. He seemed upset by it. I really just wanna take a look."

"Oh, God, Erin, don't you see what's happening here? He's latching on to you because you remind him of Jules. This isn't healthy, honey. It's not going to help either of you move on."

"I thought we were here for Dad. Why are we even talking about this? I'm fine, Mom. I just need to know what Jules was up to, that's all." Erin sighed. "He doesn't want anything from me. We just…I don't know, we just understand each other. There's nothing more to it than that."

"Sweetie, please just listen to me and be careful." Erin's mother shook her head and pushed away her food, suddenly uninterested in eating. "He's emotional and so are you. If your father were here right now, there's no way in hell he'd

336

let you drive out there. But since I'm here and he's not, God knows I can't stand in your way."

Erin shook her head. "I get it. And I will be careful, I promise."

"Alright, then. Let's get out of here and stop at the cemetery to say 'hi' to your old man. I'm not that hungry anymore, and you haven't even touched your food, so I guess we'll take it home."

Erin stayed seated as her mother stood and reached for her cane.

"There is one more thing you should know."

"Okay?"

Erin looked up at her, uncrossed her legs, and slowly stood. "I decided not to renew my lease. I'm moving out of my apartment at the end of April."

"And just where are you moving to?" Her mother looked back, a presumptuous smirk spreading across her face.

"We'll see," Erin said. "We'll see."

Cold rain hit the windshield as Erin merged onto the freeway, and she turned up the radio as she approached the curve near the Marquette University Law Library. This was where it had happened, where a random car had lost control and slammed into Jules. Though she had seen them countless times since, Erin couldn't stop herself from looking at the deep black mark on the concrete partition. She wondered every time if it was a remnant from the accident. Trying to block it out, she turned the volume even higher. Sara Bareilles' voice filled the car and she laughed out loud at the irony. Jules had loved Sara Bareilles; as a result, Erin had added several of Sara's songs to her own set.

Singing along to the music, Erin tried to curb the nervousness tingling deep inside her stomach. She wasn't sure what to expect from this evening, and she wasn't sure if she was more nervous to see Will or meet Jillian. Besides, being in Jules' house again would definitely stir up emotions—she had lied to Will when she told him she didn't know the address. She had been there before, just once. It was early December, on a weekend when Will had taken Jillian out of town to visit his brother before the holidays. As usual, Jules stayed behind to work, and for the first time, she asked Erin to make the drive out to her house. It had been strange to see her in her own element and among her own things. She was laid back and casual, so unlike the on-the-go journalist she was in the city.

"God, how can you stand living this far out?" Erin asked. Jules added another log to the already blazing fire and joined Erin on the couch and propped her feet on the coffee table. The light from the flames danced across her face when she turned to Erin.

"It wasn't my idea," she said. "But other than the drive, I do actually like being away from the city. I don't have to worry about people talking to me about the paper. I can just be a normal working mom. Half the people out here don't even know what I do for a living. I like it that way."

338

"Oh, yes, I forgot—you're such a celebrity," Erin teased, turning toward Jules with a facetious smile.

Jules scoffed and leaned her head back. "I didn't mean it like that, but you'd be surprised how many people get pissed off when they don't like what I have to say. That's one thing I really hate about writing a column. My opinion doesn't matter anymore than anyone else's, but when it's in black and white, people tend to think I actually know what I'm talking about or that my ramblings actually matter."

"Then don't be so critical." Erin's hand slid toward Jules' fingers.

"I don't want to be critical," she replied softly. "I'd rather stick pins in my eyes than criticize someone's art, but unfortunately, that is exactly what my superiors like to see. They seem to think they created some sort of expert. But let me tell you, I'm anything but an expert on anything in life."

It was clear Jules was tired of the persona the paper had created for her. As they talked and watched the fire, Erin envisioned for the first time what it would really be like to have a future with Jules. Being alone with her in that big house made her realize just how much she wanted to share a life with her, and she was willing to give up almost anything to have it. But later, when they climbed the stairs toward the bedroom Jules shared with Will, Erin hesitated on the landing. A pair of men's slippers near the front door made her feel out of place, as if she were an imposter in this house. After all, this was the home Jules had built with her husband, and somehow she looked

339

different inside these four walls than she did in the outside world, or even in Erin's apartment in the city.

"What is it?" Jules turned back and realized Erin wasn't following her.

"Are you sure you want me up there? I mean, that's *your* bedroom."

Jules smiled, lowered her chin, and raised her eyebrows. "Um, pretty sure we've been in *your* bedroom a few times."

Erin shook her head and looked away. "That's different. You know it's different."

Jules came back down the stairs and sat on the bottom step. "Now you're going to feel weird about this, after all this time?"

"It's just different being here, Jules. All of a sudden I feel like I'm intruding or something."

Jules reached for Erin's hand and pulled her down beside her. "You're not intruding here anymore than you would be if we were at your apartment. I'm the guilty one here, not you. I asked you to come. I'm a willing participant in this whole thing. Besides, I don't know what you had in mind, but all I wanted to do was go to sleep and wake up with you in the morning." She smiled suggestively before continuing up the stairs.

The rain fell more steadily as Erin reached the exit and pulled off the interstate. When she turned her car in the direction

340

of Will's house, she remembered what it had been like to wake up with Jules. They had fallen asleep facing one another in her bed, under the warmth of Jules' heavy down comforter. Erin woke before dawn. Jules was illuminated by the dim moonlight that crept through the window. Her breaths were slow and her face was calm and peaceful, as if she were a million miles away. Her hair was spread over the pillow, but one long, dark piece swept down over her left cheek. Erin wondered if she would ever have the chance to wake up with her like this again. When the sun finally rose and the morning light inched across Jules' face, Erin couldn't stop herself from reaching out and brushing the hair from her cheek. Jules slowly opened her dark eyes, and Erin was struck with an unexpected and overwhelming surge of emotion. Out of nowhere tears, slipped down her cheeks.

"What are we doing, Jules? What are we gonna do about all of this?"

"I don't know," Jules said, sliding closer to Erin. Though they had done nothing but sleep and talk the night before, they shared an intimacy unlike anything Erin had ever experienced as the dim light seeped through the curtains that morning. Being so close to Jules throughout the night and into the morning had made Erin realize that there was no turning back now. She was completely in love with Jules, and she wanted nothing more than to spend the rest of her life beside her.

It had been so hard to leave on that cold, dreary morning. She wanted to transplant herself into Jules' life and

341

stay within those warm, safe walls—but she knew it was impossible. She glanced in the rearview mirror as she drove away. Jules stood on the front porch, leaning against a post and shivering in the frigid air. She wore a tortured expression, and Erin fought the urge to stop the car and go back to her. But she knew Will and Jillian would be home soon, and even if Jules did introduce her to them, it would be impossible to hide their emotions now. The stronger the feelings grew between them, the more important it became to keep their relationship secret, at least until Jules was ready to face the truth.

Now, turning down the familiar road leading to the house, Erin's heart sank and her palms sweat. When the house appeared, she instantly regretted making the trip. Her mom had been right. This was too emotional, for both her and Will. The rain fell harder as she turned into the driveway. When the car rolled to a stop, she sat with the engine still running and the wipers slapping back and forth. She debated whether to get out of the car. But, just when she was about to shift into reverse, Will opened the front door and stepped onto the porch. He shoved his hands deep into the pockets of his jeans and smiled. He stood beside the same post Jules had leaned against on that cold morning. His wavy, auburn hair was combed back and he was clean-shaven, unlike the last time she'd seen him. Knowing it was too late to drive away now, she switched off the ignition and opened the door.

"You made it. I wasn't sure if you changed your mind," Will said as she stepped onto the porch.

"Well, I'm not gonna lie, I thought about it," she said, trying to smile.

As they stepped inside, Erin was struck by the smell of vanilla. The house had the same familiar warmth, even though it was brighter than she remembered. She shivered, shaking off the cold. There were faint voices from the TV in the next room.

"Jillian's watching *SpongeBob*," Will said with a smile, but then he quickly looked away.

She nodded and unzipped her jacket.

"Here, let me take your coat." She slid it off her shoulders and handed it to him. He turned and hung it on the rack near the door, then nervously shoved his hands into his pockets. "Can I get you anything to drink?"

"Actually, I'm okay right now, thanks." It was the polite response, but she really wanted to ask for a drink to calm her nerves.

As she walked through the house, the familiar imposter feeling returned. The aroma of something cooking filled the air as they reached the kitchen. Steam rose from a pot on the stove, and a large cookbook was spread on the black granite countertop.

"Uh, I—I'm attempting to cook some kind of pasta dish." He stuttered as he moved toward the stove to remove the lid from the pot. "I hope you're hungry."

Erin was suddenly afraid to move. She hadn't expected him to cook for her.

"Look, Will, I—"

343

"Daddy, can I have something to drink?" A small voice came from behind her, and Erin turned to see Jillian standing in the doorway. She held her breath as the little girl looked back at her with big, questioning eyes. Her dark hair was pulled back into a long ponytail and she wore a blue sweater with black leggings and a bright pink tutu.

"Uh, yeah. Sure, honey." Will gestured toward Erin. "This is mommy's friend, Erin. Do you remember her?"

The little girl looked at him and then she shifted her glance toward Erin. "She's the one who gave me the scarf."

Will placed a hand on her shoulder and stole a look at Erin. "That's right, sweetie. She's the one."

Erin faked a smile and tried to mask her anxiety. She felt as though Jillian could see right through her, like she somehow knew Erin didn't belong here.

Will filled a cup with milk and handed it to her. "Are you gonna watch more *SpongeBob* before dinner?"

She looked inquisitively at Erin. "Can I show her my room?"

Will smiled and opened his mouth to speak, but Erin cut him off.

"I'd love to see your room. I mean, if that's okay with your dad?"

"Sure. After dinner, though, okay?" He looked back at Jillian. She smiled before setting the cup down and skipping away.

344

Will turned toward the stove and stirred the pot's boiling contents. "I'd offer you some wine, but I try not to keep alcohol in the house," he said coyly.

Erin scoffed. She felt more uneasy by the minute. "Um, you really didn't need to go to all this trouble on my account. I didn't realize you were gonna cook."

Will shrugged. When he turned toward her, his green eyes seemed so much clearer than they had when she saw him last.

"Well, don't get too excited," he replied. "I'm not a good cook. But I have to say, it's definitely one thing I did better than Jules."

Just the mention of her name made Erin momentarily catch her breath. She thought, *God, what the hell am I doing here?*

"Have a seat," he said, motioning toward the table near the patio doors. The icy rain pounded against the glass as the evening light began to fade. Will pulled some plates from the cupboard as Erin sat down.

"We'll take a look at her stuff after we eat," he said, opening the refrigerator. He removed a glass bowl filled with tossed lettuce and placed it on the table.

Erin nodded, but she was beginning to feel as if Will had staged the entire event just to get her out to the house.

Will glanced in her direction. "You okay?" He stopped what he was doing. "You look terrified."

"Will, I—I just don't get what's happening here. I thought you wanted me to help you try to make sense out of what Jules was writing, but now you did all this, and I'm feeling a little out of place right now."

He leaned forward and looked out at the rain, leaning on the back of a chair for support. "I know, it *is* weird. I swear I don't have a plan or anything, and I do want you to look at what she wrote. That *is* why I asked you to come." He shifted his eyes away from the window. "I just…I don't know. I'm so tired of the emptiness in this house, and no one really knows what that feels like. They think they do, and they look at you with those fucking pathetic stares, and it just makes you feel like you'll never get over it. You know?"

"Yeah, I know," she whispered.

"And besides, if Jules is watching this whole thing go down right now, she's probably shitting her pants, don't you think?" He smiled and moved toward the stove.

Will, Jillian, and Erin picked at their food as an awkward silence hung heavily in the air. Jillian occasionally looked up at Erin and then back down at her plate.

"Jilly, did you know Erin plays the guitar *and* the piano?" Will said, looking at his daughter.

Erin stopped chewing. She wondered how he knew she played piano.

"I play piano, too," Jillian exclaimed, her face lighting up. "We have a piano in the basement."

346

Erin swallowed hard. "Well, maybe you'll have to play for me." She looked at Will, but he didn't meet her eyes. She began to sweat. The rain pounded against the window like tiny shards of glass.

"Geez, it sounds like pure freezing rain out there," he said, wiping the corner of his mouth with a napkin. "The temperature must've dropped or something. I bet the roads are getting bad."

Feeling suddenly trapped, Erin lost her appetite. If it weren't for Jillian sitting across from her, she thought she might get up, walk out of the house, and never look back, icy roads or not.

"Daddy, I'm full. Can I be done?" Jillian looked up at him and held her stomach as if she might explode.

"Can you eat one more bite, kiddo, just one?" He pointed at her plate with his fork.

Erin imagined that this was exactly the type of evening Jules must have had every night when she was home, just the three of them interacting as if the outside world—and Erin herself—didn't exist.

Jillian groaned and took one more bite, chewing slowly, as if it might kill her. She swallowed and begrudgingly looked at Will.

"I'm *not* eating more," she whined. "Can I show her my room now?"

"Well, if Erin is—"

"I'd love to see your room, Jillian. Let's go check it out." Erin pushed her chair away from the table, but then glanced at Will. "Dinner was really good. Thank you."

"Sure. Glad you liked it," he said, collecting the plates.

"Can I at least help you clean up?"

Jillian tugged at her hand and moaned.

"No, it's okay," he said, nodding toward his daughter. "You better go or she'll just keep nagging until you do."

Erin followed Jillian through the hallway and noticed black-and-white family photos lining the wall leading up the stairs. There they were, Will, Jules, and Jillian, posed like the perfect family. She tried not to look at Jules' smiling face as she cuddled a laughing Jillian in her arms. Will stood beside them, a beaming smile stretched across his own face; his hands rested on Jules' shoulders. An instant wave of jealousy swept over her and she held her breath as Jillian leapt up the stairs. Erin tried to block out the image of Jules sitting on that bottom step and the sound of her voice repeating in her head. *I'm the guilty one here, not you. I asked you to come.*

Jillian raced ahead, turning in the opposite direction of the master bedroom. She skipped down the hall, pushed her bedroom door open, and waited for Erin before scampering inside. Reaching the top step, Erin glanced toward Will's bedroom and was glad she couldn't see the large, inviting bed where she had slept with Jules.

Dancing impatiently, Jillian tugged Erin's hand and pulled her inside the pink bedroom. It was cluttered and had

348

toys, books, dolls, and dresses scattered across the floor. The day bed was covered with stuffed animals, and she wondered how Jillian managed to squeeze in amongst them. She moved a few animals aside as Jillian bounce about the room.

"This is my favorite animal," she said. "He's a giraffe. His name is Safari." Jillian proudly handed Erin the animal, then reached for a tiara that was on a bookshelf shaped like a dollhouse. She placed it on Erin's head and then stepped back, giggling.

"Well, I feel pretty royal now," Erin smiled and adjusted the tiara. "Safari is pretty cool, and I really like his name." Her eyes landed on the photo of Jules that sat on the nightstand, then moved to the black scarf that was wrapped around the bedpost.

"Mommy named him. We got him at the zoo." Jillian snatched the animal back from Erin's hands and held it against her body.

"Ah, well, it's a good name. Your mom was a pretty smart lady." Jillian turned away and Erin couldn't stop herself from touching the scarf.

"Do you want that back?" Jillian asked when she noticed Erin touching it. "Daddy said I can have the things in Mommy's closet, so you can have that back if you want it."

Erin tried to smile. She could see so much of Jules in this little girl's eyes, mannerisms, and even the sound of her voice. "No, honey, you keep it. I want you to have it."

349

Jillian picked up a princess wand. "I'm gonna spin around and cast a spell on you."

Jillian spun like a marionette on strings, but Erin knew she had already been enchanted, spell or no spell. When Will appeared in the doorway, Jillian stopped turning and walked dizzily toward Erin, who caught her with both hands when she stumbled. They laughed, and though Jillian quickly wiggled out of her grasp, Erin didn't want to let her go.

"Alright, Bug, I need to steal Erin away for a little bit. You can play by yourself for a few minutes and then you can watch TV downstairs, okay?"

"Okay," she said, nonchalantly moving toward the Barbie dolls on her shelf.

Will led Erin to a room at the far end of the hall. He pushed the door open and flipped on the light. Erin stopped in the doorway, instantly struck by the intensity of Jules' office. Will circled the desk as Erin stared at the shelves, which were lined with books. Until now, she hadn't been face to face with many of Jules' personal belongings; here, in this room, she was bombarded by objects that reminded her of Jules.

Her eyes scanned the titles, and she was shocked Jules hadn't showed her this massive collection in December. She was drawn to copies of *To Kill a Mockingbird*, resting on the shelf, and she ran her fingers over the spines of *The Complete Poems of Emily Dickinson, Leaves of Grass,* and *The Poems of Robert Frost.*

350

On the shelf below was Jules' Virginia Woolf collection. She instinctively reached for the copy of *Orlando*. Pulling it from the shelf slowly, she brought it to her nose to breathe the musty smell that Jules loved so much. Jules hadn't lied. Her copy was much more tattered, but as Erin held it in her hands she couldn't stop herself from recalling all the nights when she and Jules had sat side by side in Erin's bed taking turns reading lines from the story. Erin knew she would never have been able to interpret the meaning of that novel without Jules. But now the story was imprinted inside her head, almost like a song she couldn't forget.

Will watched as Erin's facial expression shifted. "Do you know that one?"

"Uh—yeah. Jules said I should read it," she lied. "She thought I might like it."

He nodded as she slipped it back onto the shelf and then looked down at the large, black book lying on the desk. Erin moved closer and saw Jules' name scripted in gold letters across the front.

"This is the book the paper put together for me and Jillian," he said, shifting his gaze to Erin. "But the article about you is over there."

He pointed toward some papers that cluttered the desk and then reached for Jules' work bag. He pulled out her notebook and flipped through the pages. "And here's the letter I found. It's not very long, but I really feel like she was trying to say something. I just don't know what."

Erin apprehensively glanced down at it.

"I'll give you a little privacy," he said, moving toward the door. "Take your time. I'll be downstairs."

Erin sat in Jules' chair and glanced around the room. She rubbed her face and noticed the framed master's degree hanging on the wall beside a photo of her and a group of girlfriends. They all smiled and held what looked like margaritas. Jules' laptop was closed and still plugged in, and a chewed pencil lay beside the computer, along with a pair of reading glasses. It looked as if she had just taken them off five minutes ago. Jules' presence was everywhere in this room.

Erin's gaze shifted to the notebook and the papers beside it. She didn't know what to read first. Listening to the hard rain as it hit the roof, Erin picked up the notebook. The letter was written in Jules' scribbled handwriting. As she read the words, tears welled in her eyes.

Dear Jules,

A mirror is something that faithfully reflects or gives a true picture of something else. But you need to ask yourself, what is the true picture? And, how are you faithful?

Each mirror gives a different interpretation of what it represents. The mirror on your wall allows you to see what you want to see. It can make you beautiful, or at least it tries, or it can be your worst enemy when you can't look into your own eyes. It judges you because it knows the truth. But, it can also lie.

352

The window you stare into reflects a lighter version of your own image. The image is not fully visible, but it sees you, nonetheless. That window allows you to see yourself, but it also sees what's waiting on the other side. It transcends you to a side of yourself that only you know.

And then there is water. When you stare into the river, you see yourself as the distorted, rippled woman that you truly are. But the river preserves you because it understands you. If you dip your fingers into the water, you just might feel all the warmth and cold beneath the surface. That water is alive in you.

Love is like a mirror. It's a backward depiction of what really is. Others may see you as the opposite of what you truly are. Love is real, but, like the mirror, it can be translucent and it can shatter.

So what do you see when you stare into that mirror? Do you see fire? Do you see pain? Do you see two sides of a woman that used to be one? You, Jules, are the burning mirror that reflects the sun and destroys all that lies beneath. Whatever comes in contact with you will be reduced to ashes and left to smolder.

Until you can truly see yourself and become the image staring back at you, you will be like the river. You will absorb the distorted image of the world and reflect all you hold inside. When you finally speak the truth, your water will be set free, and then your depth will flow to the ocean and you will burn no more.

Erin brought her hand to her mouth and her eyes blurred as tears dripped onto the paper. This letter was something deeply personal, and she knew Jules never meant for anyone to see it, let alone her or Will. She knew this was Jules' way of describing her conflict over their affair and her sexuality. It was sad and beautiful, and it read more like poetry than a letter. Erin was sure there was only one person meant to understand all of its deep meaning—and that was Jules herself.

The rain lightened as Erin returned the letter to the desk and wiped the tears from her face before turning her attention to the black book. A nauseous tinge shifted through her stomach as she opened the cover and paged through the countless stories Jules had written. She glanced at photos of a younger, less serious Jules, and her fingers grazed over the photo that had accompanied her column in the paper each week. It was the first image Erin had ever seen of Jules—before they even met.

Setting the book aside, she picked up the article draft, its tattered pages marked in red ink. She was queasy as she read the headline and then saw a glossy image of herself lying on the desk where the papers had been. She instantly knew where the photo had come from. Her stomach convulsed as she read and the facts of her own life spilled across the page. It seemed as if she had explained every detail of her story to Jules during an official interview, but she hadn't. She had never even discussed some of the story's content with Jules. The article included everything from her father teaching her music before his death, her teaching career, and her move to Nashville—playing the clubs, her record deal, her sexuality and previous relationships, the alcohol and drugs, and her arrest. The article also covered her move back home to care for her mother. As her anger rose, she could hear the blood pumping through her head.

There was only one way Jules could have attained most of this information, and only one person who could have given her that photo, which had been taken in Nashville just over two years earlier. Her mother had lied. No else who could have offered such private details to Jules. Shocked, she slammed her fist on the desk, wanting to tear the pages to shreds. She looked around the room, which seemed smaller than it had earlier, and tried to slow her breathing.

"Why, Jules?" She whispered, hoping Will wasn't standing just outside the door. "Why did you do this—and why did she help you?"

Chapter Twenty-Four

Will glanced at the clock and realized Erin had been in Jules' office for well over an hour. He had expected her to be surprised and unnerved by what Jules had written, but now he wondered if having her come here had been the wrong decision. As he was about to check on her, another weather warning flashed across the TV screen.

"All southeastern Wisconsin counties are under a winter storm warning," the meteorologist said. "Freezing rain and high winds are causing havoc across the area and conditions are dangerous tonight, folks. If you can avoid it, I'd advise staying off the roads."

Will sighed and looked down at Jillian, who was asleep beside him. She was peacefully lost in her own little dream world, still wearing the pink tutu she'd insisted on wearing that morning. Lifting her from the couch, he winced from the familiar pain in his back and cradled her in his arms. From the top of the stairs, he could see the light shining from Jules' office down the hall, and for a brief second it felt like old times when she would work late and he would put their daughter to bed. He tucked Jillian in and slipped out of her bedroom, but hesitated in the hallway. Other than the sound of the icy rain hitting the roof, an uneasy silence seeped from every corner of the house. He wondered what was keeping Erin so long. He walked slowly toward the office and then softly knocked on the door before turning the knob.

He opened the door to Erin sitting in Jules' leather chair. Her eyes were red, as if she had been crying, but her face was white and almost void of emotion. She held Jules' reading glasses in her hands.

"Are you okay?" He asked, unsure if he should disturb her.

She seemed dazed when she looked up at him. "No, not really," she said, placing the glasses on the desk. "I really can't believe she did this."

"She was good at hiding things, apparently," he said as he leaned against the doorframe. "So, you really didn't know she was putting all that together?"

Erin blinked slowly and shook her head. "No, I didn't. I know she wanted to, but I made it clear every time she brought it up that I had put that part of my life behind me. I didn't want her to do this, and I can't believe she did it anyway. My mom had to have been helping her. There's no one else who could've told her some of those things, because I know I never did."

"Well, if it makes you feel any better, it's a really good story—probably one of her best." He stepped inside and shoved his hands into his pockets. "It's pretty honorable what you did, giving up on your career and coming home to take care of your mom like that. And the stuff about your dad—it's just a really good story."

"Yeah, a good story," she said, looking toward the pages lying on the desk. "But if she had asked me, she would've known it's only half of the truth."

Will stayed quiet as she looked up at him; her blue eyes suddenly seemed hollow.

"I was eleven when my dad died. My mom was an absolute mess, though she must've forgotten to mention that part to Jules. I got used to taking care of things, and taking care of her. But I get it now, and I get what she and Jules were doing."

"What do you mean?" Will stepped inside the room and sat down in the window seat behind Erin. She slowly turned the chair as he moved.

"I know my mom didn't want me to come home when she got sick, and she sure as hell didn't want me to move back in with her. That was the whole reason why I got my own apartment to begin with—because she didn't want me in that house."

The wind howled and the rain hit the window like pebbles being tossed against glass.

"Don't get me wrong. My mom loves me—I know she does, but she knew I'd drop everything to come home and take over. That's why she didn't tell me she was sick in the first place. She's stubborn that way. But that's what I got used to doing after my dad passed away—taking care of her."

"Well, that doesn't seem wrong to me. It sounds like you love her a lot," Will said. She looked away from him.

"Yeah," Erin said, "but she pushes me away now when things get hard, all out of guilt, because she wasn't there for me when I really needed it. We've never really gotten past it."

It was clear that Erin was struggling with something; she looked vulnerable and afraid, so unlike the tough and guarded woman Will had met at the bar.

"There were a few things I never told Jules, but considering it's mentioned here, I know my mom must have told her." Erin wiped her tears on the sleeve of her black sweater. "There were some things I just didn't want Jules to find out because I knew it would change things between us. It would make her look at me different, and I didn't want that. I didn't want her to feel sorry for me. And my mom knew how I felt about it, but apparently she did it anyway."

Will clasped his hands in front of him and shook his head. "Why would she do that?"

"Guilt. Maybe she thought this story would change something, or maybe she just wanted me to leave," she said, her voice cracking slightly. "And Jules, well—maybe this was what Jules wanted all along. A good story."

"Maybe they both just wanted you to realize how talented you are," Will said softly. Erin leaned back in the chair, as if she hadn't heard him. She momentarily closed her eyes and then opened them again. Her chest rose and fell before she spoke again. When she did, her voice was low, as if it took all

359

her breath just to say the words. "My mom was really lost after my dad died. She drank a lot, took pills, smoked weed—she just couldn't keep it together."

Will found himself wanting to reach out and comfort her as he listened, but he hesitated.

"She was at the bar a lot, so I learned how to take care of myself most of the time," Erin said. I made my own breakfast, lunch, and dinner. I walked to school, came home, did my homework, and played my guitar, all while she was out getting drunk or high. She managed to hold down a job for a while anyway, but pretty soon that ended, too. Everything that was normal when my dad was alive just vanished once he was gone. And his cancer went fast. I mean, he was diagnosed with lung cancer in April and he was gone by August."

Will nodded.

"And then, when I was fourteen, she met a guy—Mike Delvis."

He could tell by the way the name rolled off her tongue that she strongly disapproved of this relationship.

"He worked at the Harley plant and made good money, and pretty soon they were spending a lot of time together. Then he was sleeping over at our house all the time. I hated him from the start, the way he looked me up and down when she wasn't looking. He was a piece of shit who had her fooled, and I knew it. Everyone knew it…everyone but her."

Will held his breath.

"And then one night, when she was passed out, I was in my room doing my homework and Mike came in." Erin's voice cracked again and she swallowed hard. "He tried to be all sweet at first. He asked me what subject I was working on, but I could see him looking at me. He had that pathetic, disgusting look in his eyes that only perverts like him get."

She shook her head and took another breath. "And then he touched my leg and told me to relax, so I pushed him off and told him to get the fuck out of my room. Of course, that only pissed him off, so he slapped me with the back of his hand." A tear slipped down her cheek as she looked up at Will. "I'd never been hit like that before, and it was so hard and unexpected that I didn't even know what happened at first. But then he was all over me, pinning me down, kissing me, telling me how beautiful I was, and he was sorry for hitting me. His disgusting breath reeked of brandy, and there was nothing I could do. He was twice my size, and even though I screamed, my mom was so drunk she couldn't hear me—no one could."

"God, Erin, I'm so sorry." Will reached for her hand and gently squeezed her fingers, but she quickly pulled away and wiped her eyes again.

"Yeah, well, when it was over, he went back to her room and passed out. I ran to my aunt's house and my uncle, who was a cop at the time, went over there and beat the shit out of him. Then they hauled him away."

"At least he got what he deserved," Will said. Just the thought of someone touching Jillian that way made him clench his jaw.

"Yeah," Erin said. Turns out he had a long record and he seemed to particularly like minors. They gave him twenty-five years for second-degree sexual assault."

"And you never told Jules any of this?" Will was stunned, unsure of what else to say.

"No. Other than my family and the counselors I had to see for years, I never told anyone—not even Jules. That kind of information makes people see you differently, even when it's not your fault." She surveyed his face for a reaction.

"It took a long time for my mom and I to work things out. I lived with my aunt and uncle when she went to rehab and cleaned up her act. When she got out, she was different—almost like a sad, determined version of her old self. She went back to school and finished the nursing degree she started before my dad died. Then she got a good job and worked her ass off. I eventually came home, and slowly but surely, we started to heal. When I graduated from high school, she paid for me to go to college. When I finished, I moved back in with her and tried the whole teaching gig for a few years. But then she started getting weird again. She wanted me to talk about what happened and she wanted to know every detail of my life. We fought all the time. That's when I decided that music meant more to me than teaching, so I took off for Nashville and never really planned on coming back."

"And then your mom got sick?" Will looked down at the desk.

"Yeah, and then my mom got sick. I had already made a mess out of my own career, but then I came back home, took a half-assed job, and—guess what—your wife walked into the bar. Ain't life grand?"

Will tried to lighten the mood. "Yeah," he said. "It's the best. You know, for someone who was screwing my wife, you're really making it hard for me to dislike you. But I *am* sorry. I'm sorry for all of it. I honestly don't know what else to say."

"See? There you go," she said, pointing at Will. "You're looking at me differently."

"No. Well, maybe. But not in the way you think." He shifted nervously. "I understand now what Jules saw in you. I mean, please don't take that the wrong way. You're just...I don't know...real, I guess. God, is it hot in here? I could really use a drink right now."

Erin stood and touched Jules' glasses with her fingertips. "Yeah, and I'd *really* love to get high. Things were so much easier to bury when I could get high."

Will nodded. "I do have one question, though. If you didn't tell Jules, why did you tell me all this? We barely know each other."

Erin moved around the desk and headed toward the door. "I really don't know," she said. "I ruined your life, so I guess maybe I owe it to you to let you know what kind of person she was with."

"You didn't ruin my life," he said as they moved into the hallway. "Jules did that all on her own. But you know, I still have the best part of her."

Erin looked past him as they hesitated outside Jillian's bedroom door.

"Go ahead," he whispered. "You can peek in on her. It's okay." He gently opened the door.

Jillian was fast asleep and he watched as Erin looked her over, seeming completely enamored. She walked toward the bed, knelt, and gently moved the hair away from Jillian's face. When she stirred slightly, Erin backed away. Her eyes were glassy when she turned back and followed Will down the stairs.

"You're a good father, Will," she said as they reached the final step. "You remind me a lot of my dad. He was a really good man."

He hesitated by the front door. "I'm really sorry about your dad. I lost mine when I was young, but he was a complete asshole. I can't imagine what that must've been like for you."

"Well, I'm still here. I learned to live with it."

"Yeah, but it must've been hell. For my old man, I was just a mistake he made after coming home from the army. He knocked up a woman he never really loved and then stayed with her. I spent my whole life trying not to be like him, but then I actually became him for a long time."

When she reached for her coat, Will peered out the narrow window beside the front door and nervously shifted on his feet.

"I was seventeen when he died," Will said. "He got up on a random Wednesday morning, went to work, and then ran his truck into a tree on the way home, maybe on purpose. Who knows? But, as weird as it sounds, I was glad to be rid of the son-of-a-bitch."

Erin held her jacket and gave him a look that suggested she understood his torment. He was captivated by her eyes, but feeling suddenly guilty, he glanced out the window again.

"Uh…again, please don't take this the wrong way, Erin, but it's literally pure ice out there and the weather guys are telling people to stay off the roads. We have a spare bedroom downstairs. Would you like to spend the night? Maybe consider it payback for the night I spent at your place?"

Erin's face turned serious. "Will, I—no. No, I can't stay here."

"Honestly, I insist. It's a mess out there. I wouldn't feel right about you leaving. I don't have a great track record with people I know and car accidents."

Erin scoffed. "Jesus, that's not even funny."

"Tell me about it," he said. "But, really, I think you should stay. I wouldn't even suggest it if it wasn't so icy—I swear to God."

Erin looked out the window and then back at Will, considering his offer.

"I'm sure Jillian would love to have breakfast with you in the morning," he said with a smile.

She laughed and shook her head. "That's not fair, using your daughter as a way to convince me."

She returned her coat to the rack, and he was both relieved and nervous that she had decided to stay. She kept her eyes on the floor as they moved into the living room. Walking toward the couch, it was almost as if she knew where to go even without him guiding her.

Chapter Twenty-Five

The living room was warm and comfortable, just like it had been on the night when Erin was there with Jules. She took a seat on the couch and her eyes drifted around the room. Will stood before the fire, seeming suddenly lost in thought. Though part of her regretted telling him about the assault, she also felt an odd sense of relief in letting it out—finally.

There were so many times when she had wanted to tell Jules about it, times when it had been right there on the tip of her tongue. But the words never came. Jules would have taken that information and held onto it. Unable to erase the past and unable to fix Erin's pain, the knowledge of that event would have burned Jules to the core. At the same time, it would have explained so much about Erin's fight-or-flight defense whenever things became heated between them. But Erin never gave Jules the chance, and now she wondered just how much Jules had known—and for how long.

Erin wondered if everything that had happened between them was even real or if Jules had just been playing games. A slow, hot anger boiled inside of her as she imagined her mother spilling everything to Jules. She wanted to call her mother right then and hear a confession straight from her mouth.

But when Will turned and smiled, she became calm and oddly complacent. His green eyes locked on hers and she could tell he was as tired of the fight as she was. They were both exhausted from grief and the constant barrage of unanswered questions. There were so many things they both needed to hear from Jules and so much they would never understand.

And then she noticed the white, metallic urn resting on the mantle. Beside it was a black-and-white photo of Jules that Erin had never seen before. Her stomach twisted as she focused on it. Jules was resting on the end of a pier wearing a light-colored tank top and a worn pair of jeans with holes in both knees. Her feet were bare and she looked out at the water while leaning back on one arm and resting the other on her raised knee. Her dark, silky hair was blown back over her shoulder and the familiar, somber look that had become so prevalent in the days before she died was written all over her face.

"I took that picture last July," Will said. Erin's eyes snapped away from the photo. She hadn't noticed him watching her.

Last July, Erin thought. *The art museum, the rain...*

She looked at Jules' face and wondered if the picture had been taken following that afternoon in her apartment. After that incident, Jules had distanced herself from Erin because she was so afraid of taking their relationship any further. But Erin wondered now if Jules' distance had been because she was afraid of facing her sexuality or because she was she afraid of falling for the subject of her story.

368

"You're really quiet," Will said as he moved away from the fire and sat in the leather chair near the couch. "Are you okay?"

She glanced at the urn. "I guess I just wasn't prepared to see that."

"Yeah, I really need to figure out what to do with her. She was raised Catholic—strict Catholic, actually—but she wasn't really practicing anymore. Obviously." He smiled facetiously.

Erin smirked and looked away.

"So, what did you make of the letter? Did you read it?" The fire popped and crackled.

Erin sucked in her breath. "Yeah, I read it."

"And?"

"I don't know, Will. Jules was good at hiding her feelings. You of all people should know that."

"That's bullshit," he shot back. He stood and walked toward the fire. "You and I both know what that said."

Erin tried to read his expression. He stared into the fire, and she was suddenly confused.

"What do you think it means?"

He slowly turned toward Erin, keeping his eyes on the floor. Nervous, he sat on the hearth before running his fingers through his hair.

"You said you slept with her that day—on the day she died, right?"

Erin nodded. He clenched his hands and his knees shook slightly.

"Did she tell you when she slept with me last? Did you ever talk about stuff like that?"

Erin shook her head. "No, she didn't like to talk about that side of her life."

He rubbed his face and looked up at Erin. "The night before. She slept with me the night before, and she told me that no matter what happened, to always remember she was still here."

Erin stared at him, not knowing what to make of it.

"You don't see a pattern in that? In the letter and in that comment? You don't see it?"

She shook her head.

"I think it was a suicide note, Erin. It sure sounded like one to me."

"No. God, Will. I didn't see that at all." She was shocked. "Her death was an accident. There's no possible way she could've planned that."

"I know." His green eyes stared through her. "But what if that accident was just a fucked up coincidence? What if she really was planning to kill herself?"

Erin was shocked. She couldn't believe what she was hearing. "No, I don't believe that. Not for a second. She wouldn't do that—she had too much to live for. She would never do that to Jillian."

"Really?" He replied condescendingly. "Then what did you see from it?"

"I can't tell you what she was feeling, Will, but if there's one thing I knew about her, it's that she had a very, very hard time admitting that she was attracted to women."

"You mean, attracted to you?" His eyes were ice-cold for the first time since she stepped inside the house.

"It wasn't about me. That's what you don't understand, Will. It wasn't about *you*, either. She just couldn't stop it, and she couldn't look at herself because of it. That's what I read. I don't think she ever meant for anyone to see that letter. She was just trying to explain her feelings to herself, not anyone else. She hid her real feelings and her sexuality for most of her life, and I don't know if she was ever actually going to let that out, but she wouldn't kill herself over it. No way."

Will was angry. He ran his tongue over his teeth and sucked in his breath. "Is that why you like women? Because of what happened to you?"

Erin glared at him. She couldn't believe the question had rolled off his tongue so easily, as if her earlier confession had been meant for him to interpret.

"Fuck you," she seethed. She stood and turned toward the door.

"Shit. Wait, I'm sorry." He moved toward her. "I didn't mean that. I'm sorry—I'm so sorry. I just wonder if it was something I did, that's all I meant. Did I do this to her?"

"No, you didn't. She was who she was." Erin turned to face him. "And what happened to me has nothing to do with who I choose to love. I knew I was different even before that son-of-a-bitch took my virginity. I've had counselors and therapists tell me ever since then that my inability to form healthy, nurturing relationships stemmed from the moment he raped me. But that's bullshit. I just never found the right person—until Jules came along. I was born a lesbian. That's who I am. And Jules was born without seeing gender as a barrier for loving someone. Maybe she was gay and maybe she wasn't, but she definitely wasn't straight. As hard as it was for her to wrap her head around that, loving a person for *who* they are and not *what* they are is a hard and brave fucking thing. She felt like two people trapped in one body. I don't have to understand it and neither do you—but that's who she was. It wasn't what her dad did, it wasn't what *you* did. She fought off her true feelings long enough. But, God, you men sure do enjoy toying with female emotions and twisting reality, don't you? So fuck you, Will. You were lucky you had her as long as you did."

"You're right," he whispered. His shoulders sank. Erin had pierced him to the bone with her words.

"For what it's worth," Will said, "I *am* really sorry. I don't even know why I said that. Maybe we should call it a night before I fuck this up any worse. I'll take you downstairs to the spare bedroom."

"I'm fine right here. Actually, I don't think I can stay here." Her voice was cold.

372

"Erin, please. I'm sorry. Please don't drive in this mess. It's not safe."

"Fine, but I'm leaving first thing in the morning."

"Okay," he said, unable to meet her eyes. "I'll grab you some blankets. The bathroom is around the corner if you need it."

"Got it," she said, turning away. She stomped toward the bathroom, once again ignoring the family photos on the wall.

She stared into the bathroom mirror, trying to calm her nerves and regain her composure. She knew Will hadn't meant what he said about her assault, and she also couldn't believe his interpretation of that letter. Jules would never leave them that way—never. She may have been sad and confused, and trying to work through her feelings, but she wouldn't have left them that selfishly, even if she was writing that story behind Erin's back.

The house was dark and still when she emerged from the bathroom. The icy rain and wind continued to pound against the windows, and Erin reminded herself that leaving now would be foolish. She turned the corner and glanced into the living room. Will was gone, but he'd left a blanket, pillow, and pair of pajamas in a neat pile on the couch. She realized the pajamas must have been Jules'. She was surprised he would offer them to her, but she knew she couldn't bring herself to put them on— not here, not in Jules' house.

Will must have fed the fire when he came down since it blazed brighter than it had before. She took a seat on the couch

373

but then looked toward the stairs, wondering if she should apologize to Will. But Erin decided it was probably best to leave things alone. They were both in turmoil over the things Jules had done, and there was nothing either of them could say to take it all away. She pulled her knees to her chest and hugged them close to her body. She glanced at the urn on the mantle and, as Will had mentioned earlier, she wondered if Jules could see her now. Here, in her house, with her husband and daughter. What would she say if she knew?

She pulled Jules' pajama shirt close to her face and unfolded it. The faint, familiar smell of Jules' perfume engulfed her as she draped it across her knees and rested her head on the soft fabric. She didn't want to cry anymore and she didn't want to think anymore, but her body shook while she held that shirt in her hands and buried her face in its scent. The entire night had been surreal, and she knew she shouldn't have come. She hugged her knees and tried not to make a sound as she cried.

She was startled when Will gently touched her shoulder, and she gasped for air as he sat down beside her. Sobbing, she looked at him and saw her pain written on his face. He pulled her toward him, and when she tried to push him away, he wrapped his arms around her. She didn't want to give in to him, but the more she fought, the more he tried to hold her. Finally, she realized there was really no reason to fight him. She gave up and melted into him, allowing herself fall apart. They were silent as her tears saturated his shirt and he held her firmly, yet gently.

374

When she began to calm down, Erin wiped her face with her sleeve and pulled away. Will had been crying, too. He rested one hand on his knee and the other on the back of the couch. He smiled, as if trying to hide his own pain.

"You're so angry with her, Will, and you have every right to be. In some ways, I am too." Erin's voice was a whisper. "But I still love her, and I feel like I can't breathe without her. Nothing seems real to me without her—nothing."

"I know," he said softly. "I feel it, too. I wake up every day wishing she was still here. I *am* pissed off at her, and I don't understand her, but God, I miss her."

Something shifted between them as they stared at each other in the firelight.

Will looked away and lifted his hands to his face before returning his gaze to Erin. She froze when he leaned back and moved closer to her face. His breath was warm on her skin and she moved toward him, as if she wasn't in control of her own body. They both hesitated, afraid to move as their faces touched and their lips grazed. Erin's heart raced as Will caressed her cheek and then pressed his head to hers in the same gentle way Jules always had.

Unable to stop herself, Erin closed her eyes and kissed Will's lips. He exhaled and gently moved his hand to the back of her head, pulling her closer. The kiss deepened, as if all the turmoil and emotion from the last few months was seeping out. Soon they peeled off their clothes, letting them fall to the floor like all the tears they'd cried over Jules. Will's touch was gentle,

375

and Erin sighed as his lips touched her neck and he slowly leaned her back onto the couch. Will lifted his head and looked into Erin's eyes. As she stared back at him, her walls crumbled. Will and Erin studied each other's faces and he traced his fingers over her lips as she ran her fingers across his rough, unshaven face. She lifted her head and kissed his neck as he slowly moved his hand down her side, then slipped it behind her back before pushing himself forward. She tilted her head back and gasped. He buried his face in her hair, moving slowly and gently as his warm breath covered her skin.

She gripped him tighter as tears slipped down her cheeks. He was crying too. Will and Erin held each other tightly, as if they couldn't let go.

"Do you want me to stop?"

"No," she whispered, wiping a tear from his face with her fingertips.

As they moved together, Erin realized how sensual the moment was. Jules was the last person either of them had been with. She was unsure if it was the overwhelming emotion they both felt or if it was the release they both craved, but they fed on each other's movements and gave in to one another both physically and emotionally.

When it was over, they lay on the couch breathless and drained. The night's emotions had consumed them both, and Erin fought the urge to cry. She looked at the urn and tried to forget everything she and Will had done and said since she walked in the door that evening. She didn't want to think anymore. Will's breaths were slow and deep, as if he was asleep, so she rested her head on his chest and listened to his beating heart. Its steady rhythm reminded her that they were both still here—and they were still alive.

Chapter Twenty-Six

Will stirred as the soft morning light seeped through the curtains. The sound of the icy rain had stopped, replaced now by the gentle chirp of birds gathered around the feeder that Jules had placed just outside the window last summer. Erin's warm body was heavy on top of him; her slow and steady breathing signaled that she was still fast asleep. He didn't want to move or wake her, so he stared at the ceiling and tried to remember how long it had been since he and Jules woke up this way. It felt strange to hold someone else, but he couldn't stop himself from touching Erin's smooth skin or running his fingers through her soft hair. He understood now why Jules had fallen for her. She was beautiful, strong, and fragile all in the same package. He wanted to make love to her again, but then his eyes shifted to the photo of his wife on the mantle and a tinge of guilt crept up inside of him just as Erin began to stir.

She lifted her head, wiped her eyes, and rested her chin on his chest. He smiled, unable to look away from her blue eyes.

"Has anyone ever told you how gorgeous your eyes are?" He moved the hair away from her face and tucked it gently behind her ear, just like he had always done with Jules.

378

She looked away and rested her head on his chest. "Do you really want me to answer that question?"

He laughed softly. "Well, Jules always did have good taste."

Erin's body shook as she laughed.

"Daddy?" Jillian's voice suddenly called out from the top of the stairs and Will instinctively jumped up, nearly pushing Erin to the floor.

"Shit, I'm sorry," he whispered as they flung off the blanket and scrambled for their clothes.

"Daddy?" Jillian called out again, and he could tell she was coming out of his bedroom now.

"I'm downstairs, honey," he answered pulling on his pants as Erin quickly pulled her sweater over her head.

"Where in the hell are my pants?" She looked panicked by the sound of Jillian's feet coming down the stairs.

"Over there," Will pointed as she tossed him his shirt and he quickly slipped it on. He walked toward the stairs to distract his daughter as Erin finished dressing.

She buttoned her jeans and smoothed her hair just as Jillian appeared in the doorway holding her stuffed giraffe.

"Morning, sunshine," Will said enthusiastically as his heart thumped ferociously in his chest. "You're up really early."

"Why weren't you in your bed?" She looked over at Erin, who waved nervously from across the room.

"Well, sweetie, I got up really early and made my bed already before I came downstairs to talk to Erin."

"She stayed overnight?" She looked confused and eyed Erin suspiciously.

"Yeah, honey. See, there was an ice storm, and Erin lives in the city where Mommy worked. She stayed overnight because it was too dangerous for her to drive back home on the icy roads."

"Oh." Jillian lost interest. "Can we make pancakes now?"

"Absolutely," he exclaimed. He knew he was over-doing it with the enthusiasm, but Jillian didn't seem to notice. Instead she turned and headed toward the kitchen.

Once she was out of sight, he turned back toward Erin, who was folding the blanket that had covered them all night long.

"I'm so sorry," he said, moving toward her. Her lips curved into a smile, but there was a change in Erin's eyes. "Please, stay for breakfast."

"Sure," Erin mumbled. She lifted Jules' crumpled pajamas from the floor and began to fold them again.

Jillian chattered all through breakfast. She rambled about her best friend, Allison, and the dog Will promised they would get this summer. He watched as Erin smiled and drank in every word. She looked over at him occasionally, catching him staring, and then quickly shifted her eyes back to Jillian. He could tell she had regrets.

Erin was quiet as Jillian bounced off down the hallway after they finished eating, and Will began to sweat. "Are you okay?"

"I'm fine," Erin whispered as she helped him wash the dishes.

"Erin," he said, taking the towel from her hands. "Talk to me. Are you really okay? I swear, I didn't plan for—"

"I can't do this," she said, backing away from him. "I can't take her place here. I can't do this."

"No one is asking you to do that." Will reached for her hand and forced her to look at him. "What happened last night just happened. We didn't plan it, and it doesn't mean you're replacing anyone. We're both just lonely and we both loved her. Jules was my wife—no one can replace her."

"It was my fault," she mumbled, looking out the window toward the icy river. "It's my fault she's not here right now. If she hadn't been with me that day, she would've been home on time and she would be here right now."

"You don't know that," he said. He tried to pull her toward him, but she pushed away again.

"I should go," she muttered, turning away. "I need to get back."

"Erin—"

"No, Will, I need to get out of here. This is too much for me right now. I'm sorry, I really am, but I can't be here."

"Okay," he said, knowing there was nothing he could do to stop her.

381

"But," she said, "I really want a copy of the article. Can you do that for me? There are some things I need to find out."

"Of course," he replied, dropping the dish towel on the counter. "I can photocopy it. But about that article...there's something else I should probably tell you."

She turned to face him.

"I asked Jules' boss to run it, but they need your permission."

She blinked. "Why would you do that?"

"I don't know." He leaned against the counter and stared at the floor. "I guess because she believed in it, and she believed in you. I didn't understand what that meant until now, and I feel like I owe it to her."

"She believed in me?" Erin shook her head and glared back at him. "She was trying to get rid of me—that's what she was doing. That's what she and my mom were *both* doing. It had nothing to do with whether she believed in me or not, Will. She wanted me out of the picture and out of your life so she could go back to pretending."

"You don't know that," Will said. "We'll never know that." Erin turned away, but he continued to speak. "I think she loved you and she wanted you to remember what you're capable of. That's what I think."

"Says the guy who also thinks she wrote a suicide note," she shot back.

He was shocked by her sudden coldness. "I'll get you the copy."

He brushed past her and went up the stairs. She followed and watched from the doorway as he photocopied each page of the article, and then the photograph.

"Thanks," she said quietly, staring at the books lining Jules' shelves. Will handed her the copy but held firm to one end as she tried to pull it away. When she finally looked up, he let go.

"I'm sorry if you think last night was a mistake," Will said as Erin's eyes softened. "I loved my wife, but I don't think last night happened by accident. She brought us both here. Don't forget that."

He left her standing in the doorway and moved toward the stairs. But before his foot reached the top step he heard voices below. His heart sank when he descended and saw Jillian talking to Sarah, who had just come in from outside. She seemed annoyed while wiping her feet on the rug by the front door.

"Did you forget I was coming to get her today? She doesn't even look ready to go."

He glanced up the stairs. Erin was visible from below, standing in the doorway to Jules' office. "Uh, yeah. Crap. I totally forgot, Sarah. Where are you going again?"

"We're going shopping and to a movie. How could you forget? I just sent you a text yesterday to remind you."

"Yeah, Daddy. Aunt Sarah said she told you to put it on the calendar and you forgot. I have to get dressed really quick now."

Jillian rushed by him and bounded up the stairs, noticing Erin frozen like a statue in the doorway.

"Aunt Sarah, Mommy's friend Erin is here. She stayed overnight!" Jillian ran toward her bedroom.

Will clenched his eyes shut, but then quickly opened them. Sarah glared at him as if he had just committed an indescribable crime.

"So," he said. "I take it the roads are better since you drove all the way out here?" He ignored Jillian's comment.

"What the fuck is going on, Will?"

Sarah looked up at Erin as she slowly made her way down the stairs.

"Uh, well, Sarah, this is Erin," he nervously said. "And Erin, this is Jules' younger sister, Sarah."

Erin attempted to smile when she reached the bottom step and moved around them to grab her coat off the hook. Sarah continued to glare at Will before turning her dark eyes toward Erin.

"You're the Erin from her phone," she said. "You're the Erin from the video."

"Sarah, I can explain," he said as Erin slipped on her jacket.

"Can you tell Jillian I said goodbye?" Erin grabbed her purse and avoided Sarah's accusing eyes.

"Wait, no. Hold on, Erin." He stepped toward the door, attempting to block her.

"Yes, Sarah, this is the Erin from Jules' phone, and yes, they were having an affair."

He stared at Erin as her eyes lifted to meet his.

"She told me everything."

"Wow. Okay then. I guess it's really nice to meet you, Erin." Sarah shook her head and walked off down the hall.

"I'm sorry," Erin whispered. She grasped the doorknob, but Will placed his hand on the door to stop her from opening it.

"I can handle her, don't worry." He smiled slightly. "Can I call you, at least, just to make sure you're okay?"

"Yeah, sure." She looked up at him one last time. "Tell Jillian I said goodbye, okay?"

"Okay."

She slipped out the door without looking back. As Will closed it behind her, he gripped the knob and held his breath again.

"Sooo, let me get this straight. You're fucking her now, too?" Sarah's voice came from behind him, and he turned to find her staring him down as if she was a drill sergeant.

"I don't have to explain this to you," he said, moving past her and toward the kitchen.

"The hell you don't, Will," she said, following close on his heels. "She must be pretty good if you've *both* done her. Hell, maybe I should fuck her and find out for myself."

"Jesus, Sarah. It's not like that. Knock it off."

"Then how is it, Will? Explain it to me, please. I really wanna hear this. How the hell did you end up fucking the same woman that my sister was apparently also fucking? Is this some kind of twisted game?"

"Wow, Sarah. You think you have this whole thing figured out, don't you? Not that it matters to you, but how am I the bad guy here all of a sudden?" He turned back to face her. "Your sister was having an affair, not just a fun little fling. They were having a full-on affair and Jules loved her."

Sarah stared at him suddenly speechless.

"Yeah, I can't exactly explain that one to you, since I was acutely unaware of the fact that my wife enjoyed fucking women. But it's true—all of it."

"Even the cocaine?" Sarah pulled out a kitchen chair and sat down slowly, as if Will had taken her breath away.

"It wasn't hers—it was Erin's." He sat down across from her. "Jules was trying to get her to stop using, so she took it from her."

Sarah shook her head. "Now that part sounds like Jules."

"Yeah," he mumbled.

"But really? You slept with her Will? Why? Why would you do that?"

"It just happened. She came out here to read some things Jules wrote, and then the ice storm ended up being worse than expected, and —"

"And then you fucked her."

Will sighed as the guilt once again began to creep. "It wasn't like that."

"Jules hasn't even been gone two months, Will. Not even two months."

"She's been gone a hell of a lot longer than that, and we both know it," he snapped back. He stood and forcefully shoved his chair toward the table.

"Ready, Aunt Sarah?" Jillian scampered into the room dressed in purple leggings, an orange T-shirt, and the same pink tutu she'd worn the day before.

Sarah and Will couldn't help but laugh as they looked down at her smiling face.

"Sweetie," Sarah said, "let me help you pick out a different outfit." She glanced at Will.

He smiled as Sarah and Jillian disappeared up the stairs.

Later that afternoon, Will and Father Tom sat on a stone bench outside the brick building where they regularly attended AA meetings. Tom puffed his cigarette, holding Jules' letter in his fingers as his eyes moved over the page. He sighed when he finished, removing his reading glasses and handing the letter back to Will.

"What do you think?" Will shivered and zipped his jacket all the way up to his chin.

Tom dropped his cigarette on the sidewalk and ground it in to the concrete with his tennis shoe. "Well, it's pretty profound, and given everything you just told me, I do think she was struggling with some inner demons."

"Inner demons?" Will scoffed. "I guess, if that's what you wanna call them."

"What do you see when you look in the mirror, Will?" Tom asked, turning toward his friend.

"I see myself. I don't know what you mean." Will folded the letter and shoved it inside his pocket.

"Precisely," Tom responded. "But in that letter, Jules is talking about mirrors and reflections and how all of it is perceived. She isn't talking about suicide. She's talking about perception and understanding. She's talking about two sides of the same person, and how they look from different angles."

"I'm not following."

"She was having an affair—but not only was she having an affair, she was having an affair with someone of the same sex."

"Thanks for the recap, Father." Will's tone was sarcastic.

Tom laughed. "She talks about the judging eyes in the mirror, the backward depiction, and the translucent image—"

"Okay?"

"She's talking about herself, Will—not being able to face herself for what she did. She's talking about her own guilt."

"You really think so?"

"I can't be sure, but that would be my guess. I'd have to agree with your friend Erin. I don't think this letter is about suicide. Jules was far too smart for that. From an outsider looking in, I think she loved you both and she didn't have the faintest idea what to do about it."

Will looked down at the cracks in the concrete.

"Call it God, call it fate," Tom continued. "But sometimes the unknown has a funny way of stepping in and taking the decision out of our hands. Personally, I think that's what happened with Jules."

Will looked up again. "What do you mean?"

"She couldn't decide, so fate decided for her."

"So she died for her sins. Is that what you're telling me?"

Tom smiled and gently patted Will's knee. "Absolutely not. Jules knew what her sins were, and I think she confessed them pretty clearly in that letter. *That* was her confession to herself. I think her death was a random act of God, and because of that, she never had to decide what to do. Maybe that was her absolution."

Will took a deep breath and rubbed his stubbly face. "Maybe, maybe not. I guess we'll never know."

"Unfortunately, no, we won't know—at least, not in this life."

"Geez, who knew you were so philosophical?" Will smiled and jammed his hands into his pockets.

389

"Yeah, I gained that once I gave up the bottle. Funny the clarity you gain when you sober up." Tom pulled another cigarette from the pack. He lit it and a puff of smoke rose between them. "So, what have you decided to do with her ashes? Besides leaving them above your fireplace."

Will sighed and shook his head. "I still don't know. I mean, her mom wants me to entomb them, but I don't know. That doesn't make sense to me. It sorta defeats the purpose of cremation, if you ask me."

Tom took another long drag from the cigarette. "You know, if you read that letter again, I think your answer to that is right there, too."

Will thought about the words again. He hadn't seen it until Father Tom pointed him to it, but the answer was suddenly obvious. "The river? You think the river?"

Tom stood, exhaled the smoke, and put one hand into the pocket of his black pants. "They were her words, Will, but the decision has always been yours. It seems pretty clear to me, though."

"God damn," Will whispered. He stood and placed a hand on Tom's shoulder. "Thank you. You're a goddamn genius."

Tom dropped his cigarette and pointed a finger at Will. "Now, you see there? God had nothing to do with that one."

They laughed and stepped into the building as the regular crowd rolled in for the five o'clock meeting.

390

Chapter Twenty-Seven

Erin sat on her bed and stared at the photocopy of Jules' article. She read the words over and over, and though Jules' had painted Erin's life in a beautiful tapestry of words, Erin was still shattered. She wondered now if everything they'd experienced together was just Jules' selfish way of advancing her career. Writers were good liars; she had always known that to be true. Her logical side didn't want to believe that Jules could actually be that cunning, but her jaded side knew she might be.

Even through the hurt, Erin felt as if she'd betrayed Jules by sleeping with Will. Yet she found it hard to erase his face from her mind. The soft, gentle way he'd touched her was so sweet and unexpected. His arms had made her feel safe and protected, just as Jules' arms had done, but she knew they couldn't let anything like that happen between them again.

Her phone buzzed as she read the article again. It was another text from her mom, who had been trying to reach her all day. Erin didn't want to respond because was too angry to talk and needed time to figure out how to handle the situation. However, she couldn't ignore it because the message was more direct than the others had been: *You have ten minutes to answer me before I call the police and report you missing.*

Erin rolled her eyes. She picked up the phone and typed a reply. *I'm fine. Not feeling good. Been sleeping.*

Her mother answered immediately. *Oh, well, good to know you're not dead and you thought to call your mother. Rose and Joe will be here at six. Bring rolls...please.*

She groaned aloud. She dreaded the thought of going to the family's weekly Sunday dinner. Though she wasn't at all in the mood for small talk about the weather and college basketball, she knew it just might provide the perfect opportunity to confront her mother about spilling her secrets to Jules.

She glanced at the clock and realized she was supposed be to her mother's house in an hour. She knew she should shower, change her clothes, and head to the store for rolls, but instead she stared down at the piece of paper in her hands, unable to move. She closed her eyes and thought of Jules, but then felt Will's breath on her neck all over again. It had felt so good to wake up in his arms. She hadn't felt that in so long; Jules never stayed until morning, and Tina never felt that comforting. But had Will held her for the entire night, pulling her close and caressing her skin. Yet she wondered if he had been holding on to her or to Jules' memory. Either way, she convinced herself, it had been a mistake.

Erin swung her legs over the side of her bed and opened the nightstand drawer. Inside was an old wristwatch that

392

had belonged to her father, a birthday card he had given her on her eleventh birthday, the green-covered copy of *Orlando* from Jules, and the half-empty vial of cocaine. She picked up the card and remembered the day her father had given it to her. His cancer had just been confirmed, and though she was terrified, her dad had been optimistic—as usual. He had always been a glass-half-full kind of man. He had sat beside her on the couch, smiled, and handed her that simple envelope with his grease-stained hand. There was a picture of a smiling sun on the face of the card, along with the simple message, "Happy Birthday." When she opened it, a chipped black guitar pick had slipped out of the card before she read his words:

Erin,

You are my sunshine, my only sunshine. You are beautiful, you are perfect, and I love you more than you will ever know. Always remember that.

Love,

Dad

P.S. Keep practicing that C major chord. You'll get it, and I'm pretty sure this might help.

To most people, a tiny piece of plastic like that guitar pick wouldn't mean anything, but it meant everything to Erin. Her father was passing on his legacy and even at that young age, she knew what a precious gift that pick was. Her father always used it, and it was so worn on the edges that she sometimes wondered why it didn't break mid-song. Though he wasn't religious or superstitious, Erin's father had always told her that

393

sometimes it wasn't the guitar itself, or even the strings, that made the music sound right—sometimes it was all in the fingers and having the right pick. She didn't dare risk using that pick now, though; instead, it was tucked safely inside the case of the old Gibson guitar she used the most. That guitar, the chipped pick, an old wristwatch, and the card were the only things she had left of the only man she had ever loved.

She lay back on the bed and held the card tightly to her chest. Things had been so much easier when her father was alive. She wondered what a different person she might be now if he were still here. She knew her mother sometimes blamed herself for Erin's torment, and she knew how hard her mother tried to make up for what had happened with Mike, but all Erin wanted to do was forget.

She closed her eyes and remembered the week following her overdose. She had come home from her mom's house one late afternoon to find Jules sitting on the steps outside her apartment. Jules seemed leaden and tired, but she smiled sweetly as Erin made her way up the stairs toward her.

"What are you doing here?" Erin asked.

Jules rose to her feet, took off her sunglasses, and squinted in the sun. "I was in the neighborhood. I wanted to see how you were doing."

Erin eyed her suspiciously while slipping the key into the lock and turning the knob.

"Uh-huh," she said as Jules followed her in. "And when you realized I wasn't here, you just decided to loiter outside my door?"

Jules shrugged her shoulders. "I was supposed to do an interview on this side of town, but the guy cancelled at the last minute."

"You could've called. I would've come home sooner if I knew you were waiting." Jules didn't look at her.

"It's okay. I wasn't waiting long, and I needed a break anyway. I didn't mind."

"My mom called you, didn't she? She told you I was on my way home."

"Maybe."

Erin sighed. "I'm okay, Jules. Really. You don't need to check up on me. I took the week off from work, I've been seeing the doctor like I'm supposed to, and I'm spending every day with my mom and my aunt. I'm okay."

Jules' hands were shoved into the pockets of her tan pants. "I'm sorry I ran out on you. I should've listened to you. I should've taken the drugs away on that first day instead of doing them with you."

Erin leaned against the counter and watched Jules shift nervously.

"It wasn't your fault. This is the same thing I did in Tennessee. It was just a relapse, that's all. I knew I was playing with fire when I started doing it again, but I'm done now. I don't need it anymore. I shouldn't have called you and dragged you into all of it, or said all the shitty things I said to you. You were right—that wasn't me."

Jules stepped toward her. "I'm glad you called me. I can't stop thinking about what would've happened if you didn't."

Erin studied her face, but Jules still didn't look her in the eyes.

"Look at me, Jules." Erin reached for her hand, but Jules kept her eyes on the floor. "Why can't you look at me right now?"

"Because I feel responsible, and the last thing I ever wanted to do was hurt you. God, what you've been through—"

"Stop. Just stop." Erin pulled Jules close, and Jules wrapped her arms around Erin as if she might never see her again. "It wasn't your fault. I'm okay now."

Erin opened her eyes as the memory faded. She stared at the ceiling and zeroed in on Jules' words. *God, what you've been through.* Erin hadn't noticed that day, but Jules had acted differently; the way she held Erin was the way a mother holds a scared child when she wants to protect her from something. She must have known about Mike and the rape. It would've made perfect sense for her mother to spill while Erin was unconscious in the hospital.

Erin sat up and stuck her father's card back in the drawer. She then removed the book and brought it to her face. It smelled like the musty books on Jules' office shelf, and it made her long for Jules' touch all over again. She set it down quickly and then picked up the vial of cocaine. Rolling it between her hands, Erin tried to convince herself that she just needed to stand up, walk to the bathroom, and flush it down the toilet. But instead, she clenched her eyes shut and saw Mike Delvis' face as he pushed her down, placing his strong tattooed forearm over her neck, making it impossible for her to breathe as he ripped at her sweatpants with his large, calloused hands.

The pain of that moment had haunted her for twenty years, but she had never used it to excuse her actions. She was so angry at her mother for telling Jules because it only meant the situation robbed her of one more thing. As the anger boiled over, Erin grabbed the framed photo of her and Jules that she kept on her nightstand. She threw it across the room and it crashed against the oak door, the glass exploding into tiny shards.

She clutched the glass vial in her hand and paced back and forth. It was hard to breathe, as if the walls were closing in. She couldn't stop the images that flashed through her mind like snapshots in a slideshow—Mike coming into her room, his hand on her leg, the look on his face when he slapped her, the redness of his face as he held her down, the demented look in his eyes as he penetrated her. The pain she felt at that moment had left a permanent mark. She couldn't forget it, no matter how hard she tried. She had pushed those images and feelings down inside of herself for years, trying to forget, trying to pretend it had never happened, trying to love herself again so she could find the courage to love someone else.

But the cruel ache and stabbing pain of those memories rose again, and this time she couldn't stop them. It was as if Erin was fourteen years old and back in that bedroom all over again. She dropped to her knees and clasped her hands over her ears to drown out the screams in her head. All she had wanted that night was for someone to save her, for someone to hear her— but no one came. And now there was no one to save her tonight—not her father or her mother, not Jules and not Will. It was just her, again.

She pushed herself up from the floor and stared at the white powder behind the glass. She wiped the sweat and tears from her face, unscrewed the cap, and moved toward the bathroom. Jules wasn't there to stop her, and she had nothing left to lose. Erin flipped the light switch and turned the vial sideways to fill the cap, but then she caught a glimpse of her reflection in the mirror. Her eyes looked strange, as if they'd lost all color, and the only thing she could see staring back at her was the hollow, empty shell of a woman that looked nothing like her. She studied the vial in her hand and felt a new anger tugging at her subconscious. Without thinking, she turned on the faucet and watched the powder slip down the drain until there was nothing left. She dropped the vial in the trash and then splashed cold water against her face, letting the sting bring her back from the hot hands of a temptation she knew all too well. She stood up straight, reached for a towel, and looked in the mirror again. Slowly, the color returned to her face.

Rushing out of the bathroom, she snatched the photocopy of Jules' article from the bed and ignored the shattered glass on the floor. She slammed her apartment door and bounded down the stairs to her car. Speeding across town, she tried to remember what it was like to lay next to Jules. Even through her anger, she still wanted to feel the softness of Jules' lips on her skin and smell the sweetness in her perfume. She missed Jules' laugh, the way her shoulders shook, the way she bit her lip, the crease in her forehead when she was thinking, and the way her voice bent around the syllables of Erin's name. She wanted to understand why Jules had written those words and what she was planning to do with them. After all the times Erin had told Jules not to write that article, she couldn't believe Jules had done it anyway—and she needed to know why. Pulling up to her childhood home, Erin knew there was no way she would leave that house until she understood exactly what her mother and Jules had been doing.

Pushing through the door, Erin noticed her aunt and uncle seated at the table. Her mother stood between them, attempting to pour a glass of milk. They all stopped in mid-conversation to stare at her.

"Sweetie, are you alright? You're late. We were getting worried." Erin's mother set down the milk and limped toward her without using the cane.

Erin dropped the photocopy on the table and glared back at her. "Can you explain this to me?"

399

Her mother froze. She gripped the back of Joe's chair and looked at the crumpled paper. Her face instantly turned red.

"Tell me you have a good explanation for this, because I really want to hear it," Erin said, gritting her teeth. "I really want you to tell me that you and Jules weren't in on this together and that you didn't lie to me yesterday when I asked you that question straight out."

Joe and Rose exchanged glances and then looked down at the table. Her aunt clasped her hands in front of her and briefly closed her eyes, almost as if she were praying.

"If you calm down, I can explain it," her mother said, motioning for Erin to sit. "But you need to calm down first, honey."

"Mom, tell me you didn't tell her about Mike. Please tell me she didn't find out about that from you."

Her mother looked at the floor.

"You told her." Erin clenched her eyes shut and lifted a hand to her forehead. "Why? Why would you do that to me? I loved her, and you drove her away. You were pushing her away from me so I would leave again. Did you think that letting her write this would convince me to go back to Nashville and try again? Do you really want me gone *that* bad?"

"God, baby, no. That's not why she did this, and you do have what it takes. She knew that—we all do."

Her mother moved toward her, but Erin took a step back. She stopped short, glanced down at the article, and then raised her hand as if pleading for Erin to understand.

400

"You're missing part of that story, honey. There's more to that article. She wrote an introduction, and it wasn't about you—it was about her."

Erin shook her head. "What?"

"Yes, she asked me for the information to fill in the holes that she didn't know, and I gave her the picture. She was going to show you and tell you before they ran it, but her boss put on the brakes after she read the introduction. She wanted Jules to fully consider it, but Jules didn't want that. She was going to tell you, and let you read it first—all of it, I swear to God, but she wanted to be sure first."

"What are you talking about?" Erin looked into her the faces of her mother, aunt, and uncle, desperately trying to understand what each of them already knew.

"You need to read the introduction, honey. Then you'll understand."

Erin shook her head.

"It was about how difficult it had been to realize who she was and how your story inspired her to start living *her* truth. If she had it her way, this would have come out already, but her boss didn't want to run the introduction and Jules wouldn't let the story run without it. She was finally trying to tell the truth, honey—about all of it."

Erin's throat began to close, and she sank into the nearest chair. "She was coming out?"

Her mother sighed and then smiled slightly. She rounded the table and sat down beside her. "Yeah, baby, she was. In grand fucking fashion, too."

"Oh my God." Erin gasped, recalling the words Jules had said to Will on the night before she died. *I am still here. Whatever happens, just remember that.*

"But she still wanted me to leave, and you're pushing me to go. Why? And don't hand me this bullshit about reclaiming my career because you know I don't need that anymore, and I know there's something else you're not telling me."

"You need to tell her, Vi," her uncle said in a low, deliberate voice.

Erin's mother covered her face.

"Violet, tell her, or I will," Joe said, his voice more stern now, yet Erin's mother kept her face covered and shook her head.

"Tell me what?" Erin said, looking around the room at her relatives. "Dammit, someone say something."

"He's out, Erin—Mike is out of prison," her uncle said. Her mother uncovered her face and put a hand on Erin's knee.

"Wait, what?" Erin's stomach turned. He's supposed to be gone another five years."

"He made parole and he's back in the area because he has family here," her uncle said. "But he can't contact you, or your mother, or else he'll be in violation of his parole. I have

402

some contacts down at the station keeping tabs on him, so you don't have to worry."

"That's why I want you to go, honey," Erin's mother said, turning toward her. "I want you to be happy and play your music and not worry about me—all of that. But mostly, I just want you to be safe. I don't want you to walk into the 7 Eleven on Oklahoma Avenue one day and just randomly bump into him. I know what that would do to you, and I can't watch you fall apart like that again. I just can't."

Erin stared down at the table. She felt numb and had a hard time catching her breath, as if there was no oxygen in the room. "How long has he been out?"

"About four months," Joe replied.

"So Jules knew, too?" Her mother slowly nodded.

"Honey, she loved you. She loved you so much that she was willing to let you go so you could be safe and happy. That's all any of us want for you—you have to believe that."

Erin pushed her chair back from the table and stood up. "So, she was coming out, and then staying with Will so I would leave and go back to Nashville—all because of Mike Delvis?"

She was dizzy as she walked toward the door.

"Honey, where are you going? Please don't leave like this," her mother pleaded.

"I'm going home. I can't be here right now."

"Let me drive you, honey." Rose walked toward her. "You can tell me no, but that sure as shit isn't going to stop me. Joe will pick me up later. Vi, you sit your ass down."

403

Erin didn't have the strength to argue. She took one last look at her mother, who suddenly seemed older, as if she had aged ten years within the last ten minutes. "I love you, baby. I'm sorry."

Erin walked out the door.

Chapter Twenty-Eight

Will stood at the end of the pier. He stared at the water as large chunks of ice floated by. A week earlier, the river had been covered in a sheer layer of snow, but it had only taken a few mild days to break the shell and free the current. Though the air was chilly, he sun was warm on Will's face. He closed his eyes and listened to the calm breeze as it moved through the trees.

He longed for peace, and he knew he needed to make that accord not only with Jules, but also with his father. Maybe Will's father had never loved him, at least not the way Will needed him to, and maybe Jules hadn't either, but he needed to let it go. He needed to forgive his father for everything he hadn't been, and he needed to forgive Jules for everything she couldn't say. Two days earlier, Will had visited his father's grave for the first time in eleven years. After staring at that barren rock for what had seemed like hours, he said aloud the words that usually echoed inside his head.

"You were a mean, self-righteous son-of-a-bitch—and I'm not you. I'm not the reason you hated your life, and I'm not the reason you took your own life. I won't let your anger rule me anymore. I hope wherever you are, you hear me, you fucking bastard. We were better off without you. This is the last time I'll ever come here, so I hope you found your peace."

Will had felt lighter when he walked away, as if saying those words out loud meant his father would finally understand the cruel seed he had planted inside his son. He was done with anger.

After his talk with Father Tom, Will decided to spread Jules' ashes in the river behind their home. The house had been constructed strictly out of fear at a time when, consumed by losing her, his only goal was to win her back. But Jules never fully returned, and now he knew that she might not have even surrendered to him in the first place.

Jules had always been part of her surroundings, no matter where she was, so it only seemed logical to release her back to the thing she loved most about this place—the water. Though her mother and sister weren't completely on board with this plan, they both agreed it was the right thing to do after reading her letter. All he needed to do now was tell Erin. To find his peace with Jules, he needed Erin to be there, too.

Two weeks had passed since they'd spent the night together, but neither of them had reached out to the other. Though he didn't regret what they had done, he knew deep down that it was a mistake. He had started to dial her number several times but always stopped himself, thinking she would say something, anything, to break the silence between them if he waited long enough. But she didn't.

Jules would have turned forty-one the previous weekend. Though he and Jillian had baked a cake and celebrated in their own way, he'd found himself wishing Erin was there with them. She was the only person who could understand the deep, hollow feeling of missing Jules.

Looking out at the water he realized just how much things had changed in one year's time. He had planned a surprise party for Jules the previous year but, as usual, she'd figured out his plan. He was never good at keeping secrets from her, and she could read his face like an open book. So when he told her he had found a babysitter and she should pack a bag for the night, she called him out.

"I know about the party," she said with a coy smile on her face.

"I don't know what you're talking about," he said, dodging her eyes. "I just thought it would be fun to spend the night at a hotel in the city."

"Uh-huh. Nice try, honey, but you forget—I've spent years learning how to read people and getting them to answer questions. It really wasn't that hard to figure it out."

Will shook his head as she pecked him on the cheek and then walked up the stairs. He was disappointed that she had figured it out, but being who she was, she was gracious anyway. That night, he watched from across the room as she laughed and talked with friends. Her smile was bright and wide, and her eyes sparkled. When the night ended, she leaned on his arm in the hotel elevator, drunk and sleepy. She pulled him close and kissed his lips.

"Thank you," she whispered. "That was the best birthday of my life."

It was hard to believe that he was planning to spread her ashes and attempt to let her go just one year later. He knew he would never stop loving her, but he had to find a way to move on with his life. If he didn't, he would be trapped on this carousel of memories forever. If it weren't for Jillian, he thought he might just join Jules in that water, but for the sake of doing one thing right with his life, he knew he owed it to his daughter to be the father he'd never had.

Walking back toward the house, he thought about Erin and her father. Though her father left far too soon, he'd managed to instill his love of music in her, molding her into the gifted musician she was today. As his boots thumped along the pier's wood planks, he wondered what gift he would pass on to his own daughter. Jules had been the artistic one. She was the gifted writer and the philosophical thinker. Will only knew how to build things, and now he was struggling to find enough work to keep himself busy. Even today he was waiting for an email from a potential client. It was the job Ray had helped him to bid on. It was a dream opportunity to restore an historic Queen Anne Victorian on the other end of town. The owner had promised to answer him by email today.

Stepping back into the house, Will glanced at his watch and realized he had two hours before he needed to pick Jillian up from school. Though he'd checked his email less than an hour earlier, he couldn't resist looking one more time. He sighed, sat down at the kitchen table, and opened the laptop. His heart raced when he saw the client's name in his inbox. He opened the message, scanned it, and released the breath he didn't realize he'd been holding. She gave him the job—and the money was good. Finally, something was going his way.

Jules would have loved the old house. As his excitement rose, he realized that, for the first time since they met, she wouldn't be there to share his joy. He closed the message and leaned back in his chair, but then he noticed another unread email, this one from Jules' boss. Surprised, he leaned forward again and clicked on Nancy's message. As he read, the world began to spin. When he reached the end, he shook his head and then read it one more time.

Dear Will,

I'm writing to let you know that I received a call from Erin Quinn regarding the article you and I discussed. She corroborated the facts and gave permission for us to run the story, but only under the condition that we run the article in its entirety—including a personal introduction written by Jules. Initially, I had asked Jules to omit this introduction, but out of respect for her, I've decided to go ahead with Ms. Quinn's request.

However, before we put this in print, I think it's important that you read the introduction and give it your full consideration. I've attached it to this email. I should have mentioned this when we last spoke, but truthfully, this introduction was the real reason I was apprehensive about publishing this work. I knew that publishing it would change everything for Jules and would most likely alter her life and her career completely. What I didn't realize was just how important that would be for her, and how much she really needed it.

I wasn't truthful when I told you she wouldn't admit what happened between her and Erin. Though she never actually said it with her voice, she spelled it out in the best way she knew how—in her writing. She was a brave woman, and I am so honored to have known her. I'm very sorry for not including this sooner, and for not being the supportive boss (and friend) she needed. Though I know this won't be easy for you to read, I would sure feel better if you gave us your blessing to use it.

> *Thank you, and I wish you all the best,*
> *Nancy*

Will's hand shook as he clicked on the attachment. When the document opened, it looked like a thousand other columns Jules had written. As he read it and soaked in its meaning, however, he finally understood everything his wife had been hiding.

> *Facing the Mirror - by Jules Kanter*
> *Over the span of my sixteen-year career at this newspaper, I've met thousands of talented people who, at times,*

410

have moved me beyond words. Whether it was in the graceful steps of a dance or in the beauty of a voice hitting just the right note, these artists have had the ability to transcend me to a place where I truly believe anything is possible. After all, that is the job of an artist—to inspire. Inspiration can sometimes make us feel invincible. But without it, we might find ourselves staring into the mirror and repeating the age-old universal question, "Who am I?" Unfortunately for many of us, inspiration can be elusive. Many of us hide from it instead of allowing it to lead us, and in turn, we lose our sense of knowing who we really are—or who we are truly meant to be.

In the story to follow, I will introduce you to a woman who has undeniably changed my life. As cliché as it sounds, I knew there was something astounding about her on the night when I first heard her voice belting out a cover tune in an average bar on the east side of this city. I had no idea back then just how incredible her story would be or where it would inevitably take me in my own journey. But this woman is a true artist. She is as naturally gifted with a guitar as Hemingway was with a pen or Michelangelo was with a brush. You wouldn't know it by her smile, or even from her amusing, snarky banter, but the road to success for this artist has been paved with gaping potholes, detours and, yes, even a few wrong turns. Still, her talent far exceeds her shortcomings. And, despite all the realness this artist exudes, her ability to attain a certain level in her career was marred by an identity she was forced to deny. Though being gay doesn't show on her face, reduce her talent

411

or make her any less deserving, this remarkable woman was asked to either keep her sexuality a secret or lose the very thing she deserved—success.

The story of this talented Milwaukee native should remind us all that no matter who we are or what we do, we should never be afraid to stand up, speak the truth, or show our true colors. Though the costs are great at times, and we find ourselves forced to let go of what's considered safe, it's denial that hurts us so much more in the end.

With this in mind, it's time for me to speak my truth. For years, I have hidden deep inside my own skin—always denying and always hiding my true colors. It wasn't until I met this incredible artist that I finally found the courage to face the mirror and see myself for the very first time. I am a mother, a wife, a writer—and I am gay. The admission of my sexuality does not define me; it is simply one part that makes up the whole "me." I believe love is universal and, as in art, it comes in all forms. My greatest hope in making this confession is to inspire others who are like me to do the same. Perhaps then my daughter (and your children) can grow up in a world that embraces the beauty of diversity with pride and without the need to assign labels or reduce the beauty of human difference.

So thank you, Erin Quinn, for leading me toward my mirror. You helped me to see the world through clear eyes, and for the first time, I am capable of knowing love on a level I didn't believe possible. To all those who struggle in the same ways that I have, I encourage you to trust your art (whatever it

might be), live your inspiration and above all, always speak
your truth. As another great artist once said, "The truth will
make you free." And it does.

    Will leaned back in the chair and stared at the screen. This is what Jules had meant when she'd said those words to him on the night before she died. She was admitting who she was, and she knew the consequences would be heavy if this article ever ran. But what was she planning to do? Was she planning to force Nancy's hand and push for the story to run? Was she planning to end things with Erin, or was she planning to leave him and go to her? If she truly was gay, how could their marriage have ever survived? Before he could change his mind, he hit reply and typed *Run it*. He sent the message and closed the laptop, then wiped the sweat that had formed on his brow.

    He wanted to drink and he wanted to escape, but instead, he pulled his phone from his pocket and looked out at the water one more time before dialing Erin's number. He nervously tapped his fingers on the table as he waited for her to answer. He didn't know why, but all he wanted now was to hear her voice. It didn't matter how wrong it was, or why they had fallen toward each other in the first place. It was Jules who had built this secret. She was the one who had crafted this house of cards with her own two hands and then conveniently escaped before one quick breath blew it down. It had collapsed on all of them, pushing them into the same unorganized pile that had existed long before Jules learned how to stack the deck. There was no rebuilding that house now. They had all played their hand. There was nothing left to win—and nothing left to lose.

Chapter Twenty-Nine

Erin's phone buzzed as she pulled another glass from the cupboard and began wrapping it in newspaper. She didn't recognize the number and thought about ignoring it all together, but then she changed her mind and picked it up.

"Hello?" She held the phone between her cheek and shoulder while placing the wrapped glass into a box on the floor.

"Hey," Will said softly. "It's me."

She caught her breath at the sound of his voice. For the first time, he hadn't called her from Jules' phone.

"I know you probably don't want to talk to me, but I had to call you—"

She interrupted. "I never said I didn't want to talk to you, Will." She sank to the floor with her back against the cabinets. "I've just had a lot happen in the last couple weeks. I should've called you. I guess I just didn't really know what to say."

"Is everything okay? Are you okay?"

There was genuine concern in his voice, and the guilt crept up in her throat once again. She knew he deserved at least a phone call and an explanation for her silence.

"Well, honestly, no. I'm not okay, but I will be." She breathed into the phone. Though she had made up her mind to leave, telling him about her decision was harder than she'd expected. "I'm leaving, actually. I decided to go back to Tennessee."

He didn't respond.

There was no taking back what had happened between them, but Erin also knew there was no point in taking it any farther. Though part of her wanted to take refuge from her grief with Will, she knew that grief would fade in time, and once it did, they would be left with the same memories and unanswered questions. They would always wonder who Jules would have chosen.

"I can't stay here anymore, Will. There's just too many reasons for me to leave, and it's time to move on."

"Yeah, I know what you mean. But when? When are you leaving?"

She held her breath and closed her eyes. Once she'd learned the truth about Mike and made up her mind, she set her plan in motion before she had time to think it through or change her mind again.

"I ended the lease on my apartment a month early, so I need to be out of here by Thursday. I'll be staying with my mom for a few days, but then I'm leaving on Sunday morning."

Will sighed. "God, that's so soon."

"Yeah, I know."

"For what it's worth, Erin, you were right. Us sleeping together was a mistake. I get that now." His voice was soft. "But I want you to know, I don't regret it. For some weird reason, I think we both needed it."

"Yeah," she said, remembering the warmth of his arms wrapped around her. "And I *am* sorry, Will. I'm so sorry for getting in between you and Jules, and for not understanding what it was like from your side. She really did love you. I hope you know that."

"I do," he said. "I understand now how hard it was for her. I just wish she would've talked to me, or at least tried. I don't know what I would've said, but I wish she would've tried."

"I know. I wish she would've talked to me, too." Erin glanced at the boxes stacked around the room. Her apartment suddenly seemed foreign, so unlike the private sanctuary that had hidden her and Jules from the outside world.

"I, uh...I also want you to know I got an email from Jules' boss," Will said. "She mentioned that you called her?"

"Yeah, I did. About that, Will, there was more to that story—"

"I read it," he said, cutting her off. "I told her to run it."

Erin closed her eyes and held her breath. She hadn't been sure how Will would react to what Jules had written, but she wanted the truth to be told. Nancy had sent Erin an email with Jules' introduction. Erin had been standing behind the bar just before the start of her shift when she received it. She picked up her phone and clenched her eyes shut before reading it. There were no customers waiting and the bar was quiet, so she walked into the back alley and opened the email. As she read Jules' words, it seemed as if the world stopped moving, as if everything was waiting for her to react. She remembered how giddy Jules had been on that warm fall day when they walked along Atwater Beach—how Jules had said she felt good because she was writing something important, something meaningful. When she finished reading, she wondered if Jules had written the introduction that day.

Erin had been so wrong to think Jules wanted to forget about her and go back to her old life. The only thing Erin didn't understand was why Jules had been secretive about the article and its introduction.

"Are you still there?" Will asked.

Erin took a breath, thankful he had agreed to let Nancy run the introduction. "Yeah, I'm here," she said.

"Like I said, I get it now." His voice was somber.

"Thank you," she said, her eyes filling with tears. "She never meant to hurt you, Will."

"I know. I'm trying to believe that this wasn't about me, but it still hurts," he said. "And here's one more thing…" His voice trailed off as if he was trying to catch his breath.

"Okay?"

"I finally decided what to do with her ashes." Will paused and took a deep breath before continuing. "I'm going to let her go in the river. Her parents are flying in this weekend, and I'd really like you to be there. We were planning on Sunday morning. I know you said you're leaving, but is there any possible way you can make it?"

"The river," she said. She closed her eyes and leaned her head against the hard surface of the cabinet behind her.

"Yeah, just like she said in the letter."

"I'll be there." Erin wiped her face and tried to hold back her tears.

"Okay. We'll be down there at ten, on the pier behind the house."

"Okay. I'll see you then." Her voice shook and she swallowed hard.

"See you then," he said and then hung up.

She swallowed and wiped her face before setting the phone on the floor. Feeling overwhelmed, she looked around the room. So much had happened here, and though the past year had seemed so dark and cold, part of her was sad to leave it behind. There were so many memories of Jules here. From the early days when they first began spending time together while sitting on the back deck to the final days when they lay silently entangled in Erin's bed afraid to let go, this apartment would always hold residual memories of everything they had once been.

Erin looked toward the front door and remembered that warm spring night when Jules had stepped inside for the first time. They'd been drinking and she'd tripped on the same rug she stumbled on when she was here last. That first night, Jules laughed after she stumbled and innocently reached to steady herself against Erin's arm. Though Jules didn't know it then, it was those small gestures that made Erin realize they were something other than just friends.

Erin had kissed Jules for the first time in this kitchen, and she had broken down her walls in that bedroom. They had laughed together, cried together, and confessed their feelings for one another all within the confines of these walls. But, when Jules wasn't there, Erin had also spent so many nights alone in her bed with the burning ache of just wanting Jules beside her. Later, Erin had torn Jules to shreds with her words while fighting withdrawal from cocaine and antidepressants. But still, Jules always came back. Even when Jules had countless other places she should be and more important things she needed to do, she was always with Erin. If the walls of this old house could talk, Erin knew their story would only be one of many—but it was also one like no other.

Erin stood up from the floor, remembering something Jules had said late one night. It was after one of the first times when Erin had played an original song for Jules. Knowing how gifted Jules was with words, Erin had been terrified of how amateur her lyrics might seem. When she finished, Jules was quiet. She slowly exhaled and fixated on Erin's face with her deep, dark eyes. Jules lay on the bed, her head resting on her hand, and just when Erin had thought that playing the song had been a huge mistake, Jules smiled sweetly and moved toward her.

"You are such an artist," she whispered. She leaned in close and grazed Erin's face with her fingertips. "Talent is talent, but artistry is the result of real experience. Artists always crave knowledge of the unknown—that's why they keep searching, and that's why they feel more than most people." She took Erin's hands into her own, tracing Erin's skin with her fingers. "Artists like you seek out things that cowards like me hide from. Promise me you'll never hide, Erin. And please, don't ever stop reaching for the things you want. If you do, the world will miss out on something really fucking amazing."

No one had ever understood her the way Jules did. Erin closed her eyes and remembered the first time they had locked eyes, when she was singing on stage nearly a year ago. Erin had known from that first glance that Jules was something different—s something good.

"You were always the real artist, Jules," she said aloud. She took a deep breath and looked around the room before continuing to pack. It wasn't long before she heard heavy footsteps on the stairs. Seconds later, her aunt and two of her cousins moved through the door, bickering as usual.

"Hey, sweetie," Rose said, approached Erin with a wide smile and outstretched arms. "These two bozos brought the truck for the couch and anything else you need to get out."

"Damn, Erin," her younger cousin said as he flopped down on the couch and swooped his bangs out of his eyes. "This thing is gonna look sweet in my apartment. You didn't tell me it was this nice. I almost don't want my dumbass roommates sitting on it."

Erin laughed and lifted the box of glasses from the floor.

"Well, you bought it, Timmy. It's your problem now."

"Man, I bet this couch has some good stories, hey?" He raised his eyebrows suggestively. Erin laughed, but her aunt shot a dirty look in his direction.

"You know, I did read a lot of books this year, kid," she said. "And my favorite place to read was right there where you're sitting. I'm sure the guys will love that story."

"Yeah, if I can tell them you were naked," he said. His brother tossed a pillow from across the room, smacking him directly in the face.

"What, Joe? Like your friends don't think she's hot? Yeah, right." Timmy was joking, but his brother scoffed and glanced nervously at Erin.

"Boys, get your asses going. We don't have all day," Rose said. They stood, lifted the couch, and stumbled across the room before clumsily making their way toward the door. Rose rolled her eyes as they attempted to maneuver it down the stairs. "Good God, be careful! The last thing I need is to rush one of you to the damn hospital."

Erin smiled and then cringed.

"How're you doing, kiddo?" Rose asked. She pulled a kitchen chair out from the table and plopped into it while

422

waving her hand in front of her face as if she were having a hot flash.

"I'm okay," Erin said as she opened another cupboard and began removing plates. "It seems kinda weird leaving again, but I'm doing okay. It'll be good to get back."

"Yeah, we sure do hate to see you go. But as your mother always says, you never really did belong here."

"She actually said that?" Erin stopped what she was doing and eyed her aunt.

"Well, honey, she didn't mean it in a bad way. She just knew you were always cut out for more, that's all."

"Yeah," Erin scoffed. "That's usually her guilt talking."

Rose shook her head, pursed her lips, and brushed her fingers across the tabletop.

"Erin, I know you don't like to talk about everything that happened, but your mother does harbor a whole lot of guilt over all of that. We were all pissed off at her, and disappointed in her for not keeping her shit together, but no one could possibly punish her any more than she punishes herself."

Erin looked at the floor. Rose had taken her in after that awful night, and she had been the one who comforted Erin and stayed with her when she was too afraid to sleep alone. And then, when she had driven Erin home two weeks earlier, she had swept the shattered glass from the floor and stayed with Erin all night. Even though she had four children of her own, Rose had always been a mother to Erin, too.

"She knows what she did to you, but she also loves you very much," Rose continued. "Watching you drive away is going to kill her."

"Then why is she letting me go?" Erin lifted her hands and stared at her aunt. "I want to be here for her."

"Because, sweetie, you need to make your own way in this world. You two cannot keep bouncing off each other over things that happened in the past. Yeah, she messed up when your father died. She messed up bad by bringing that pathetic excuse of a man into your lives. But she wasn't the one who committed that crime—he was."

"I've never blamed her for that, Rose, never."

"Yes you have, Erin." Rose nodded. "You've always blamed her for not seeing who he was and for not saving you from him, but then you feel guilty for blaming her, and she feels guilty because you feel guilty. It's a vicious cycle and you need to let it go. Both of you do."

Erin sighed and took a seat across from her aunt. "Can you promise me one thing?"

"Anything, honey. Anything."

"Can you promise me if she gets any worse, or if anything happens—?"

"I will call you, you have my word. You don't even have to ask." She reached out and tightly clutched Erin's hands. "Don't forget, I was the one who got you back here this time. Trust me, she hasn't let me forget it."

424

Erin smiled and tightened her grip on her aunt's hands. "Thank you for always being there for me, Rose. You've always been my safe harbor. I mean that."

Her aunt's face lit up as her sons walked through the door. "And you've always been my grateful child, unlike the four other spoiled brats I managed to raise."

Three days later, Erin stood in the empty living room and took one last look around. She had been a different person when she stepped foot in this apartment for the first time. She had been angry with her mother and missing Nashville like crazy, but she also knew that staying in Milwaukee was the right thing to do. That had been two months before she met Jules. Now she was almost scared to leave, and she wished Jules was there to keep nudging her forward, the way she always had.

The familiar thump of the morning newspaper hitting the bottom step made her turn toward the door. Holding the doorknob, she held her breath and closed her eyes. Leaving the room would make everything seem final. Tonight was her final set and shift at the bar, and then on Sunday she would say goodbye to Jules for the last time before heading back to the life she'd known before any of this had become her reality. So much had happened, and so quickly, but it was time to let it go. Erin lifted her head, took one last look at the empty room, and then stepped outside. She closed the door behind her and then took a deep breath before locking it and descending the stairs. She picked up the *Journal Sentinel*, which was lying on the sidewalk

425

in its usual place, and dropped the key in her landlord's mailbox. Once inside her car, she looked back at the house and wondered about the people who might occupy that small upstairs apartment next. They would have no idea how profound her time there had been.

As she was just about to start the engine, she caught a glimpse of the newspaper lying on the passenger seat. The banner in the top right-hand corner of the front page displayed a small picture of Jules. It was a lead-in to her article inside. In bold black letters, it said, "Facing the Mirror – with commentary by Jules Kanter."

Erin's heart leapt as she unrolled the paper and turned the pages. And then, there was Jules again, smiling at her with those beautiful eyes. The photo that appeared with this column was different than the one the paper usually ran. It was a stunning black-and-white masterpiece. Jules stood in front of a white wall looking casual in a white blouse and worn-in boyfriend jeans. One side of her shirt was casually untucked and her right hand was shoved in her pocket in that sexy, childish way that had always driven Erin crazy. But her face was the most stunning part of this image—it lit up in a way that took Erin's breath away. It looked as if she had just burst out in a loud, cheerful laugh and the expression had been captured it in the split second before it was gone. Even in the stillness of the image, Erin could almost hear that laugh.

Jules' words and her confession were all there, followed by Erin's story. She had asked Nancy to modify a few

426

details; mainly that she was moving back to Tennessee to pursue music again in some form, but with a better understanding of who she was because of everything she had endured in the past year. Music meant something different to her now, and because of Jules, she wanted to find a way to bridge her music and her teaching ability. An infectious smile spread across Erin's face as she read the words. It was all there, every word—and their secret was finally out.

Later that night, she played her final set at the bar to a full house. She performed every song that reminded her of Jules, along with four original songs that Jules had helped her to write. With her mother, aunt, uncle, cousins, and friends looking on, she thanked the crowd for embracing her music. She raised a glass and toasted Jules one final time before stepping off the tiny stage and closing that chapter of her life. With tears and hugs, she said goodbye to her work family and then drove back to her childhood home.

Lying in bed that night, before she let the memories of this house creep into her head—both good and bad—she thought of Will and Jillian. She imagined her own father standing in the doorway with the old Gibson in his hands and a wide grin stretched across his face.

"You're gonna be great, kiddo," she imagined him saying. "Just keep playing."

On Sunday morning, as Erin placed the last bag in her car's backseat, the ache of leaving began to set in. Her mother limped from the house and walked toward her. She tried to smile, but Erin knew she was faking it. This was the moment they had both been dreading. Though there had been so much damage and wreckage between them, Erin's mother was the only woman alive who truly understood her now. Rose was right. It was time to stop blaming each other and finally let go of the past.

"You all done?" Her mother asked, leaning on her cane, just as Rose pulled up to the curb. The brakes squealed slightly as the car rolled to a stop.

"Yeah, that was the last thing," Erin said, trying to choke back the fear that had kept her awake most of the night.

Rose approached them slowly and then slipped an arm around her sister.

"Erin," her mother said, "you call me when you get tired, or when you stop to pee, or even if you just feel like telling me to go fuck myself. You call me, okay?"

Erin laughed, but her eyes blurred. She reached for her mother and then held her tightly. "I will call you, I promise. Please call me if you need me. Please don't shut me out," she said. "I love you, Mom. I love you so much."

Her mother pulled away and then rested a hand on Erin's cheek. "You are your own woman. You are the strongest person I have ever known and that had *nothing* to do with me. This place is part of your past, but it's not part of your future. That's why you have to go, and that's why I'm making you go. But this isn't goodbye. You'll only be eight hours away, so don't say that to me, okay?"

428

"Okay," she whispered.

"I love you, beautiful girl," her mother said before turning back toward the house. "I'm not going to watch you drive away, if that's okay with you."

Erin nodded and Rose leaned forward to hold her tightly in that comforting, close hug Erin had learned to depend on. "I will take care of her, I promise you, honey," Rose whispered before kissing Erin's cheek. "Go live *your* life—on your terms."

Erin tried to hold back the tears, but it was no use. "I love you, Rose. Please make sure she's okay, and don't let her lie to me. Please."

"I won't, honey. I won't," she said, pulling away. "Now go before you change your mind or that crazy woman comes out here and begs you to stay."

"She'd never do that." Erin laughed.

"Yeah, but it was nice thought anyway," Rose said with a smile, wiping her cheek.

Once behind the wheel, Erin took a deep breath and slowly backed out of the driveway. She waved to Rose and took one last look toward the house. Her mother stood in the front window. She had decided to watch after all, tears streaming down her face she blew Erin a kiss. Though part of her wanted to stop and run back to her mother, Erin smiled, blew a kiss in return, and drove away. She stopped at the end of the street and looked in the rearview mirror. That quiet street appeared as it always had. A woman walked her dog on the sidewalk beside

429

her, as if it was just a regular day, and Erin knew life here would continue on. It wouldn't be her last time in Milwaukee or at her mother's house, but leaving felt different this time.

She shifted her eyes to the road ahead. There was still one thing she needed to do before she could leave her guilt behind.

Chapter Thirty

Jillian squirmed in her dress and poked a stick into the river using small, circular motions, causing the water to ripple and flow away. She looked at her father and smiled. She wouldn't understand the profound importance of this moment, and she might not even remember it in years to come, but Will smiled back and took her hand to lead her down the pier toward the water's edge.

Earlier in the day he had shown her the latest newspaper with the story Jules had written. Even though she was too young to understand the words, she had sat on her father's lap as they looked at the picture of Jules for a long while, soaking in her silent laugh before placing the article inside of the black book and closing the cover. Someday soon, and in the blink of an eye, Will knew Jillian would be old enough to read the stories Jules had written, and she would know the real woman her mother had been. But regardless of what those words said, or how Jillian chose to interpret them, he hoped their daughter would understand that out of all the things Jules had done in her life, having Jillian had been her greatest victory of all.

431

Standing side by side, Will and Jillian watched the dark, flowing water. Holding Jules' urn beneath his arm, Will could almost feel her there with them. It was a warm, calm, and pristine day—the perfect day to say goodbye. He knew this was what his wife would have wanted. Though he would never truly let her go, he knew now that release was what she had needed all along. Just like he needed to let go of his anger, Jules needed release from the lies she'd created to hide who she really was.

As a warm breeze circled around him, Will heard footsteps and felt vibrations in the pier's wooden beams. He turned to see Jules' mother, stepfather, and sister walking toward him. He smiled dolefully as they took turns wordlessly embracing him. There was nothing they needed to say to each other now. He had given them a copy of Jules' letter, and though they would never really understand its meaning, they all felt the impact of her words.

Just as Will glanced at his watch, Erin appeared from behind the house and walked toward their gathering. She waved and her long auburn hair blew softly over her shoulder. Jules' mother sighed. Accepting her daughter's relationship with Erin had not come easily to her, but as Erin stepped onto the pier, Sarah took her mother's hand. "She loved her, mom."

Jules' mother looked away as Will moved toward Erin. But then he hesitated, unsure if he should embrace her. She smiled sweetly and reached for him. He held her close as the scent of her perfume surrounded him, and he couldn't help but think of Jules.

432

"Erin!" Jillian shouted, bounding toward her.

"Hey there, pretty girl. I'm so happy to see you! Gosh, I think you got taller."

Will smiled, but then cleared his throat. "Erin, I know you've already met Jules' sister, Sarah, but this is her mother, Deb, and her stepfather, Bill."

Jules' mother eyed Erin carefully and then apprehensively extended her hand.

"It's really nice to meet you." Erin shook Deb's hand and smiled with her head tilted slightly downward.

"It's nice to meet you, too," Deb replied, looking Erin in the eyes. Will could see the tension beginning to disappear from his mother-in-law's shoulders. He knew exactly what she was feeling. Erin had the same impact on him when he woke up hung over in her apartment so many nights ago.

"I know technically we've already met, but I'm Jules' sister," Sarah said, reaching out to shake Erin's hand. "I wasn't very nice to you the last time we met, and I'm really sorry for that."

"It's okay," Erin said, the corner of her mouth rising slightly. "I can't say we met under the best circumstances. But, wow, you look so much like Jules."

Sarah laughed. "So I've been told."

"Well, okay," Will said. "We're all here, so I suppose we should get this show on the road." He lowered his head and repositioned the urn under his arm. He took Jillian's hand and led her to the edge of the pier, where he stopped and looked out across the water. He sucked in his breath.

"Jules loved all of you," he said, turning back to Erin and Jules' family. His eyes drifted across each of their faces as he twisted the cover of the urn. "She was never an easy woman to understand, but we loved her anyway."

Deb wiped a tear from her cheek as Will knelt beside Jillian and looked into her sweet, dark eyes. The water gently lapped against the pier as Sarah pulled Jules' letter from her pocket. She stood shoulder-to-shoulder with Erin and read the words out loud as Will tipped the urn and the ashes slid into the water. White dust rose in the air and quickly disappeared. The river consumed the ashes almost instantly. It seemed as if Jules had always meant been to mix with the water flowing off toward a place where they couldn't follow it.

Will's throat tightened as Jillian took in the moment with pure innocence. She was Jules' true legacy. Though he felt the heavy responsibility of teaching Jillian to be the woman Jules would have wanted her to be, he was also consumed with pride over their daughter's sheer beauty. Jillian was a living reminder of everything Jules had been.

He stood and took his daughter's hand as he stared at their distorted reflection in the water below. Erin's likeness was behind them, and though he couldn't make out the expression on her face, he knew she must be feeling a deep pain—because he felt it, too. When he was finally able to turn back toward the family, he saw that they were each saying goodbye in their own

434

way. Everyone stood quietly for a long while, even Jillian, and watched the river flow. One by one, they broke from a trance-like state and walked away toward the house.

With Jillian beside him tugging at his hand, Will walked back with Erin. She was quiet. Jules had been the center of both of their worlds. Though they had orbited around her for so long, he knew they had to veer off in different directions to discover who they were and what they could be without her.

"Can you stay for brunch?" Will stopped on the lawn as the family trailed into the house ahead of them. Jillian stayed close to him and looked up at Erin.

"No, I should get on the road if I want to get to Nashville at a decent time," she said, looking toward the river again.

"Okay." He nodded. They turned and walked around the house to her waiting car. "But before you go, I have something for you. Can you wait just a minute?"

She shoved her hands into the pockets of her jeans and squinted in the sun. "Sure."

"Okay, stay right there." He jogged toward the house, pushed through the door, and snatched a book off the bench near the stairs before racing back to her with his heart beating fast.

"Why are you leaving? I don't want you to go," Jillian whined as her father jogged back toward them.

Erin knelt and brushed the dark curls from Jillian's face. "Well, sweetie," she said, "your mom told me once that if you wanna find something special in this world, you can't be afraid to go look for it. So that's what I have to do."

Jillian smiled. "Can I come?"

"Maybe someday, kiddo, but you know, I think we'll see each other again. I can feel it."

As he listened to the conversation, an invisible rope tightened around his neck, making it hard to breathe. The book felt like a brick in his hand.

Erin rubbed Jillian's arms. "But, until I see you again, you keep playing that piano and practice real hard, okay?"

"Okay," Jillian whispered. She wrapped her arms around Erin's neck and Erin drew in a deep breath. She kissed Jillian on the top of her head and looked into her eyes again before pulling away.

"Take care of your daddy. Make sure he eats his vegetables and he doesn't stay up too late." Erin tapped the tip of Jillian's nose with her finger. "But now you should go find some cake. I bet there's some in there somewhere."

"Okay." Jillian smiled and then skipped off toward the house.

"Here," Will said. Erin's eyes were still locked on Jillian as she rose to her feet and Will handed her the book. "I know it's not much," he said, "but I wanted to give you something of hers. It's that Virginia Woolf book, and I...the last time you were here, you said the two of you talked about it, or that she wanted you to read it, or something. I thought

436

maybe…well, I don't know. I just wanted you to have it, I guess."

Erin took the book in her hands. Her eyes glassed over and she ran her fingers along the cover. The wind picked up slightly, blowing the hair from her face.

"I wish I liked to read more," he said, "but most of those books are wasted on me." He slipped his hands into his pockets and looked at the ground. "I know Jules would want me to save them for Jilly, but I saw the way you looked at that one, so I just thought you should have it."

"God, Will, I don't even know what to say," she whispered. She gripped the book and then lifted her eyes to meet his.

"You don't have to say anything. Just take it. Please."

Erin nodded and pulled the book to her chest. "Thank you."

"Don't mention it," he said. His throat tightened again.

"You know, Will, I didn't want to feel anything for you," she began, shifting her glance toward the road. "I wanted to hate you, but I—I just can't do it. I loved her so much, and I always will. I don't know if this will make sense to you, but now I know why she couldn't leave."

He instinctively reached for her hand. "I don't know what she was planning to do, and maybe I don't wanna know, but I get it, too. I understand why she loved you."

Their eyes met and there was a heaviness between them. He could read the wounded look in her eyes, but he also

437

knew something was driving her and she was itching to go. There was nothing left for them do but say goodbye. Jules had unintentionally brought them together, but as he stood there, wanting nothing more than to drown in Erin's blue eyes, he knew she needed leave. He would never be big enough to fill the empty space inside of her that Jules had left behind, and she could never fill the empty space inside of him.

"Good luck to you, Will," she said, moving in to embrace him one last time. "Take care of that little girl."

"I hope you find everything you're looking for, Erin. I mean that. You deserve it," he said as they pulled apart.

She bit her lip and turned away. As she opened the car door, she looked back and hesitated, but then she smiled and slid behind the wheel. Will watched her eyes in the rearview mirror as she drove away.

Once Erin's car had disappeared down the road, he turned back toward the house. He could still hear the sound of Jules' voice in his head telling him that everything would be alright and, in time, he would understand and forgive her for everything she had done. He knew now what it meant to be alive and to be sober.

Everything stung. The pain of losing Jules, the ache of watching Erin drive away, and the fear of watching Jillian grow up too fast. But he also knew Father Tom had been right all along—he was stronger now, and it was time to get back to living. He reached into his pocket, pulled out the original copy of Jules' letter, and walked back down to the river. He sat alone on the pier and read her words one last time before dropping the paper into the water.

"Goodbye, Jules," he said as the letter slowly drifted away.

Chapter Thirty-One

Erin stared at the neon gas station sign ahead, shivering and blowing into the steaming cup she held in her hands. She glanced at the clock on the dashboard and leaned against the headrest. She debated between pushing on and calling it a night to hide away in the cheap motel across the highway. She couldn't wait to see the friends who were waiting for her in Nashville, but she was also terrified of reclaiming her life there.

What if I just keep going south? She thought while watching the blurred headlights on the interstate below. *What about New Orleans?* Maybe the boulevards of that swanky, historic city wouldn't be as cruel or as cold as Milwaukee's concrete jungle or the unforgiving Nashville streets that she already knew so well. What if she turned west? She could be on the sunny coast of California within a few days—or, better yet, she could point her car northeast and find herself in New York, where she could reinvent herself in any way she chose.

Growing anxious, she glanced at the book that sat on the passenger's seat beside her. It was Jules' copy of *Orlando*, the one that Will had given her. She picked it up and lifted the cover. The smell of musty pages filled the air as she flipped through, noting the highlighted passages and dog-eared chapters

440

that Jules had clearly marked. She knew some of those phrases well.

Nearing the end of the book, she turned one more page and then noticed several neatly folded and flattened pieces of paper, which obviously didn't belong in the book, tucked tightly into the binding. Switching on the light inside the car, she freed the papers and slowly unfolded them. Squinting in the dim light, she made out the words "Dear Jillian" scribbled in Jules' handwriting. Her heart dropped as she stared at another letter from Jules. This one was addressed to her daughter, and she clearly hadn't meant for it to fall into Erin's hands, but yet here it was. Unsure if she should read it, Erin held it tightly in her fingers. She closed her eyes and wondered what to do. *Nothing is random*, she thought before opening them again. She took a long, deep breath.

Dear Jillian,

You're sleeping next to me while the cold October rain falls heavy on the roof above us. The sound of the rain, mixed with your sweet, peaceful breathing, makes me realize there's nowhere else in this world I'd rather be right now. I'm holding your hand, even though you don't know it, and I can barely catch my breath because you are the most beautiful thing I have ever seen. But, even as I watch you, I'm torn because there's so much I need to tell you—but I can't, at least not yet.

Right now my mind is adrift with the heavy implication of making a choice that seems impossible to carry out. I can hear the sound of my watch ticking on the bedside table, and just the sound of it makes me anxious. It reminds me that time is running out. I'm so tired, baby girl, but right now all I can do is stare at you. Your face is so familiar to me. Sometimes when I look in those beautiful brown eyes of yours, I feel like I've known you all my life. Somehow, even when it felt like the universe was keeping us apart, I knew you would come along when you were ready. You're strong that way. You were born with a rare intuition that doesn't belong to me. You are fearless in so many ways and I want to protect you from everything, but I can tell, even now, that you won't need me to shield you for long. You are brave, Little Bug, so much braver than I could ever be. You aren't afraid to go your own way. I pray you never lose that bold, unabashed force that's leading you toward the woman you're meant to be.

As much as your bravery leaves me in awe, it also reminds me of just how feeble I am. Though I've tried desperately to fight it, I've fallen completely in love with another woman. By the time you read this letter, you'll already know this to be true, because she and I will be together—at least, that's my hope. But even with as young as you are right now, I want so badly for you to be the first person to whom I address this pontification.

Your father loves me—don't ever doubt that. We had a wonderful and fantastic love affair once, too. But he loves me far beyond the depths of anything I could possibly reciprocate, and now I know why I never could. There were times when I did love him very much, and times when I thought I could again, but

442

even in the safety of his arms, surrounded by his love, I still felt incomplete. It was never his fault. It was always mine. I have always known who I am, even when I was too afraid to admit it.

I didn't ask for the love that came along and changed me. In fact, I never thought love like this was possible for me. But just like I knew you would come, I somehow always knew she would eventually find me, too. I've been afraid to love her back, but I can't hide it anymore, so I'm going to give myself to her—if she'll still take me. I don't want to hurt you or your dad. I hope you know that. Your father is a good man, but together, we sometimes bring out the absolute worst in each other. Until I had a mirror right in front of my face and finally understood the woman I really am, I couldn't see all that was wrong with the life we had built together. I only hope that once enough time passes, we'll forget the hurt we caused each other and focus on the most important thing—and that, my brave and fierce little girl, is you.

I hope that by the time you read this letter, you'll understand that my love for you has absolutely no end. I really do hope you learn from my mistakes because the art of living a good life, sweet girl, is to be true to yourself—and to those around you. I haven't always been true, but I promise you, I'm trying.

Above all, please be true to yourself, and always be brave enough to love who you love—no matter the cost. Love is a terrifying force of nature that can sometimes rob you of everything, strip you bare, and leave you completely exposed.

But it can also fill you with so much joy that not even the devil himself can take it away. Someday soon you're going to look up at me with those big eyes and ask if love is it really worth it since it hurts so much. No matter how many times you ask me this, my answer will always be the same. Even if it kills you, real love is always worth the risk. She is worth the risk I'm taking now.

If you find love like that, don't fear it, honey, embrace it. Even if your brush with true love is brief and filled with unexpected shades of gray, it will still be worth more than a lifetime spent inside the black-and-white walls we build around our hearts when we're too afraid of being hurt. Love has so many brilliant and fantastic colors. Always reach for those colors. They are everything that's real and beautiful in this world. If you fill your life with that vibrancy, in whatever form it takes, I promise, you will never feel empty.

Virginia Woolf once wrote, "I see you everywhere, in the stars, in the river, to me you're everything that exists; the reality of everything."

You are my reality, and <u>you</u> are my everything. Sleep well, Little Bug. I can't wait to see you in the morning.

Love,
Mommy

Erin blinked heavily, but she couldn't cry. She simply refolded the letter and tucked it back where she'd found it. She wondered if Will had known this confession was hidden there. Had he read it? Was this the real reason he'd given her this book? An unfamiliar and peaceful calm came over her as she returned the book to the seat beside her. She thought of Will at home with Jillian—and she thought of Jules. Everything seemed surreal. The answer to her most burning question was now perfectly clear, but Jules was still gone.

Erin drew in a slow breath before turning the key in the ignition and shifting the car into gear. Before taking her foot off the brake, she looked down at the book and placed it in her lap. For some reason, having it there just felt right, as if it brought her closer to Jules.

She glanced at the parking lot ahead and the open road beyond. There was no sense in turning back now, or in stopping to consider her options. She needed to keep moving, and over-thinking would only take her back to the places where she had already been. There was only one way she could go, and that was forward. The road ahead was daunting, but it was also full of possibility. Wherever she would land, she'd know that love—although painful—had been the one thing that led her there. It would also be the one thing that would lead her home—wherever home might be.

CPSIA information can be obtained
at www.ICGtesting.com
Printed in the USA
FFOW03n1919080618
47052019-49383FF